UNCHOSEN

ERIN RIHA

Cover design by Ashley Ruggirello

Book design by Ashley Ruggirello

eBook: 978-1-942111-84-9

Hardcover - 978-1-942111-88-7

Paperback - 978-1-942111-87-0

REUTS Publications
www.REUTS.com

For anyone who ever felt second best

CHAPTER ONE

*F*ish guts and oily sewage swirl in the gutter to my left. I will not step in it, even if it takes knocking over the fluffy debutantes blocking my path. They continue toward me, oblivious to my plight, and I turn my rickety woven cart toward a fruit stand.

The oppressive, mid-afternoon sun reflects off the paver stones, drawing the cloying stink of death from the withering fruit. The freckle-faced boy manning the stand eyes me and my cart. I flash the sunburned boy a shy, submissive smile as I run my gaze over his pyramids of shiny pomelos and fragrant grapefruits, pretending I have change to waste on an afternoon treat. The girls' chatter grows louder, and I lean over the table to hide my now familiar face behind the fruit. Even the noisy bustle of the port surrounds me with the sensation of slow decay: the grumbles of sailors wheeling and dealing; the gentle lap of stagnant gulf water; and somewhere, a radio.

"*—marks the second time in as many months that such a large shipment of Nordanian zinc has been reported missing. In other news, humanitarian efforts are underway to assist displaced Orthodox families stranded along the Osterstani corridor after fleeing an oppressive—*" The radio cuts out as I lean in to smell the grapefruits, like the well-to-do women I've seen over the past two weeks since I was given the market run — since my world turned upside down.

The radio cuts back in, and the boy turns up the volume.

"—*the first time in three years a girl from Peninsula City has been invited to the National Institute for Women. Sources say Miss Thatcher has already caught the eye* . . ."

A cold shiver tumbles down the back of my neck despite the thick, humid air. I crinkle my nose at the memory of the girl who slept next to me for so many years. The so-called friend who pretended to root for me, all while needling her way into stealing what I'd earned. I didn't see it coming. I was foolish and stupid. I won't make that same mistake twice.

Something shiny catches my eye. I squat to pocket the silver piece on the ground and neatly tuck it into my skirt. Every coin counts when you owe a debt like mine.

"Oi!" The shop boy barks at me, seeming to have decided I'm no better than the vermin in the gutter behind me. "Either buy something or move on."

I blink up at him and press my reddish-coral lips together into a docile smile. It's one of twenty-seven smiles Headmistress Moyle taught me in my training for the institute, and I like to think my lipstick compliments this purpose exactly.

"Ain't you understanding me?" He tries to make himself look bigger, spitting on the ground. I edge back, brushing into a voluminous sleeve of cool silk linen.

"Watch where you're going!" a high-pitched voice squeaks out behind me. I whip my head toward the trio of girls who are now blocking me from passing them on the esplanade.

"Excuse me, misses," I say with a little curtsy I'd once thought I would use to pay respect to foreign dignitaries. Not that these girls would know the difference between a cordial curtsy and a kumquat. I edge to the right, to pass them away from the gutter. But the redhead blocks my way.

"This is the high street, urchin," she says, a cruel smile curling her thin, un-glossed lips. Her eyes are cold blue, her white skin freckled but not tanned. She's spent her days indoors; the market is merely a way to waste an afternoon. Her friends giggle behind soft hands that hide nothing.

"I'm not an urchin, miss," I say through gritted teeth, nodding at her with deference.

"You're not?" Her pretty black friend steps toward me in such a way that I have to step back. Her cheeks are rouged, and the off-putting shade reminds me of over-ripe nectarines.

"Could've fooled me," the first says, pushing me toward the gutter.

"Oh, I know what she is, Gilly," the friend says.

"Francine," scolds the third, a blonde so fair her skin almost blends into the stone wall behind her. "Leave her be. She's had it rotten enough lately."

"That's right," Francine says to Gilly, ignoring their other friend. "She's not even good enough to be an urchin."

"Oh," Gilly says, her eyes flashing. "I saw that. *Unchosen*. Her picture's posted at city hall." I wince. I knew it was only a matter of time until it was made official, but my stomach churns just the same.

"Of course, you know what really happens up at that estate. I mean, you've heard about CJ and his friends," Francine says, sharing a giggle with Gilly, as if they're sharing a vicious inside joke.

"Ladies," their pale friend cautions.

"What? As if it's not obvious?" Gilly steps forward. "This little slut obviously disqualified herself. Probably got caught crawling between his sheets—or legs, more likely. Can't imagine he'd willingly let her filth into his bed." I lift my chin and meet her sharp gaze.

I grit my teeth and feel my nostrils flare as my stomach

tightens into a hot coil of indignation. Her grin spreads, as if she's enjoying my reaction as much as an afternoon operetta.

"Well, she got what she deserved, then," Francine says, standing even with Freckles. "Now she's just a pathetic, nasty *Unchosen*."

Freckles snorts and laughs, shaking her head. "She's not even pretty. I don't ge—"

I don't hear the rest of her insult. I lunge forward, elbow first, hitting Freckles in the stomach. She knocks into Francine with a gasp, and the two of them tumble backward, landing ass-first in the gutter. They sit there for a long, breathless moment, their dresses soaking up the oily sludge like discarded tea bags.

Then they squeal like pigs. The boy at the citrus stand doubles over with laughter. A loud whistle comes from behind me—a police whistle—and the boy catches my eye.

"Run!" He waves, as if telling me to go through the building behind him. I stare, open-mouthed. He hands me a pomelo. "Go! What are you waiting for?"

"You're helping me?"

"Those twits deserve to fall in the gutter if they wear ball gowns on squid day."

I suppress a grin and tug my cart behind me as I run through the dark storeroom. It's musty and filled with vats of heaven-knows-what, stacked three tall. But behind me, angry squeals and a deep, authoritative voice keep me moving away with my head ducked. Finally, I push through another door and onto a quiet street. Even here, I can hear the commotion from the high street, but I brush myself off and turn left, rushing along in the direction I'd intended to go.

Just ahead is a small plaza with a dry, chipped fountain and a handful of pigeons that look like they're one orange short of a bushel. At the apex of the fountain are the steps to city hall. I can't help myself. I cut across the pavers to where a sign has been posted on the notice board.

There's Arden. Looking a mess with red, puffy eyes and frizzy brown hair. Cripes, she even has dirt on her cheek. Next to her photo, it reads: *Congratulations to Arden Thatcher on being chosen to attend the National Institute for Women.*

Below her picture, though not any smaller, is my own photograph. My dark mahogany hair is smooth and shiny, my naturally bronze skin tanned and rosy in all the right places. My smile is straight and white, and my brown eyes are clear and bright. I look like I've learned four languages. Like I've read every book on the list of *200 Books for Well-Read Girls.* Like I know how to fold a napkin into a swan, and a dove, and a damned Brandeiss emu. Like I'm the ideal Nordanian girl, and not the daughter of an Espancian whore.

But next to my photograph, it says: *Neve Ruiz, Unchosen, is thanked for her application to the institute.*

That's it.

I did everything that was asked of me, and in record time. I only had six months from the time Conrad and Headmistress Moyle discovered Tatiana was pregnant until the application deadline. But none of that matters because Arden was picked instead. Now, she's living the life I worked so hard for, and I'm stuck living hers. It's worse than that, though—she wasn't anything, while I'm Unchosen.

Angry shouts echo off the buildings behind me, and I know it's time to go. I don't look over my shoulder. I have a feeling that if I do, I'll see the constable chasing after me with whatever ridiculous allegations those fluffy harpies fed him.

A dark alley lingers to the right. I duck down it, holding my nose as the stench of human waste fills the space. I hope it doesn't seep into my clothing too badly. The whistle echoes off the buildings as the constable draws close, and I press my back into the cool, shaded stone. People rush past, their feet clomping. It seems a little excessive for what would have been labeled an accident, or been simply ignored, if it had happened between men.

But then, I'm no longer afforded any sort of protection or the benefit of the doubt.

I'm Unchosen, and Unchosen girls are not to be trusted.

After a few moments of silence, I poke my head out from the alley. The road is quiet; only a few passersby meander down the street. I keep my head down and start back in the direction of the estate.

"So much fuss," a voice says from across the way. A man with tanned skin sits at a bistro table, a book open as he sips spiced tea from a small ceramic mug. Even from here, I can smell the cloves, cinnamon, and something bright and almost lemony wafting from the teacup. I stay where I am, taking him in. He's pleasant-looking, with dark, chestnut-brown hair and shiny brown eyes behind black wire-rimmed glasses.

"Yes," I say, because it seems the only thing to do. He holds my gaze, and I feel rooted to my spot, as if I need to wait for his permission, or maybe his reassurance that he won't take me straight to the constable.

He tilts his head, and I can't place his expression. It makes my stomach pulse with a hot ache.

"You'd best be on your way, then," he says, turning a page in his book. "I'm fairly certain the distraction went the opposite direction, but one can never be too sure."

"If they come back . . . you won't?"

"What could I possibly say to a lynch mob?" He shrugs, as if it's the simplest thing.

Relief floods my stomach as I nod my thanks and resume my journey. As I walk away, I feel his gaze fixed on me. I look back over my shoulder, but he's focused on his book, a smile curling his lips into something that transforms his face.

He blinks up at me, and the smile disappears. My stomach tightens into a hard, cold knot, and I take off toward the estate, whispering a little prayer that I can make it back before the constable finds me.

CHAPTER TWO

By the time I get back to the estate, the steamy kitchen is a welcome embrace compared to the rancid stench of cloying orange groves and foul fish-stink from the bay. I've been here for seven years, and I've never gotten used to the odor. The only thing that made it bearable for so long was the knowledge that I was writing my own ticket out of here. I came with one goal, and I worked with singular focus from the time I arrived to achieve it. My mother saved up for my ticket to get here. I'm certain it was more money than she'd ever had at once in her entire life. I try not to think of what she did to get it.

But get it, she did. She spent it just as quickly and pushed me onto a train that took me the long way here, to where she'd been promised I would have a chance at a better life. I was hopeful. I was eleven. And I was stupid.

I arrived and met Carla, Arden, and Tatiana. As soon as I put eyes on Tatiana, with her bird bones and princess lips, I knew that I was second best. If Tatiana hadn't been an idiot and gone to bed with Samuel Fisherman, I'd still be second best. I would have never known the taste of hope. I would have never let myself believe.

When I left, my mother's parting words were, "It's an opportunity, Nevesh, not a prize. Keep your chin up and do me proud." If I'd known this was going to be the outcome, I would have never left her side.

"Neve!" Gaia's sharp voice comes from near the stoves, where something fishy is braising in something citrusy. If I never eat another piece of fish the rest of my life, it'll be too soon. I push my cart toward a third-year kitchen girl. She has the wide-eyed look of a girl who will stay in the kitchen of a home on the peninsula the rest of her life.

"Now," the voice snaps again, and I make my way over to the cook. Part mother hen, part drill sergeant, Gaia perpetually smells of garlic and onion and orange zest. I've seen her make men cry, but she protects her kitchen girls with everything she has.

"Yes, Gaia," I say, sniffing at whatever it is she's braising.

"You're wanted upstairs," she says. "I suggest you clean up. Put on something that doesn't stink of sweat." Upstairs can only mean one thing: Conrad has summoned me. After the events of this afternoon, I can't imagine it's going to be good.

"Why are *you* telling me?" Usually, it would be Headmistress Moyle summoning me on Conrad's behalf.

Gaia turns with a scowl on her face, one hand on the soft, subtle indent at her waist.

"Because I'm telling you," she snaps. "Now, scoot!" She smacks my butt with her hand towel and I scuttle for the door, leaving her to mutter things under her breath about useless girls.

I make it all the way to the stairwell before I stop myself. The day after Arden left, Carla and I were shuffled to a dark, damp room in the basement. Of course, that's not what Headmistress Moyle called it. She referred to it as a "charming, garden-level" room. If by charming, she meant it had a view of a patch of clover, then she was spot on.

We're not the only ones down here, of course. Gaia maintains the largest room, nearest the kitchen. She claims she can't be troubled with traipsing up and down the steps in the middle of the night to check the proofs on her dough. The others down here are other unfortunate beneficiaries whose stock has been squandered. Girls whose complexions turned on them, girls whose waistlines exceeded whatever stupid number Conrad deemed "desirable," girls who were caught publicly with boys in the village and haven't yet been relocated.

And always, there are rooms for the Unchosen and the leftovers. I'm Unchosen, and Carla is left over. But you'd never know it by looking at her. She swings the door open just as I approach, and her white teeth cut a bright, cheerful smile across her dark complexion.

"You're home!" she says, her caramel-brown eyes twinkling, even in the poor light. I cringe at the word. This place has never been home. I push past her into our room and squat next to my bed, pretending to re-tie my shoes as I tuck my new silver piece into the bag hidden inside the hole in my mattress.

When we were moved, I worried I wouldn't have time to get the little caches of money I've tucked away over the years. A piece here, a piece there. Nothing much. But over six years, it adds up. I've split it now, most of it hidden inside the mattress, a smaller amount hidden inside a ball of stockings in the back of my traveling chest. I've never had a real plan for it, but knowing it's there, slowly growing, has always given me a sense of peace.

"Neve, what are you doing?" Carla hisses from the door.

"I just need to chan —"

"No time for that!" she says, nearly breathless. "You've been summoned!" She tugs on my arm, pulling me up and right back out the door.

"So I've heard," I say, frowning at the positivity radiating off my roommate.

Carla is sweet and friendly, and if people in the town got a good look at her, it could invite all sorts of potential problems. Where I'm sharp and dramatic, and curvy where my undergarments help me out, Carla is sweet and vulnerable, and practically broadcasts "easy prey." Conrad can get the most reimbursement for her beneficiary contract if she remains sweet and sheltered.

I can handle myself. I have street smarts and the savvy to keep my wits about me, even around men. I will never forget the incredibly uncomfortable morning I spent with Headmistress Moyle where I learned far more about the things that allegedly go through every man's head when faced with an attractive woman than I ever would have wished to. But even Carla must see that I'm in no state to meet with our benefactor.

"I smell terrible," I say, waving at my dress. "I nearly stepped in the gutter."

"He's already been waiting an hour," she says.

"An hour?" I frown. That's too much time. It can't be about what happened on the high street. "What do you suppose it is?"

She stifles a little giggle, but she can't hide her smile.

"I think . . ."—she draws it out with a mischievous glint in her eye—"he's found you a match!"

My heart flips, but it doesn't feel good. It feels fatal.

Of course. This is what I'm here for. A future. Just not the one I deserve.

"You might be leaving here soon," she says, blinking quickly.

"Maybe," I say, letting her push me out the door and up the stairs with a quick squeeze and a bounce.

When I reach the door to the main residence, the lock sticks.

It's not that it's actually locked. But the lock on this door is old and loose and sometimes slips. I groan, but pull two hairpins from my head. After my third scolding for being late to housekeeping duties, Gaia pulled me aside and showed me how to feel for the pins in the locking mechanism using toothpicks. I was never late again.

The second pin slips into place, and I open the door. The white marble floor tiles are shiny, and the cross breeze that flutters the sheer drapes reeks of sour brine and fermented candied oranges.

Conrad's office doors are thrown open, letting in the light and the air. He sits at his desk, reading over some papers, his bald gray head bowed as if in prayer. If the papers have anything to do with money, then it makes sense. There's very little that he does without financial motivation. It's not a secret that he married his wife—who was, from what I understand, a toothsome, quiet girl several years his junior—because she was the only child to the owner of the largest acreage of citrus groves on the peninsula.

I tap gently on the door and step back, lowering my head. For a short time, I was taught to only lower my eyelids for a moment, then lift them again slowly with the intention to flirt. Now, I just remain submissive.

"Neve, please come in," he says. His voice is upbeat as he points toward the settee against the windows to his right. As I sit, he remains standing, hands casually in his pockets, hips back and relaxed. He looks victorious. My stomach turns sour.

"I have news for you," he says, as if waiting for me to ask him what it is. But of course, I've been trained. When I say nothing, he leans over, as if speaking to a stupid dog.

"As of this morning, I have secured interest in the remainder of your contract," he says.

My throat goes dry. Because, while it's possible that some nice, sweet-natured man might come asking for sweet, gentle Carla, I can't imagine what kind of man would come asking for the girl Unchosen.

"You may speak," Conrad says, waving at me as if that's all it takes to share his joy. His large, diamond-studded watch reflects off the overhead light, blinding me, and I flinch. He frowns.

"Who is he?" I ask, schooling my face to keep from giving away my hand. Conrad arches an unimpressed brow, but then smiles indulgently.

"His name is Jarls Von Brandt. He's recently come into some

extensive property north of here, and he has what has become a very successful business. Not that any of that would mean anything to you," he says with a flap of his hand and a condescending smile. "He's become an important associate of mine, however.

"You will meet him tomorrow night. He will join us for dinner, and you will be the guests of honor." I can tell by the expectation heavy in his expression that he wants me to be excited. Or to thank him, at the very least. But I can't bring myself to say anything more. Once again, despite all my hard work, my fate is taken from me. Even if I wanted to get out of here, or find my own suitor, it's no longer an option.

"Neve," Conrad says, his grin tight. "Say something."

I look up into the cold eyes of my benefactor, feeling the challenge held within. *Be grateful. Be gracious. Be quiet.* I press my lips into a tight smile, forcing the skin around my eyes to crinkle. I've practiced this smile in front of a mirror and can conjure it on a moment's notice. If he knows, he says nothing.

"What wonderful news," I say, forcing the right amount of excitement into my inflection as seems appropriate. But what is appropriate? Conrad doesn't know what I gave up to get here, how hard I worked, staying up all night to memorize Swendish conjugations and the strange hierarchy of the Brandeissland Parliament.

I will make sacrifices. But I won't sacrifice my freedom. I won't sacrifice my own happiness, or what I've worked for. What I deserve.

"What's this?" CJ enters the room. Conrad's son and heir shoots me a grin, his white teeth gleaming, his perfectly manicured hands pressed together.

"We've found Neve a match," Conrad says, his tone light, and yet, with a note of danger that wasn't there before. "Isn't that right, Neve?"

I swallow and force what I hope appears to be an overwhelmed, bashful smile.

"Yes, that's right."

"Wonderful! Congratulations!" CJ says to his father. He leans against his father's desk, crossing his arms over his chest. Despite his golden hair and sun-kissed skin, there's a sharpness to him that wasn't there a week ago. It's in the way he blinks his icy blue eyes more than he should. The way his foot taps against the floor just a touch too fast. I always thought he and Arden were just using each other, fooling around and pretending no one knew. But he seems changed with her absence. On edge.

"Assuming, of course," I interrupt, feigning a demure smile, "that they like what they see at dinner tomorrow night."

"Formalities, of course," Conrad says. He tilts his wrist, checking the time on his heirloom watch.

"Of course," I mimic.

"You'll be relieved of your duties tomorrow starting at three, so that you may prepare," Conrad says, effectively dismissing me.

I thank him and go back downstairs in a blur. My mother's words come back to me as my brain spins with fears and ideas. *It's an opportunity, Nevesh, not a prize.* Well, I'm going to need another opportunity, in case this one is as bad as I suspect it will be.

CHAPTER THREE

I thought I had more time. It's only been ten days since Arden was shipped off to what was supposed to secure *my* destiny. And in just as many days, her stock has risen and gossip is in her favor.

Meanwhile, I'm Unchosen. Never mind that I was the first-choice candidate. Never mind that I can recite the given, middle, and family names of all the ambassadors to Nordania and bake a perfect crabmeat soufflé timed precisely for the fish course. No, I'm to be shuttled off to skies-know-who as quickly as possible because this may be as valuable as I'll ever be.

I worked *so* hard so that I'd never have to rely on another person again. But that's exactly where I am.

Gaia catches me in the kitchen the next morning before I can go on my errands. Even early in the morning, she smells like garlic and rosemary, and when she directs me into the storage locker, my mouth waters.

"What are you going to do?" She bunches her apron like a nest and drops golden potatoes into it one at a time.

"What am I going to do about what?"

Her hand smacks the backside of my head faster than I can react.

"Ow! Gaia!"

"Stop being smart with me, girl. You don't have the time." Her wide nostrils flare, and she returns to choosing a potato, looking it over with far more care than the previous ones.

"What have you heard?"

"Nothing good," she says, her tone dark. "I know . . ." She leans over, reaching for a glass bottle of herbed oil sitting directly next to me. "I know about your nest egg."

"My what?" I ask blandly. But if she knows, she knows. It doesn't matter how secretive I've been, how careful I've tried to be to hide it. And if *she* knows about the money I've been pilfering away, who else does? She shushes me just then.

"Now, now, none of that. I doubt anyone else knows, but I've seen you stuffing coin in your pockets. Found some tucked away in an apron on the line once."

I don't respond, neither acknowledging nor denying. Instead, I pluck a potato and pinch off a long eye.

"What are you saying?"

"Smart girl like you? You could make something more of yourself than ending up trapped in a house with a man willing to pay bargain pricing for the privilege of using your womb."

A shudder starts to roll down my back, but I tense my muscles. I've trained for this. I can mask any unexpected reaction.

"I expect," Gaia continues, as if this is just a hypothetical and not my soon-to-be life, "if I ever found myself in that position, and I had the means to purchase passage out of here, I might take advantage of this afternoon's schedule and book passage to the mainland."

"Where?" I scoff, but I keep my eyes on Gaia.

"Oh, I wouldn't know," she mumbles, taking the potato from my hands. "I've heard rumblings about Osterstan."

"Osterstan?" I hiss. "You must be joking." Osterstan has long been regarded as the most backward-thinking nation on the Mittle continent. About thirty years ago, they shut their border to Swendenland, whose only possible crimes against humanity include producing chocolate, mining gemstones, and fur farms. To be fair, the notion of a fur farm saddens me, and I always knew that given the choice, I would refuse to wear the stuff. But it hardly seems justification for shutting off all land access to a country.

In the humanitarian mission that followed, Nordanian forces joined with Sudersberg to cut a supply line through Osterstani borders. Today, that train line runs daily from Sudersberg to Swendenland, allowing fresh produce and other supplies not grown in Swendenland to reach its people so they don't starve. All I've ever heard on the radio and read in newspapers is that the natives in Eastern Osterstan are grateful for the business it brings.

Osterstan proper is unreasonable and barbaric. Osterstan is *not* the place for someone like me.

"You can't be serious," I say again, when she hasn't responded.

"I only know what I've heard. They have good laws for refugees," she whispers, plopping a handful of potatoes into her pouch with much less care.

"I'm not a refugee," I snap. Her shoulders soften, and I realize my mistake. If I fled Nordania for Osterstan, that would make me a refugee. Of course, Gaia has sussed out my Espancian roots, no matter how quiet I've tried to keep it.

"There's a big world out there beyond ball gowns and fish courses. More than you know. Perhaps it's time you start caring about the world beyond your pretty little nose."

"And I *know* what I've read," I say. "Osterstan is dangerous and repressive and—"

"You ever stop to think who's writing those books you read,

girl? Or do you believe everything you read?" Gaia's brown eyes are hard and imploring.

But I shake my head. "I have other options."

"Do you, now?"

I nod, and she slams the jar of oils back onto the shelf.

"Things have changed, girl. Arden is at the institute, and you may be sore in the cheeks over it, but it's done, and unless you do something quickly, your future is going to be done just as quickly."

I suppress the urge to shudder. But it has me thinking.

Arden didn't have a snowflake's chance in Espancia of beating me for top girl here, and yet, she made it out. Maybe I can make it out as well.

"Thank you, Gaia. I'll think about it."

She shakes her head and leaves me in the locker. But she's right. Maybe it is time to take matters into my own hands.

CHAPTER FOUR

*J*arls Von Brandt needs a tissue.

And he's asked me to get it.

I wonder if he's accustomed to the women he meets wanting to flee the room upon introduction, and if this is his way of beating me to the punch.

I know that as an Unchosen girl, I can't expect Declan Levingston. But I at least thought Conrad would secure me a husband born within a decade of me. Jarls Von Brandt is what I would call a squishy man with a red nose and a narrow mouth. His coloring combined with his last name makes me think he must be heir to some sort of middling fortune. Or at least some sort of business enterprise.

Especially since his first words to me after Conrad's introduction were, "Be a good girl and get me a rag for my nose."

Charming.

With a deep breath, I return to the sitting room where he and Conrad are swirling amber liquid in short glasses. The ice clinks as the liquid sloshes, and when I pass Jarls the tissue, his eyes wander down my arm, settling on my chest. I break out in chills, but this only seems to embolden him.

"You have lovely skin, Nell."

"It's Neve, sir," I say.

"What is?"

"My name, sir. It's Neve."

"I like the way you call me *sir*, Neve."

Bile coats the back of my throat, and I suppress a shudder as his chapped fingertips brush mine. Conrad says something, and Jarls steps back, scrubbing the tissue against his nose. It comes away pink, and he plops the dirty rag in my hand.

"Dinner is served in the dining room," Gaia says from the doorway with an air of occasion. She grins at the men, and once they've gone through to the room, she casts me a dark glance.

"Put it here, girl," she says, offering to take the filthy tissue from me. "Chin up."

I go into the dining room and take my seat, directly across from Jarls. Conrad sits at the head of the table, and a place at the opposite end of the table is cleared. CJ must not be joining us.

The men talk about matters of national business and delve into international politics through the salad course. When the bouillabaisse is served, they're debating what should be done about Osterstan. Headmistress Moyle glazed over the readings I did on Osterstan, as they're not one of Nordania's allies. In fact, their moral values are considered so misaligned with our own that Nordanian women are discouraged from even visiting.

"The corridor must be protected. We have that right," Conrad says. Jarls nods, running his finger along his upper lip.

"I think there are more like-minded people than you think." He catches my eye, and I force a benign smile. His eyes drop to my chest again. It takes everything in me not to cover myself up — and to keep my fish broth down.

"What do you think, Neve?" Jarls asks, suddenly directing the conversation to me. Conrad becomes very still, but his eyebrows lift, as if he wonders what I might have to add to this. I set down my spoon and sit back in my chair.

"I think that no matter where you are in the world, you're likely to find like-minded people." The men stare at me for a long moment, and then Jarls chuckles. Conrad nods at me, approving. I feel sick with it. I don't want his approval. I want him to forget about all of this and leave.

"You're correct there," Jarls says, pointing a chubby finger at me. "The trick is to know where to look for them. For example, there are certain interests, shall we say, that might be harder to find like-minded individuals with than others."

"I don't follow," I say, sitting straighter as one of the younger girls takes my unfinished soup.

"Say you have someone," he says, leaning onto his elbows and picking at something between his teeth, "who has a particular interest. And it's an interest that is perhaps very personal to him. Something that means a great deal, but that he's very private about. Because it's that personal. Do you follow?"

"Yes, I think so." Out of the corner of my eye, Conrad is quiet, which makes my shoulders tense.

"Obviously, for one man to have such a personal interest, it would mean the world for him to find someone to share that interest with."

"Yes, of course."

"But how is he to locate someone with that same interest, if he is so private about it?"

"Well," I say, frowning down at the table. This feels like a test, and I'm not sure if I want to pass it. "I would imagine that at a certain point, he would have to take a chance. Take a gamble and put himself out there. It's the only way he'll truly know."

"Ah," he says, grinning and leaning back in his chair, pointing his fat finger at me again. "But what if some might frown upon that interest?"

"Why would they frown upon it?" I ask.

He shakes his head as Conrad goes stock still. "Reasons," he says, waving his hand in the air. "People have all sorts of reasons for disapproving of so many things. Coffee. Whiskey. Skirts above the knee . . ." His words are simple and straightforward, and yet they make me feel dirty.

But something tells me this is his ploy. He wants to make me uncomfortable. So instead, I lift my chin and meet his eye.

"People are entitled to their opinion."

He nods, sucking on his teeth as the kitchen girls appear with our entree: more fish, surely.

"What if you disapproved?"

"Disapproved of what?" I ask. "Are we still speaking in generalities, or have we moved to you telling me what it is you are interested in?"

"Neve." Conrad's voice is low and lethal as he lazily grips his knife.

"She's a wicked one, isn't she, Connie?" Jarls laughs, spearing a square of white, flaky fish covered in a syrupy citrus glacé and stuffing it in his mouth.

"That she is," Conrad says, his focus now on Jarls with consternation. "And you are a guest in my home. Either get to your point or leave my girl alone." A shiver rolls up my spine at the way Conrad's laid claim to me. I place a small bite of fish on the back of my tongue and give it a cursory chew before I swallow it back with iced tea. The tea almost rids the citrus glacé from my tongue. But not entirely. Instead, it coats the back of it, nearly gagging me as I swallow more tea.

"I'll speak plainly," Jarls says, leaning onto his elbow and chewing with his mouth open. "You know we're negotiating a marriage contract."

I nod. He does the same.

"If I take you on, you won't be my first."

My eyebrows arch, but I don't say anything.

"I'm not in mourning or anything. Don't get that in your head. You'd be number three."

"Number three?" I ask, frowning.

Conrad clears his throat. "Jarls is a practicing apostle in the Fundamentalist Church of the New Lightbringer." My stomach drops. Part of my truncated education with Headmistress Moyle was to cover the cultural norms and religions of Nordania. The Church of the New Lightbringer is a denomination—but the Fundamentalist faction is another thing entirely. It's particularly prevalent in the westernmost corner of the Great Plain. Mostly because it's remote and nobody bothers them.

They also engage in the practice of plural wives.

"You want me to be your third wife?"

"Aye," he says, his eyes darting below my chin again. This is getting pathetic.

"Neve is a quick study and very capable. She's adaptable, and I think she'd be a perfect fit into your marriage, particularly considering what you've expressed to me."

It takes everything in my being to keep a neutral expression on my face, much less keep my dinner down. My stomach practically boils in outrage.

"We've got a bit of a conundrum with my second wife," he says, openly picking his nose at the table. He wipes it on the tablecloth and then sits back in his chair, taking a long swig of his wine. "She's a tiny thing, fragile constitution and all. Doctors don't give her a good prognosis."

"Is she ill?" I can't tear my eyes off the mucus smeared on the tablecloth. Still, my voice is softer than I mean for it to be.

"You'd think, the way she moans so much," he says with a sharp chuckle. "No, she's only just with child."

The blood drains from my face as I take this man in. He's drinking wine and speaking so cavalierly about the woman he's gotten pregnant—the woman whose doctors don't think she'll survive the pregnancy. And he's here, wanting to bring me in as his third wife.

"What will happen to her?"

He recoils and looks at Conrad, then back at me. "Only God

knows, child," he says, suddenly sounding like a different man. "But if God deems it time for her to come home, then you'd be wife number two."

As my gut turns cold and queasy, I set my fork down. I've hardly touched the dish, but I don't think I could eat another bite if I tried.

"That would be quite the honor for a man of your stature, Jarls," Conrad says. His eyes meet mine, the hidden message clear as day: *get it together, now*. I nod, keeping my face as blank of emotion as I can muster.

"Yes, so it would seem."

"Glad you see it that way."

My cheeks flush with an emotion I can't immediately define. But as dinner wraps up, I find it hard to keep focused on the conversation. I nod and smile when it seems necessary, but it's about all I can do beyond the swell of panic in my chest.

"What do you say, Neve?" Jarls asks suddenly. I realize a question has been asked and both he and Conrad are standing next to the table.

I don't say anything.

CHAPTER FIVE

"Can I interest you in a cuppa, sir? Miss?"

Jarls continues walking right past the waiter outside the cafe. My spine stiffens at the salutation, recalling the way I've been treated since my face turned up in the window of city hall. Now that I'm with this man, despicable though he may be, I'm worthy of their time again.

I hate it. I want to hate them. And yet, more than anything, what I feel is relief.

"The air is so sticky," Jarls says, spittle pooling in the corner of his mouth. "Foul-smelling, even."

I nod in agreement, as a well-trained girl is supposed to do, even though the cooling air has left a thin layer of damp chill on my exposed arms. Conrad nudged us out of the house before I could object to a walk in just this lightweight cotton dress.

"In Umberland, the air is fresh and pristine. Good for the skin."

I nod again, picturing a map of the land along the northwest central coast of Nordania. If that's true, then based on his splotchy complexion, he must be more of an indoors guy.

"You would benefit from it," he adds, his gaze dipping to the square cut of my neckline. I may as well be wearing a bullseye there.

"Does it get cold?" I ask, trying to turn the conversation away from whatever it is he's thinking of.

"Yes, of course. We have four seasons there. You've never truly lived until you've waded into the pools of the Christentine Lagoon on Midwinter's Eve. It's brisk and refreshing. A balm for the soul."

Again, something tugs at the back of my head.

"Is this a tradition among your people?"

"My people?" He scoffs, and it's an ugly sound. It occurs to me that there is something inherently foul about him, something rotting from deep within. "If you mean the pious people of the New Lightbringer, then yes. But they are not *my* people. To say such a thing would be blasphemy."

"I apologize, sir," I say. His nostrils flare as he stops and turns toward me. He lifts my chin with two fingers. His hand smells like fish. It takes everything in me not to gag.

"You'll learn soon enough," he says, then continues walking.

We pass taverns and bistros, flush full of people getting their fill of fun for the night. The light spills out onto the promenade, reflecting off the pooling water and making it glow. I imagine, if someone painted a picture of this scene, it would look ethereal, romantic even. But beneath the glow, the air reeks of fish entrails and desperation. Sweat runs cold between my shoulder blades, inching down my spine like mercury.

"I want to be blunt, my dear," he says, turning up a narrow side street. "My aspirations are to increase my brood, as God's will may allow. It is a man of many children who can truly count his wealth and find a place in God's heaven."

My stomach coils into barbed wire, and my throat is too dry to articulate anything other than a vaguely affirming sound.

"I've studied your form, and your hips appear to be the right width." My blood runs cold, and I curl my fingers into tight fists.

"All your papers are in line. You've bled, you're healthy, good teeth, etcetera."

We approach the next street and its pleasant, warm glow of more people and life. Safety. But he stops, blocking me from view, hiding me in the shadows.

"Conrad has assured me that you're still intact. But I need to ask, just the same. It would be a sin to our Heavenly Father to bring a girl who has already been broken in by another man."

I open my mouth, trying to find the right words. Headmistress Moyle never prepared me for such brusque conversation. Of course, she made it clear that men could be more frank, more abrupt, crass even. And of course, I was aware of it, having overheard coarse language from some of my mother's patrons. But this? A strange man, sizing up my hips and asking about my hymen?

"No," I say, struggling for words.

"No?" He repeats my word, his nostrils flaring. Something lascivious flickers across his eyes.

"I mean, yes, I am still . . . intact." I hate the word as it comes out of my mouth.

Disappointment crosses his bloated features, but he seems to decide something nonetheless.

"There's no need to lie," he says, stepping closer. I back up and hit the scratchy limestone wall. A foul stench reaches my nose, and I notice a puddle of something dark and thick that I don't want to step in.

"I'm not lying."

"Hmm," he says, stepping closer still, his sour breath brushing across my nose. "You'll be a third wife soon enough, then. But perhaps we could still do something about this price Conrad wants."

I can't hide the gasp. "How much does he want?"

He scowls at me. "Such a filthy question . . ." He leans in, as if he's going to kiss me, and I press my hands into his soft chest.

"Please, sir. This is inappropriate."

"Say that again," he says. My stomach tightens, the urgent flare of fear filling my chest. I try to sidestep him, but he blocks me with his arm.

"No, sir. Please take me back to—"

"The first thing you'll need to learn about being a good, devout wife, is that you must heed your husband completely," he says, fingering a strand of my hair. I push against him again.

"Please stop. This is enough."

"The lady asked you to stop." The voice comes from the street, behind Jarls. I try to lean around him to look, but the figure is backlit. I can't see his face. The voice is soft but severe, with a slight accent.

"The *lady* is to be my wife," Jarls sneers. "Go mind your own business."

"And yet," he says, stepping closer, "it would seem that she wants you to stop." He moves nearer still, and I can just make out the curve of his face, the warm brown eyes that stare with mild disinterest from behind black-rimmed glasses.

"Where I come from, a man's property is his to protect and defend," Jarls says, curling his fingers around the back of my neck. I shudder with revulsion. His sneer tells me he doesn't miss it.

"Where I come from," the man says, stepping closer, "a woman is not property." His accent is thicker now, and his vaguely familiar bronzed features and golden flecks to his dark hair make it clear he's not from Nordania.

"Ah, another Osterstani refugee? If things are so wonderful there, then why are you here? And why are Nordanian women not allowed to travel to such a heathenistic place?"

The man shrugs, but there's a tension to his shoulders as his eyes lazily fix on Jarls's fingers digging painfully into my neck.

"If your God condones the way you're strangling your—what

did you call her? Soon-to-be-wife? Then perhaps our definitions of what qualifies as 'heathenistic' are incompatible."

Jarls pulls back his hand, letting me go, and I stumble sideways into the wall, my cheek scraping against the stone.

"You've made your point," Jarls seethes. "Now, move on."

"I don't think I could, in good conscience, do that."

"I don't care what your asinine conscience says."

"I will not leave you to manhandle this woman when she does not consent to it."

"Jarls," I say, finally finding my voice, "I want to go home." Something sinks in my belly, and I realize it's the first time in seven years that I've ever referred to Conrad's as "home." Nordania is not home, has never been home — *will* never be home. But right now, I need to be away from this man, from this situation. And I don't need to be saved by some stranger who may or may not be any safer to be around.

But Jarls turns on me, his eyes wide and his nostrils flaring.

"I'll return you when I say it's time to return. If I'm going to pay, then I'm going to take my damn time. As for you — "

The stranger's fist is faster than Jarls's mouth. Jarls's nose crunches, and he loses his balance, stumbling backward. The red-hot pool of anger stewing in my stomach reaches a breaking point. I stick out my foot. The only thing louder than his nasal wail as he topples backward over my foot is the thud of his rear end landing in the shallow puddle of skies-knows-what.

"Are you all right?" the stranger asks, his voice soft.

The stranger is holding me by the wrist, and I only now realize that he tugged me out of the way. I stare down at the soft, loose hold he has on my wrist, and then up at him. His familiar eyes fix on mine, and for a split second, the veil drops. There's a question behind them, something soft and squishy and vulnerable.

"You imbecile!" Jarls sputters.

The stranger returns his attention to the man on the ground.

"What a shame," the stranger says, still holding my wrist. His touch is so gentle that I don't have any doubt I could pull my hand from his and he'd let go. Strangely, though, I don't.

"You'll pay for this," Jarls hisses, pushing to his feet. He steps closer, and the stench is so foul—sour and acid mixed with something fishy—that I gag.

"You'll want to get changed. I cannot imagine wanting to be seen smelling—or looking—like that. No Godly man would ever allow anyone but the Lord himself to see him in any state less than his holiest."

Jarls freezes, as if the stranger has said the magic words. I fight a smirk.

"Find your own way home," Jarls hisses, and then turns on his heel, leaving me in a dark alleyway with a stranger.

I pull my wrist from his grip, and as I suspected, he lets go immediately.

"I suppose you'll want me to thank you?"

"I don't suppose anything. I don't know you," he says. His face is blank again, still half-hidden in shadow. "But I would hope a woman wouldn't deign to marry a man who considers her his property."

The judgment in his voice is too much. It cuts right through my core. My knotted stomach fills with angry heat. I try to take a deep breath, to cool it down, to stop the bubbling anger from exploding as it often wants to, but the breath catches, rattling on its way out.

"I can't imagine anyone wanting someone like that," he says, almost as an afterthought. But it's enough. The heat boils into my chest, and I can't keep it down.

"You don't know the first thing about me. And for the record, this woman wishes only to survive in a world where she's been battered down at every turn. Do you think I *want* to be married to that man? Of course, I don't. But I don't have a choice in the matter."

"We always have a choice."

"If you believe that—if you truly believe that . . ." I sputter, realizing I've lost my cool and trying to reign it back in. "Then . . . then you're a naive fool."

His pupils flash in the dim light, and I realize I'm just called a stranger a fool in a dark alleyway. I take a step back, toward the light.

"Now, if you'll please, I am tired, and I have quite a walk back to where I belong in terribly uncomfortable shoes."

Before he can object, I turn on my heel and start back up the well-lit street. I don't know what awaits me when I return to Conrad's, or how I'll be received when I return alone. Or if the marriage offer even remains on the table. It's not a good marriage —the thought of having to reproduce with that vile man is enough to make me want to vomit—but it's a *marriage*. Some girls don't get that lucky. Some girls end up in workhouses or brothels—or worse.

Hot tears threaten to fall, and I pick up my pace, hoping for the second time in as many days to make it back to the estate before the news of my actions can ruin my future yet again.

CHAPTER SIX

I'm filled with dread. There's no way Jarls didn't realize exactly what happened in that moment. That yes, the dark stranger punched him and likely broke his nose, but also that he tripped over my foot. That I stuck it out on purpose. That the reason he's now covered in vomit is because I wanted him to be.

My feet hurt as my too-small, heeled slippers pinch my toes and clack against the paver stones. But it's the least of my problems as I realize just what Jarls said. *If* he's willing to pay Conrad's price . . . does that mean he's still negotiating with Conrad? If he's not willing to pay the full contract rate, what happens? Would that even be possible? I have come so far, left the only family I know to come here for the chance at a new life full of honor, and I could still end up in a workhouse.

I step on a stone and the flimsy sole of my shoe does little to protect the ball of my foot from the sharp edge. I curse under my breath, attracting scowls and disapproving glares from passersby who surely recognize me. Without Jarls at my side, they no longer hide their disdain for the Unchosen girl leaning against the side of a tavern in the dark, clutching her foot.

I take a deep, cooling breath—in through my nose, out

through my mouth. Losing my temper again right now won't do me any good. But there's a sharp edge to the heat tying my stomach into knots, and it aches like something relentless and hopeless.

"Are you okay?" The now familiar voice of my dark stranger comes from over my shoulder. I look back at him, to where he stands a respectable distance away, beneath the glow of a streetlamp. He's not unpleasant to look at. Tall, with wide but trim shoulders, long arms and legs, and a long face. Still, his cheeks look fuller than I would have expected for someone so narrow, as if, given the opportunity to smile, it might transform his face. He wears a lightweight suit that looks like something someone might purchase in a traveler's shop. He tucks his hands into his pockets, revealing suspenders—something out of fashion in Nordania—but they look right on him. Charming.

"Miss?" His voice is full of concern now, despite the fact that his veneer is still fully intact. In the lamplight, he steps closer. I recognize him from outside the café yesterday, when I was running from the nightmare debutantes.

"You?"

"Me?"

"I saw you yesterday—at the café."

"You made quite the entrance. Though I fear I was less helpful than I hoped to be, as trouble follows you nonetheless."

"Yes," I say softly. He's heard me lose my cool, and it's really only my own self-preservation that makes me think back to Headmistress Moyle's lessons about how to interact with unfamiliar men.

"I would like to walk you home, if that would be acceptable?" The way he phrases his question makes it even clearer that he's from somewhere else. Or at least, that Nordanian isn't his first language. I remember the conversation he had with Jarls.

"You're from Osterstan?" I ask.

"Yes."

"What are you doing here?"

"Traveling."

"Do you ever answer questions with more than one word?"

"Yes." A smirk floats the corners of his mouth upward, and I can see just a hint of what those cheeks can do to his face. The frivolous thought does something strange to me, and I shudder, trying to rid myself of it.

"Are you chilled?" he asks, working at his jacket.

"I'm fine — " But before I can protest, he has draped his linen jacket over my shoulders and resumed the proper distance between us. I hadn't realized how much the night air had chilled my arms. His jacket is warm, and smells like floral detergent and something sweet and bright that I can't place.

"Who are you?" I ask, pinching the lapels of his jacket and pulling them over my chest.

"My name is Rafael, family name Rostami."

"Is that how you introduce yourself in Osterstan?"

He grins, and my stomach tightens. His eyes light up and he nods, adjusting his glasses by the corner of the dark wire frame. Then he starts to walk in the direction I'd been heading before I pulled off to check my shoe. I cautiously walk next to him.

"Thank you for your jacket, Rafael."

"You're welcome . . ." He arches his eyebrows and waits for me to introduce myself. I let out a sigh.

"Neve." He waits, as if on the edge of his seat. "Family name Ruiz."

"It's lovely to meet you, Neve-family-name-Ruiz."

I smile and walk next to him under the lamplight.

"What are you doing on the peninsula?" I ask.

"That is a more challenging question than I fear is appropriate for first impressions."

"What does that mean?"

"It means, I will tell you now that I am traveling before I

return to my commitments. But that, alas, my travels are coming to an end."

"Your Nordanian is good," I say.

"Is it such a surprise that I would speak the common language of trade? Most of us do in Osterstan. Old Osterstani is a thing of the past. Though, I would be lying if I said I didn't crave hearing it again."

"So . . . you're returning to Osterstan, then?" The thought of this man, who's visiting from a region I only ever hear about in clips of new reports, an embattled region plunged into strife and suffering—a place that he will soon return to—fascinates me. I can't keep the curiosity off my face.

"Yes, of course I'll return to Osterstan. It is my home."

"Is it . . ." I begin, then shake my head, not finishing the thought aloud. If this is his home, he may find my questions about it rude. But he waves his hand, as if coaxing me closer.

"Is it what?"

"Is it safe?"

He lets out a laugh that echoes off the buildings, and it's hard to keep the smile off my face.

"Yes, it is very safe."

"Oh."

"I understand that there are some . . . misconceptions about my country," he says, waving his hand again. "But it is a warm, loving place to live, and I do look forward to my return."

"So, why did you leave?" I ask, and then quickly look away. Headmistress Moyle would have my head for questioning him. But he doesn't seem too put out by it.

"I suppose, for the same reason anyone leaves their homeland. To see what else is out there." He's quiet for a moment as he seems to consider something. He moves a fraction closer and drops his voice. "Forgive me for saying so, but you aren't Nordanian. Surely, you can relate? Coming from Espancia?"

A shudder ripples through my body. I've done everything in

my power to hide my roots, and for the most part, I've succeeded. My accent is all but gone, with the exception of when I become truly angry. Which is rare anymore. And I've learned to apply my makeup to soften my prominent Espancian features —shading my cheeks so that my nose looks more narrow and pert, shaping my lips with color so that they don't look quite so full, lining my eyes so that they look like the classic doe-eyes of my Nordanian sisters and not the often-sexualized slant of my Espancian mother.

"What makes you think I'm from Espancia?" I ask. He slows his step slightly and opens his mouth. Then closes it again, as if stopping himself.

"I apologize if I was incorrect. I recently traveled through Espancia. Perhaps it was just fresh in my mind. It was my favorite place I've visited on my travels. The food alone has starred among my nighttime fantasies."

My cheeks flush at the way he phrases his words, and I find myself smiling, wanting to agree. I miss my mother's cooking so terribly that I occasionally wake up thinking I can still smell her plantain-wrapped corn pies.

"It is okay with me if you do not want to talk about Espancia," he says, his voice quieter still. "But if you do, I would like that, too."

I nod, catching his eye. He watches me, the same indifferent, passive mask over his features, but he doesn't look away.

"Thank you . . . no," I say softly. We walk along the curve of the road as the high street comes back into view, and with it, the noise of revelers out for a night of fun and little consequence.

"Was it something I said?" I ask, even more softly. He frowns for a moment, and then, seeming to understand my question, cracks a little smile.

"It's the way you walk."

"The way I walk?" I stop where I am, suddenly self-conscious.

"Yes," he says, leaning back on his heels, hands back in his pockets. "Like you were born a queen and anyone who disagrees can go to hell."

I don't bother to fight the grin that spreads across my cheeks. I don't know what to say, so I just nod my thanks. He chuckles.

"No one has ever . . ." I hesitate and lower my voice yet again. "Not to sound strange, and I don't think you meant it this way, but I don't think I've ever been paid a higher compliment."

His eyes widen like saucers, and the smile drops.

"I meant it as the highest form of compliment."

Something passes between us, a commonality, or an understanding. The two of us, strangers in a strange land, walking under the dark of night, knowing little more about one another than our place of birth and our names. And yet, I feel more bonded with this man than anyone I've met since I arrived in this country.

"Where am I taking you?"

A flush passes over my body, and then I realize what he's asking.

"It's this way." I point to where the high street curves away from the port, and we continue walking. The air thickens, and the fishy stink lingers as we move away from the bustle of the port. When we turn onto the road toward Conrad's estate, his eyes travel to the canopy of magnolia trees, to the thick ropes of moss twining between them.

"This is not your family home, then?" His voice is light and conversational, but there's something deeper there, as well. He seems genuinely interested. He waits for my answer, as if there's an imperative purpose to his questions.

"No, it's not."

"Are you a beneficiary? For the institute?"

My blood runs cold, and I tug his jacket tighter. But the plain interest in his face is enough to make me let my guard down. Perhaps just enough to be dangerous.

"I was. I mean, I still am a beneficiary, but am no longer in the running for the institute."

He nods, his eyes wandering down the first row of orange groves at the edge of Conrad's property.

"So, you are now seeking marriage? A husband?"

My defenses climb, and I feel the urge to defend myself to this man. "I'm seeking a way to pay off my debt to my benefactor."

"That is so strange."

"What is?"

"That you would owe your benefactor money. Isn't the definition of a benefactor someone who gives freely? Why would you owe a debt to one?"

His words leave me stumped. I shrug and shake my head.

"That's the benefit of being an outsider, I suppose? That you can see things that insiders don't?"

"I suppose," he says, though his expression is troubled. He slows his pace as we reach the main road into the estate, looking back toward the town. "And your debt will be paid by that man?"

The distaste in his expression is clear, and for a moment, I forget myself. I've been able to speak so freely with him, perhaps because I know I'll never see him again. Because he's a traveler, just passing through, never to be seen again.

"Yes, he will pay my debt," I say. "And in return, I will marry him."

"That is your wish? To marry a man like that?"

"Of course, it's not," I say before I can think twice. Clouds pass over the moon, casting us both in shadow, making it hard to read his expression. But his shoulders remain relaxed, his hands in his pockets as he leans back on his heels. I don't know when we stopped walking, but we're just outside the main gate. I should walk away. Wish him a good night, return his jacket, and thank him for escorting me to the property.

Instead, I step toward him.

"I worked hard. So hard. I should have been chosen to go to

the institute. But I wasn't. And now, I'm trapped. I don't have a say in these things. If I tried to speak up, it wouldn't go well for me. You understand?"

"I understand," he says, but his eyebrow ticks with judgment, or disapproval. I'm not sure which. "If you could choose, though, you would not choose that man?"

"Of course not," I hiss.

"But you would still choose to be a wife?"

"I don't know," I say. "Why? Are you offering?" I mean it to be a joke, but I've never been particularly funny. It doesn't land.

"Of course not," he says, too lightly. It hurts. I shouldn't let it. I should be tougher than that. But I feel my shoulders cave in slightly. He lifts his palms.

"I am sorry, Neve Ruiz. I did not mean offense. I just have no desire to take a wife."

"And I suppose, you don't have any desire to have children? Or if you do, that you'll get to it when you get around to it?" His features pinch slightly, but he shakes his head.

"Having children is very important to Osterstanis."

"But you have no interest."

"It's never been something I considered. Not seriously, anyway."

"Oh? How nice for you to have that option."

"Yes, I suppose it is." He speaks plainly, and it starts to infuriate me. I feel my stomach coil into a snake of anger, ready to strike. I breathe in through my nose and out through my mouth.

"Don't do that," he says, nodding at me.

"Don't do what?"

"Fight your instincts. Be yourself."

I stare at him. This stranger who presumes to know so much about me, who presumes too much.

"This is ridiculous."

"What is?"

"You. Questioning my ability to choose my life. Bragging

about how you don't want a wife. How you don't need to choose one—your privilege in this world—all while you're walking me home after a man who claims to be Godly tried to . . ." I shudder as I struggle to find the right words to describe what he interrupted before.

He opens his mouth and raises his palms, as if placating a wild animal, and it's too much. I fall over the edge as red seeps into the corners of my eyes.

"And another thing. You should be so lucky as to have a wife like me. I am *incredible*. I will be an amazing wife. I speak four languages. I know Morse code. I can cook, and cook well. I can sew and manage a household, and I know how to endear myself to household staff and earn their respect. I can send and receive messages on a telegraph and plan a formal dinner party in five countries, and I would take care of you better than anyone has ever taken care of you. I would make your mother look like a wild animal who tries to eat her young."

I stop, slapping a hand over my mouth. His eyes are wide with amusement, but there's something else ticking there beneath the surface. Anger, perhaps? I may have gone too far.

"What about love?"

"What about it?"

"Doesn't love have a place in marriage?"

"Not for me."

"No?" He frowns, but his interest is piqued. "You've never loved?"

"I loved my mother." My use of the past tense gives me pause, and I see a flicker of something cross his features.

"You would do all of that for a husband and never expect love in return?"

"I wouldn't do it out of love."

"No?"

"You're forgetting something fundamental."

"What's that?"

"I have to survive."

He is quiet for a long moment. He stares at me, studying me, and I feel exposed, raw, vulnerable. I want to coil in on myself, but I fight against it, rolling my shoulders back and standing straighter. He nods, as if he's decided something, and then walks through the gate toward the estate.

I walk alongside him as he nods to himself. His brow is set, but he remains quiet as we approach the estate.

"Fine, then," Rafael says as we reach the wide steps that lead up to the pillared entrance.

"Fine?" I ask.

"I would like to speak with your benefactor, please."

I stare at him for a long moment and barely recognize the sound of the heavy, white oak front door opening behind me.

"Miss Neve?" Leo, Conrad's valet, sounds confused.

"Leo," I say with a gracious smile. "Mr. Von Brandt had . . . an emergency. He asked Mr. Rostami, here, to see me back."

"I would like to speak with her benefactor, please," Rafael says, his accent stronger now, as if he's playing it up.

"Sir?" Leo frowns and looks between us.

"It's really okay, Mr. Rostami," I say with a cordial curtsy. "You've done more than enough in seeing me home."

"I'll wait here," Rafael insists.

"Please," I say, removing his jacket, realizing Leo must have thought it strange to see me wearing a strange man's clothing in the dark of night. "Have a safe trip home, and thank you for seeing me back safely."

Rafael takes his jacket, but merely folds it over his arm.

"Miss Neve, perhaps it is best that you return to your room?" Leo's voice is soft, and yet, unflinching. But I'm frozen, my core heating with uncertainty.

"I will simply reassure your benefactor that nothing amiss happened tonight," Rafael says, his voice low. "I would not want my actions to have led to any trouble for you." Cool relief floods my chest, and yet there's still something that leaves me unsettled. Something I've missed.

"Say your goodnights, Neve," Leo says. Leo technically holds no authority over me—yet I wouldn't dare disobey him, and he knows it. I nod at Rafael, and he nods at me, the same bland expression over his handsome features. And yet, there's something slightly different about his posture, about the way he carries himself as I climb the steps and pass through the house. It's not until I have changed and climbed into bed, trying to fall asleep to the sound of Carla's soft snores, that I realize what it was that lifted his shoulders, that relaxed his forehead ever so slightly.

It looked just a little bit like hope.

CHAPTER SEVEN

*T*he money is gone.

I couldn't sleep last night. Every time I started to drift off, memories of the night before would inundate me with terrifying clarity. By the time the sun rose, I felt sweaty and sick to my stomach with the knowledge that yet another piece of my future could have slipped through my fingers so easily.

I rinsed off before anyone else rose, feeling both sweaty and chilled as the lukewarm water rinsed my flushed and feverish skin. I dressed in clothes I could move in, shoes I could walk in, not putting to words what I was planning. I would go into town later this morning for Gaia, and she would understand. She was the one, after all, who told me I should go to Osterstan.

I reached under my bed, digging my fingers into the clever little slit in my mattress that I'd made when I was moved into this glorified closet of a bedroom in the basement.

I reached deeper, grasping around for the little pouch of coin I'd placed inside. My fingers felt nothing. By the time the fear crept into my cheeks, I knew it was gone. But I didn't stop looking. I flipped the mattress, tearing the fabric apart from the springs. I turned the bed frame itself around, in case it had somehow fallen somewhere I couldn't see it.

"Neve?" Carla's soft voice cut through the chaos in my head, the way it always could. Her soft hand landed on my back as I shook my head.

"It's gone."

"What's gone?"

"It's all gone."

"We'll find it," Carla says, unhelpfully. I turn around. Her face is calm, knowing.

"You knew?"

"Your savings?" Carla says with a little nod. "Well, I know you kept some money. I wish I had some. But I never leave here." She gives a sheepish laugh and guilt seeps into my chest. I'm not sure Carla has left the estate since she arrived a few months after I did. She's always been a few steps behind me and Arden, her placements and chore assignments always an afterthought.

"It's all gone."

"What about the others?"

"What others?"

"You used to keep coin in different places, right?"

I close my eyes and pinch the bridge of my nose. If she noticed, then it's possible others did, too. Probable, even.

"I never said anything," she says quickly.

"I know."

"So, did you check the other places?"

"Look around us, Carla," I say, motioning to the minuscule room that contains just enough room for our two mattresses on rickety frames and a bar to hang our clothes. "Where else would I hide it? It was all in the same place."

"How much was there?"

"Enough," I say. There was enough in there for me to book a passage out if I ever needed to—just me. Her eyes widen. But I don't correct her assumption.

"Someone was in our room."

Her eyes widen further, and then she shakes her head.

"What?" I ask.

"I saw Conrad down here yesterday."

"Yesterday?"

"Last night. You were in the village? With Mr. Von Brandt?" She frowns and shakes her head again, as if trying to convince herself that that couldn't be the case. But I have little doubt. Von Brandt clearly has something Conrad wants, and he doesn't want me running off.

"Speaking of," she says, a mournful pallor dulling her brown cheeks.

"Speaking of what?"

"Conrad has sent for you."

I swipe on a layer of demure rose lipstick to steel myself for whatever is to come.

Conrad's sitting behind his ornately carved, walnut-wood desk, shuffling papers. He doesn't invite me to sit, so I remain standing opposite him.

"Seems you had an eventful evening." His words are lazy and bored. There's no benefit to responding. Yet another one of Headmistress Moyle's lessons. A cost-benefit analysis of when to speak and when to remain silent. I simply stand before him.

"Your contractual debt is considerable."

"Yes, sir."

"This isn't enough." Something hard clinks against his desk, and I look down to find my pouch of coin. It somehow looks both heavier and smaller than I remember. My stomach coils tight, and I let my canine tooth pinch the inside of my bottom lip.

"You've done well, Neve," he says, leaning back in his chair, pressing his elbows into the arms and steepling his long, gray fingers. "You should've done better, considering the investment I made in your last-minute preparation, but you did what was asked of you. When you consider the investment I made in Arden and her pay-off"—he runs his eyes over me with something like disappointment, and then shrugs—"it balances out."

I'm not sure what he wants me to say. So, I remain silent. *Silent and submissive*, Headmistress Moyle would have said. *When in doubt, remain silent and submissive.* I suppress a shudder that wants to destroy my composure and instead, roll back my shoulders.

"Of course, you are more impressive than Arden. Better trained. Your intelligence far superior. You understand the value of loyalty. You're a loyal person, aren't you, Neve?"

My stomach tightens to stone, like hardened lava rock as I nod. "Yes, sir."

"I have business interests around the world, as I'm sure you've surmised. You're very bright. I've never doubted that."

I'm not sure what to say, so again, I say nothing.

"Not everyone has the same interests as I do, and it can be difficult to protect those interests. But my interests are Nordania's interests. I will always be, first and foremost, a Nordanian. You know what it's like to be a loyal Nordanian, don't you?"

"Yes, sir." My fingers freeze against my thighs as my lungs tighten. His icy blue eyes hold mine with his implicit threat. After all, he knows exactly who I am and where I come from.

"Very good. I wouldn't want you to forget that that's what we're here for. The most important value of all." He reaches for a document on his desk and runs his fingertips over it, considering. "I want you to consider that statement very carefully when I tell you that I consider you to be family."

My stomach tightens, the shell of lava cracking, threatening to boil over. This man is not my family. Until six months ago, he didn't even notice that I was putting in all the extra work at night, helping Tatiana study for her time at the institute. She would've made it, too, if she hadn't gotten pregnant by some village boy. That's when Conrad noticed me. He considers my success his, but it was my own.

Only when I failed to secure a spot at the institute did it become my fault.

"Family protects family. You understand that, right? You, perhaps more than anyone, understand that. Don't you, Neve?"

"Yes, sir." I don't know where this is going, but something tells me I'm not going to like it.

"I would never send family out into the world with someone who is a virtual stranger without a safety net. I hope you know that." His eyes flicker up to me, and he picks up the money pouch. My money pouch.

"I'll hold on to this for you. Invest it. It's a good, healthy sum. It will do you a lot of good, and I'll be happy to return it to you— with interest—if you can accomplish what I need from you." The air between us feels denser, thicker. I frown as the hard pit in my stomach heats.

"I'm sorry, sir, but I don't understand?"

He leans forward, folding his fingers together against the desktop.

"You really are quite the lucky fool, aren't you?"

The cruel shift in his tone makes me straighten my spine. But I say nothing.

"I don't know how you managed to find, much less catch the eye of the incoming Osterstani Trade Minister . . ." His gaze flickers to mine, as if wanting to catch my reaction. The satisfaction in his posture makes it clear I've given him exactly what he wants. He nods, stroking the side of his chin with his thumb.

"It's quite the coincidence, really. He's set to take over the role any day now. But his whereabouts have been unknown . . . until now."

I frown, trying to work out this change in events. I'm not

entirely sure what has happened, but a chill rushes down my spine nevertheless. I don't know what to say, so again, I say nothing. There's often more power in saying nothing than saying something just to fill the air.

"I'll need you to send me, shall we say, information. Keep me apprised as to the things you see. Rumors you might hear. On a regular basis, I will expect you to send me coded telegrams— international telephone calls are still a rarity there and would draw far too much attention—and occasionally, I'll need you to send and receive packages. Connect with my business associates. All for my business interests, of course—the family business. And I'll need you to do this without attracting the wrong sort of attention."

"I don't follow. . . . Are we talking about . . . Rafael? I mean, Mr. Rostami? I thought—"

"Yes, well, I thought your ship had sailed. But your wiles are far craftier than I gave you credit for."

"Are you asking me to do something . . . ?" I pause. I know exactly what he's asking. But I decide to play at being careful with my words so as not to accuse the man holding my future in his hands of something offensive, to play the part of the naïve ingenue. "Something that might raise eyebrows?"

"I would never ask you to do anything that would be illegal under a Nordanian court of law." His words are crisp and cutting. "I simply ask you to protect our family's interests. Just as I would protect you as part of our family."

"Will that include sending information that might pertain to my new husband? My new family?"

He is quiet for a long, tense moment. He leans back, complacent, and shrugs one shoulder.

"I suppose that depends on what sort of dealings your husband or your new family engages in."

His threat is clear. *Do what I ask of you, or consider yourself in danger.*

"My new husband being . . . Rafael?"

Conrad shrugs again. I take a deep breath, and it's as if I've just inhaled a fine mist of something that feels a whole lot like hope.

"And if I succeed?"

He tilts his head and taps his fingers on the desk, next to the pouch of money—*my* money.

"If you succeed, then in one year, I will send you the sum of your paltry savings here, with interest."

This is a trap. It smells like a trap, it sounds like a trap. And yet . . . if I can do as he asks for one year, I could have enough to find my way out of whatever terrible situation he might send me into.

"Who knows," he continues, a knowing smirk curling the corner of his mouth into something truly terrifying. "If you can manage to keep your legs closed, you might even find yourself in a position to walk away with both an annulment and the means to live on your own.

"Of course," he says, tapping his fingers on the desk, "the offer that Jarls made is still on the table. If this doesn't seem to be something that falls within your considerable skill set . . ." His eyes dip down my body, and then back up, just slowly enough to make my stomach clench. "Well, I'm sure I could persuade Mr. Rostami to consider one of my other girls."

My chest swells. It's hard to breathe.

He's offering me a path to freedom. Actual freedom.

I'll only have to betray the man who wants to save me. The man who already has saved me—twice, in fact. A hard, uncomfortable pit settles in my gut, telling me this is wrong. That I shouldn't bring this—whatever it is—onto his head. Perhaps I should just take the other offer?

But then, I remember the feel of Jarls's chapped fingers against my skin. A violent shudder wants to wrack my shoulders, but I hold it in, biting hard on my bottom lip. I wonder what I could do to stave off Jarls for a year. It seems unlikely, considering how much he wants to *expand* his family. I suppress a shiver.

I don't know what exactly it is that Conrad wants me to do once I'm there, but if I could walk away at the end of the year with enough money to write my own way in the world, wouldn't it be worth it? And maybe, I could even control the fallout. Maybe I could tell Rafael? I immediately dismiss that thought. It would be foolish to assume I could trust a powerful man with my life like that.

A knock sounds at the door behind me. My stomach sinks, but Conrad raises a finger.

"Just to be clear, in case you decide to change your mind or betray me—remember the company I keep. It would take nothing for me to ruin whatever life you think you've built in that godforsaken country. Loyalty is everything. And disloyalty will be severely punished."

The air in the room seems to thin and still, as if his words alone, the severity of them, can control such a thing. My heart thumps in my chest, as though it realizes sooner than my brain does that this life, the one that Conrad has provided, isn't really over. It may never be over. Not really.

"Come in," Conrad says, standing and stacking the papers on his desk. Our conversation is over, which can only mean one thing: this is happening now. I have to agree to his terms now.

"What do you say?" Conrad says under his breath as the door closes behind me and footsteps approach.

I don't have a chance to respond before my nose is met with the scent of lilacs. Lilacs, and fabric detergent, and something sweet that I can't place.

"Hello there, Neve-family-name-Ruiz."

CHAPTER EIGHT

I can do nothing to keep my jaw from dropping. Rafael stands next to me, wearing a pale blue linen suit and gray suspenders over a crisp white, button-down shirt.

"Trade Minister," Conrad says, passing the stack of papers to him.

"Mr. Laarsworth. Pleasure to see you again." His smile is charming, but there's still a stiffness to him, something I notice as he adjusts his glasses by the corner of the frame.

"Neve has become like a member of our family," Conrad says, holding Rafael's gaze. An odd, vaguely paternal smile takes over Conrad's face, as if he's playing at being a father figure. I work hard not to roll my eyes.

"And now, she will become a member of mine." Rafael doesn't flinch away. After a long moment, he turns to me and takes my hands in his, once again holding them just loosely enough that I know I can pull them away at any moment and he'll let me go.

"Of course," Rafael continues, "only if she wants this."

"Pardon?" Conrad asks, his voice clearly unsettled.

"Forgive me," Rafael says to Conrad, and then turns back to me. "It is customary in my country that we allow the woman a say in the matter. If you do not wish to become my wife, I will honor your request. I will still honor the contract, as well," he says with a brief nod to Conrad, who has gone stony still. "But I will not force you into anything you do not wish to be party to."

The weight of the decision settles into my shoulders. Rafael is willing to buy out my contract, to pay off my debt, and let me go. But if I do, I will have nothing. I will be free, but I will have nowhere to go, no way to earn a living, and the title of Unchosen will follow me for the rest of my days. If I go with Rafael, I will be beholden to him as his wife, but also to Conrad. But if I do as Conrad asks, in one year, he'll give me my money back. With interest.

Rafael doesn't want to be married. He said so himself. But also, I told him I don't see love as a part of marriage. He knows what I want out of this, what I can give, and he's still standing here, offering this to me. I don't understand what he has to gain from this arrangement—he said himself he's never pictured having children—but then, Conrad's other words come back to me. *If you can manage to keep your legs closed, you might even find yourself in a position to walk away with an annulment.*

Rafael's expression is hard to read, but there's something gentle, even encouraging behind his warm brown eyes. Conrad stares from the corner of my eye, his glare a warning. One I'd do well to heed.

"Yes," I say, squeezing Rafael's hands. My gaze flickers to Conrad in answer to his implicit question—the one he posed just before Rafael arrived. "Yes, of course I will be your wife, if that is your wish."

"It is," he says.

"Wonderful." Conrad's wry tone cuts through the moment.

"You will find the agreed upon payment in your coffers by the day's end," Rafael says, not letting go of my hands.

"Of course," Conrad says, waving his hand as if money is the least of his concerns.

"Shall we?" Rafael says, and I realize it's happening now. He's going to take me away from here now. Not later today, not tomorrow — *now*.

I walk out the door, my arm threaded through his, having made two promises to two different men. My future has never felt so tenuous, or so bright.

CHAPTER NINE

*T*he wicker headpiece digs into my scalp, and my neck aches with the stress of it all.

"You will be a sweet bride," the woman in the back of the chapel tells me, smoothing out the purple and white homespun ribbons that hang from the side of the headband. Apparently, in an Orthodox Osterstani wedding—something Rafael's mother would never forgive if we skimped on—the bride is meant to look like a cloud, ascending to the heavens. The groom is marrying her in an attempt to ascend to the holiest of places himself.

But as I look in the mirror, I can't help but giggle—then clamp my hand over my mouth. I look like a child's unwrapped birthday present.

"Do not be ashamed of your gleefulness." The woman with the same coloring as Rafael shares a knowing smile. "There is much to be excited for today. Not least of all the wifely duties that will find you after the sun sets."

That's a sobering thought. My gut tells me Rafael won't actually expect me to make good on those duties, but then, I didn't expect him to insist upon a traditional Orthodox ceremony either. And if consummation is part of the package . . .

One thing at a time. First, I need to figure out how to see through this veil of ribbons and tulle so I don't accidentally walk into a wall.

The woman seems to anticipate this and tells me to take her arm.

"I understand your mother cannot be with us today," she says, tutting her tongue. I wonder what Rafael told her and her husband, the priest, when he asked for this ceremony. They didn't seem fazed, and didn't even ask if I was pregnant. Surely that would be the only reason someone would ask for such a quick wedding ceremony?

"It is the mother's job to give away the young bride, to prepare her for the things to come. After all, 'From womb to womb flows godliness.' I won't presume to take on that role, but I will stand in and do my best to support you. You deserve some support today." Her cheeks are pink and full, her hazel eyes watery and kind, and I feel the overwhelming urge to either push her away or hug her. It's an uncomfortable feeling, so I simply smile and say nothing.

She walks me into the chapel where Rafael is waiting, wearing a long white tunic and white pants, his feet bare. Though, beneath all the veils, his feet are the only thing I can see clearly. His feet are large, and his toes long, his toenails nicely groomed. I find it a strange relief to know the man I'm about to marry takes care of his toenails.

I'm thinking about toenails as I'm getting married.

The woman walks me over to him, and he turns me by the elbows to face him. Then slowly, one layer at a time, he lifts my veils. As the priest speaks in the background in what I assume is the old language, Rafael's face becomes clearer and clearer. When he lifts the last veil, the priest stops speaking and the chapel is filled with a warm weight. The air feels heavy, heavier than I can put words to. Peaceful, almost.

Rafael's warm brown eyes focus on mine from behind his glasses, but his expression remains guarded, unreadable.

"You look beautiful," he says at last, lifting my gloved fingers to his lips and pressing soft, chaste kisses to each of my knuckles.

The man says something to him, and Rafael nods. He begins to slowly tug on the fingers of my gloves, until he's removed one completely. The priest approaches, holding open a liturgical book. Rafael places my glove across the pages, and then works on the next. The priest begins speaking again in old Osterstani, and Rafael removes my second glove.

The priest nods to him, and I could swear Rafael's cheeks flush pink. He casts me a strange, apologetic look, and then kneels before me. I flinch when I feel his hand coil around my ankle.

"Lift your foot, dear," the woman whispers behind me. I do, and Rafael slowly, carefully, unlaces the strange bootie I'm wearing. He removes it, then the thin stocking beneath it. He moves on to the next, and then presses a kiss to the ground between my feet. When he stands, he looks a little flustered. It's a look I haven't seen him wear yet, and I can't ignore the shift in the room. Whatever this ritual is that we're performing has weight to it, and I already feel the ties between us binding in some spiritual way.

"Neve," he says, drawing my attention back to him. "It's time for our vows."

"Oh," I say, my stomach tightening. I don't know how I will understand the language to repeat it.

He seems to sense my anticipation and smiles. "We just say what we feel. What we promise to each other. It is personal. It is not meant to be pretty or elegant. Not rehearsed." It's the one human element amidst the divine.

I don't know what to say. What am I meant to promise this man? This man who I have no intention of remaining married to, much less consummating this marriage with. This man who I've already betrayed by simply accepting his proposal?

The priest motions to him, and he clears his throat.

"Neve," he begins, and his hands shake slightly beneath mine. "I promise to be a good, fair, and just partner to you."

I don't know what I was expecting, but it wasn't this. This isn't antiquated or patriarchal. But maybe it really is like he said? It's about speaking his truth, not saying something he's rehearsed.

"I promise to protect you and keep you safe, always. I promise to consult you and value your opinion whenever possible. I promise to give you everything you need and to listen when you ask for more."

He takes a deep breath, and his hand shakes. I give it a supportive squeeze and run my thumb on the underside of his palm in support. He frowns, staring at our hands, and I wonder if I've made a mistake. If I've done something too intimate or just unwelcome. But then he runs his thumb along the inside of my wrist.

"I can't promise to be perfect, and I can't pretend to believe I can be everything you would hope for in a husband. But I will always try to be your friend — " He stops, as if he was about to say more, and then thought better of it.

That's it. Those are his vows to me.

They're not romantic. I don't feel loved or adored. But I do feel valued. Respected, even. For a girl like me, an Unchosen girl, it's more than I could have hoped for. And yet, I find myself longing to know what he kept back.

The priest says something else and nods to me. It's my turn. I take a deep breath and let it out.

"Rafael, I promise to be kind and considerate, and to be dutiful to you." The words are out of my mouth before I realize they're something Headmistress Moyle would've told me to say. I give a little shake, trying to get her out of my mouth.

"I promise to respect you and to speak my mind when you ask it. I promise to listen and to be your friend when you need one. Even when you don't . . ."

These aren't the vows I imagined I'd be making, but they feel right. They feel like something I can strive toward — that I would want to strive toward — and they don't feel like lies. I'm sure God knows I'll have lies enough to fill a marital bed soon.

"I vow to honor your family and your traditions. But I also vow to tell you when I disagree and to try my very best not to let my temper get the best of me — " It's out of my mouth before I can stop it, and I freeze. Fortunately, everyone is smiling, even Rafael. His cheeks are full, and in this moment, free from his normal guarded expression, he looks at me with something that resembles adoration. I feel my cheeks flush and look down.

"Thank you," Rafael says, squeezing my fingers gently. "That was beautiful."

I'm not sure I agree. It felt clumsy and unorganized. But it also felt honest. And I suppose honesty is the best gift I can give him for now.

The priest speaks again in the old language and starts to walk around us, his wife walking in the opposite direction. They continue to walk in circles around us until I start to feel unsteady with their motion. As if expecting it, Rafael squeezes my hands, and I hold his gaze.

They stop moving, and Rafael moves in, pressing his lips to my cheek. He kisses my other cheek, and then leans in. He hesitates.

"May I kiss your lips?" His whispered words tickle my lips.

I nod, not wanting to break the spell with my own clumsy words, and his lips brush mine. It is chaste and over quickly. He's being congratulated by the priest, and his wife is hugging me.

The rest of the day is a blur. We change into traveling clothes and have a light lunch before we board a ferry across the bay. It's not until the port is disappearing into the horizon that I realize I never got to say goodbye to Carla.

My stomach twists, and I feel Rafael watching me, studying me. But he says nothing, chewing silently on a bit of flatbread as we glide over the open water.

We board a train next, and cross the rest of Nordania in a blur. People call me Mrs. Rostani, and I nod and smile. Even in such a short amount of time, people don't see me as Nordanian anymore. When I'm on the arm of an Osterstani man, they seem to assume I'm Osterstani. Rafael seems pleased by this.

But as we approach another port town and a large Osterstani ship comes into view, it all comes crashing down.

I'm married.

I'm married to an Osterstani man, and we're going to live in Osterstan with his Osterstani parents.

I've said vows to this man—that, shockingly, I mean to keep —*and* I'm going to report back to Conrad with whatever it is he wants. I'm going to spy on my husband, who even now, watches me with the weight of responsibility as if it's his pleasure to carry. I hope I can get through this and keep both myself—and my soul —intact.

CHAPTER TEN

*T*he ship rocks in the port as the bellboy carries my spartan luggage ahead of us.

"Here we are, ma'am," the bellboy says, stopping in front of a nondescript cabin. He speaks with a rich accent that reminds me of Rafael's, only less refined. The bellboy holds the door for me. He waits outside the door once I've entered, and I feel awkward, as if I've forgotten something.

"My apologies," Rafael says, rushing into the room with me. The bellboy then enters, relief apparent on his face. As he moves around the room, turning on the lamps, I shoot Rafael a look.

"What?" he asks.

I shake my head, holding my tongue. He wraps his long fingers gently around the back of my head and presses a kiss to my temple. My chest squeezes with an emotion I can't place. But then I notice the bellboy's eyes fixed on us. It's just for show. I let out what I hope doesn't sound too much like a relieved sigh. He hesitates next to what I assume is a closet door.

"I can unpack my things," I say, shaking my head. The boy's eyes dart to Rafael's, and his features slant with awkwardness.

"You'll be needing the maidenhead?"

"The what?" I ask.

"Yes," Rafael says, wrapping an arm around my shoulder and giving me a placating squeeze. "Bad timing and all, but alas, you cannot fight nature."

The boy nods, solemnly, and then unlocks the door and shuttles my suitcase inside.

"Where is he taking my things?" I whisper.

"Do not worry," Rafael says. "You don't have to sleep in there."

"Sleep in where?" I say with a frown. The bellboy reappears, the room behind him still dark.

"If that will be all?" The bellboy stands at attention. Rafael nods and passes him a large Osterstani coin. The boy grins as he tucks it up his sleeve.

"Oh, and congratulations"—he nods to me—"and best wishes" —he nods at Rafael— "upon the occasion of your wedding." I smile demurely, as it seems I'm meant to do.

"Thank you," Rafael says, pressing another chaste kiss to my temple as the door closes. He steps away from me a little too quickly, going straight for the mystery room. I follow him as a light flicks on and see a small, spartan space without a porthole. It contains a narrow bed, a nightstand, and a wash basin. That's it.

"What's this?" I ask, blocking the door.

"It's a traditional maidenhead suite." His voice is cool and matter-of-fact as he lifts my suitcase off the luggage rack.

Something rings in the back of my mind, but it's buried among the meager Osterstani history and culture I read about and immediately forgot.

"It's where women who are menstruating sleep for the duration of their courses."

My cheeks flush at the same time I lose the ability to speak, and he pushes easily past me, bringing my suitcase back into the main room.

"This is where I'm meant to sleep when I'm . . . on my

courses?" I nudge into the bed. It's hard as a rock, and the blankets are thin and itchy.

"That's the idea," he says, placing my suitcase on the larger luggage rack in the main room and lifting his own.

"Why?"

"It's traditional," he says. "It's not something that all Osterstanis observe, but the more devout ones do."

"Like your mother?"

He presses his lips together in a tense line.

"Like my mother."

"But I'm not . . ." I hesitate, feeling my cheeks flushing hot. I've barely known this man for more than forty-eight hours, and already, I've shared so much personal information with him.

"I thought you might be more comfortable if I slept in a different room," he says, stopping next to me in front of the door, his suitcase in hand.

"Oh."

"This seemed a good solution."

"You're going to sleep in there?" I ask, frowning at the bed.

"I won't have you sleeping on that terrible bed on our wedding night," he says quickly. "I don't want to scare you away so quickly." He tries to make a joke of it, but there's something vulnerable and sweet in his delivery that twinges my heart.

"How do you know it's a terrible bed?"

"Common knowledge," he says with a shrug. "Punishment for woman's original sin and whatnot."

"That's barbaric!"

"That's why I won't ask you to sleep in there." He cups my shoulder with his hand, and for a moment, I wonder whether I should volunteer to sleep in the maidenhead room after all.

"Thank you," I say, feeling ungrateful for everything he's already done for me. With a curt nod, he takes his suitcase into his room and starts to unpack. I get to work, as well. It will be a solid four-day journey along the northern Mittlesee to reach the westernmost city of Albahar in Osterstan, so there's no use living out of a suitcase.

"Do all Osterstani apartments have rooms like that?" I call from where I'm shifting my pajamas into a dresser that's bolted to the wall.

"Some do, some don't," he calls back. There's something to the way he speaks that makes me think he's being purposefully dodgy. I remove my stockings, and they reveal a thin brown package. I'm about to pick it up when I realize it's probably from Conrad. I quickly shut my suitcase and shove my stockings into the open drawer. I cross the room and lean against the doorframe, watching him tuck his luggage under his meager bed.

"Does yours?"

"Does my what?"

"Does your apartment have a room like this?"

He nudges his case and shifts it, just so.

"No."

"No?" A wash of relief comes over me, followed by something much murkier and more confusing.

"I don't have an apartment."

"You don't?"

He rises to his feet and stuffs his hands into the pockets of his trousers. His suspenders stretch, and I find the maneuver simply charming.

"I have a townhouse in the Old City."

"Oh."

"Yes."

"Well, does your townhouse in the old city have a maidenhead room?"

"Yes."

"And is the bed terrible?"

"I don't know," he says, frowning. "I suppose we'll have to ask my mother."

"Your mother?" He crosses the small space, removing his

jacket and folding it over his forearm. He approaches the doorway and leans against the opposite side. There's nothing overtly threatening about the way he's standing, and yet, I feel intimidated.

"Yes, my mother. She's the only one who's slept in there."

"Oh," I say, letting out a little sigh. "I thought you were going to tell me she still lives with you."

"She does," he says. I feel my eyebrows fly upward. "But then, so does my father."

"Your mother, the super traditional one, lives with you?"

"She lives with us, love."

I stare at him for a moment as he nudges his glasses up his nose.

"It is traditional in Osterstani homes for multiple generations to live together. Strengthens the familial bonds and whatnot." His face is bland. It's hard to glean any sort of opinion.

"Oh, okay."

"You won't be expected to change their bedsheets or anything," he says, tucking his free hand back into his pocket and standing a little straighter. "But I'm sure my mother will make a point of teaching you the pertinent things—you know, family recipes and whatnot."

I swallow hard around a big lump. A memory, faint, of my own mother, squatting in our small flat with me, stuffing okra and pork into mounds of ground corn and pork fat. Teaching me to always cup my hands, never squash.

"If that's okay, of course?" Rafael tilts his head, his eyes searching.

"Yes, fine," I say, clearing my throat. "Is she a good cook?"

He crosses his arms over his chest and shrugs. "She's a traditionalist. She'll be glad to pass on the recipes, the ways of things, to the next generation."

I nod, looking down at the narrow space between our knees. It's so strange—two days ago, I didn't know this man. And now, we're standing in a married couple's suite on a ship to a strange land.

"This will be okay?" he asks, his voice lilting with anticipation, as if he's waiting for my approval.

"I've never lived with family—" I stop as his brow furrows. "It was only me and my mother when I was a child." He nods as if he understands. But if he still lives with his parents—or rather, they live with him—then he doesn't truly understand.

"Does your moth—"

"Should we get dinner?" I ask, feeling agitated.

He nods, straightening his back, and slips past me toward the door. He holds out his arm, motioning for me to join him. As he twists the door handle, he pauses and places a gentle hand on my lower back.

"I know that our arrangement may be a little . . . well, perhaps it wasn't what you hoped for." I open my mouth to disagree, but he shakes his head. "Nonetheless, I want you to know that I meant everything I said in my vows. What is mine is yours, and that includes my family. If you would like to be a part of our family, it is yours for as long as you wish it to be."

My throat tightens, and I nod.

"Thank you."

"Yes, well . . ." He removes his glasses and blows on them, as if cleaning his glasses is the simplest way out of an intimate moment. Then the door is open. He nudges me through it, and we're back to playing the roles of happy newlyweds.

CHAPTER ELEVEN

"*This* is it?" I ask, staring up at the tall, orange brick house sandwiched between two others, and then two more, and so on, to form a row of houses about ten long. Exhaustion from our journey seeps into the corners of my eyes as I blink up into the reflecting sun. The building stretches three stories above the green front door. Once we arrived at the port of Albahar, it was still a fairly long cab ride from the chipped-paint, clapboard buildings along the port, through a brown-and-orange bricked commerce district, and into the whitewashed blocks that Rafael explained was the financial district. By the time we turned onto the paver stone streets of the Old City, I was too exhausted to appreciate the trimmed greenspaces and carefully maintained brick row houses.

"This is it," Rafael says, setting our suitcases down for a moment before running up the steps, taking them two at a time. Before I get out of the cab, I reach into my bag for a tube of lipstick and fortify my nerves with a layer of soft plum. I press my lips together and with a deep breath, follow him out of the car.

He raises a palm before I can get too close. "Wait here just a moment. My family will want to welcome you. It is tradition."

I nod and stay where I am. Honestly, the last thing I want to do right now is go through a formal meet-and-greet. Part of me had hoped we'd arrive in the middle of the night and be able to deal with the rest of the world in the morning. Not to mention the package I found tucked into my luggage courtesy of Conrad. It contained telegraph paper, pre-addressed and stamped envelopes, stationary, and a package addressed to *W. W.* with no explanation. Part of me wanted to open the package and see what it was, but another part of me knew better than to know too much.

I look down the street as I wait, watching pairs of people walk back and forth. Osterstan hasn't been what I expected. For starters, listening to Nordanian radio and reading the news would have you believe the entirety of the country is war-torn. It's not. Sure, it's a little shabby around the edges, and it's clear that some parts of the city seem dated, or like they could use a touch-up with paint, but it feels fairly modern. Far more cosmopolitan than Peninsula City.

A man and woman walking next to each other grow near. I smile at them, but the woman averts her eyes, and the man scowls at me. They pass without greeting me, and I am about to check my armpit to ensure I don't smell when I hear the man hiss, *"Nordanian sludge"* under his breath.

The woman stares back at me, and for a moment, I think she might look apologetic. But then she spits. Actually spits.

At me.

I'm used to negative attention following me. Heck, I'm Unchosen. But this level of vitriol feels biblical.

Fortunately, her aim is terrible. It doesn't even come close to reaching me, but that's not the point. I don't know what to do, what to think. I wonder if it would have been different if Rafael had been standing next to me. But also, I realize that part of me expected that I would be able to blend in better here than I had in Nordania. The entire journey here, if I was addressed by anyone, it was with nothing but respect. I was Mrs. Rostani or Madam to anyone who spoke with me. Nobody even asked to see my papers because they, I suppose, assumed I was Osterstani. They only looked at Rafael's. But now, this? It seems things are far from that simple.

"Here she is," Rafael says from the top of the steps. I turn my attention to where he stands, flanked by two people who are clearly his parents. The woman to his right is tall, almost as tall as he is, with sturdy shoulders. Her dark hair is pulled back into a severe chignon at the base of her neck, and she wears a collared, short-sleeve dress that hits her legs at mid-shin. It is blocked in black, white, and emerald green, and looks both chic and maternal. It's more revealing than I'm accustomed to seeing on a woman, but I don't dislike it.

"This is your wife?" The man to his left speaks in a richer accent, from beneath a silver-gray mustache. It's dignified and sits above his full lips, making him look like a wizened professor or military general. He wears a pressed white shirt unbuttoned at the neck, tucked into loose gray silk pants. His suspenders are green with gold clips, and when he holds his hands behind his back, they accentuate his broad chest.

"Come to us, girl," his mother says. "Let us have a closer look at you." She presses her full lips into a thin line, her gaze bland as it rakes over me. I leave my suitcase where it is and ascend the steps. They don't move when I reach the top, so I stay where I am, one step down.

"This is my Neve," Rafael says with a pride that makes my cheeks flush. "Neve, these are my parents, Nima and Benham."

Nima's gaze doesn't soften as she takes me in. If anything, her jaw sets harder when her eyes flicker up to my face. She looks somewhat disappointed, as if she's just sniffed a rotting orange. Benham looks bored. As if he has a better use for his time than to meet his son's new bride.

"You expect us to welcome her into our home? Have you even been blessed by a proper priest?" Nima says, as if I'm not standing right here. My stomach tightens, and I dig my thumbnail into the pad of my index finger, trying to release some of the building tension.

"Yes, of course, Maman," Rafael says. "In an Orthodox ceremony. She wore the crown. I unlaced her boots. The priest and his wife welcomed us into the church." She doesn't look any more impressed.

"What do you have to say, girl?" Nima says. I don't miss the fact that she doesn't use my name, despite having been given it.

I give a demure curtsy and bow my head. I don't recall the exact customs of Osterstan, but it seems like a general show of respect and as good an idea as anything.

"It's a pleasure to meet you."

She stares down at me, her steely gray eyes boring into me, as if looking for a fault to wedge her way into.

"She is to stay here?"

"Nima . . ." Benham says.

"Yes, of course. She is my wife."

"Perhaps she would be more comfortable elsewhere for her first night?"

"Maman," Rafael says, his face pinched with strain.

"She looks as though she would fit in well at the Black Magnolia."

"Nima—"

"That's enough, Maman," Rafael says, his voice clipped and his forehead tight. It's the most emotion I've seen on his face, save for the briefest of moments during our wedding ceremony.

"Nima," Benham says, exhaustion creeping into his voice. "They've traveled far. Can we not save the interrogation for the morning?"

Rafael darts past me down the steps to collect our luggage. The whole time he's getting them, Nima glares at me, and Benham pinches the top of his ear, as if that will release pressure somewhere else.

"Come, my love," Rafael says into my ear, pressing a kiss to my shoulder. I fight the surprise and give him my sweetest smile. I feel Nima's eyes on me, scrutinizing and skeptical, and try to let out a little laugh. Rafael does the same.

"Forgive me," I say, trying to sound soft and unthreatening. "It has been a long journey."

"Yes, I'll show you to our rooms," Rafael says.

"Rafi," Nima says, caution in her voice, but Benham silences her with a look and lets us pass into the house.

Inside the door is a small vestibule with warm wood paneling and a slate floor. We pass through into a long space that houses both a formal living room and a dining room. To the right is a wide staircase that disappears into the ceiling alongside a solid wooden banister. Rafael climbs the steps and motions for me to follow. We reach the second floor and continue walking down a dark, narrow hall to a door at the very front of the house. He opens this door and waits for me to enter, much like he did on the ship.

The room is dark but well-appointed, if a little formal. Orangey wood paneling comes up the wall about one-third of the way, and above it is a green, gold, and peach wallpaper displaying exotic flowers and zebras. It's a lot to take in. And yet . . . I don't hate it.

Light filters into the room as Rafael opens the thick, navy velvet drapes, displaying a large bay window that spans the width of the room. A small breakfast table with two armchairs rests in the recessed window. Dust motes flicker in the air. Rafael stands, backlit by the window. I can't see the expression on his face, but he stuffs his hands into his pockets and rocks on his heels.

"We can change it, if you prefer. This is your home now, so we can do whatever makes you happy. I want you to feel welcome."

I look back at the room and take in the large four-poster bed with a heavy damask bedspread and about a dozen fussy pillows. At the foot of the bed is a navy velvet chaise lounge chair. On the opposite wall is a fireplace, and down from it is another door. I walk toward it and turn the handle.

Beyond the door is a bathroom complete with a green porcelain soaking tub and green marble sink. The wallpaper continues into the room, offset by glazed tiles that meet it halfway up the walls. It is dark in the room, even with the etched glass lamps, but I can see it would be a comfortable place to clean up. Directly across from the door I just passed through is another, and when I open it, I find that I'm standing inside the maidenhead room. It is small and dark and spartan, just like the one on the ship.

"We can alter this room as well, if you like."

"I'll be sleeping here?" I ask, feeling claustrophobic in the windowless room. My stomach tightens, as does my throat.

"Not unless you choose to."

Reality slams into me. We are husband and wife now. Under the same roof as his parents. We will be *living* as husband and wife.

"The sofa is very comfortable," he says, nodding at the chaise. His face is distant and again, unreadable. I wish I could read him just a little bit better. To know what it is he really wants, what he really means.

"I don't wish you to live your life sleeping on a sofa," I say, speaking truthfully but not as openly as I perhaps should.

"Some couples choose to sleep in individual beds."

"Do they?" I ask, but there's something in his tone that has me cautioning against celebration.

"Yes, some do. Though it's not traditional in this part of Albahar."

"In this part of town?" I ask, not following.

"The Old City is not just a historically protected neighborhood. It's also where the largest population of practitioners of the old faith live." His voice doesn't carry much hope or levity, and I understand his meaning. If we were to replace the large bed with two smaller ones, people would notice. It could be an issue.

"Wouldn't your mother prefer that?"

"My mother would prefer you pregnant already."

I snap my head to face him, and I can only imagine how wide my eyes are. He snorts and can't contain his laughter as he shakes his head.

"You can't be serious."

"My mother is a true believer. She wants to see me 'go forth and multiply.' To her, the greatest sin would be for a woman not to birth as many babies as the good Lord deems her worthy of." I arch a brow. Considering I have no plans to birth, much less conceive any babies any time soon, I can see our relationship is doomed.

"She's not going to warm up to me, is she?"

He shrugs. "I think you have more in common than you may realize."

"I don't know anything about her, so I'll take your word for it."

He steps out of the way, and I move back into the main bedroom. He begins to unpack his things and shows me where I can put mine. It's so strange to see my entire life contained in a single suitcase.

"What's that?" he asks, nodding toward the package taking up a solid third of my luggage.

"Oh, just a gift from my benefactor," I say, setting it aside. "I'll open it later, in private. If you don't mind."

He shrugs and returns to unpacking.

"I will show you the top floor a little later. My office is up there, and I fear we will find it in the same state in which I left it. Or worse—the telegraph machine was likely running the entire time I was gone on my travels."

My interest piques, but I try not to lean into it too much.

"Another time, then," I say.

"Yes, of course."

He shifts past me to put away more clothes, and then back to his suitcase. That's the way we spend the evening. Quietly moving around each other, trying not to step on each others' toes. His small kindnesses continue when he asks me which pillows I prefer and whether I would like a sachet for the cedar-lined wardrobe. I thank him as he continues with his own unpacking and wonder how it will feel to betray his confidence. A cold shiver rushes down my spine, and I shudder at the unpleasant sensation.

"Are you cold?" he asks, concern marring his brow.

I shake my head and smile. "No, not cold."

He nods and resumes his task of unpacking, leaving me to incorporate my own sparse clothes into the small existing wardrobe. I wonder how I'm going to make it through this, when it already makes me feel this uneasy.

CHAPTER TWELVE

The kitchen is at the back of the first floor. It's a cheerful space, full of light and color. The cabinets have been painted red, with shiny brass hinges, offset by handmade glazed tiles. The countertops are bright white heirloom marble, betraying years of love and abuse. Everything forms a U-shape around a pristine white cast iron stove with beautiful arched legs. It's far from new, but it looks well-loved and well cared for. The air is warm and smells rich and inviting—distracting. I startle when I finally notice Nima standing next to the long peninsula, sipping what smells like a hearty, spiced tea and nibbling on a seeded pastry.

She glares as I enter.

"Good morning, ma'am."

"You may call me Mother."

I swallow hard. *Mother* is a title that is not given freely in Espancia. But judging by the severe angle of her heavy brow, it seems this is non-negotiable.

"Yes, Mother," I say, cringing as the word passes my lips. I approach the peninsula and stand opposite her, taking in the spread in front of me. The seeded pastry she's eating is shaped like a bowtie and crusted in a blend of sesame, poppy, and caraway seed. But on the tray in front of her rests a variety of other pastries—some with thick, gem-colored compotes, others with rich blends of cheese and fruit, and still others glazed in bright icings.

"Tea?" she offers. I nod, though I'd much rather have coffee. She pours some from a silver teapot into a small ceramic mug and passes it to me. The aroma is thick and heavy as it hits my nose, but when I sip it under her watchful glare, it's surprisingly light. I still prefer coffee, but the cinnamon and clove blends with the vanilla and honey and something vaguely floral.

"Pocked pasty?"

"Excuse me?"

She nudges one of the seeded pastries toward me. "These are called pocked pastys. They became popular during the Mittlesee Embargo twenty years ago, when Rafi was a little boy and there was little fruit or milk to fill the pastries with." There's something in her gaze that makes me want to shrink into the floor, but I refuse to falter. I take the pastry and bite into it. The seeds fall everywhere, and the pastry flakes apart, contributing to the mess. It's not an easy thing to eat, but it is delicious. The buttery dough blends with the savory toppings, and I moan in appreciation before I realize what I've done.

She narrows her eyes, but says nothing.

"This is delicious," I say, dabbing at the corners of my mouth with a napkin. "Thank you."

She nods and sips her tea. We keep standing there, awkwardly, in silence until I realize that I haven't actually seen Rafael this morning.

"Where is Rafael?" She narrows her eyes again, as if I should know.

"He is at work."

"Oh," I say. Then I frown. The way she's watching me, I know that she suspects I didn't know he'd already left for the day. So I just nod.

"When will he be home?"

"At the end of his work day."

Right.

We continue to stand there in silence. Her, watching me as I try to eat the flaky pastry with some dignity. Me, failing miserably to do so. When there are no crumbs left for me to eat, I stare at her, waiting for her to say something else.

"Thank you for breakfast."

"Yes."

She stays where she is.

"I suppose I'll go now?"

"Go where?"

I stand, stuck in place. I don't know how to answer her question—or what it is she's really even asking.

"I, uh . . . suppose I'll visit the neighborhood?"

She frowns. Wrong answer.

"Or I guess I could familiarize myself with the household?"

Her frown deepens.

"What would you suggest? Where should I begin?"

"If I was a devout, Godly woman—which I am—I would probably begin with the bed."

"The bed?"

"You'll want to strip the sheets. Change them. Your husband should not sleep on such filth."

I frown, and curl my fingers into fists as a hot ember of fury ignites in my belly.

"Excuse me?"

"I assume you bled last night?"

I cock my head again. I don't understand. If I was bleeding, shouldn't I have been sleeping in the stupid maidenhood room?

She crosses her arms over her chest, and a smirk tugs at the corner of her mouth. She looks very much like the cat who caught the mouse.

"The neighbor works at the port. He's a sea traffic manager. Very prestigious appointment."

I nod, waiting for her to continue.

"He told his wife, who stopped by this morning with a gift of new marital sheets."

My stomach coils into a hot, twisty mess, and I let out a deep breath.

"Ma'am—"

"Mother," she practically hisses.

"Mother," I say through gritted teeth. "Please forgive me. Your customs are unfamiliar to me. If you would speak plainly, I think we would both be better off."

"She explained that you had your monthly courses while you were on the ship. You slept in the maidenhood room the whole voyage. Such a shame, since without consummation, you are not man and wife." There's a low rumble of a threat in her words.

My stomach twists tighter, and I rub at the right side, where it aches the most.

"Right," I say, unable to argue with anything she just said.

"So, I assume the sheets will need changed from the filth of your sin." Her eyes are so hard and hateful on me, as if, by merely having sex with my husband, I would become unworthy of him. Not just that—it's as if, even though it would literally take both of us to consummate the marriage, I'm the one who has sinned. Not her precious son.

I feel the heat rising from my stomach into my chest. Fast. Too fast. I can't lose my temper. Not now, and not with this woman. She turns and starts to head for the kitchen door. She's going upstairs. I rush to catch up to her.

"Mother," I say, trying to endear myself to her, to squeeze around her before she can get to our bedroom and find out that not only are the sheets as white and clean as they were when the bed was made, but that only one side of the bed is rumpled.

She keeps walking, and I only just get around her to block her way at the bottom of the steps.

"What is the problem? Surely you didn't lie about your condition before you were wed?"

"No, of course not," I say, shaking my head.

"Then what is it? Why are you blocking my way, girl?"

She still hasn't called me by my name; I wonder what it will take for her to do so. A strange part of me wants to earn that level of respect from this woman who so obviously hates me. But as she glares at me, waiting to catch me in a lie, I realize that it would be too easy to get caught in a web of deceit. So instead, I decide on the truth.

"The sheets aren't dirty, because we haven't consummated the marriage."

She steps back, and while there is victory in her expression, there's also something that looks a lot like disappointment.

"Surely you aren't still on your monthly courses?"

"No, I'm not," I say, not clarifying that I haven't had my courses in weeks. "But neither was I ready to do something so important on my first night in a strange place after such a long travel day. I was exhausted and overwhelmed with all the newness. It's been . . . well, it's been a lot."

A mix of suspicion and sympathy crosses her face, but she doesn't back off.

"So, no. We have not yet consummated the marriage."

"You took vows to be an obedient and submissive wife, correct?"

I frown at her. Those weren't the vows I took, and when I don't answer immediately, she leans in.

"You are to honor your vows. My son is a blessing. He is a miracle, and he has been blessed by our Heavenly Father. He is destined to carry on his legacy. He has chosen you, and your union has been blessed in our church by our righteous and holy creator. You are his vessel to eternal life, and you will do your duty."

I stare at her, truly speechless. And suddenly very cold.

"I will monitor your condition, as I'm sure you will as well. God willing"—she makes a motion and looks upward as she does it—"you will be with child before the new year, and we will ring in midsummer with a new babe. Then, everything will be settled."

She reaches out, and her hands land on my hips, pressing on them a bit as she studies them. Just like Jarls did. I flinch away from her and wrap my arms around myself.

"You'll do nicely. Wide hips are good for birthing God's miracles."

I step backward up the steps with a nod and mumble something about needing some rest.

"Girl," she calls after me. I freeze at the top of the stairs and look down at her. The light hits her face strangely. It makes her look sepulchral, an enemy.

"If I discover you've brought sin into our house—into Rafael's bed—I will put an end to this little mockery of a marriage." That ember of anger flares back to life, and this time, I can't seem to stop it from burning up.

"There is no mockery, ma'am."

"*Mother*," she hisses.

"I have a mother," I practically spit at her. She flinches. "And she would never speak to me this way." Her eyes are wide and oddly triumphant. I turn and speed walk to our room, locking the door behind me, pressing my body against it until my breathing calms. Once it does, the heat returns to my stomach. It rises, higher and higher, until I can't take it anymore. I pick up a pillow and scream into it. The scream peals against my throat, leaving it raw and aching, and still I scream more. I scream until I'm breathless and panting on the floor.

I don't know how I can be married to someone I know so little about, whose family thinks so little of me and seems to have no interest in welcoming me into his life. Someone who vowed to protect me, and yet has left me to the wolves, left me hiding here, sobbing in a heap on the bedroom floor. A year is going to feel like a long time, but as I lean against the wood paneling, catching my breath, I want nothing more than to get Conrad what he wants and make it to the end of that year. I need to make my own way in the world.

CHAPTER THIRTEEN

"*W*ill you be all right today, love?" Rafael says as he clips his suspenders into his silk and wool blend pants and walks back toward the bathroom.

I sit on a chair in front of the bay window in our bedroom, picking at a pocked pasty as I try to rub my plum lipstick off my coffee cup.

When he returned home after that first day, I still hadn't left our bedroom. I hadn't eaten lunch, and when he asked me to come down for dinner, I tried to argue against it. I would've been fine sneaking down in the middle of the night, picking at leftovers. But he pushed me to tell him what had happened.

Halfway through my recollection, the corners of his wide mouth were pinched, and by the end of it, he'd taken off his glasses and pinched the bridge of his nose. He stood there for a long moment, polishing the lenses slowly, methodically. Then he put them back on and excused himself.

I didn't dare leave the room, terrified that he would come back with some new bit of information that he couldn't live with and would send me on my way. Or that he would force me back downstairs to apologize to his mother.

When he returned, though, his face was solemn, and he looked even more tired than he had when he arrived home. He walked to the wardrobe and extracted a dress I didn't know was inside. White silk, with buttons down the front, it looked like it would fall just below my knee. Shorter hemlines seemed to be the fashion in Osterstan, though I didn't actually have any evidence of that beyond catching sight of his mother's shins.

We dressed for dinner, and he escorted me downstairs, hand in hand. When we arrived at the dinner table, he rearranged the chairs so that he sat next to me instead of across from me. His mother said nothing throughout the meal, leaving me to listen to his conversation with his father. They talked about shipping and trade and the weather. Things I knew very little about, especially as they pertained to Osterstan. But I remained focused throughout, trying to commit as much to memory as I could.

At the end of the meal, his father offered him a cigar and a brandy while "the ladies cleaned up." Instead, Rafael pulled my chair out for me. He took my hand and led me back upstairs. For a moment, I was afraid he would change his mind about not pushing me to consummate the marriage. But he didn't. He simply exhaled and asked if I enjoyed my meal. Then he took a shower and tucked himself into the blankets on the chaise. He slept well enough, it seemed, though my sleep was fitful. I stayed in our rooms the next day. Then, after two days of staying in the bedroom, I finally decided to venture outside into the neighborhood. But I only made it three blocks before it felt unsafe, given all the hissing and insults that were levied at me. I turned home as soon as a child spit at my shoes.

"Love?" Rafael's voice cuts across the room as he emerges from the bathroom.

"Yes?" I haven't gotten used to him calling me that. I'm not sure I will.

"I don't want you to spend your whole day in this room. This is your home. You should feel free to move through it as you please."

"I'm fine, Rafael," I say, picking up the book I've been reading.

I've amassed a little pile of books that I've taken to reading in front of the wide bay window. The one I'm currently reading seems a little scandalous to exist in such a devout household, but it only makes the time pass faster.

He sighs and squats down next to me. He cups my hand in his, and I realize that this is the first time he's touched me in this room. It feels shockingly intimate and heat pools in my cheeks.

"I don't want you to be fine. I want you to be comfortable."

I cross my ankles and fluff the pillow at my back.

"I'm perfectly comfortable."

He presses his forehead to my knuckles—another strangely intimate move—and then stands. He steps back, hands in his pockets, and looks down at me.

"You'll be ready tonight? At seven?"

I nod, a little rush of nerves scuttling through me.

Tonight, we have a dinner with his colleagues. I don't know what to expect; he hasn't given me anything to go on. I've asked for books I could read to hone up on my knowledge of Osterstani customs. But he pushed back, telling me it's good to have an outsider's perspective at "these things." I don't know what that means. I don't even know what to wear. He crosses the room and pulls open the door on the wardrobe.

"I forgot," he says, and I look up, watching him hook a dressing bag on the outside of the door. "I have something for you."

I stand and cross the room.

"What is it?" I ask once I'm standing next to him.

"I wasn't sure if you'd been shopping?"

I look down and shake my head. There's a part of me that feels ashamed or embarrassed for not yet going to the shops. For still being so dependent on him. I've literally been trained for this life. Although, perhaps the institute would have trained me better still? Not that it makes an inkling of a difference.

"This should do," he says. He pauses as he passes me and brushes his lips against my temple. It's chaste and brief, and yet it feels like such an intimate show of support. I nod at him in thanks and wish him a good day.

For the next thirty minutes, I stare at the dress hanging from the wardrobe door. It's a floor-length, ivory silk gown with cap sleeves and a keyhole at the neckline that dips down between where my breasts should go. It is simple and elegant—what I've always dreamed of wearing, attending an event like this. It doesn't feel real.

But I've trained for this. I can do this.

I work at my makeup, spending a little extra time on the shading around my nose and eyes, making my long nose look a little rounder at the tip. I add heavier bronze shadow in the crease of my eyelids. And yet, I keep my lipstick neutral and demure. I don't actually know what the style is for Osterstani women, but as a new bride, it seems wise to use a lighter hand. My armor, as my mother would have called it, is battle ready.

I style my hair up, curling my long, dark tresses so that they fall down the back of my head like a waterfall, landing just below the nape of my neck. When I step into the dress, it's a near perfect fit. I look elegant, refined, and not at all like I was ever Unchosen.

Rafael arrives, having already changed into a dark, formal suit complete with a bow tie, and when I carefully walk down the steps, he watches me as if he's sizing up the fit of the gown. His mother sits in the formal living room, her eyes narrow, but she says nothing.

A black cab waits outside for us—it's different than the others I've ridden in, with shiny hubcaps and an official-looking insignia on the hood that I can't make out clearly in the dim light. It rattles along the paver stones of the Old City and out into the traffic of the busy Albahar streets. It's an odd mishmash of vehicles that fill the streets of the city proper: automobiles, like our cab, but also coaches pulled by horses, carts pulled by donkeys, and even little carts attached to bicycles and motorbikes. The city has a lively, unpredictable energy so different from that of Peninsula City—far more frenzied, and foggy with vehicles of all sorts. And yet, though I haven't seen it, I sense an underbelly far more similar to Nordania and Espancia than would appear.

We pull up in front of a large building with pillars out front. It reminds me of Conrad's estate on the Peninsula. I take Rafael's arm when offered, and together, we walk up the steps and into the building. As soon as we enter, a large chorus of people call out his name. It's the press. They call to him, shouting questions, and the noise is almost too much to handle. He pats his hand over mine, as if he knows I wasn't expecting this.

But why wasn't I expecting this? I had all week to ask him what to expect, to nudge him into giving me details he clearly knew but did not share. I could have prepared for this. And I didn't. Did I do it on purpose?

"Rafael!" a voice calls from within the press corps, and Rafael stops, nodding at him.

"Yes, Yosef."

"What do you have to say about the new sanctions imposed upon—"

"Did you not already ask me that just this afternoon?" Rafael says easily as the rest of the press laughs, good-natured. "Tonight, we're here to raise funds for orphaned children of the corridor. And this is the first event to which I've had the opportunity to bring my wife."

That sets off another round of questions, which Rafael laughs off just as easily as the first. I smile, as if I'm keeping a particularly good secret.

"If you'll excuse me, I'd like to enjoy our dinner so I can dance with my wife." Another round of laughter follows, and Rafael turns us toward the main doors to the event. As he winds us through the interior, he's stopped every few steps to talk to someone or another. If I had to guess, I'd say it took another twenty minutes before I finally sit in my seat at a table for six. An older couple sits on the far side of Rafael, and two empty seats remain to my left.

"Wow," I say, once Rafael sits down. He lifts his water glass to his lips and arches his eyebrows. "You're like a celebrity."

He laughs, and it might be the first time I've seen it reach his eyes. Once again, it truly transforms his face, and I think for a moment that I could get used to seeing that smile.

"I am the trade minister. Not a celebrity."

"I hardly see the difference, what with the way everyone's reacted. Your title is new, correct?"

"Yes."

"And you were elected to this position?"

Something pinches in his face as he shakes his head.

"I was appointed. Technically, my seat was inherited." He waves it off, as if it makes his position less impressive. His father's interest in Rafael's work now makes more sense—if it was inherited, it certainly affected his own legacy. Rafael doesn't say any more, and someone stops to shake his hand. He laughs with the gentleman, and though I can't hear what he says over the general noise of the ballroom, I smile when he looks in my direction.

"What exquisite luck!" A grating voice floats over my shoulder, and I turn to see a bloated, balding man with an over-waxed mustache leering over me. He wears a plum-colored suit, a large brown feather pinned to his lapel, and there's something in his glance that makes me want to change tables. Something knowing.

"Hello," I say.

"William Whitey," he says, holding out a hand. "Espancian

delegate to Osterstan." His hand is small. That's the first thing I notice. It's also clammy when I shake it.

"Neve Ru—Rostami," I say, catching myself. I realize this is the first time I've introduced myself by my new name. Not only that, but introducing myself as an Osterstani, who used to be Nordanian, who was born Espancian—to an Espancian man.

"Of course! The trade commissioner's new wife. Lovely to meet you!" He steps to the side slightly and nudges a slight, awkward-looking woman in a long-sleeved, slightly wrinkled plum gown. The skirt hangs oddly, and I realize it is weighed down in feathers that match the one on William's lapel.

"My, aren't you a lovely thing. How in the heavens did the institute miss out on someone like you?" Unease cripples me. I can't move, much less come up with something clever to say in response. There's an unspoken threat beneath his words, but he shrugs as if nothing has just passed between us.

"This is my wife. I'm sure you'll have many things in common." He nudges her toward me, and I take in the woman in the feathers—a woman who can't possibly be any older than me.

"Neve," I say, reaching out my hand to her. Her hand curls into mine, her fingers delicate and cold. Her skin is pale, and her eyes are as flat and unadorned as her thin brown hair, which hangs limp around her shoulders. Yet there's a spark of something there. Something I want to get to know.

"Zerah," she says. Her name is familiar, and as I study her expression, I know her in an instant. She was at the institute. And she's not anymore.

Which means, she knows Arden.

And Arden knows I'm Unchosen.

"Nice to meet you—"

"Look at these two," Whitey says, his voice grating as he shakes Rafael's hand with a little too much effort. Rafael winces. "Getting on like flies on meat."

Zerah shuts her eyes and slowly exhales. I press my lips together, fighting a laugh, as she opens her eyes.

"Yes," Rafael says with a kind laugh. Whitey shifts toward Rafael, abandoning us to shop talk. Zerah clears her throat. She arches a thin, sparse eyebrow.

"You need a life raft?"

"What?"

She nods down to where I'm still clutching at her hand. I let go, startled by my gaffe. She snorts as she takes the seat next to mine.

"So, how'd a Nordanian girl get into Osterstan?" she asks, reaching for a basket of bread and plucking a round, flat roll. She offers the basket to me, and I take a piece, despite the fact it's not time for this yet. The salad course hasn't even been served. Assuming there is a salad course. I don't know what kind of food they're going to serve. So far, the food that Nima has prepared has been rich, hearty stews full of legumes and spices. I can't imagine we'll be eating such heavy food next to a dance floor.

"It's just a piece of flatbread," Zerah says, biting into hers without any decorum. "Either eat it or don't. Nobody cares."

I cast a glance around the room and realize nobody is looking at me. Nobody is watching these two girls from Nordania pilfering from the bread basket before the meal has begun. I tear a piece off and tuck it into my mouth. It's good. Buttery and tender-crisp. After a few bites, I get a subtle taste of garlic and something else a little sweet and nutty.

"This is delicious," I say.

"Yeah," she says, as she chews, "they don't mess around at these things."

"Have you been to many?"

She shrugs. "Some. He's not exactly top of the heap, but he tries to be heap-adjacent."

The laughter that comes out is sharp and positively un-ladylike, and I clap a hand over my mouth to keep the bread from tumbling out. An amused grin works into half of her face, and she takes another bite of bread.

"Good to see you can take a joke. Most people I meet at these things can't."

The brilliant ring of silver on crystal cuts through the room, and people file into their seats. Rafael presses a light, chaste kiss to the top of my head as he sits. Speeches are given, and the courses begin. The salad course is unique from any salad I've ever had. Delicate greens are dressed with a soft, nutty cheese, pine nuts, and mulberry-poppyseed vinaigrette. The soup course is some sort of broth— Rafael explains it as a lamb consommé with leeks and dates. When our entree arrives, a ripple of joy runs across the room, and I stare at the bulbous thing sitting awkwardly on my dish in a puddle of broth.

"Stuffed onions," Rafael explains. "A special treat usually reserved for holidays."

I nod and watch him slice his open. Lamb, rice, dates, figs, and a litany of spices tumble out onto his dish. The older couple at our table digs into theirs, and Whitey does the same. I look at Zerah as she pushes it around on her plate.

"Not your favorite?" I ask.

She crinkles her nose. "Not an onion person." There's something hollow in her words that begs for more questioning, but it's just prickly enough that I know not to dig.

When dessert arrives, Rafael grins and can hardly hold himself back. The dish is a creamy-looking cake that isn't quite solid.

"This is my favorite," he says. "Custard apple cream cake. Custard apples are a local treat, and they blend it with tangy goat cheese and poppyseed sauce. Try—I think you'll love it." I arch my eyebrows, and he laughs. It occurs to me that I've seen more emotion on his face during this meal than I have at any point during our short relationship. His eyes light up behind his glasses, and I see flecks of green-gold in his brown irises. The laugh lines around his cheeks and temples crease, transforming him into what anyone with a pulse would call beautiful. I've never noticed beauty on a man before, and I like it.

I slide the side of my fork through the cake, and it cuts easily. It doesn't look like any cake I've ever eaten. I sniff it and inhale the tangy-tartness. Rafael grins, nodding for me to try it. Slowly, I close my lips around my fork. The moan that comes from my throat is less than ladylike. But it might be the most delicious thing I've ever eaten. It's less a cake and more like a dense custard, with sharp, bright citrusy notes—but without the cloying sweetness of the Peninsula oranges. The brightness reminds me of sunshine in a very specific way, and paired with the heavy creaminess of the base, it melts on my tongue, and a moan escapes my throat.

Rafael's grin sharpens, and his eyes dart to my lips. A different sort of smile spreads across his. Something mischievous and hungry.

"You like it?"

I nod, pressing my fingers to my lips, as if to hide something improper.

"Don't do that," he says, reaching for my fingers and holding them in his hand. "If you enjoy it, let it be known." I swallow the dessert and look at my hand in his.

"It's delicious."

"These are some of my favorite foods."

"They're delicious." I laugh at my inability to come up with a different word, and thankfully, he joins in.

"I'm glad you like them." The gratitude in his words feels personal. For a moment, it feels like we're seeing eye-to-eye on something I can't quite name.

Our moment is interrupted by the clinking of another glass. Someone makes an announcement, and the speeches start in earnest. I've eaten more food than I think I have in a very long time, and my stomach is full and warm. It's hard to keep my eyes open, despite the impassioned orators.

Rafael stands suddenly, and there is a shower of applause. I realize I've missed something important, and he squeezes my shoulder as he goes to the stage. He shakes the hand of the last speaker, and then takes to the podium.

"I know everyone has just digested their custard apple cake, so I won't take much of your time for fear of actually putting you all to sleep."

The audience laughs. There's even a couple of cheers in appreciation. It's impossible not to smile. Rafael goes on to speak about the importance of protecting children and families trapped in the Osterstani corridor—a region to the east that has become an important bridge between Swendenland and the rest of the Mittle Continent. Before the railroad that spans the corridor, Swendenland was essentially cut off by the way Osterstan's borders cut into the Mittlesee. The train lines were protected by Nordanian and Sudersbergian forces.

But nowhere in my reading have I heard about children and families being trapped anywhere.

"As Osterstanis, the family unit is our lifeblood. As much a part of who we are as our circulatory system is to our bodies. If we do not protect this most sanctified unit, we lose our identity, our purpose. This work tonight will mean that dozens of families will sleep warm, safe and sound among their people. Thank you for being here, and now, I'll get off this stage so you can dig into the mulberry liqueur and still have enough time to dance it off."

Cheers and laughter fill the hall. Rafael shakes hands with the presenters, who pass him a plaque that I must have missed before. It takes him a while to return to the table, but when he does, he leans over and cups my cheek. His eyebrows lift in question, and I nod. He brushes his lips against mine, as chaste as our wedding kiss. The crowd cheers more, and I realize the show he's just put on.

This is what I'm here for — to be the politician's wife. This is what I've trained to be. But I realize I will have to learn the difference between the two men: the quiet, humble, hard-to-read man I married, and the effusive showman who just dazzled and inspired a crowd.

Music strikes up from the opposite side of the ballroom from a six-piece band. It's not a song I'm familiar with. The strings are plucked quickly with a passionate frenzy. I feel the vibrato, the tremble of each note, deep in my gut. It's hard not to sway to the lilting rhythm.

"Dance with me?" he asks, the crisp politician's smile still on his face — the one that doesn't quite meet his eyes.

"Yes, of course," I say. I take his hand, and he leads me across the room. I feel eyes on us as he leads me to the dance floor. There are only a few other couples, and they shift out of our way. When the song is over, everyone claps, Rafael included. I look to the band, to join in and show my appreciation. But they're clapping and looking at us.

I feel awkward, as if I'm the butt of some joke. The band strikes up another song, and more people move to the dance floor, as if eager to dance to the song they've been waiting for. The floor fills in, and I can feel the tension drain ever so slightly from Rafael's shoulders.

"You're something else," I say, quietly enough that only Rafael can hear.

"Meaning what, precisely?"

I arch an eyebrow, and he chuckles.

"You're important here."

"I suppose so."

"Why didn't you say so? When we first met. Before . . ." I stop myself. *Before you paid for me to become your wife*, is absolutely the wrong thing to say right now.

His face transforms as he nods hello to someone who passes

us. Then he spins me slightly, so that his back shields me from the crowd.

"I didn't want it to color our interactions." His brow is tight. "Not that there was really much time for it, anyway. We didn't exactly have a long courtship."

"You're suggesting we *had* a courtship?" I ask. He chuckles, and it reaches his eyes. My chest warms.

"Everything happened so quickly. I just . . . I enjoyed keeping everything simple."

"We had time. We had four days on that ship, and we barely discussed anything."

"I know," he says, dipping his head. It's a strange thing to see him do. The man of the hour, revered and celebrated by so many people who paid what I can only assume is a lot of money to be here tonight—showing me a submissive nod.

"I'm sorry," he says, and there's real concern in his eyes. "Is this something you can forgive?"

I shake my head, and his face drops. "It's nothing to forgive," I say quickly, realizing what my response must have looked like to him. "I like to feel prepared. I would have liked to feel more prepared for this evening. I hope I haven't made any mistakes."

"You were perfect," he says, lifting my knuckles and gently brushing his lips against them. Then he presses them to his lips again, and holds them there. It's different. There's something that feels like the spark of something real.

"Rafael!" A large man claps him on the back, and they chat as I stand awkwardly. Rafael introduces me, and the man apologizes for the interruption. I try to listen in, to pick up any bit of information that might be useful, but it becomes apparent that Rafael is needed elsewhere. I excuse myself and wind through the ballroom, ducking my head in greeting to all the strangers who catch my eye. There's a wary intrigue in most of their glances, and I wonder how much of it comes from the same place as the neighbors in the Old City who hate me because they think I'm Nordanian.

I duck into the bathroom, grateful for the quiet. The air is cooler, more peaceful, and I let out a deep breath. I didn't realize how much tension I was holding around my ribs until I feel the muscles release. I touch up my lipstick, giving myself another coat of armor. Something tells me the night is far from over, and I'll need it.

As if on cue, a toilet flushes in one of the stalls. The woman who emerges is stunningly beautiful, with shocking white-blonde hair and thick dark eyebrows. She doesn't look much older than me, but there's a worldliness to her that resets my guard.

"Well, if it isn't the woman of the hour."

CHAPTER FOURTEEN

"*I* was wondering if I would have the chance to rub elbows with you." Her teeth are white and straight behind her crimson lipstick, and the way her top lip bows so perfectly makes her look like a fashion doll.

"Hello." I'm not sure what else to say.

"Are you having fun?" She runs her delicate, bronzed hands beneath the water of the sink.

"It's been lovely," I say, keeping my shoulders back.

"If you don't mind my saying," she says, rubbing a tiny bar of soap between her hands, "you look awfully southern for a Nordanian bride."

My stomach tightens into something sharp and painful.

"Oh?"

"Mm-hmm," she says, eyes focused on her hands, rinsing the suds from them. She shakes the water from them and turns off the faucet, reaching for a small hand towel that sits on the sink. "Oh, I won't say anything. That's not my business, and frankly, it's no one else's. Not that they'd notice. They hear 'Nordanian' and immediately assume you're one of those institute whores. Or that you're trying to invade them. Not that they're unjustified."

Her accent is similar to Rafael's, but subtler, more refined. There's something about her, about the way she speaks—I couldn't tear my eyes away if I tried.

"But you know?" I say, not disputing or playing dumb. It seems there's no point.

"Of course," she says. She puts the towel back in place and leans her hip against the sink. "It's in your walk."

I laugh. I don't think it's what she expects, and she laughs as well.

"You're not the first person to say that, if you can believe it."

"I believe it," she says, tapping a fingertip against her lips thoughtfully. "Irina." She holds out her hand for me to shake. I accept it.

"Neve."

"Yes, I know."

I shrug, because of course she knows. Everyone here knows.

"It's in the hips," she says. When I frown, she nods toward them. "You have the perfect hips—and I hardly expect I'm the first to comment on them. Your new mother must be particularly happy with them."

I press my hands against them, as if that will minimize them or make me feel less aware of the way they flare.

"She has, and yes, she seems happy enough." I keep my words diplomatic, but it's as if she can see right through me.

"Welcome to Osterstan, where a woman's waist to hip ratio is of national importance." She flashes a wry grin. I'm not sure what else to do, so I mimic her expression.

"Are you happy here? In Osterstan?" Her words are light enough, but the way her eyes hold mine, it feels like there's something far more significant passing between us. I only wish I could understand what it is.

"Yes," I say, cautiously. "I'm still learning the city, and the family dynamics . . ." She lets out a sharp laugh and nods.

"Yes, I can imagine. Rafael's mother is famously devout." She wrinkles her nose. "Devout *and* opinionated. Dedicated to the old faith, and even older ways." She arches a perfectly shaped brow, as if to emphasize just what she thinks of those older ways.

There's an intimacy to the way she speaks. I wonder if this meeting wasn't just down to chance. If perhaps she sought me out. I wonder if she doesn't just know Rafael casually, but if there's a more intimate connection there.

"Yes, she is . . . devout."

Irina's smile curves into something sharper.

"Of course, a girl like you must be used to difficult living situations . . ."

Everything in me tightens, and I can sense it. She's two syllables away from outing me, making it clear that my being Unchosen hasn't left me at the border.

"But if that ever changes . . . if you find yourself unhappy . . ." She picks up a black clutch purse that I didn't notice and pulls a small card from inside. She hands it to me. There's nothing more than a number written on it. It looks to be a telephone number.

"It's been lovely to finally meet the woman who snagged Rafael," she says, and then pauses, her head tilting. "I love your lipstick. It suits you." Then, before I can respond, she ducks out of the bathroom.

The card burns against my hand, and as the bathroom door starts to open again, I quickly tuck it into my bra. Two older women enter, and their faces brighten upon finding me in the bathroom. I quickly wash my hands and excuse myself.

When I return to the ballroom, I spot Rafael. An uneasy frown casts a shadow over his face as I catch his eye. He's talking to Irina and William Whitey. Zerah stands next to him, as if she's trained her whole life to stand in the shadow of a truly mediocre white man.

"There she is," Irina says as I approach. Rafael wraps an arm around me, his fingers pressing into the small of my back with tension.

"I understand you've already met?" Rafael asks.

"Yes, only just." I nod toward the bathroom.

"It is like our secret clubhouse," Irina says with a wink.

"Of course, it is," Whitey says with a sharp chuckle. "You women keep your secrets where we can't get at them—yet."

Everyone laughs because it's the thing to do, though something about his words and the way Whitey's eyes prowl across my skin makes me want to squirm.

"Well, I'll leave you to it. Good to see you, Rafi," Irina says. My throat tightens as my stomach flares with unidentifiable heat. She leaves, and Whitey helps Zerah into a lightweight jacket.

"Careful," Rafael says under his breath. He tucks a stray lock of my dark hair behind my ear, disguising his warning as something far sweeter.

"What?"

"Be careful around her." He nods to where Irina stops to talk to another man. The woman standing with them looks on, her soft features sharpening into something bordering on lethal.

I nod, not really understanding, but not about to ask for clarification.

"We would love to take you up on that offer, Rafael," Whitey says, clapping him on the back.

"Oh, yes?" Rafael looks awkward, but the diplomatic smile doesn't slip from his face.

"Get the girls together, they'll be thick as thieves. And I've recently spent some time in Nordania. Attended some state dinners and such. I am sure Neve would love to catch up with someone as good as an old friend." Whitey's eyes fix on mine, as if he's trying to impart something to me. I simply nod and smile. Zerah is just behind him. She shuts her eyes again, as if counting to ten.

I think I would like to spend more time with Zerah. That much would be easy, in any case.

"I'll set it up. Get back to you with some dates," Rafael says, shifting as if we're going to leave.

"This week, then?" Whitey says, his voice insistent and brash.

Rafael's eye tics, and I catalog it in my list of his reactions — I'm pretty sure this one classifies as annoyed.

"We'll see what we can do," Rafael says.

"Lovely to meet you, Neve," Whitey says, reaching for my hand and shaking it. He holds my wrist a little longer than seems necessary and nods down at where our hands are connected. He pulls his jacket sleeve back, exposing his watch. It's engraved, presumably with his initials: *W.W.*

It clicks. Conrad's package — the envelope addressed to W.W.

"Yes," I say quickly. "This week would be perfect."

Rafael's eyebrows lift as I tug my hand away from Whitey and shift to Zerah.

"I must confess, I've been lonely for female friendship since I've arrived. I would love to get to know my fellow Nordanian a bit more, if you're open to it?"

Zerah frowns, but it's not unwelcome. It's considering, as if she might actually enjoy something her husband drags her to for once.

"That would be lovely."

I give her a quick hug, feeling Whitey's hawkish watch, and after a moment, she hugs me back.

Rafael escorts me as we leave the event, my heart racing as I try to catalog everything that happened. I think I'll be processing it all for quite some time.

CHAPTER FIFTEEN

The weekend arrives with a gust of rain and wind. My breakfast tray is waiting for me when I wake up. It's been so strange sharing a bedroom with Rafael, but not really interacting with him. He's gone when I get up, but there's a note tucked beneath a cup of steaming coffee.

Saturday is a day of rest for the devout . . .

I grin, realizing that this is his way of telling me the coast is clear. I take a long sip of the brew and fortify myself.

I dress in a simple tan button-down dress that puffs slightly at the shoulders and sweeps across my knees before ending mid-calf. When I get to the kitchen, Rafael is sitting there, reading the newspaper next to a coffee press and a plate of day-old pastys. I'm coming to appreciate how functional and simply stylish Osterstani clothes are. Every dress I've inherited has pockets—and not merely decorative ones.

"Good morning, love," he says. "How did you sleep?" I can't remember when he first started calling me that, but it feels like something I can hang on to, to remind me that this thing between us, while decidedly un-romantic, is real. That it's not about to end on a whim, and I'm not in danger. Yet . . .

The events of the previous night floated through my head like the crank on Gaia's laundry machine as I tried to fall asleep last night. As soon as I would forget the way everyone eyed me with suspicious curiosity, I'd think of Zerah and that feathery dress that looked all wrong for a girl who seemed to be decidedly un-fussy. And then, there was Irina and her loaded questions, her familiarity with Rafael—only to be outdone by William Whitey's revelation.

He's Conrad's associate, the one I'm meant to pass something along to. He was so insistent on our meeting, and now, I understand why. Part of me wonders if I can trust Rafael with this sort of thing, if I could just be honest and explain that I need to meet with him, that I still owe my benefactor some level of loyalty . . . but that would delve into that slippery gray area of lies. And lies are so easy to unravel.

Or perhaps I could blow it off. I could say screw it and just accept my fate as wife to an Osterstani politician. Rafael doesn't appear to have an unreasonable bone in his body. Perhaps he would understand the difficult position I'm in?

Just then, Nima shuffles into the kitchen in an elegant embroidered housecoat and woven slippers. Even on the sabbath, she looks like she could lead an invasion.

"Good sabbath, Maman," Rafael says, lifting his cup of tea to her. She gives him a sweet smile, and then her eyes land on me, standing next to him and the coffee press. If there was such a thing as an expression that growls, that would be what she did with her face. She takes a fig from the fruit basket and leaves just as quickly as she arrived.

Yeah. I can't let go of my chance at freedom any more than she can accept me as her daughter.

"How was your sleep?" Rafael asks again, nodding for me to join him. He presses the coffee grounds down, and then pours the brew into a large ceramic mug, nudging it toward me.

"I slept well," I say. He arches an eyebrow.

"I didn't know that tossing and turning were the symptoms of a good night's rest."

I sip the coffee and suppress a smile.

"I may have been a little over-excited from the night's events."

"I understand," he says with a little nod. He watches me for a long moment, his expression unreadable, as if wanting to decide something and coming up empty.

"Do you—" I stop what I'm saying and look around the space, as if I'll find someone hiding between the cupboards. I lean forward, and he does the same. "How have you slept? I mean, do you mind? Sleeping on the chaise?"

He removes his glasses as he shakes his head.

"Your comfort is most important."

"That's very kind," I say, setting my mug down, "but it's also not what I asked."

"You would make a good barrister," he says, polishing his lenses one at a time.

"Don't change the subject," I say, giving him a teasing smile.

"If I'm being honest"—he replaces his glasses on his long, regal nose—"it's not the most comfortable place to sleep."

My stomach twists on itself. I feel guilty.

"We could trade off?" I suggest. "Or I could sleep in the other room?"

He shakes his head.

"The other room is adjacent to my mother's rooms. The walls are not permanent—it used to be her maidenhead room. She will know when you sleep in there, and she will be vigilant."

I realize what he's saying. After all, she as much as told me that she will be tracking my cycles.

"That's going to be a headache, isn't it?"

"Possibly," he says, suppressing a knowing grin. He leans forward, and there's something tentative in his expression as he presses his fingertips into the table. "If I'm being honest, my hope is that this will not be a permanent solution."

"Oh."

It's as if the floor slips out from beneath me. I am entirely reliant upon his goodwill, and if he doesn't see my place here as permanent, then no good can come from this arrangement.

His eyes widen, and he shakes his head. "All I meant is that we might grow to be comfortable enough to share the . . . space. Whatever that might mean. In our friendship . . ." He struggles for words, and it's endearing. And yet, there's also a little twinge of disappointment that I choose to ignore.

"Rafael —"

"Rafi."

"What?"

"I wish that you would call me Rafi. It's what my family calls me. You are my family."

And Irina. Irina calls him Rafi, as well. I decide not to mention this, saying simply, "Oh."

"Yes . . . if you feel comfortable."

"Yes . . . Rafi."

He smiles, and it stretches into his cheeks, plumping them. Something changes in his expression; it opens, and I see him — really see him — for the briefest of moments. Something unfamiliar rushes through my veins, making me light. It feels like one of those moments that life freezes for you so you'll remember.

A bell rings. He looks over his shoulder and rises.

"I wonder who that could be?"

I follow him into the living room. With the vestibule door closed, voices echo, though I can't hear clearly what is being said. The door opens, and Rafael steps out of the way.

"What a wonderful coincidence!" William Whitey stands on the precipice of the living room. Zerah is behind him, looking immensely uncomfortable in a hat festooned with a large, brown-black feather that looks both scratchy and too rabid to be considered fashionable.

"Mr. Whitey, what a surprise," I say, unsure of what else to say.

"You remember my wife, Zerah?" He nudges her toward me, and she stumbles slightly. I don't have to look at her to know she's shut her eyes and is doing that deep breath thing she does. "Of course, you do. You two were tight as mice last night."

"To what do we owe the pleasure, Mr. Whitey?" I ask. Rafael's lips are pressed into a thin line, and his right eye tics.

"Well, would you believe we had an errand to do first thing this morning in the Old City? But then we got here and realized it was the sabbath—and then, we remembered you lived just around the corner! And you were so insistent that we visit together this week. So, well, we thought we'd just drop by for a visit." Whitey's nasal voice is grating, and the way his eyes latch onto mine makes his intentions clear. He's here for whatever it is that Conrad sent to be passed along, and the sooner I work out how to get it to him, the sooner he'll leave me alone.

"What a treat," Rafael says, his diplomatic smile drifting back up into his features. "Although, as you mentioned, it is the sabbath, and my family observes."

"Yes, but you don't, correct?" Whitey says, pointing a wide finger. Rafael's smile tightens. "Modern Osterstani that you are. You are devout, but don't let it impact your service to your family and your country. Correct?"

"Yes," Rafael says, his teeth a little tighter than before. "I see you listened to my speech at the swearing-in ceremony."

"Indeed! And I can see that your wife hasn't been treated to a proper shopping trip. Otherwise, she would be wearing the latest fashions."

I look down at my dress and suddenly feel very exposed. I look at Zerah. Her lips are pressed together as though it's the only thing stopping her from speaking her mind—although, I wish she would. It would probably be funny.

"You're right," I say, before Rafael has to defend me. "I

haven't made the time to shop yet. I've still been adjusting to the different hemlines popular here and haven't been eager to navigate that quite yet. I'm sure Zerah can relate."

Zerah casts me a look that makes me think she's saying, *What did I ever do to you?* I press my lips together to keep from laughing, and there's a flash of something in her eyes that tells me we're on the same page.

The truth is, I wouldn't mind doing some shopping with Zerah. For one, I haven't seen the city since I arrived and we rode through it in a cab. And two, as much as I appreciate the few dresses that Rafael—Rafi has tucked into the wardrobe for me, none of them are quite my style. I wouldn't mind having something that feels like it's my own.

Just then, Nima passes through again. She catches Rafael's eye, and I realize quickly that part of her observation of the sabbath must include a moratorium on speaking. I do recall that some practitioners eschew all forms of labor on the sabbath, including any sort of meal preparation.

And speaking.

Saturdays might just be my new favorite day.

"If you're open to it, I would love to see the city markets," I say to Zerah. Her eyes flicker around the group, and Nima glares at her.

"Yeah, let's do that," she says.

"Wonderful! Gives us old codgers a chance to catch up on our former bachelor ways. A little male bonding never did anyone harm. Say, do you have some mulberry liqueur, Rafael? I must admit, I'm a bit of a fiend for the stuff."

Nima's eyes flash with shock. I'm guessing that imbibing alcoholic beverages isn't part of the sabbath. She excuses herself, wordlessly.

"Yes," Rafi says, his expression tight. "Just through here, in the kitchen." Whitey shows himself through as Rafi takes my elbow and leans in.

"I'm sorry," I say, grinning.

"No, you're not," he says, a playful grin quirking the corner of his lips.

"Thanks just the same," I say.

"If you find something, tell them to add it to my account. If you have any trouble, tell them to contact the house directly or send for Emil."

"Emil?"

"My assistant."

"Did Emil pick out that dress for me yesterday?"

"No," he says, with a frown. "I did."

"Oh." My cheeks flood with warmth.

"Have fun," he says.

"You, too," I say with a wink. He glares at me as I slip out the door before he can change his mind.

We take a cab to the central market, and I'm inundated with the swell of hundreds of shoppers, looking for the best deal. The market is a mix of booths full of trinkets, colorful scarves, and leather goods in all the shades of the rainbow; carts with handheld snacks that smell of cinnamon, cumin, and yeast; and brick-and-mortar shops with greeters to keep the doorways clear of crowds.

Zerah takes her hat off as soon as we reach the market. She carries it loosely between two fingers, as if it's not precious. I ask her about it, and she snorts.

"Emu feathers."

"Emu? Like the land bird?"

"The one and only. It's what William made his money in."

"Is there money to be made in emu feathers?" I ask as she sniffs a cart that passes by. The vendor fills paper cones with small round nuts roasted in cinnamon, sugar, and cardamom.

"No," she says with a smirk. "Honestly, I don't know how he

makes money. Perhaps at one point, there was money in emu feathers, but from what I see, nobody but me is wearing the damn things."

"They look . . . heavy," I say, trying to be diplomatic.

"They look hideous. They poke and scratch and smell awful. You know, I think they shed some sort of emu dandruff."

"Hmm."

"You want to know something?" She looks conspiratorial. "He's terrified of them."

"Who? William?"

"Yep." She eyes a scarf, touching it with her fingertips while I try to hide my surprise.

"He's afraid of emus?"

"Yep."

I press my finger to my lips to muffle my laughter. She follows the motion, and a shrewd grin flirts with the corners of her pale lips.

"That's . . . unfortunate."

"Yeah." She arches an eyebrow, and with that, drops the hat on the ground and keeps walking.

We approach a split in the road for traffic, and once we cross the street, she points to a shop on the right, tucked back between a stand displaying wooden carvings and another one with beaded jewelry. The greeter at the door casts us a wary glance, but after a moment, opens the door. I want to ask Zerah how she's found the Osterstanis treat her, since she looks far more Nordanian than I do, but once I enter, I'm swept into a new world.

The shop is bright and colorful, the walls lined with dresses and sweaters and even pants for women, all cut in interesting styles far different from what I've seen in Nordania. She approaches a navy silk dress with long sleeves that button at the wrists, and a high, overtly-demure rounded collar. It doesn't look anything like what I've seen her wear thus far, and yet it looks just like her.

"Will you try that one?" I ask.

She shakes her head and steps away from it.

"I have a wardrobe. It's complete." She speaks as if repeating something she's heard over and over again. And yet, her eyes linger on the dress. "You need something that doesn't make you look like Rafael's mother."

I feel my eyes widen and look down at my dress, realizing that in all likelihood, that's exactly what I'm wearing: her cast-offs.

"Ladies, how may I assist?" A narrow man with a long face and small eyes approaches, his prejudice showing. Zerah shrugs with vague indifference.

"I don't know if there's anything here for you, Mrs. Rostami," she says. I see his eyes flicker between us, and I realize what she's doing.

"But did you see this one in the back?" the man says, motioning for me to follow him. "We just got it in from our dressmakers, and this poppy red would be so lovely on your complexion . . . I'm sorry, what was your name, sweets?"

Zerah looks anywhere but at the man, and all I want to do is laugh with her.

"Neve," I say, far preferring my own name to Rafi's. The man holds up a pretty red dress with a high neck, cap sleeves, and a belt that tucks in the waist. The buttons down the front are opalescent, a delightful pop of luxury, and they go all the way down to where the hem hits just below the knee.

"Neve, I'm Fas, and I'm going to get you out of your mother-in-law's clothing." I can't suppress the snort that comes out, and he grins.

❦

An hour later, I've charged six day dresses, two evening gowns, and a trousseau's worth of undergarments to Rafi's account. When Fas tells me the amount, I feel guilty, but one look from

Zerah tells me that it's the least I deserve for playing the role I've been given.

Fas kisses both of my cheeks once we've finalized the delivery arrangements, and I wear the poppy-red dress out of the shop, along with some comfortable tan-and-black, menswear-inspired heels that have a chic T-strap at the ankle.

We stop by a makeup shop, and I spend entirely too long admiring the rainbow assortment of eyeshadows and rouge, the creamy lipsticks of every color from raspberry to aubergine. Zerah watches me with a bit of wary intrigue, but I notice her admiring a coral lipstick that would match the natural flush in her cheeks. I buy it, and a soft red for me. For a moment, I think she won't accept it. I tell her that she doesn't have to, but that it never hurts to have a secret weapon to give you a little more confidence. She frowns, but then tucks it into a pocket in her dowdy jacket. I consider it a victory.

We reach another traffic break, and she hesitates. The salt-and-seaweed scent from the port hits my nose, and I realize we must be getting close. It's not nearly as suffocating as it was in Peninsula City. There's a freshness mixed in with it here that makes it much easier to breathe. Zerah draws suddenly close, gripping my hand as she studies my face, as if searching for something.

"Can I trust you?" For a breathless moment, I hold her gaze. But there's no doubt in my mind when I answer.

"Yes."

Her hazel eyes meet mine and lock on them. Something tenuous and electric passes between us, and I know now that whatever comes next will bond us in a way I can't revoke.

"Don't say anything," Zerah says, her inflection deceptively neutral.

She lets go of my hand and wraps her arm around my back, turning me down the cross street, and then into a shadowy, nondescript stairwell. The steps are narrow, iron, and steep, with grates that press into the bottoms of my new shoes. I imagine they leave their mark, the same way her arm around my back, her hand against my waist, is leaving its mark, sending a different kind of awareness through me.

We reach the bottom of the steps, and she continues walking me out of the stairwell and into what appears to be another market. This one, though, is very different. Quieter, dingier, and far less trafficked. The streets are a mix of neglected cobblestone and hardened earth. The street from above spans the width of the avenue, casting everything in shadow, filling the space with the phantom echo of ghost shoppers. Storefronts line the shadowy street, but there are no carts, no stalls, no one peddling their wares to the few passersby who shield their faces. I notice strange things in the windows—a baby doll with its back turned to the glass in front of a darkened shop, a travel poster for the Osterstani Highlands saying *"Wish You Were Here"* in front of what looks like a plant nursery.

"Inspections can't happen if the shops are closed," Zerah whispers. "You just have to know what you're looking for to tell if they're open or closed."

As far as I can tell, every shop we pass is closed. But it's clear that there are deals being made and wares being sold. I watch my step, trying to do my best to keep my new shoes out of the puddles of refuse and what smells like wastewater.

"You want that, go to the Magnolia," a woman hisses at a man as he falls backward, catching himself against a brick wall. He catches my eye, and there's something glazed and unnatural about the way he stares. I've seen that look before—on CJ when he would return home early in the morning.

"Keep your eyes down," Zerah hisses, squeezing my waist. A strange current, both electric and soothing, zips through my body. Before I can dwell on it, she pushes me toward a flimsy door with eight dirty glass panes. Inside, the shop smells like herbs and plants, but it looks like a chemist. It's compact and cramped. A long table fills most of the shop, covered with powders and colorful glass vials with cork stoppers. The walls are lined with overstuffed shelves. There's a counter in the back left, and behind the counter, a woman with kind eyes who looks like she can't be any older than Rafi.

"Hello, sweets," the woman says from the back of the shop. Her voice is soft and reassuring. Her dark curls are pinned back in a low bun, her fringe hanging just low enough into her eyes that it looks neglected instead of fashionable. Zerah lets go of me, and a shiver wracks my body.

"Hello, ma'am," Zerah says, more familiarity in her voice than I've heard her use with anyone else. It doesn't take a stretch of the imagination to infer that this woman is a chemist . . . or something like it.

"How are you feeling?" she asks.

"Fine," Zerah says. "It worked as you said. Thank you."

"Of course. Do you need more?"

"Yes," Zerah says, her voice a little cautious.

"It won't hurt to have it on hand. Just in case."

Zerah nods, and waits.

"Who is this?" the woman asks, nodding at me.

"I'm—"

"My friend," Zerah interrupts. The woman nods.

"Do you need the compound? The tea?"

I frown at Zerah and shrug.

"Just a minute," Zerah says, rounding on me as if merely giving the chemist her back gives us privacy. The chemist nods, understanding creeping into her features. She ducks into the back, I assume to work on Zerah's order—whatever that might be.

Zerah nudges me into the corner and steps a little closer, picking up a box of tea and showing it to me. It's chamomile and doesn't seem particularly remarkable.

"I think we are in the same position, so if we are not, I apologize."

I don't say anything, but I meet her eye and wait for her to continue.

"If you would like to protect yourself . . . to have some protection from your husband . . . or to give you some time until you're truly ready . . ." Understanding dawns over me, and I realize that she's obtaining a form of birth control here. "Or if you would like to have something on hand in case something . . . in case of an unintended result . . ."

"I understand," I say quickly, wanting to reassure her. She stops talking, and I shake my head. "We have not . . . I don't need anything like that."

She looks surprised, and it seems like a slip, like she didn't intend to show her surprise that Rafi and I have not consummated the marriage. Then I realize my mistake. I just confessed that we are not truly married. Panic edges into my chest. She simply nods, understanding softening her posture.

"If you would like to have something on hand, there are risks to coming here. It's not forbidden, but it is frowned upon. It would be easier to obtain it now than to return again on your own."

"I understand," I say, considering the option.

"You will need to keep it hidden away, particularly in your house." She leans a little closer, taking the chamomile tea from me. "The old faith still abhors this practice. Family values and whatnot."

"I see." I think for a moment, and after a long pause, I shake my head. "I don't think it's a concern. Not yet . . ."

"If it becomes one," she says, holding my gaze. We understand each other. Two Nordanian girls, married off to men from foreign countries, trying to protect ourselves. She returns to the chemist, and I stay where I am, watching her pay for her tinctures, tucking them into inconspicuous packages and then into pockets on the inside of her jacket.

That's when it hits me—she has to lay with William Whitey, to perform her wifely duties with a man who must be at least fifteen years her senior, who I find repugnant. A man who works with the likes of Conrad. A man afraid of his own emus. And this is what she's had to resort to in order to protect herself. My stomach tightens into a hot, sharp ball of barbed wire, ready to burst and embed itself into everything around me like shrapnel.

As if she can sense it, she turns around and meets my gaze. She tilts her head and smiles. It's such a sad smile, a little bit of gratitude for my company, or for being her secret keeper, or I don't know what. It douses me in cool calm, settling me in a strange way I don't think I've ever experienced. She approaches and nods to the door. I nod in return, and we exit quietly.

We climb the staircase again and filter back into the traffic of the high street, arm in arm. Her weight tethers me to the moment in a way I don't think I realized that I needed. But then she tenses, and her movements become tight. Her eyes dart from left to right as she begins to weave us through the traffic a little differently.

"Zerah?" I ask.

"Someone is following us."

I look over my shoulder, and she jerks my arm, pulling me around two men who argue about a sport.

"Don't look," she hisses.

"Who would be following us?"

"We just left the underground market. It could be anyone."

It's one thing to know that we were just in some sort of black market—another thing to put words to it. Based on what she said earlier, it wouldn't look very good for the new Nordanian wife of the modern, yet very much devout Osterstani trade minister to be seen in a shop that peddles family planning tinctures. It could be anyone, from a rival, to an officer of the law, to a reporter.

"This way," she says, tugging me across the traffic break and down the cross street. She lifts her hand, and a cab stops for us. She nudges me inside and looks back before climbing in herself. She gives the driver instructions, and we're quiet the entire ride back to the Old City. My heart is racing, my cheeks warm, and I realize after a long moment that the electricity from before is back —her hand is braced on top of mine. I don't pull it away. Neither does she. It's as if we're literally holding each other together. Neither of us speaks, but neither do we let go of each other, tethered together to reality through something so tenuous as our hands.

We return to the house, and Rafi stands immediately, his eyes floating over me with a bit of surprise that makes me feel warm and safe.

"How was your visit?" Rafi asks, approaching to wrap an arm around me. "You look flushed."

"It was nice," I say.

"I don't see packages or purchases," Whitey laughs, still holding a glass full of a brownish-purple liquid. The decibel of his nasal laugh hits a nerve that makes my neck spasm. "Always a relief when a woman is able to practice some restraint."

Zerah closes her eyes.

"I hope you did not refrain from getting what you need," Rafi says. The way he says the word *need* harkens back to when we said our vows, and I hear how important this seems to be to him.

"I arranged for the items to be delivered. I should be well outfitted now."

"I like the one you've come home in," he says with soft appreciation. I feel my cheeks flush, and the discomfort isn't entirely unpleasant.

"Thank you. The shopkeeper was kind. Very helpful."

"And you, wife? What have you done with your hat?" Whitey's voice has a sharpness to it that wasn't there before. The hairs on the back of my neck prickle, and Zerah touches her hair with the skill of a truly great actress.

"I don't—I had it just a moment . . . oh, William, I must have left it in the cab. Shoot . . ." Her face falls, and I press my lips together to keep the amusement off my face.

"You must be more careful with those little luxuries," Whitey says. "We don't want people to think you're ungrateful. Or that I don't take care of you the way I should."

That's not a word I would ever apply to Zerah, but she nods submissively, and he seems pleased enough by her response. He approaches and stumbles, spilling the liqueur down the front of her dress beneath her jacket.

Zerah squeaks in surprise as I gasp. Whitey mumbles his apologies while casting dirty looks at Zerah, as if it was her fault. Rafi goes to collect towels to clean up, and when he returns, I help her dab up the liquid from her dress so it no longer drips onto the floor.

"Shoot," I say. "It's soaked right through."

"It's fine," she says, her mouth pressed into a thin line.

"No, you'll borrow something of mine to wear home."

"What? So I can look like your mother-in-law?" She says it below her breath, but I laugh just the same.

"Better to get it out of my house."

"I'll help you with those, Rafael," Whitey says. "Women can be so clumsy. Thank goodness for the stronger sex, am I right?" Rafi grunts and turns around, so I can't actually see his reaction to what Whitey said. It doesn't sit well in me, but I nudge Zerah upstairs just the same.

We dig into the wardrobe and find a plain white housedress that looks like it will fit her. I leave her to dress in the bathroom. There's a knock at the door, and when I crack the door open, I'm surprised to see Whitey there instead of Rafi.

"You have something for me?" His voice is low, his meaning clear. It's time for me to pass along whatever it is that Conrad entrusted me with. I nod and motion for him to wait. I step away from the door and dig into my suitcase under the bed for the envelope.

"I don't have patience for this, girl. In the future, figure out a way to get messages to me faster, or it'll be your hide on the line."

"I'm not your servant," I hiss, passing him the envelope, happy to get it out of my possession. He tears into it and reads a letter, then looks inside the package. He doesn't look entirely happy, but he doesn't look nearly as agitated as he did when he forced his way into my bedroom.

As if he can read my mind, his expression changes. He looks up at me, stepping nearer.

"You'll be whatever it is I need you to be, girl."

"That's not the arrangement."

"As an Osterstani citizen," he says, stepping even closer as I back up into the foot of the bed, "it would be an utter shame to be tried for treason, espionage, or other crimes against your country."

"I'm not—" I start to say, but my conviction isn't there because I don't actually know that I'm not. I married an Osterstani citizen—is that how it works?

"You've figured it out, haven't you? And imagine what would happen if the wife of the trade minister was convicted of espionage? He would be a national embarrassment. He would lose his position and likely hang for crimes against his country. Is that really your intent?"

I swallow hard as he steps closer, his knee against mine.

"Especially when there's already so much for people to find buried in your husband's coffers." He stays still for a long moment, and I don't dare take a breath.

"Love?" Rafi's voice is hard, and Whitey stumbles into my shoulder, coughing hard. I don't have a choice but to grab hold of him, as if breaking his fall. I don't understand what just happened, but Rafi stands in the doorway, his face hard, his expression as unreadable as ever, while Whitey continues coughing against the side of the bed.

"Oh, dear," Whitey says between coughs, the package I handed him now gone—though the side of his jacket looks a little more padded than it seemed before. "So embarrassing. I swallowed oddly, and it went down the wrong pipe. Thank you for catching me, Neve."

Whitey grips my shoulders, pretending to right himself. The meaning in his hardened gaze is clear: play by my rules, or you'll regret it.

"Yes," I say. "Of course. It's my pleasure."

Zerah emerges from the bathroom at that moment, the dress she's borrowed transforming her, showing off her figure, even with the heavy jacket still covering her arms and a bulky, albeit featherless scarf still wrapped around her neck.

After our guests have left, Rafi is quiet for a long moment.

"You would be honest with me if something bothered you, correct?"

His eyes are open and clear, his hands at his sides, open instead of stuffed in his pockets, like usual.

But I can't tell him this. I don't actually know what I just did. I passed something to Whitey from Conrad, like a fool, and now, all I can do is trust his word. And if his words are, in fact, trustworthy, then I'm not the only one in this marriage with secrets.

"Yes, of course," I say.

He nods, but looks disappointed. I feel the same.

CHAPTER SIXTEEN

"*S*mells wonderful in here," Rafi says, setting down his briefcase. His voice is like a beacon for Benham; his father walks down the stairs to greet him before I can. They kiss each other's cheeks, and then Rafi approaches.

"It will have to do," Nima says, carrying a dish of curried cauliflower I tried to roast and ended up frying. Badly. I still think she turned up the heat too hot, and it burned before it ever had the chance to sauté. His eyes track to me, and his eyebrows arch in mild curiosity.

My back aches, and my eyes burn. My arms are sore and exhausted, and there's flour and poppyseed stuck beneath my fingernails despite the fact that I spent a solid thirty minutes cleaning them beneath the weak pressure in our bathroom sink. So much poppyseed . . . who knew Osterstan was the world's largest producer of poppyseed? Of course, Nima made it crystal clear that in Osterstan, we call the part we eat *nigella* so as not to confuse anyone into thinking that we're morphine addicts. After yet another week of ignoring each other, Nima decided that today was the day that she would teach me how to make her mother's nigella swirl bread.

Apparently, teaching me meant that I was the one to knead all six loaves of yeast dough for twenty minutes each. It also meant that I was the one to grind the poppy seeds. I had no idea how difficult it was to grind down such a little seed. If I'd known that cooking of this caliber was going to be in my future, I would've spent more time in the kitchen with Gaia, like Carla and Arden.

Arden, whose face was featured in the newspaper today— something that Nima tutted at when I paused to read the article. The reporter seemed to think she was a front-runner, and that Declan Levingston, son of the Nordanian prime minister, was showing signs that he'd like to marry. The thought didn't burn as hot as it once may have. But it seems safe to say that while she's been busy finding ways to get Declan's attention, she hasn't been digging tiny poppy seeds out from her nail beds.

It also seems safe to say that she doesn't have a mother-in-law who looks at her as though she's worse than dirt. Although today, there was a slight difference. Not for the positive, but there seemed to be a new tension or imperative to teach me how to do this. As if it was critically important.

Of course, if she knew I'd started my monthly courses the night before, she'd likely feel differently.

I had told Rafael, and while he looked vaguely squeamish at the mention, he didn't say anything about me sleeping in the maidenhead room. If anything, it endeared him to me a bit more.

"Did you prepare tonight's meal, my love?"

His mother's back straightens out of the corner of my eye.

"I tried," I say, nodding at Nima. "Your mother tried to coach me. I fear I was a poor student."

"Not everyone has the gift," Nima says, approaching Rafi and offering him her cheek, which he kisses. "That is why a man keeps his mother so close."

Rafi's lips curl in a knowing smirk as he shifts away from his mother and wraps me in a hug, holding on a little tighter and longer than I expect. A couple weeks into our marriage, and I still don't feel like I have a good sense for his emotions, but something feels off here. His mother's eyes narrow on us, at this western-style display of emotion. But she says nothing, retreating to the kitchen for cloth napkins, or silverware, or maybe holy water to fix my terrible cooking.

"Are you okay?" I whisper as he presses his temple against the top of my head.

"Just a long day," he says, giving me one last squeeze before he lets go. When I look at him, he does look tired. There are dark smudges under his dull brown eyes, and I wonder how long they've been there. It's not the sort of thing that would appear overnight. At least, I don't think it is. Perhaps the weeks of sleeping on the stiff sofa have taken their toll.

Still, he looks rumpled, as if he barely sat at all today. His shirt is slightly untucked around his suspenders, his glasses smudged, and his hair mussed as if he'd been tugging it in frustration.

"Let me guess: a visit from Pietersun?" Benham says.

Rafi snorts and shakes his head. "That would have been a delight."

"Oh, my boy!" Benham claps his son on the shoulder with a sympathetic grin. "We shall discuss this after dinner."

Rafi's eyes meet mine, and he seems to make a decision in that moment.

"No, that's all right. It would feel good to talk at dinner."

Benham stiffens, his eyes landing on me.

"That hardly seems appropriate."

"To discuss my workday with my family?" He presses a hand to my back, making his sentiment clear. My heart races, knowing that this is what I've been waiting for—the chance to hear some of his "shop talk."

Benham flinches. He presses his hands on his hips, ready to respond, when Nima passes through the door bearing a beautiful loaf of the nigella swirl bread. I gasp, wondering how in the world it came to look so good. I feel the corners of my mouth tilt upward as Rafi squeezes my shoulder.

"That looks wonderful, love," Rafi says.

"I was able to salvage this one from the freezer," she says with a modest smile. My stomach swoops like I've just fallen down a steep hill. Rafi's right eye tics.

Nima serves the men hearty helpings, then herself. Only then does she pass me the scant remains of the dinner I worked so hard to prepare. My cheeks flush hot as something even warmer churns to life in my stomach. I breathe in slowly through my nose, imagining that cooler air working its way down to my belly—but then Rafi trades his full plate for my empty one. He serves himself from what remains as he discusses his day.

"There are reports of a storm offshore," Rafi says, scraping the last charred bits of cauliflower onto his plate. Nima glares at me, watching Rafi take the meager portions she's left behind for himself. She excuses herself to get some hibiscus tea, and I lean in.

"Please, Rafi, this is too much food."

"Let that be a lesson to her, then."

"You should not be in the business of teaching your mother lessons, Rafi," Benham scolds, though his words are restrained.

"Really, you must be starved after the day you've had. And I can't possibly finish this."

"It's done, *my love*," he says, his look sharper than I expect. My stomach tightens yet again, and I'm suddenly not hungry for any of it.

"The United Trade Association ambassador arrived today," Rafi says as Nima returns. Both his parents straighten in their seats.

"Rafi," Nima says, squeezing his wrist, "wouldn't you rather discuss this with your father after dinner?"

"It appears there have been unapproved shipments coming

through our port at odd hours of the night, moving black market items."

A new tension floats across the table, and I feel the heat in my stomach dissipate as ice-cold straightens my spine. This is it. Conrad would want to know about this development. Or at least, I think he would.

"Black market items, you say?" Nima scoffs uncomfortably, her eyes flicking to mine. "This hardly seems appropriate dinner table conversation."

Rafi turns to me. "Osterstan has long tried to stop the trafficking of illegal items and harmful practices. Perhaps it is idealistic, or puritanical, but it is in our nature. My role is a large one, to keep these harmful things out of our borders, and today, I discovered that under my watch, I have failed."

His father sits straighter and clears his throat.

"It can't all be left on your shoulders, son."

"The dates align with my tenure—not yours."

"Criminals will take advantage of a transition. You will right the wrong."

"Gentlemen, this seems hardly appropriate for conversation in front of . . . well, a virtual stranger."

"Enough!" Rafi slams his fist on the table, and his mother is quiet. "That is enough, Mother. How long before you accept the fact that I have married? That Neve is the lady of the house? And instead, she feels unsafe in her own home, resigned to hiding in her bedroom all day, tolerating your unfair criticisms?"

"How dare you speak to your mother that way!" Benham roars, startling me. I sit, frozen in place, staring at the wood grain on the table. I've never heard such vitriol at close range—not since I was a child in the slums of Espancia, anyway—and sitting between these two men who are essentially fighting because of me is horribly uncomfortable.

"She has done nothing to earn your cruelty."

"Oh, come now, Rafi," Nima says. "She is not your wife. She confessed as much."

"What?" Rafi turns to me, the shock of betrayal cutting into the mask he usually wears.

"I—" I don't know what to say, and I just sit there, my mouth open.

"Without consummation, there is no marriage," Nima hisses, a self-righteous smirk on her face. "She is little more than a whore and more deserving of residence at the Black Magnolia."

Rafi is quiet and stone still for a long moment, too long. I don't even see him take a breath. Then he stands, his chair flying back behind him, falling over and knocking into the loveseat with a crash.

"My marriage is not up for discussion," he says, his voice soft and deadly. Despite the arguing that led to this point, this is the first time I've actually felt afraid. "What happens between me and my *wife* will remain between *me and my wife*. If you disapprove, you know where the door is."

The blood drains from his mother's face as he storms out of the room, through the vestibule, and out of the townhouse. He slams the front door behind him, the door to the vestibule swinging open behind it. The three of us remain silent, staring at the food that nobody seems hungry for. I stand, picking up both my and Rafi's plate to wrap in the kitchen for later.

"Leave them," Benham says.

"I was just going to—"

"Leave them. Nima will take care of her son. That's her job." Nima lifts her chin, her eyes meeting her husband's, and I realize that this is some sort of impasse, a line drawn in the sand. My stomach tightens into a hot knot, and I don't fight it back.

"Don't worry about it. It's my job to care for my husband." I pick up both dishes when Benham slams his fist on the table.

"My wife is right. You are not yet a part of this family, and this is a family matter. Leave the dishes, and leave us."

The heat in my stomach boils up my chest, into my throat, and I look at Rafi's seat. To the empty vestibule where he went, leaving me alone to be treated like this. I set down Rafi's plate with its meager ingredients, and then turn to look at Benham. He stares at me with such heated disdain. The violence of his oppression fuels the anger boiling in my belly, and I'm helpless to stop it from bursting.

"Fine," I seethe.

I slam the dish into the table.

Nima screams as the dish cracks, shattering into dozens of pieces as potatoes, lentils, lamb, and the damned nigella bread go flying. Benham stands, his face red, but I turn on my heel and walk up the stairs, going straight to the room where I've spent most of my days. I turn the lock on the door and don't bother to muffle my screams with a pillow this time. Instead, I throw pillows, books, shoes, anything I can get my hands on. I work my way through the bedroom, the wardrobe, the closet, the bathroom. I finally feel my skin cooling down, slowly, slowly, from the top down. And then the tears come, and I once again find myself on the cool tile of the bathroom floor, holding myself together.

I don't know how long I lay there before I hear the lock click. Rafi crouches, touching my cheek, and then curls up next to me on the hard floor.

"I'm sorry," he says, tucking a frazzled bit of hair behind my ear. I don't know what to say. I'm not sure I could, even if I did. My mouth is dry and hot. I'm still angry that he left me like that. I'm angry that his parents yelled at me for trying to do what it is I vowed to do. In the ceremony they insisted upon. And yet, they still insist I'm not a part of their family, despite Rafi's promise that I would be part of his.

That part stings, and I don't know why. I don't particularly like his mother, and I hardly know his father. His father treats me like I'm not worthy of his attention, that I'm not worth the time it would take him to get to know me. His mother has hardly taken the time to get to know me either, and the time she has spent has been used to work me to the bone, and then criticize and diminish my contributions. And yet, at the end of another day, I'm just a girl, crying for her parents to notice her. To see her value. To choose her.

"I'm sorry, love," he says again, running his fingers along my cheek, down my jaw.

I shake my head, as if telling him that it's nothing, that it's okay. But I can't make the words come off my tongue, and it's like he knows.

"There's no excuse," he says. "I do wish you had told me that you confessed the lack of our consummation to my mother—"

"I'm sorry—"

"No," he says, pressing a finger to my lips. It's warm, and I realize just how cold I am at the moment. Chills rush down my arms.

"No, you owe me nothing. But I do wish that you had told me she was asking such personal questions. She has no right to dig like that."

"She is your mother," I say. "She wants grandchildren. It is the most important thing to Osterstani people."

"I know she does." He sighs, as if the very idea of that conversation exhausts him. The one where we admit that we are not headed that way. "But neither of them has the right to treat you like anything other than their son's wife."

He sits up and helps me up, as well. "Can we get off the floor? Talk a little bit where you aren't shivering so badly? I would hate to think that my inattention has cost you your health." I bite my bottom lip, shivering as he helps me to the sofa. He wraps a blanket over my shoulders and sits next to me.

"We haven't talked about our past, because there hasn't been a need. But I do feel that I've been unfair."

I take a deep breath. The night of the event comes flashing

back, the way Irina spoke to him with such familiarity. A part of me wants explanations, and another part of me doesn't want to know. To acknowledge that she knows him in a way that surpasses what I'll ever know. To feel the humiliation of being bested.

"I must admit, I am out of my depth here. I've had only one serious relationship. It was . . . unexpected. Neither of us intended to fall into it, and yet, we did. Once we admitted to ourselves that it was real, that we had feelings, it was too late to do much about it. There were always secrets, all kept in the name of protecting the other, but in the end, I was the one who paid the cost."

I don't understand. I don't know what he means, and it's all too unspecific. Then it clicks. *Irina.* The way she used his nickname, how she knew what his mother was like, the mystery that surrounds her. It seems to make sense. And it would explain his distrust of her.

"My father is the one who helped me through the aftermath. It was . . . I was not capable of seeing my way through. Since that time, he has been supportive, but almost over-protective. Despite the fact that I am twenty-eight years old and fully an adult. That I have inherited the family seat in government and everything else I'm entitled to. He saw me at my lowest, and I believe he's trying to be protective."

"You think he sees that we don't love each other?" I say, speaking as plainly as I can. He flinches.

And the mask falls.

I see him clear and true for the first time, possibly ever. His eyes are glassy, his jaw soft. He brushes the hair behind my ear and shakes his head.

"Yes."

I take a shaky breath and force a wry smile. "He's observant, then."

"It's not that simple, though, is it?"

"What do you mean?"

"Just because we don't feel anything now—that we didn't feel anything from the start—doesn't mean that we won't ever feel something. Maybe even something wonderful?"

I cock my head, uncertain of where he's going with this.

"You feel it, right?" he asks, suddenly uncertain, vulnerable. "The potential?" His hand freezes on my cheek, and the warmth radiates through me. I feel something. I don't know what it is, whether it's friendship or something more, but I do feel it. It's a sense of calm. Peace even. I suppose I had just attributed it to his demeanor, but perhaps he's right, and it's something else. Perhaps it is us?

I nod.

He lets out a deep breath, and a sweet smile curls his full lips. It's the most beautiful thing I've ever seen and almost takes my breath away. It doesn't touch his cheeks, but it reaches his eyes. They glint with pure, joyful hope.

"Neve? May I share the bed with you tonight?"

I laugh. Loud. Inappropriately so. He flinches.

He looks so exhausted, I don't even think twice as I nod. But then I do. "You, uh . . . you remember what I told you yesterday? My courses?"

"Oh. Yes?" He tilts his head, as if waiting for me to tell him something more. But I see what I need to see right then. He has no problem sharing a bed with me while I'm on my courses. In that regard, he is not his mother's son. I nod again.

That night, I fall asleep feeling his weight and his warmth on the other side of the bed. And when I roll over a few times, unable to sleep, I feel his hand reach for mine in the dark, beneath the blankets.

And we fall asleep, just like that.

CHAPTER SEVENTEEN

*T*he ballroom is resplendent, sparkling beneath the light of a dozen crystal chandeliers. In my limited reading about Osterstan and Osterstani culture, I had always been led to believe that it was an impoverished country, both culturally and actually. But it's becoming more and more clear with each passing day just how limited my education truly was.

Indeed, as women spin around the ballroom in a whirl of shimmering silk and satin, and the men, with their metal-adorned suspenders and shined shoes gather in conversation, the overall sense of luxe is beyond anything I could've imagined for even the institute. However, the food at this event is much milder: a roasted bird of some sort on a bed of greens, with pomegranate seeds and the revered mulberry gracing the plate in some sort of reduction sauce.

It's too sweet for my taste, reminding me a little too much of the fermented oranges littering Conrad's groves that came to smell like the most terrifying and tense years of my life. To this day, I can't figure out who the hell wanted to buy those damned oranges.

Zerah is here tonight, thank goodness, but then so is William Whitey. He cornered me when we first arrived, waiting for Rafi to turn away before he gave me a message to memorize: *Today, there were ten-foot waves, and I saw two jellyfish. They were bloated, which is good luck according to local custom.*

I'm certain it's a code. But for what, I couldn't begin to guess.

I don't know exactly what he has running with Conrad, or what they have their hands in. But if I can keep my nose out of it for another eleven months, there's a good chance I could walk away from this.

After dinner, Rafi excused himself, looking distracted, his brow furrowed. I haven't caught up with him since, though right now, Rafi catches my eye from across the room, his brown eyes glinting gold in the lamplight. It's hard not to flush in appreciation —or guilt.

"There's the lucky girl," a familiar voice says from beside me. Irina dangles a champagne flute next to her hip. The bubbles appear almost pink as she holds it next to her bias cut, rose-gold gown. With her fair coloring, she shouldn't be able to pull off that color, but somehow, she does. She does it well. I'm not the only one who notices the way it accentuates the flush of her ample décolletage, which is almost indecent in the way it makes her look like she's naked. The way men and women alike admire her as they pass us.

"Still happy?" Her question is perfectly casual and delivered with a lightness that belies what I believe her intentions to be.

"I am," I say with a nod. Then I lean a little closer, feeling like I can perhaps confide in her now, since I do think she's the one Rafi was talking about—his past relationship. "It's been much better since Rafi had words with his parents."

"Did he?" She arches a perfectly dark eyebrow and stifles a laugh. "I would have liked to see that."

Part of me would have liked to see it, as well. The truth was, he didn't go to work the next morning, and instead sent me to a litany of appointments while he announced he would take a late morning. His mother protested, insisting that she should come along with me. Once I realized that the appointments were to meet with doctors and establish medical care, I was grateful he insisted I go alone.

I was pleasantly surprised to discover that my doctors were all progressive and open minded. And my internist was, thankfully, a woman who conducted a brief examination and told me to return when I was no longer intact to spare me unnecessary discomfort. When I'd returned home, the house was near silent, and Rafi was sitting on the settee.

"Make yourself comfortable," he'd said, and then he kissed my cheek and left for the office. He never did say what transpired between him and his parents, but a few hours later, his mother offered to make me lunch. It was so startling that I declined, and then was starving by the time we had our late dinner. There have been no unkind comments since.

"I'm happy for you," Irina says, crossing her arms and sipping her champagne. Her lips are so soft around the rim of the glass, and I find myself staring, wondering what she did to achieve such a sensual flush with her rouge.

"What are you doing here?" I ask. "This is a different cause tonight, correct?"

"Yes," she says, lazily, "but still a good one. Fundraising for women in professional school. Women should be encouraged to seek out the full extent of their ambitions."

Of course, I knew the topic for tonight's benefit, but I suppose I hadn't really considered it. Something about the way she phrased it, though, sits uncomfortably, like a bit of clam shell stuck in my heel.

"Not to speak out of turn, but I thought this cause would resonate with you, in particular."

"You did?" I'm cautious with my words. She nods, running the edge of her champagne glass along her lower lip. A thin layer of lipstick smears on the glass. It makes me flush with heat.

"You have worked very hard to achieve your goal." Her gaze is pointed, as if she can see right through me. For a moment, I forget which goal we're talking about.

"Thank you for saying so," I say, shaking my head and watching Rafi work the room. "But it was truly a coincidence and my good fortune that led me to Rafi."

"No, I do not speak of your husband," she says, turning to me, putting her full attention on me. "I'm talking about the institute. Your failure to be chosen."

My stomach goes cold. My shoulders stiffen, and my neck tightens. I don't dare look away, waiting for her next move. Over the past few weeks, I'd forgotten what it was like to hear that word—or the implication of the word: *unchosen*. Unworthy. I could only imagine what Nima would say if she knew. And this woman, who shares a history of some sort with my husband, knows my greatest secret—or at least one of them.

Irina flaps her hand and returns her focus to the ballroom at large. "I would never say a word. All I mean is that I understand. To work so hard in life, to learn a trade, a skill, a discipline: a woman should be able to utilize that skill and not be punished for it."

Her words move me, and I feel them settle deep inside me, taking root somewhere not quite my gut, but somewhere far more tender and permanent.

"I thought I lost my cape, but William found it." Zerah pouts next to me, a sheen of sweat coating her hairline. The hideous, brownish-purple cape she wears is weighted down by a thick layer of emu feathers along the bottom hem.

"Oh dear, you're the emu wife, aren't you?" Irina says with a look of horror and glee.

"Yes . . . though sadly, that's not the worst thing I've been called," Zerah says, smoothing out the horrid accessory. She looks up at Irina, and her gaze freezes.

"Hello, then," Irina says, holding out a hand. "Irina."

Zerah is quiet for a long moment, and I interrupt.

"This is Zerah."

"Zerah," Irina says, her eyes knowing. "Yes, I followed your time in the institute. I hope it was everything you hoped it would be."

It's the first time I've heard someone outright mention it. Zerah's cheeks flush, and her mouth sets into a hard line.

"I learned the lessons I was meant to."

"That's usually the way it goes," Irina says, draining the rest of her champagne. "And I do hope your husband's birds are well?"

Zerah frowns.

"I hear the large animal doctor has been to see them? At least a handful of times?"

Zerah looks uncomfortable with the change in subject. She shrugs.

"Emus get seasick, too." Her eyes flicker to the floor, then back up to Irina, as if deciding whether to trust her. "It's too bad they can't get sick on cue . . ."

Irina suppresses a smile, but not her suspicious gaze.

"I must excuse myself. I see the ambassador to the Southern Unified Territories, and I need to have a word. Good to see you, Neve."

Zerah continues to remain stiff, as if a pallor has been cast over the night, and the ballroom suddenly seems too noisy and hot.

"Would you like to get some air?" I ask. She nods, and I turn her in the direction of the rear balcony. I look over my shoulder, trying to catch Rafi's eye. He's deep in conversation with an older couple as a harried waiter stands next to them, as though waiting for his "in." Rafi will find me when he needs to.

We weave through the crowd and down a long, wide hallway

with a tall, arched ceiling. The floor is tiled in overused black-and-white marble. The cracks are filled with something that looks like gold. A series of heavy teak doors stand on either side of the hallway, giving the space an odd, carnival funhouse sort of feel. We pass them all, until we end up on the wide, enclosed veranda overlooking a large orchard. The grounds are home to the various orchards where they grow custard apples, pomegranates, and almonds, among other things. This orchard looks ancient, the trees are gnarled and curved toward the sky.

"Who was that woman?" Zerah asks.

"Irina . . ." I hesitate, realizing that I don't know her last name. I shrug. "Rafi knows her, though he told me to be careful around her. I think they used to date."

"Really?" Zerah frowns, surprised by that. Fortunately, she doesn't seem to want to dwell on the topic. My connection to Arden would out me, and even though I'm curious about why Zerah seemed so uncomfortable talking about her time at the institute, it feels safest to leave it be for now.

I shrug and stare out over the orchards. Only a few people mill around the veranda, and the late summer breeze feels good over my shoulders. I'm wearing one of the new evening gowns—a black, strapless dress that gathers at the bust and falls on a bias to the floor, swirling around my ankles.

"Are you happy, Zerah?" I ask, realizing that Irina didn't care to ask her this same question. Zerah arches an eyebrow.

"What kind of question is that?"

"I don't know. Isn't it fair to ask?"

"That's not something I worry about."

"Hmm." I nod, leaning against the railing, looking out over the trees again. "I suppose I don't either. But tonight, looking at what they're raising money for—perhaps we should be thinking about it?"

"We are not these women, Neve."

"Aren't we?"

"No."

Her words are crisp and neat, leaving little room for argument or confusion. But there's something more to it, too. I turn to meet her gaze, and there is indeed something there. Something messy and thick. I don't know what it is, or how to navigate it. But neither do I have a chance.

Because right at that moment, a scream cuts into the night.

CHAPTER EIGHTEEN

a loud crack cleaves the night in two. It's so loud, so violent, I'm not convinced the building hasn't fallen off its foundation.

"What . . . ?" I turn and look at the doors that open to the hallway. Another thunderous crack comes from inside, louder this time, followed by more screams.

"Gun," Zerah whispers, her skin pale and her throat working hard.

"We have to go."

"Where?" she asks, her eyes panicked.

"We can't stay here. There's nowhere to hide." We're completely exposed on the veranda, with nothing to stop someone from reaching us.

"But they're inside." More gunfire sounds from within the ballroom, and my heart drops. Rafi was in the ballroom. I didn't even tell him where I was going. I don't know where he is, and he doesn't know where I am. If whoever is in there with weapons and ill intent wants to find two Nordanians who can't hide, they can do exactly that. The only way out is the way we came.

"We have to go in."

"No."

"We must."

"Neve —" Zerah freezes, her hands stiff, her fingers bent oddly at the first knuckle.

"I've got you," I whisper.

Taking her by the shoulders, I direct her inside. We keep to the wall, sliding slowly along it, listening for clues. The ballroom ahead is sealed off, the doors shut. The small windows are dark and reveal nothing. As if the lights have been turned off.

We move slowly, on our toes, creeping along the wall, when suddenly everything goes dark. Zerah sucks in a breath, and it gets caught in her throat. She coughs; it echoes off the curved ceiling like a hunting call.

"Shhh," I say in her ear. I try the handle on the first door. It's locked. I curse under my breath and keep moving. Slow and steady.

The sound of a crash, wood on wood splintering, bounces off the walls in the ballroom ahead, followed by terrified screams. I nudge Zerah faster until we approach the next door. Gruff, harsh voices get louder on the other side of the ballroom doors. I push Zerah faster and faster, as the voices get louder and louder. We reach the next door just as I hear a handle click on the doors down the hall. I try the handle on this second, mysterious door, and thankfully it turns. It opens, and I push Zerah inside, slipping in behind her. I close it quickly behind us, just as the door at the end of the hall squeals open.

I slide my hands along the back of the door and find a lock, clicking it in place, and then step back into the pitch dark room.

"Zerah," I whisper into the room. I hear her hiss something, but it's not my name. When I find her, she's shaking so violently that it's hard to get a hold on her.

"You have to calm down," I whisper, wrapping my arms around her, coaxing her to sink to the ground where she can sit and not have to rely on her shaking legs. I don't know what is going through her head, but she's clearly terrified. In the dark, as we're hiding from who-knows-what, I don't know what to say to help her. So instead, I just rub my hands up and down her arms.

A loud crack from outside shakes the walls. Like the splintering of a wooden door. There's another pop, like gunfire, and more screaming. Zerah cries against me, and I hold her tight, breathing in the sweet verbena scent of her soft hair.

"You're going to be okay," I say, smoothing my hands up and down her arms, pressing my cheek against the top of her head. "We're going to be okay. Someone will take care of whatever is happening out there."

"They're looking for us."

"How do you know?"

"Because it makes sense. It all makes sense."

"What makes sense?"

"William said he would know tonight for certain."

I frown, but keep rubbing her chill-bumped arms.

"That could mean anything," I whisper into her hair.

"I don't think so. He seemed fairly certain something was going to happen tonight."

"He could have been talking about—" I stop before I say anything more. Because what I was about to say was, *He could have been talking about giving me the message to pass along to Conrad.* I clear my throat and shake my head.

"He could have been talking about anything. What is his business here in Osterstan? Does it have to do with his emus?"

She shakes her head. "He's selling the emus. He's waiting for them to arrive and go through customs so they can then pass into Swendenland."

I frown. Why would they need to come to Osterstan before going to Swendenland? Why wouldn't he just ship them the long way around and avoid Osterstan altogether?

There's a crash against another door in the hall. She buries her face into my shoulder, and I hold her tighter, stroking the back of her head.

"My benefactor," she whispers, frantic, as if she has to get this off her chest. "He would make threats. I once saw him shoot a man who owed him money. I had to hide. He was so angry when I didn't return. He found me, though, in a dark, abandoned building. I spent the night there, just hiding. It was so cold. And then he found the building . . . knew I was inside. He kept firing the gun into doors, through walls."

I don't know what to say. Her story doesn't make sense. I don't understand.

"He wasn't going to stop. I returned, and he punished me. I survived, but . . . I hate . . ."

I don't exactly know what happened to her, but I know how to finish that sentence as she shakes in my arms.

"The dark. You hate the dark." She nods against my collarbone, and I hold her tighter. "It's okay. I have you. I'm not going to let anything happen to you."

She continues to shake, her shiver rattling her teeth with dangerous force.

"Do you believe me, Zerah? That I'm going to protect you?" I lift her chin and force her to look at me. There's only a tiny bit of light coming in from just under the door, but it's enough to see the reflection of light against her eyes, to see the deep pools of black that are her pupils. Her shivers abate, ever so slightly, and I brush a piece of her hair behind her ear.

"Yes," she whispers, with a little nod. She cups my cheek and repeats herself. Her touch is soft and warm, and for a brief moment, in spite of everything else that's happening, I believe myself. I believe that we are safe.

And then the door explodes.

CHAPTER NINETEEN

$\mathcal{B}$linding light streams across the room. Zerah cowers away from it, while I try to shift so that I'm better shielding her.

"Zerah? Neve?" Whitey's nasal voice calls from the doorway. The door is splintered, broken into jagged pieces fit for a bonfire. Zerah's shoulders stiffen, and I fold myself over her even more.

"It's safe. You can come out now," he calls again. A security guard steps across the splintered wood and crosses the room to where we sit, huddled on the floor next to a bookcase. I hadn't even considered what was in this room. I couldn't see a thing, but now that the light spills in through the door, I can see it's some sort of office or bookkeeping room.

The guard reaches down, and I pat Zerah's back.

"It's okay," I whisper into her ear. She lets out a breath, and I'm not sure if it's relief or disappointment. I nudge Zerah to take the guard's hand first, and he helps her across the room as another one helps her climb through the splintered wood door.

"I'm so glad you're okay, my dear." Whitey's voice carries across the room, grating against the last nerve I have left. I stand on my own. The guard returns to help me navigate the wood splinters. I don't really need the help. I can see and walk just fine. Part of me wants to say this, but instead, I hold my tongue.

"You're both okay," Whitey asks, though it seems less a question. If I didn't know better, I'd say that was disappointment, not relief. But when he checks Zerah's pulse and whispers something in her ear that I can't hear, it does seem like he is legitimately concerned.

"Where is Rafael?" I ask.

His eyes are round, and flicker to the security guard and back.

"I must be honest, Neve," he says, pulling me to the side. "I haven't seen him since earlier, when he was speaking with the . . ." He hesitates and lowers his voice. "I hate to do this, but sometimes delicate things must be discussed. I saw him in the foyer shortly before I came looking for my wife. I had just made it to our table, thinking Zerah might have come for a reprieve. But then the gunshots went off, in the foyer where he'd been speaking with . . . well, there's no delicate way to say this. He was speaking with that radical woman. You know, the Sudersbergian madam."

My stomach drops, and I frown.

"The 'Sudersbergian madam'?"

But as soon as it's out of my mouth, I wonder if I don't already know. My stomach twists as he leans in a little too close for decorum.

"I believe she goes by the name Irina."

Ice cold slithers down my spine as my stomach tightens into a hot ball of anger. I'm not sure which is going to win out when a guard approaches.

"We need to escort you outside, so that the building can be cleared."

"Yes, I understand," Whitey says, motioning for both me and Zerah to go with them.

"We'll need you to come this way. The foyer is a crime scene." Whitey nods, his face paling.

He gives Zerah his arm and places a hand against my back. It feels predatory, and I walk faster, trying to distance myself while my brain runs in circles. I can't see straight. Because, while a white-hot anger rises from my stomach into my chest, my neck tightens as I realize what Whitey said—that he saw Rafi in the foyer.

The gunshots went off in the foyer. It's now a crime scene.

I'm hardly aware of my feet on the ground as we're whisked through a side door that looks like it's been painted closed. There's no path outside, and I feel every single divot from the grass and rocks and flowers I crush beneath my shoes. But my legs keep moving. I keep walking. I reach the front of the building, where the other revelers huddle in pairs and small groups all over the grounds. A woman looks dazed as she stands on top of a petunia plant and her husband rubs her back. A man stares at the building, hunched over, while someone else speaks to him, as if coaching him through breathing exercises. A trio of gentlemen lean against a stone gate, passing a bottle of amber liquid between them. I scrutinize all their faces.

None of them are Rafi.

I stop at one group and ask if they've seen him. They haven't. I go to the next. Another group thinks they saw him in the foyer. Another hasn't seen him. I work my way from one group to the next, and the next, and the next, until my panic has won out and the icy fear threatens to tighten around my throat.

Then I notice the small group standing at the base of the steps to the entrance. They're not moving, not panicking. Just . . . standing. Fidgeting. Some whisper to themselves, rock themselves.

These are the loved ones. The next of kin. I take my place among them and stare at the constable in a police uniform speaking to one of the event organizers.

There's nothing to do but wait.

The woman next to me is older, with paper-thin skin and blue veins that are far too visible along her neck beneath her gray skin. She looks sort of familiar. I think I saw her speaking with Rafi earlier, before I left with Zerah? She looks up at me, and something silent passes between us. What if Rafi is dead? What if he was on the receiving end of one of those gunshots? The rational part of my brain says it may be for the best. I would be free. Rafi would never find out how I've betrayed him. Surely Conrad wouldn't fault me for his death?

A violent shudder rips through my shoulders at the thought that my life would somehow be better off without him. The older woman takes my hand and squeezes it. Another shiver rolls through my body, and at that moment, the door to the foyer opens. I can't bring myself to look, and her chin wobbles.

"Neve." Rafi is running down the steps toward me. I feel the shock and relief course through me like a mudslide. A heavy, thick emotion catches in my throat, and I'm tongue-tied; I can't form a single word. He wraps his arms around me and buries his face into my neck. He's holding me, and I'm shaking, and then he's telling me I need to let go. I don't understand until I look and realize the police chief is coming to talk to the woman whose hand I'm still holding.

"I'm so glad your man is safe," the woman says, her voice thick. I think I nod, or say thank you, but it's all so fast, like sensory overload. All the heat and the chill of too many emotions leaves me shivering. Rafi places his jacket over my shoulders and leads me to a cab. I'm vaguely aware of passing Whitey and Zerah.

"You're safe, my love," Rafi keeps whispering the whole ride home, but I'm shaken. I'm so thoroughly shaken, and I don't know what it is that's shaken me. Rafi presses a kiss to the top of my head and nausea washes over me, sickened with myself over my earlier thought that I might be better off if he was dead. Of course, it was only natural to think it through—or so I tell myself. It was my emotions taking over. I would never wish anything bad to fall on his head. I give him a little squeeze, and he squeezes back.

We make it home, and for the first time, I allow him to hold me as we fall asleep. But I don't sleep. I can't shut off my brain, can't stop hearing the sound of the gunshots, or the screams, or the feeling of Zerah's frail shivers against my arms.

It's half past two in the morning when I wake suddenly. The strange, cryptic message Whitey wants me to send to Conrad unspools through my head. I can't make sense of it. I replay it again in my head, but don't see anything suspicious about it, or at least nothing that could potentially sound like word of a shooting. But then, I don't think Whitey is a violent person. An opportunist, certainly, but not a murderer.

Still, the violence was so close. The terror I felt not knowing where Rafi was, or what would happen to me if he had died, only reiterates what I already knew: that I can only depend on myself. And the best way I can do that is by doing what I promised and securing my future.

I sneak down the hall, past Nima and Benham's room, and up to the third floor to Rafi's home office. It sits in the back of the house, overlooking the dark, narrow alleyway between the blocks of row houses. For a moment, I think I hear steps down the hall, but when I look, I don't see anyone. I tiptoe up the steps, taking them one at a time. I reach the landing, and then curse under my breath when I find the door locked.

I pull a hairpin out of my thick braid, then another, feeling an odd sense of muscle memory from having done this so often at the top of a different stairwell on the peninsula. I try to keep the noise to a minimum as I slip the thin wire into the keyhole and feel for the recesses in the lock pins. Just like I used to do at Conrad's. I find the grooves, and the lock unbolts with an echo.

I freeze, waiting for any sign that someone has heard me. There's nothing, so softly, I let myself into the office, shutting the door as quietly as I can. I then turn on the telegraph machine. It's a surprisingly new model, and thank gods, it's quieter than the one Headmistress Moyle taught me on. I type out the message verbatim as I remember it: *Today, there were ten foot waves, and I saw two jellyfish. They were bloated, which is good luck according to local custom.*

I read it through, and then hit send.

It's loud. Louder than I want it to be, louder than I expected. I look around for a hiding place, in case someone hears and comes upstairs. I press myself against the wall between the door and the tall cabinet and wait as the rest of the message rattles out. Finally, it's quiet. Too quiet. I strain, listening for commotion downstairs. It's dead silent.

The machine beeps again, churning out a confirmation that it's been received. I hold my breath, waiting for someone to burst into the room. What would I say? What excuse would I use? The machine goes quiet. I wait for the count of five . . . then I shut down the machine.

I move through the door, poking my hairpins into the lock again and clicking it shut. Just then, something creaks from below. A door, a floorboard—I can't be certain. I hold in place, frozen, straining to hear someone or something.

But nothing happens. No one finds me. I sneak back downstairs and silently tuck myself back into my marital bed. Rafi rolls over, his arm curling around my waist. A rush of something sticky and cloying washes through me, but this is my way out. And after seeing what could happen if I don't take care of myself in this world, I'm going to do what it takes.

CHAPTER TWENTY

*R*afi spends the morning in and out of his upstairs office. Every time he comes to the kitchen to refill his coffee, I hold my breath as my heart rate hammers out of control. As if he's figured out what I did last night. That I broke into his office and betrayed his confidence. But he doesn't.

Nima is in rare form this morning. There's no scowling when he chooses coffee over her beloved spiced tea. Instead, she putters between the kitchen and the dining room, humming to herself. She's refilled my coffee cup between poaching eggs and frying up thin strips of pork. She even goes so far as to warm a loaf of nigella swirl bread that I made. I know it's one of my loaves because one side is taller and rounder than the other side.

She's been far more tolerable since Rafi had words with them, but this morning is something else entirely. Between that and Rafi coming in and out, I'm tense and jump at every interruption.

And that doesn't even account for the attack from last night.

I caught a glimpse of the headlines on Benham's newspaper this morning. The reports appear to blame it on an ultra-progressive domestic terrorist. Which doesn't answer any of my questions. Not that I can formulate them.

Soon enough, we're sitting around the dining table. It's loaded with fried ham, poached eggs sprinkled with paprika, slices of poppyseed bread, and calamansi juice. I've never heard of or seen calamansi juice, but Nima pushes it toward me, saying that it will be good for me. I don't know what that means, but it's a little sweet, and smells like a mix of lemons and limes. So long as it's not orange or orange adjacent, I won't complain.

"Rafi, enough," Nima says, just as Rafi passes back through from the kitchen with more coffee. Benham walks down the steps, his hands pushed into the pockets of his loose silk pants, putting a strain on his green suspenders.

"Sit and eat something before you wear a ditch in the floor." I press a smile to my lips as Rafi stops, as if he hasn't noticed the spread on the dining table. "You work too hard, Rafi. I heard you upstairs last night, burning the midnight oil. Your beautiful wife made nigella bread, and we have calamansi juice."

He freezes, his brows narrow, and I swear my heart stops. But when his eyes catch mine, there's laughter in them. I'm not sure what's so funny, but he walks over and kisses the top of my head. I assume he's noticed my wonky bread.

"What has gotten into you, Maman?" Rafi sits next to me as Benham takes his chair at the head of the table and unfolds the newspaper. Nima loads up his plate with ham, and then moves to mine.

"I'm only caring for my family. It is my life's work. And I'm grateful that you are all safe and sound."

Rafi sips his coffee as if to conceal his laughter. I sit still, afraid to break whatever spell has fallen over Nima to put her in such a good mood.

"You are on top of this, yes?" Benham grumbles, his face hidden by the newspaper.

"Yes, of course," Rafi says, his tone darker. His right eye tics. Rafi and I both watch Nima pile more ham on my plate.

"It says here you stayed until the scene was cleared?"

Rafi leans back in his chair and removes his glasses, pinching the bridge of his nose. Nima adds another strip of ham to the stack she's built. Then she sets the dish down and picks up the poached eggs.

"Eggs are good for you," she says with a little smile.

"At least you did not leave your post."

"Of course I didn't, Father," Rafi says.

"An extra egg for good measure." Nima winks at me, and it might be the most disturbing thing I've seen in the entire time I've been here.

"When the leaders leave their posts, the terrorists win."

"The terrorists didn't win. I'm not even sure they were terrorists."

"Of course they were," Benham says, lowering the newspaper, his brow low and sharp. "What else would you call what happened last night?"

Nima refills my glass with more calamansi juice and nudges it toward me.

"Drink. It's good for you."

I eye the glass and the three eggs sitting on my plate next to a veritable mountain of ham. For a moment, I wonder if she's poisoned it. I look at Rafi, but he's tugging on his hair in frustration.

"It was a young man, misguided and desperate. Hardly a terrorist."

"Typical." Benham folds the newspaper and sets it down on the table with a little too much force.

"There is extra iron and good proteins in the ham. Ham is wonderful."

"Thank you," I mumble, not sure what level of crazy to tap into.

"You are still young, Rafi. You need to steel your backbone. You cannot be so soft in a time of crisis."

"With all due respect, Father, you were not there last night. You did not see the look of abject terror in the boy's eyes."

"You would sympathize with the terrorist, but not the dead?" Benham's voice carries more anger this time, and Rafi freezes.

"Of course not. My sympathies are with everyone who was affected last night."

I sip my juice, and no sooner have I set the glass down than Nima is refilling it.

"Typical," Benham says again. He shakes his head as he uses a bit too much force to cut into his ham. "The younger generation takes the wheel, and it all goes to hell."

"Why haven't you tried your eggs? They'll be more nutrient rich while the yolks are warm," Nima says.

"Enough!" Rafi says, cutting into the chaos of our family breakfast. He glares at his father. "I am dealing with a matter of national security. It is being managed. That is all you need to know."

"How dare—"

"That is all that needs to be said about the topic." Rafi's words are final and cutting. Benham lets out a shaky breath, but says nothing more, simply picking up his newspaper and unfolding it.

"Your eggs are cooling, sweets," Nima says, nodding at me.

"What is happening here?" Rafi asks, pointing between me and his mother.

"What do you mean? I'm providing for my family. Your wife is as good as my daughter."

"What happened this morning?" Rafi asks, a wash of deep concern over his face as he focuses solely on me. My stomach drops as I recall what it felt like to creep into his office early this morning. I open my mouth, but nothing comes out.

"I did laundry," Nima says.

"Laundry?" Rafi says, his eyes flickering back to his mother, who wears a knowing smile.

"There's nothing like removing a stain from the bedsheets. Though such talk is hardly appropriate at the breakfast table." She winks again.

I tilt my head, trying to think about what sort of stain she might have found on bedsheets.

My monthly courses.

I slept in that bed instead of in the ridiculous maidenhead room.

She knows. She knows that I'm not observing the traditions.

A smirk flickers the corner of Rafi's lips as he stands from his chair.

"A word?" He holds out his hand to me, and I stare up at him. He arches an eyebrow, and then says, "Wife?"

I take his hand and follow him into the kitchen as Nima watches us with a gleeful look. It's terrifying. Once we're in the kitchen and he's certain the door is shut, I approach quickly.

"I'm sorry. I'm so embarrassed, but I think I bled—"

"Of course you bled." He seems startlingly nonplussed.

"I know she follows the old faith, and I would never want to intentionally disrespect her. I think we've made strides in our relationship and—"

Rafi starts laughing. Hard. I've never seen him laugh like this before. He has to hold on to the countertop to keep from doubling over. I frown and wait for him to snap out of whatever this is. Maybe he's hysterical? Between last night and now . . . maybe he knows I betrayed him in the middle of the night and . . .

He takes a deep breath and wipes at his eyes. He's laughing so hard, he's crying.

"Would you like to fill me in on whatever is so funny?"

He laughs once more, and then steps closer, taking me by the shoulders.

"She thinks you're pregnant."

"What?" My jaw drops, and then I put it together. She

obviously found a blood spot on the sheets. Headmistress Moyle did say that that could happen during the first time. But why would she think I'm pregnant?

"Does she think you're that potent?" I ask with a little chuckle. Rafi laughs and shrugs, leaning back against the counter, arms crossed.

"I'm sure she's tracked your cycles."

"No . . ."

He shrugs. "What else does she have to keep her busy?"

"Oh, boy."

"Or girl."

I snort-laugh, and then he does, and before I know it, we're both laughing beyond control.

"What do we do about that?" I ask. He shrugs and shakes his head.

"When you don't grow a baby, I suspect she'll figure it out."

"And then go back to hating me?"

"By then, perhaps she'll think you're pregnant again."

"So what do I do?"

"Learn to love calamansi juice?"

We both laugh, and then he wraps his arms around me and hugs me. It catches me off guard, but after a moment, I coil my arms around him and hold him as tightly as he holds me.

"Are you all right?" he asks softly.

"With the fake pregnancy? I'm feeling just fine."

He laughs and shakes his head. "I mean, after last night."

I let out a shaky breath and step back, breaking the hug. He looks a little awkward with his long arms hanging at his sides.

"I'm fine," I say, crossing my arms over my chest and leaning against the counter next to the stove. I want to talk about anything except me and how I feel about last night. It would be too easy to slip up. "How are you? Really?"

He looks like he's about to tell me he's fine, that it's all going to be okay. But then he hesitates. Presses his lips together between his teeth. Lets his shoulders drop, just a bit.

"It was terrible."

I stay where I am, realizing that only last night, when he was holding me together, this man saw someone die. He saw the body —bodies. I cross the distance and reach for his hand, squeezing it. We both stare at our hands, at the way mine fits inside his.

"The gunman couldn't have been more than fifteen or sixteen. I think he was—" He squeezes my hand, although I don't think he realizes it. "I think he was looking for me."

I gasp, and his eyes meet mine.

"Instead, two older men stopped him and met the end of their lives. Then, realizing what he'd done, the boy turned his gun on himself. I don't know how many shots were fired. Frankly, it's a wonder more people weren't injured. He wasn't in his right mind."

"My father is right." Rafi removes his glasses and cleans the lenses. "He was a terrorist, but not in the way his generation thinks of terrorism. This boy was targeting me for political purposes, because he hates—" He stops again, and his pupils dilate as he stares at me. Then he blinks and shakes his head. "He's gone. And I will keep you safe. You know that, right?"

"Of course, Rafi."

He smiles.

"You call me Rafi now."

"You asked me to."

We're still holding hands. His touch feels warm and comforting. Good. The distance between us feels tighter, closer, and I'm not sure when that happened. His warm brown eyes flicker to my lips, and I suck in a sharp breath.

The doorbell rings.

My stomach flutters, and we both laugh.

"Never a moment . . ." he says, and he leaves the kitchen. I stay where I am for a moment, gathering myself. There's something he's not telling me. I can feel it. I just can't put my finger on it.

Perhaps our secrets will become too much to bear. Or maybe not. Only in time will we see.

CHAPTER TWENTY-ONE

Zerah stands in the vestibule, her face pale and tight. She's in a wrinkled dress that hits just past her knees. A heavy shawl drapes around her shoulders, weighed down by a layer of emu feathers.

"Neve, am I early?"

I frown, my gaze flickering to Rafi.

"Early?"

"For our date?" She catches my glance, and there's something that's she's trying to communicate without words, something that I don't understand. I sense it's something important, however, and within a few minutes, I'm putting on my trench coat.

Rafi kisses the top of my head and tells me to stay safe, his words light and yet so sincere that it gives me pause. Nima tries to send me out the door with a poached egg, and we leave before she returns with it.

The high street is quieter than usual today, as if people have been frightened away by the news from last night's events. Zerah remains quiet the entire walk, carrying the tension high in her shoulders. I find myself wanting to rub some warmth into her arms, her shoulders, her neck, just to help her relax.

She's less careful than before when we approach the stairwell to the underground market, and I follow her, wordlessly.

"Wait," I say, stopping her once we're at the bottom of the stairwell. "Are you all right?"

"Fine," she says, her words clipped. "I just need a draught."

"For what?" Anger pools in my stomach, and I clench my hands into fists.

She frowns and hikes the shawl up a little higher on her neck.

"Just in case."

I let out a breath, but it does little to cool the ember of anger in my gut. I wrap an arm around her back, and we walk together to the chemist. When we enter, the chemist takes one look at Zerah and invites her into the back room. I explore the overstuffed shelves of the small shop, sniffing the rose hips, the chamomile, looking at the black aster powder. I find a small glass jar of crushed yellow powder — ground calamansi seed.

"Can I help you find something?" The chemist approaches, her gold-brown eyes kind and sympathetic. She takes the jar from my hand. "Something for morning sickness?"

"Oh, no," I say, shrugging away. "That's not — I'm not . . ."

"I see," she says, putting the jar back on the shelf. I look around the shop again, and it's a hodgepodge of everything. Everything but Zerah.

"Is she . . . ?" I nod back toward the room Zerah had disappeared into.

"She'll be back on her feet in a few moments." The anger builds into something frenzied and afraid.

"Right."

She cocks her head, and her dark eyes flash with recognition.

"You are the trade minister's new wife, yes?"

My instinct is to lie, but once again, it seems foolish. It would be too easy to get caught up in it, and something tells me that a little honesty could go a long way with a woman like this.

"Yes," I say softly.

"I think you'll find my shop keeps its secrets better than most."

"How well do most keep their secrets?"

She shrugs one shoulder and moves back behind the counter. She ducks her head behind the curtain closing off the back room, and then returns.

"How are you finding married life?" She doesn't look directly at me as she thumbs through a book of some sort, but there's true curiosity in her tone. I'm not sure what she's looking at, but it seems easier to talk about it with someone who won't look me in the eye while I talk about something personal.

"Fine," I say. She arches an eyebrow, but doesn't look up. "I think I'm lucky."

"I think many women would agree with you." There's no humor in her statement, but neither is there discord.

"All I mean is that he's gentle. Patient. Our relationship is . . . I think it's unique."

"Aren't all relationships?"

"Yes, but I mean . . ."

"What? What do you mean?" She looks up at me, genuine curiosity in her brown eyes.

"We are friendly," I say. Her expression is blank. She doesn't interrupt, just waits for me to explain. "That is all we are. Just . . . friendly."

She laughs. It's not an unkind laugh, but it is a laugh nonetheless. It makes me feel both angry and defensive.

"You married a man who looks like that, and you are friendly? That is all?"

"Yes." I lift my chin and fold my arms over my chest.

"Good for you," she says, and it's genuine. She almost sounds . . . relieved? But that doesn't make sense. She roots around behind the counter and emerges with a small green tin. It looks like a tea tin, but something tells me there's more to it than meets the eye.

"I have this for you. As a wedding gift, if you would like."

"What is it?" I ask, crossing the small distance to the counter.

"It is a tea." I frown as she opens the lid, and I take a deep breath. It smells like carrots and ginger.

"What kind of tea is this? Did you blend it yourself?"

"Yes, I did. It's a natural contraceptive." My eyes flash to hers, and she meets my gaze. "Just in case things become more than friendly. Especially given the pressure you must be facing. A woman can never be too prepared." Then she winks, as if we're in on some kind of joke together.

I giggle.

I actually giggle. I tell myself it's a combination of nerves and tension and not having slept well last night. But the truth is, there's something about the idea of taking this tin home, what it means, that makes me . . . well, excited. Giggly.

"Oh, you definitely need to take this with you."

"Take what?" Zerah frowns from the doorway behind the chemist. Her skin looks clammy, but the color is back in her cheeks.

"Precautions," the chemist says, tucking the small tin into my hand. I nod my thanks and tuck it into the inside pocket of my jacket.

"Thank you," I say, feeling the weight of reassurance in my pocket.

We leave the shop, and Zerah is still quiet. I feel the chemist watching us through the window as we walk, arm in arm, down the dark, dank street. I turn around and meet her appraising, troubled gaze. If I didn't know better, I would swear she was taking measure of me. As if trying to decide what she thinks. I wonder why it matters.

When we're back on the high street, I stop to buy some nuts and tea, and then I force Zerah to eat one. Soon enough, she's sharing the snack with me, the color returning to the rest of her complexion and her step picking up a little faster. There's something about the way this all just happened that makes me wonder how many times she's been through this.

"May I ask a question?" I ask.

"You can ask, though I may not answer." Her voice is tight, and I can feel the tension in the tether between us.

"Does William . . . he's not hurting you, is he?"

Her neck is tight, but she shakes her head.

"No, he wouldn't know how to. He's mostly harmless."

"Forgive my saying, but he doesn't seem entirely harmless if you have to visit the — "

"Watch your mouth on the high street," she hisses, darting into a rickety stand with scarves for sale. I wait until she's done perusing the small shop, and then sidle up next to her as we cross the traffic break.

"I only ask because I care. You do know that, right?" I speak softly, gently. She nods, and I see her expression soften.

"I perform my wifely duties. He requires no more, no less. In that sense, he is fair. But I do not want to give him children, and he doesn't need to know that."

"Do you worry what will happen if he were to find out?"

"He is not Osterstani," she says, veering to the right and toward a greenspace. "He isn't so prudish about such things." She finds a bench, and we settle on it, shoulder to shoulder, nibbling on the nuts and carmelized sugar that remains at the bottom of the paper cone.

"Don't get me wrong," she says, her breathing getting a little faster. "I am not attracted to him. I never could be." Her hazel eyes are clear, almost pleading, as if she's begging me to understand her meaning. Something snags in a deep, warm place inside me, but I don't quite understand. I reach for her hand and squeeze it.

"Of course."

"You understand?" She cocks her head and studies me. "That there is no way I could ever be attracted to him . . . to any man . . ." Her voice is a near whisper, like a wish. I nod. Of course, he's not right for her. She is delicate and rich with emotions. She needs someone to keep up with her. He is none of those things.

"Yes, my friend. I understand."

She smiles, a sweet almost wistful smile parting her lips. I shift, and the tin in my pocket rattles against the metal bench. The smile falls, and she pulls her hand from mine.

"I have something for you," she says, reaching into her pocket and retrieving an unsealed envelope.

"What is this?"

"It is from my husband." Her voice is hollow. My throat tightens with guilt.

"You've read it?"

"Yes." She doesn't make any effort to hide it. I open the envelope and pull the letter out. It appears to be another message, but there's something off about this one.

Mark misses his two brothers. Please inquire at your earliest convenience. Snow may come early.

"What does this mean?" I mumble to myself.

"Funny," Zerah says, her eyes hard. "I was going to ask you the same thing."

I stare at her for a long moment, and she shakes her head and looks away.

"I don't know what it means."

"I believe you."

"You do?"

"But I also think there's something you're not telling me."

I'm quiet for a long minute. She crumples the paper cone,

discarding it in a bin, as I fumble for the right words. She's right. I'm not telling her something. Something big. I'm not telling her about how I've been spying on my husband. How I've been working for her husband and my benefactor, passing secret messages between them.

"Do you love him?" Her voice is cutting, and it takes me a moment to realize she's talking about Rafi.

"What?"

"You have the tea."

"Yes."

"I thought I understood, but . . ."

"I . . ." I think for a long moment, and then sigh. "I respect him. Greatly. And we are friends, I think." I sigh as she wraps her arms around herself. "We have become closer recently, and . . . I don't know. I suppose I only want to be prepared. Just in case. Isn't that what it's about? Having something like this?"

"Do you know what William said this morning?" Her voice is harder, cooler, and much more plain. I shake my head, waiting for her to continue. "He sounded like a madman. I wasn't going to tell you. I honestly thought, if this is true, she'll find out soon enough on her own. But . . . maybe not . . . ?"

"I'd find out what?"

"He said Rafael was there. When the gunman arrived. That the gunman was looking for him."

I'm frozen. I can't say anything, couldn't if I tried.

"And when he found him, Rafael was willing to talk to him. That he did—as if they already knew one another. That the only reason he fired his gun was because Rafael gave him the go-ahead."

"That can't be true," I whisper.

Zerah shrugs. "He prayed with the gunman."

"What?"

"He got down on his knees, with the gunman, and together, they prayed. They prayed for Osterstan, and when they stood, the gunman fired his gun." Pigeons turn away as I stand and step back. As if moving away from her words can make it less true.

"That doesn't sound—that doesn't make sense."

"Your husband knew the gunman, Neve. The police visited this morning to ask William questions about what he observed. They said they have intercepted correspondence between his congressional office and known Nordanian financiers. His recent whereabouts are unknown—which is suspicious, because all Osterstani nationals are protected when they travel abroad.

"You've said it yourself—his mother is a zealot. Everyone knows she is. What was he doing in Nordania when you met him, Neve?" I frown. In all the time we've been together, I don't actually know this. I've never actually pushed for an answer.

"I—I don't know."

"Do you really think it was a coincidence that you met him just before he returned to Osterstan?"

"Yes, I thought so . . ."

My breath is quick, my spine cold and my skin clammy. I don't know what exactly it is she's trying to say. It's as if I can see all the pieces of the puzzle, but there's still one missing, the keystone that could put the whole thing together, and I can't figure it out.

"Neve, they're investigating Rafael for organizing a terrorist attack. The weapon—it was made from Nordanian gunmetal."

"No, that's not possible," I say, frowning. "Nordania doesn't make gunmetal."

She sighs, as if preparing to talk me down. "Copper is a key component to gunmetal. That's what Nordania exports more of than anything else in the world." She's quiet, as if giving me the time to catch up to her. "Nordania makes guns, and this gun was made in Nordania. Where Rafael disappeared to. And nobody knows what he was doing there before he met and married you."

I'm quiet for a long moment. So is Zerah. I feel her fingers thread through mine, and then she wraps her other hand around the back of my hand, giving it a squeeze.

"But he can't . . ." I sputter, unable to find the right words. "He wasn't . . ."

"They'll sort it out," is all she says, giving my hand another squeeze.

The breeze flutters across my face, sending a slick chill down my neck and shoulders. Suddenly, everything seems so up in the air. What if he did? No, he can't have . . . but what if he did?

"This morning, he defended the gunman to his father," I whisper. Zerah closes her eyes and lets out a breath. "He said the gunman was young. That his death was a tragedy just as much as the death of the victims."

"Neve," Zerah whispers, shaking her head with regret.

"What am I supposed to do?"

She wraps an arm around my shoulders and rests her temple against mine.

"Stay safe. Stay vigilant. And maybe . . . come up with a backup plan? Just in case?"

My stomach tightens, but there's no heat there, no warmth. It's something much colder and far more terrible than when the anger spirals out of control. It's something I know, something I've known for a long time. For the first time in forever, I thought I had found a way to live without a backup plan.

I've only now realized that some dreams are just nightmares in pretty clothing.

CHAPTER TWENTY-TWO

The breakfast table is quiet, as it has been for the past few days. I've had time to process what Zerah said about Rafi, and I've looked at it every which way. The problem is that I keep hitting a dead end. The problem is that I can't seem to help from appearing suspicious.

I sent another message to Conrad, including some details I'd heard Rafi talking about around the house. I've felt both less and more stressed as I sneak upstairs at night to send messages to Conrad. Last night, I could have sworn I heard someone upstairs after I left. But Rafi was asleep next to me, and Nima's footsteps are far too heavy.

"You're going to be late," Benham says, lifting his tea to his chapped lips. Nima tuts under her breath and goes to the built-in credenza behind him to light yet another incense holder. The weather has taken a sharp turn over the past few days, with the seasonal rains moving in to drench everything. The house itself has picked up an earthy, loamy odor that I find refreshing. But Nima resents it, takes it as a personal affront. As a result, I've been choking on the heavy, musky stink of incense.

"Maman," Rafi says, lifting his hand as if to stop her by the motion alone. "The house does not need so much incense. My colleagues are starting to complain."

"Complain about what?" She tuts again, flickering a lighter at the long stick coated in what I would consider to be non-essential oils.

"My clothing is giving them headaches."

"They have weak constitutions. They must adjust to working in the same office as such a strong man."

"Maman, it is not about what they must or must not do. It is about consideration."

"It sounds as if they are not being considerate to their boss," she says, blowing out the flame on the stinky stick.

"Should I not be the one to set a good example for my workers? To make for a comfortable and inviting office?"

"I think this smells strong and inviting —"

"Maman, enough!" Rafi's face is red, his mouth pressed into a thin line. I've only ever seen him this upset with his mother once before, when she insulted me. Her eyes widen, and Benham stands.

"Is it not enough that I ask you to stop?"

She casts her eyes between the two of us, and a knowing smirk flickers across her lips.

"Oh, I see. The two of you are thick as thieves, and your companion has you doing her dirty work. Far be it from me to aid in your patriotic and Godly duties."

Whatever calendar she'd been keeping must have expired. I've reverted back to being just his companion and not his wife.

"It's fine, Nima," I say, pushing away from the table, my breakfast largely untouched. Both she and Rafi look at it instead of me as I move for the stairs.

"Love?" Rafi catches me at the base of the steps, his fingers coiling around my wrist. I flinch, and he notices. He lets go, stepping back.

"Are you well?"

"I'm fine," I say. "Just tired." It's the same excuse I've given every day this week. Honestly, I'm the last thing from being tired.

"Tired, she says?" Nima calls from the dining table, hope in her voice.

Rafi closes his eyes and lets out a long breath. When he reopens them, he shares a knowing smirk with me, but I can't seem to muster the energy to reciprocate. I'm not certain that Zerah is right. That she heard correctly, or even that Whitey should be trusted. But I haven't found anything to make me feel comfortable that Rafi isn't somehow responsible.

The fact remains that he was there, he was privy to whatever happened. It seems to be that there were only a handful of people who engaged the gunman, and he is one of two who survived that interaction.

The bell rings at the door, and Rafi lets out a frustrated sigh before turning to open it. He does, and when he returns, he's holding two letters.

"For you," he says, passing them both to me. I look down at them and recognize the handwriting on both.

"I'll take these upstairs." I turn to climb the steps, anxious to be alone with this mail.

"Neve?"

I stop, but don't turn around.

"You would tell me, right?" A chill rushes down my back as I stand, frozen. I don't know what he's asking. Or if he's asking anything at all.

"Would you?" I ask.

"Yes. My love."

"Of course," I say in an almost whisper.

"Don't hold back, Neve. Not from me."

The air between us soothes, and I continue upstairs, locking the door behind me.

The first letter is from Zerah, and its meaning is plain.

Neve,

Please come visit today. I have much I wish to tell you. Perhaps I could even show you.

Zerah

The second is more cryptic, but its meaning is entirely too clear. Still, as I read the second letter, regardless of how I'm feeling toward my husband, it leaves me feeling hollow and empty inside.

Neve,

It has been far too long since I've received an update. I hope you are doing well and finding your new life to be suitable. I wish that I could visit and inquire into your new life. Perhaps that day will arrive sooner than either of us expects.

Your steadfast and loyal,

Conrad

It doesn't matter how many times I read it, it doesn't mean anything different from the first time I read it. The details that I've sent to him clearly aren't sufficient. He wants to know more about Rafi's business dealings, and I wonder what message I passed to him from Whitey. I wonder if he suspects Rafi is up to something, as well—if he's working with Whitey, I suppose he would have every reason to.

All the more reason to go to Zerah today. Perhaps she has found something that will clear the air. I cross my fingers and grab my raincoat.

Zerah and Whitey live in what I've learned is called a four-quad in the South Waterfront district. I've never actually been there before; Zerah has always come to me. The neighborhood is a little rough around the edges, and it feels like it's just on the precipice of something truly great—or completely tragic. I'm not sure I—or any of its residents—know which.

During a previous war, the only bridge connecting it to the

heart of the city was bombed. It was never rebuilt for some reason, and so it's not the most easily accessible bit of land. That, combined with its proximity to the water and water taxis, makes it a cheap and colorful neighborhood, bustling with people from all backgrounds.

When I approach the address Zerah gave me, it doesn't take me long to know the two-story, gray-shingled house with chipped yellow trim is the right place. For one, Zerah is standing outside, leaning against a tall wooden fence. Chicken wire spans the distance between the posts, keeping things both out and in.

The real giveaway is the eight-foot-tall bird currently fighting a staring contest with Zerah.

I slide up next to her, and Zerah jerks. The bird growls, a loud, throaty thing that has me reaching for my ears. Zerah growls back, and the bird—I swear—rolls its eyes and runs away.

"Yeah, run away, you coward," Zerah grumbles. I stifle a laugh as she rubs her hands together.

"These are the emus?"

"These are the hellions."

"They're . . . big."

"That they are."

"Do you get along with all of them so well?"

"Oh, that one? He's fine. He'll come to regret stealing that glove later." I look at her hands again and realize that one is gloved, and the other is not. There's a chill in the air, but what catches my eye is a thin red scar extending out from beneath her cuff. She tugs her sleeves down, as if she can sense my gaze, and removes the other glove.

"How are things?" Her question is cautious but pointed. She doesn't make eye contact, but it's clear she wants to know if I've come to terms with what she's now certain of.

"Fine . . ." I poke at the chicken wire, and it catches on my lacy cuff. The fashions in Osterstan are far more interesting than in Nordania. Women wear delicate, feminine attire one day, and then flirt with hemlines and menswear details the next. I saw a woman wear a classic men's tuxedo shirt with a flouncy, feminine skirt at the market the other day, and I couldn't stop thinking of it. I bought a men's style shirt with little lace accents in my size and am trying it out today with a more traditional, calf-length green wool skirt.

"You haven't found any proof?" Her voice is low enough that I doubt even the emus can hear.

"He wouldn't leave anything around the house."

Her eyebrows lift, as if hearing the reluctant acceptance in my voice.

"Have you be—"

"Zerah!" Whitey's nasal voice calls from the top of the steps leading to their front door. He sounds agitated. "I thought I made myself clear. I need—" He stops when he sees me. His entire demeanor shifts, and he presents a sickly smile.

"Why, Mrs. Rostami! What a surprise. I didn't realize we had guests." His eyes flicker between me and his wife. "We almost never have guests." There's a minuscule breath between each word, and not for the first time, I wonder just how safe Zerah is here.

"Neve and I are going to the market," Zerah says, her voice submissive, yet clear: she is going to do what she wanted, and he won't be able to stop her. "She stopped here first because she's never seen your champion birds."

His face blanches as he casts a furtive glance at the birds in the large space next to his house.

"I didn't realize you travel with them," I say, politely.

"Yes, well, they are very needy. Can't go without a firm hand for too many days."

A bird grunts at him, and he jumps. Literally jumps.

"Well, if you ladies are going into town, would you mind

putting in an order for more feed? They've already gone through the supply we received last week."

"Of course, my dear," Zerah says, suppressing the most joyful grin I've ever seen. I wish she wouldn't. Zerah turns to the approaching emu and reaches through the wire fence to give it a little pet on the nose.

"You be a good boy while I'm gone, right?"

The emu—the same one that stole her glove—presses its head into her palm and blinks up at her with something that looks like adoration. Zerah clicks her tongue twice, and the emu turns its head toward Whitey.

"Now, you'll take care of him while I'm gone, won't you?" Zerah asks, blinking innocently between the massive bird and her husband.

"That's not necessary," Whitey mumbles, backing away from us and back up the steps toward the house. I stare at the scene in wonder until Whitey is inside. As if flipping a switch, the bird screams at the door, casts Zerah a nasty look, and then runs off to be with the others.

Zerah turns toward me, an amused look on her face. "Ready?"

"You've trained his emus to torture him, haven't you?"

The noise of the engine on the back of the yellow motorboat combined with the water splashing against the shabbily painted sides is enough to drown out our voices. Zerah wasn't in a hurry to get to the market, but it would be much faster to take a water taxi.

"I don't know what you're talking about." But she knew exactly what I was talking about. Judging by the amused glint to her hazel eyes. A larger ship passes, and Zerah braces herself for the oncoming waves. I do the same, and the small boat revs the engine and pushes through, rocking harder than I expect. It's not my favorite feeling in the world, but soon enough, the waves calm and we're back to jetting along the coast at a comfortable speed.

"He's afraid of them," Zerah says, her voice low and tight, but the mirth is evident in her words and her eyes. "They're his pride and joy. Rather, they're the reason for his wealth, which is his pride and joy. The only thing that gives him any sort of credibility in his sycophantic world." She braces herself, and I almost don't catch it as we hit another swell and rock hard to the right. I right myself as the boat does the same, turning toward the port.

"He won't tell me the full story, but I've gotten bits and pieces from some of the staff."

I frown. "His staff told you he hates the birds?"

"His staff told me he's terrified of them so badly that if he's caught alone with them, he'll piss his pants from pure terror. And you know the old saying: the enemy of my enemy is my friend."

I have to clap both hands over my mouth to keep from losing it.

"Why doesn't he just sell them?"

"I don't know," she says, frowning. "Seems like he'd be much better off without them. And so would my wardrobe."

I notice the stiff layer of emu feathers along the bottom of her jacket.

"They're really not a good fashion choice."

"He doesn't want there to be any question over who 'this institute girl' belongs to," she says with a snort.

My spine goes cold, and I sit straighter. It's been so long since I've even thought about the fact that Zerah was chosen for the institute, and I wasn't. She cocks her head at me, as if noticing the shift in my demeanor.

"Hold tight, girls," the taxi driver says. We hold on as we pull up to a long, low pier and bump right into it. I tip awkwardly, and Zerah catches me, her hands strong and warm against my shoulders.

"You okay there?" she asks, grinning at me.

"Oh, I'm fine," I say, laughing as I push off her. We climb out and make our way into the market.

The shops along the port look nothing like the ones in Peninsula City, and yet it feels as if I already know my way around. The people are different, and yet, they're the same: the cherry-cheeked boys with dirt smudges on their legs, manning their parents' produce stands; the women in fashionable attire and parasols who don't seem to have any reason to be here other than to see and be seen; the women with vacant eyes, and the men with hard, scrutinizing gazes who seem to watch after them. There's no horrible, cloying citrus scent mixing with the fishy sea breeze. Instead, it's the aromatic dried figs, the tart calamansi, and the earthy spices that cut through the briny wash of what lies beneath the Mittlesee.

The feed store is at the farthest end, next to a decrepit-looking building that looks as if it was once a grand hotel. The three-story structure stretches for what looks like a full city block, facing the port. The clapboards were once painted black, its flower boxes must've once been teeming with colorful flowers, and its copper lantern must've once been shiny and welcoming. Now, the vaguely gray building teems with brown, and bits of stubborn coastal grass. The lanterns display a dull green patina.

"Whatcha lookin' at, girl?" A man calls from in front of the building. I hadn't seen him leaning against it. His wrinkled brown jacket and pants blend into the marine layer and natural shadows of the building.

"Leave her be," Zerah says, taking me by the shoulders and directing me into the barn-looking building next door.

The feed store is exactly as I would expect it to be. It smells like hay and animal excrement.

"You don't want to mess with that," Zerah says, keeping her

voice low.

"What was that place?" I ask.

She turns a corner, and proceeds down an aisle, pretending to look for something among the chains and stakes.

"The Black Magnolia," she nearly whispers. I frown, something tickling in the back of my mind. It disappears as quickly as it cropped up.

"Technically, it's still a hotel. From what I've gathered, it used to be a fine one. Now? Well . . . it's not a brothel, per se," she says, tugging on a length of chain-links. She glares at someone down the aisle, a younger man gaping at us who then walks away, leaving us alone. "But it's not *not* one, either."

Someone clears their throat at the end of the aisle.

"You two look lost," a friendly voice says. A woman stands at the end of the aisle, and without the glamorous dress and makeup, I almost didn't recognize Irina. She wears a long, dark traveling coat in the demure Nordanian style. But beneath it all, I see loose, cranberry-colored trousers.

"Hello," I say. Zerah stays quiet, but nods.

"I believe we haven't been properly introduced," Irina says, nodding at Zerah.

"Probably not." Zerah's voice is stiff, as if trying to communicate something to me.

"Well, I suppose I should have guessed you wouldn't wander into a feed store without a purpose." Irina smiles as she runs a finger along a length of coiled rope.

"What are you doing here?" I ask.

"Oh, I had some business on this end of town and needed a clear breath."

"So you came in a feed store?" Zerah deadpans.

"It doesn't smell like fish in here, does it?" Something flickers across Irina's face, and I believe that she truly did come in here for an escape from the saltwater stench. I wonder what her reason is for hating it so much.

"Well, we were just here to order some food for Zerah's husband's birds."

"Ah yes, the famous emus," Irina says, not a hint of humor in her delivery.

"The very ones," Zerah says. Then she steps away from us, keeping her distance. "I should go place that order. I'll leave you two to chat." She squeezes my forearm and catches my eye, as if trying to communicate something. But I don't know what.

"Very nice to meet you," Irina says. "If you ever need anything . . ." She trails off, and Zerah's shoulders tighten. But she gives her a sharp, short nod.

Irina and I stand quietly in the aisle for a moment as Zerah walks away. I'm not sure what there is to talk about.

"How are you, then?"

"Fine."

"And after the other night? How is Rafi?"

"He's fine, too." My shoulders tense.

"Good," she says, unease creeping into the corners of her full mouth. "It is a difficult thing to try to persuade a man so set on destruction."

I stare at her for a long moment, trying to process what she's just said. But I can't. It seems far too direct to be what it sounds like. And yet, Irina may be the most direct person I've ever known.

"How are you? After the other night?" I ask.

"Oh, you know," she says, waving a hand as if it's nothing. But there's a tightness to her eyes. "It is hard to see men's lives come to such a violent end and know that you've failed to stop it."

"You think you could have stopped that?"

"I don't know," she says, looking away. It's the most vulnerable I've ever seen her, and it gives me pause. "Probably not. Once a man has set his mind on something—well, you know . . ."

"I do."

She nods, carefully. As if she believes that I would know, that I would understand.

"Well, I'm glad to see you. You look well. Tired, but well."

"Thanks . . ." I frown at her strange form of compliment. But she laughs it off.

"I think anyone who went to that party looks tired."

I nod. She starts to back away, and it clicks.

"Irina!"

She looks back at me, her gaze sharper. This is my chance. My opportunity to ask her exactly what happened.

"Yes?"

But the way she talks about him, the way she just spoke about that night—I hesitate. Would she ever really betray him, if she did know something damning?

"I, uh—" I pause, trying to get my thoughts together. I don't know what to ask, or how to ask it.

"Is there something you need?" Her voice is lower, her gaze sincere. I have no doubt she would get it for me, though.

"Rafi . . . he, uh . . ."

"He's a good man, you know." Irina's voice is soft, kind.

"He is?"

"Yes," she says, nodding resolutely. "That man has a very steady moral compass. Would never do anything without a solid rationale."

My stomach hardens. It's as good as confirmation that he could be involved.

"You've known him a long time?" I ask. She looks at me funny, as if I should already know this.

"I suppose you could say that."

"Do you think he would—I mean, is he capable of—"

"I think I know what you're asking, and let me be clear: all men are capable of all things. But your Rafi would never do something that falls in a morally gray area without a very good explanation. Or at least one that is justified to him."

She steps closer, her voice lower.

"That doesn't make it right, of course. And if you feel unsafe . . ." Her eyes flicker to the left, as if she can hear prying ears from aisles away. "I have the means to help."

"The means?" I ask. She frowns again, two lines forming between her eyebrows. She suddenly looks so much older than I first guessed.

"Are you ready?" Zerah calls from behind me. I jump and turn so fast that I have to catch myself against a looped length of chain-links.

"Your timing is perfect! I think we're quite finished catching up." Irina presses a hand to my shoulder blade. "Unless there is something else?" Her meaning is clear—but I'm not entirely clear about what taking her help entails.

"No," I say, slipping back into the role of the institute girl I was trained to play. "Thank you. It was lovely catching up." She smiles, and I recognize it, at long last, for exactly what it is—her own role.

"I'll be off, then."

"Off to where?" Zerah asks. Her question surprises me. It seemed as if she couldn't wait to be rid of Irina before now.

"Home," she says, a wash of disappointment and relief coloring her pale features. We part ways at the entrance. She crosses the street as we climb it back toward the water taxi stand.

"Did you learn anything new?" Zerah asks.

I nod, but don't say anything. At times, it felt like Irina and I were having two different conversations, but her words were plain enough. Irina made it clear that not only is Rafi capable of that sort of thinking, it could very well make sense.

And yet still, a part of me clings to the hope that it's not true. That none of it is true. I'm not sure what part of me that is, but if I want to survive, I'll have to learn to silence it.

CHAPTER TWENTY-THREE

*T*he streets of the Old City are full of happy festival-goers clad in white, green, and orange. It's a far cry from the Old City I'm used to seeing. Today is the Festival of the Virgin of the White Caves, a semi-obscure holiday on the Orthodox calendar, and the neighbors appear to be in high spirits.

Or at least, that's what it seems, since no one has spit at me yet.

Or perhaps it's because Rafi won't let go of my hand.

We've been to several formal events together, but this is the first informal one. It's the most public outing we've been on together, for certain. We have a security guard in plain clothes who follows us through the crowd, but everything still feels a bit off. Rafi holds my hand just a bit too tight, as if he's afraid I'll wander off, or that someone will try to kidnap me.

Somehow, I doubt anyone is that interested in me.

But people love him. Schoolgirls dressed in ruffled white dresses and orange sashes giggle as they line up to shake his hand. Grown men in green clothes pat him on the back. Even the older women in their orange dresses smile and wave when he passes.

He greets every person with the same dazzling smile that doesn't quite reach his eyes, not that anyone but me seems to notice. He makes eye contact with every handshake, repeats the name of every person introduced, and asks personal questions as often as he can about neighborhoods, jobs, and schools.

I'm wearing an orange dress that grazes just below my knees, the top collar a fringe of ruffles that crosses and ties in a sash at the hip. Of course, it's a lie. I should be wearing white. But then, that would open a different can of worms.

When he finally gets a break in introductions, he motions toward a kebab stand, and we find a seat as the vendor motions that he's on his way.

"How are you holding up?" Rafi's question surprises me. Although, perhaps what surprises me more is the fact that he's still holding my hand, his fingers laced with mine. He presses my knuckles to his lips.

"I'm fine. People love you."

"I don't know about that," he says, with a self-deprecating smile. The vendor brings over two glasses of what looks to be some sort of frothy cider. "Try it," he says, nodding to it, and finally releasing my hand. I lift the drink to my lips and find it smells of tart apples. When I sip it, it's not actually sweet, but it's definitely cider.

"It's light," I say, setting it down, uncertain as to whether I want to drink more. "Refreshing."

He grins. "You hate it."

"I didn't say that," I whisper-hiss as the vendor brings over two plates full of grilled meat and fruit on a stick, over top of a bed of spiced rice and vegetables.

"Custard apple cider is traditional at the Feast of the Virgin," he says, taking another long sip and lifting his glass to the vendor. He sucks at his teeth, as if it's hard to get it down. "All true Osterstanis love it." His eyes flicker to mine, and there's a joke in them.

It's hard to know what to think. I still don't know where things stand with him, or how much I trust him. But he is so earnest. I take another sip and decide I don't *hate* it. I just might not request it at any future events.

We eat the kebabs, which end up being a delicious marinated pork and golden stone fruit. The rice is flavored with saffron, turmeric, cinnamon, and mixed with braised onions, roasted pine nuts, and chopped golden dates. It's sweet and savory and goes down far too quickly.

"Rafi," a booming voice says. I had thought perhaps our security guard had put up a perimeter around us and wonder who has found a way to interrupt our meal, even as it's ending. But when I look up, I see a police officer in uniform. He approaches, and Rafi extends his hand.

"Officer Koprihan, so nice to see you! May I introduce you to my wife?"

"I've heard the news. Congratulations to you both," Koprihan says, though his steely eyes are narrow, as if he sees something others don't.

"This is Gilles Koprihan, chief constable of our district," Rafi says.

"It's nice to meet you," I say with a demure nod.

"Lovely to meet the woman who finally snagged this man's heart," Koprihan says. But the way he says it sets me on edge. Rafi places his hand against the small of my back, and I wonder if he hears it, too. But then he presses a kiss to my forehead, as he always does in public, and it feels like I'm overthinking things.

"Tell me you're at least able to enjoy a bit of the festival?"

"You know me," Koprihan says with a defeated smile.

"I do," Rafi says, lifting his cider in salute to the man before us. "He'll work extra hours if it means his subordinates can take their babies to the festival."

"How generous," I say with a smile. Koprihan nods, but says nothing more.

"What a meeting of the minds in the middle of a street fair!" Irina enters the space. Again, I wonder how she has been allowed entrance when others have been blocked.

"Nice to see you enjoying the festivities, Irina," Rafi says, rubbing his hand up and down my back. My instinct is to recoil away from his touch, but I fight against it. If anyone would notice, it would be Irina. And I'm still not sure I can trust her. Not when it comes to Rafi, anyway.

"I hate to break up your meal, but would you mind if we had a quick conversation? It won't take a moment," Koprihan says, his eyes flickering between Rafi and Irina. I try not to feel slighted.

"Of course," Rafi says. He leans in and presses a kiss to my temple. "I won't be a moment," he whispers. He's not usually so attentive, and I wonder about it. I watch him walk over to the corner of the square with Koprihan, next to a rose garden beneath a jacaranda tree with just the first few yellows of fall.

"Those two are thick as thieves. Have been since primary school," Irina says, sitting opposite me. She peers over the edge of my glass and raises an eyebrow. "Not you, too?"

"I think it is light. Refreshing even."

"How very diplomatic, Mrs. Rostami," she says with a wink. I can't help but let out a little laugh.

"Do you want some?"

"Gods no," she says. "Never did like the stuff."

"Have you been to this festival before?"

"This specific one? Of course. Many times. My family celebrated all of the holy days."

I frown, taking in what she's said. I suppose I thought she was Sudersbergian. But she makes it sound as if she is Osterstani. I suppose it would explain her accent . . .

"So, this one is more special than the others?"

"What makes you think that?" She frowns.

I shrug, feeling embarrassed by my assumption. "I don't know.

There are so many people here. Everyone's dressed up, and it seems very joyful — "

Her snort-laugh interrupts, and I hesitate.

"I do not mean to laugh. It's just always been such a strange holy day."

"What's it about?" I ask.

"Oh, you know, God blessed a virgin, kept her locked up in a beautiful white cave next to a spring that gave her everlasting life. Then a man came along, a wannabe prophet, and he decided to impregnate her. Wrath rained down upon him — boiling water from the skies, melting stone, all the works. The not-virgin imprisoned in stone forevermore. Supposedly, you can still hear her cries from outside the sealed cave."

"Is this a real place?" I ask. She nods.

"In central Osterstan, about ninety miles west of Ourocéu. It's more likely that what you're hearing is the product of natural gasses that have built up around the hot springs releasing. But if it serves the church, we can go with virginal cries."

I look around and see people chatting, laughing, even dancing in the streets.

"And this is celebrated . . ."

"Yes," Irina says with a knowing glance. "The lesson to be learned is that any woman who allows a man to enter her is allowing him to desecrate her holy vessel, and she deserves to be punished."

"So we dress in orange and white so that men can identify the virgins and the whores more easily?"

"You catch on quickly!" Irina grins, but it only looks cruel. I shake my head, not understanding what joy could be found in such an odd story. "In some texts," she says, interrupting my thoughts, "this story is called the rape of the holy vessel. But those who decide such things found that title distasteful and unfair to men."

I snort. She grins, and this time, it meets her eyes, as if I've passed some sort of test.

"What are those two talking about over there? It looks so serious."

Rafi and Koprihan stand close together. Rafi's head is tilted down, his glasses in his hand. Koprihan's gaze cuts to us, and a chill rushes down my spine.

"I don't know," I say.

Rafi chooses that moment to look over his shoulder. I'm not sure how good his vision actually is, but it must be good enough to meet my gaze, because I feel the connection—and sadness within.

"Mrs. Rostami," the security guard interrupts. "Will you come with me, please?"

"Be safe," Irina says under her breath as the guard leads me away. We walk over to where Rafi is shaking Koprihan's hand.

"Sir," the guard says, and Rafi nods at him. "I've been advised it is a fifteen-minute walk in these conditions to the central pavilion, where you are soon due for your speech." Rafi nods and gives him a weak smile.

"Thank you," he says.

"Is everything all right?" I ask. His brow narrows ever so slightly, and he tilts his head, as if deciding whether or not to tell me the truth.

He reaches for my hand, threading his fingers through mine, and presses a kiss to my temple.

"Everything is fine, love."

A feel a wave of disappointment, but grin through it, and we move back toward the crowd to smile and wave and be the people everyone out there expects us to be.

CHAPTER TWENTY-FOUR

*T*he house is asleep, or so it would seem. I've brought a blanket with me to toss over top of the telegraph machine as I tap out the message. It does its job, at least in part, muffling some of the loud noise, but it makes for a bulky task. I try to read the rest of the message in the dark, thinking through the dots and dashes of the military code.

After stewing on my conversation with Irina for the rest of the evening and well past bedtime, it felt like the only thing left to do was to tell Conrad what I knew. Or what I think I know.

She made it pretty clear that Rafi wouldn't do something without a good reason. And the fact that she said that the way she did? It seems like she's trying to tell me something, like she's trying to give me an excuse. But I don't know why she would try to endear him to me. It's all so confusing. But the thing that remains is that Rafi is a powerful man in a position where he could get away with something massive if he wanted to.

So, I continue to tap out the rest of my message:

No clear evidence.

R may be responsible.

I don't understand this code that Whitey and Conrad are

using, and honestly, it doesn't seem to matter. So long as no one hears me on the telegraph, nobody knows what I'm sending.

I tap out the last of the message, and then sit back and wait for a response. It's half past three here, but with the time difference, it might catch Conrad before he goes to bed. The wind rattles against the windows, and I nudge both arms under the blanket for a little extra warmth.

I need more evidence. I need to know what it is that Rafi did. Or didn't do. His desk is wide and has three drawers down one side of it. I open the top drawer and look through the scant contents. Two pens, a handful of wire clips, and some typewriter tape. The second drawer contains a bit more, but still all office supplies. The bottom drawer is locked.

"We'll see about that," I whisper, removing a hairpin as I squat down. I start picking at the lock, feeling around and listening for that satisfying *click*. Instead, I hear loud beeping.

The blanket has shifted off the telegraph as it hammers out Conrad's confirmation.

Keep me apprised.

I let out a breath as I shut down the blasted machine and decide to return to the bottom desk drawer another day. I tiptoe down the stairs, the blanket wrapped around my shoulders. When I reach the landing, I could swear I hear something beyond Nima and Benham's door. But I push on, deciding that I'm far enough now that I could make up an excuse. I slowly turn the handle on my own room, step inside, and close the door as quietly as possible.

But when I turn around, a light flickers on.

Rafi is sitting upright in bed. There are dark smudges under his eyes, his hair is mussed from sleep, and he looks more than exhausted. He looks disappointed.

"Rafi," I say, holding the blanket tighter to me. "You startled me. Is everything all right?"

He's quiet again. Just sits. Stares at the end of the bed, not even at me. That's when I know. Deep down, I know I've screwed up.

I step toward the bed, but he raises his palm.

"How long?" he asks.

"How lo—"

"Let's not do this. Please. Just tell me the truth." His brown eyes flicker up to mine. It's like a sucker punch to see the hurt in them.

"Since the start."

"Hmm." He nods, his gaze down at the foot of the bed again. His hands lay at his sides, limp, helpless. "How much did they pay you?"

At this, I frown. "What?"

"Don't play dumb with me, please."

I shake my head. "I'm not—I mean, it's not like that."

"You mean to tell me you're sending secret messages about me to someone in Nordania, and you're not getting paid? Forgive me if I find that hard to believe. You're a smart, cunning woman, Neve. Surely you wouldn't agree to a deal like that."

I look at my feet. I've never felt so small. The way he said *cunning* hit like a knife.

"I didn't have a choice."

"Of course, you did. You always have a choice."

"And what? Become the third wife and babymaker to some wannabe disciple in backwoods Nordania? You think that's a choice?"

Now, he frowns. "What is it you are talking about? I do not understand."

"My choice. You said I had a choice. And perhaps you're right. But my choice was either to marry the man you told me that I shouldn't, or to do as my benefactor told me to do and marry the nice man who had saved me twice."

He pushes out of bed, his brow stony still and tight.

"I paid off your contract. You could have chosen to leave and be alone."

I scoff.

"You would think that, wouldn't you?"

"What is that supposed to mean?"

"How could I leave and be alone? With what money? What you're saying is I could have—no, I *should* have chosen poverty over the deal I made with my benefactor."

"But surely you have some savings?"

"You can't be serious."

"Your benefactor told me you had some savings."

"Yeah, *had* being the operative word. He stole it from me. He has it still. He told me he would give it back to me if I sent him information about you for the next year. So that was the deal I got. Abuse, poverty, or moral damnation. Tell me, Rafi, which would you choose?"

I don't know when we moved, but we're currently standing close enough that I can feel the heat rolling off his body. I'm certain he can feel mine, as well.

"I didn't want to," I say, my voice softer. "I'm sorry."

"What did you tell him?"

I let out a deep sigh and sit on the edge of the bed. I tell him. I tell him about every message I sent back. The stupid, mundane details. How I didn't know what Conrad would want to know, so there were days I sent messages about what color suspenders he wore. Rafi chuckles at that.

"What will you do?" I ask. My fate is once again in the hands of a man.

He shakes his head and shrugs. "There's nothing to be done."

"What?"

"Officer Koprihan was somehow made aware of messages to and from Nordania coming from our address." My stomach sinks. Rafi shakes his head. "I'm not going to turn you in to the authorities, although I probably should. It would destroy the trust and goodwill I've built so far, and Osterstan needs that goodwill."

I nod.

"I'm not going to divorce you, either, if that's what you're wondering. That would only destabilize things. It would make it far worse than you could imagine . . ." He shakes his head, as if cutting off a train of thought. I frown, but don't interrupt.

"So I suppose, for the time being"—he lets out a deep sigh—"we do nothing."

"Nothing?"

"I assume your benefactor will expect more information?"

I nod.

"Then I will help you."

"Why?"

"Because I didn't mean to trap you with me. If I'd been a smarter man and had more forethought, I would have seen that given the situation, you were stuck. If I'd realized it, I would have given you an out before the wedding. A true out."

"Why?"

He tilts his head.

"Because it's the right thing to do."

I don't understand this man. And in this moment, my heart is telling me he's innocent. That somehow, Zerah must have misunderstood, or Whitey must've gotten it wrong. There's no way he could have been responsible for the attack at the party. Someone who, upon confirming suspicions that his wife is a Nordanian spy, not only understood, but accepted blame for the situation, could not possibly have played part in a terrorist attack that ended the lives of innocents.

"Why are you like this?"

"Like what?" He looks confused.

"Kind. I don't deserve it."

He sighs, and I can feel his breath on my lips, warm and sweet.

"I don't know that anyone *deserves* anything. I may not be responsible for how you came to be in your situation, but I am responsible for everything that has happened since you stumbled into my life." He reaches for my cheek, his fingers tracing a warm line across the soft slope. He brushes the dark hair off my forehead, tucking it behind my ear, and gives it a gentle tug. A haze of fuzzy warmth shrouds me in an unfamiliar sensation. I don't feel rooted to the moment. I also don't feel like I could move if I tried. Nor do I want to.

Everything I've heard since that night wants me to believe that this man is dangerous. Everything in my life is screaming at me, telling me to back away, to put as much distance between us as possible. But as he runs his fingertips over my hair, so close to my ear that I can hear the gentle friction between the soft strands and his rough hands, I don't run. I don't back up.

I stay where I am.

There is so much unanswered between us. He has no reason to trust me, and I have an even longer list of questions for him.

"Where does that leave us?" I whisper. I can't bear this closeness, but I'm terrified to step outside of this heady moment, to fracture everything we could have been into shards of glass.

"I don't know." He lets go of my hair, letting his hand settle along the slope of my neck. His gaze flickers to my lips, and my chest swells on a stilted breath.

He lets go of my neck and steps back. I feel cold, thudding into my feet. The haze is gone. It's once again the middle of the night in this drafty bedroom, and his eyes are narrowed, though there's nothing unkind in them. It's more like surprise.

"It's late. No good decisions are made after midnight."

And with that, we return to our marital bed, to our respective sides. I feel like I've been tossed out and back, like a rowboat before the breakers. I'm buzzing with too many emotions to name: frustration and guilt, fear and embarrassment. I've been careless and foolish. I shouldn't have put myself in this position. Nor should I trust him moving forward. It's too dangerous to let my guard down.

But when I feel his fingertips brush my hand as I lie there in the dark, I take his hand in mine. Maybe that makes me the biggest fool of all. Or maybe sometimes, even the biggest fool just needs someone to hold her hand.

CHAPTER TWENTY-FIVE

"*S*he's not staying for lunch, is she?" Nima says, her brown eyes so narrowed, they're almost crossed. A few days have passed since our jaunt to the feed store, and I've been anxious to catch up with my friend. In that time, I've continued to watch Rafi, but every time, he catches on. He speaks louder, or invites me into the conversation with his father. I don't know what to think, but my gut is still telling me that Zerah, who arrived just as Nima was setting the table for Sunday lunch, was wrong about him. I think Rafi is innocent.

"Maman . . ." Rafi warns his mother.

If Zerah hears any of this, she doesn't show it, politely making conversation with Benham in the living room. She tugs at the buttons on her cuffs as he sips fig wine from a short glass.

"She is not a believer," Nima hisses under her breath as she fills my glass to the brim with calamansi juice. I lift an eyebrow, realizing that in Nima-land, I'm pregnant again, and therefore susceptible to catching Zerah's incurable heathenism. Rafi suppresses a smirk aimed at me, but I turn away, ignoring it, and busy myself with folding napkins on the built-in buffet.

"And I thought all believers welcomed non-believers into their homes?" Rafi says with a little wink.

"Non-believers are welcome in my house. But that girl . . ."

"That girl is hungry," I say, not realizing that the words have slipped out of my mouth. "She's been invited, and she is my friend." Nima's glare refocuses on me, and I feel the weight of it. Her eyes flicker to my stomach, and then back up to my face, as if debating whether or not I'm in any condition to bear a scolding.

"I do not think it proper for you to spend time with a girl who smells like . . . that." My anger boils too fast for me to stop it.

"Smells like what?" I hiss. "Fresh air? Laundry detergent? Something that doesn't reek of incense?"

"This is not proper conversation within earshot of a guest," Rafi hisses under his breath as he pinches the bridge between his eyebrows.

"You know what I mean, Rafi," she says, edging closer. "She has the smell of death about her."

"Maman, that's—"

"You can smell the filth and the sin on her. I bet she doesn't even sleep in her maidenhead room."

"Neither do I," I hiss. Rafi freezes, and so does Nima.

It's been a long week. On top of watching everything Rafi does—as if, by simply observing him, I could figure out whether or not he's secretly involved in a terrorist plot—Nima has been putting me through the ringer. She's forced me to make different types of stuffed breads every day. My arms are sore and exhausted every night when I fall asleep with my back to my husband.

My husband, whose eyes seek me out right now.

"Rafi!" Nima gasps, her eyes flicking back and forth between us. "You know what the good Lord says about—"

"Maman, that's enough. My marriage is mine, not yours. I will conduct it as I see fit."

"Rafi! You bear an obligation to—"

"I said *enough!*"

Nima stares at him, her mouth gaping like a fish dangling by a hook. But then Rafi's focus shifts to me, and he nods toward the kitchen.

"Neve? A word?"

I let out a sigh of hot air and set down the fork I only just realized I'd been pressing into my palm. I flash Zerah a look, and she frowns, but stays where she is on the sofa with Benham.

We pass into the kitchen, and after a long moment, Rafi turns on me.

And laughs.

"I never thought I'd see the day . . ."

"Are you okay?"

"My mother—she didn't have a word to say. Not one." He braces himself against the countertop, and it's strange. It is funny. He's right. His mother always has something to say, and I found a way to shut her up. But there's a disconnect, too, and I can't seem to find the humor.

"You're not mad?" I ask.

"Oh, I'm not happy that you just told my mother that I'm sharing your bed while you're on your courses. I guarantee you we'll be hosting no less than three clergymen a week until she hears one of us making that horrible bed creak at night."

"I'll sleep there tonight," I say. "I'm nearly due for my courses, anyway."

He tilts his head, and his glasses slip down his nose ever so slightly. He takes them off and pinches the bridge of his nose.

"That's not what I meant."

I stare at the floor.

"I just meant that there are certain things between a man and wife that the man's mother doesn't need to know."

"Like the fact that in the eyes of her 'good Lord,' we're not actually man and wife?"

The words are out of my mouth before I can stop them. I wait for heat to flood my cheeks, or the awkwardness to permeate the kitchen. But it doesn't. When I look up, Rafi is watching me. I lift my chin, not entirely sure what I'm trying to say.

"I've told you, that doesn't matter to me."

"I know," I say quickly, stepping back. But he grabs my shoulders, leans down, and presses his lips to mine. It's fast, but his lips are soft and firm, and this is no quick brush in front of a stranger in a weird chapel across the Mittlesee. He ends the kiss, pulling back, but holds me in place, leaning over so I can't not look at him.

He looks . . . worried. Uncertain. Vulnerable. I stand frozen, the anger coagulating into an unfamiliar ember in my belly.

"What matters to me is your respect. Our vows matter to me." His words are whisper soft. "I vowed to be good, fair, and just. To be your partner. To protect you and keep you safe. I still do. I want to always be your friend, and to always listen, and . . . if you need more from me —"

"I don't," I say quickly. Because I don't really want more from him. Do I? His hands are warm and soothing against my arms, and despite the awkwardness of this moment, I don't pull away from him.

"I realize this must be difficult. Being surrounded by people who see you as having a singular purpose. And others . . . "—he nods toward the door, at Zerah beyond—"who are working at growing a family." I look away, afraid he'll see the secret I keep for her. "To live under the same roof as a woman who is tracking your cycles and choosing menus full of aphrodisiacs and virility-enhancing fruits and vegetables."

"She's doing *what*?"

Rafi laughs, and finally lets go. I rub the chill bumps along my exposed arms.

"I don't need anything more than what I currently have. But if you do . . . I won't fault you for it. I'll give you . . . if you need to be a mother . . . ." He can't even get out the rest of the sentence.

There's an inherent discomfort in the way he speaks, as if he never thought he'd ever say those words to me.

"You don't want children?" I ask. He eyes me silently, cautiously, and then slowly shakes his head once. Twice.

"It's not that I don't want them," he says quietly. "Yes, it is expected of me. This position passes through the family, after all. You may as well know. . . . There were those in power who felt I should not take the seat until there was a reasonable chance I would sire my successor. But to be blunt, I've never been one for tradition, and I never really thought children were in the cards for me."

"Oh."

"I like them just fine. I just . . . I suppose I never really pictured having them."

The door flies open, and we both startle. Benham stands in the doorway.

"Can I help you hurry this along a bit before your mother starts actively inhaling Mrs. Whitey?"

I try to catch Rafi's eye, but he's out of the room before I can. I follow him, and Benham holds the door for me. But as I pass him, his old, wary gaze returns. I don't think it's a stretch of the imagination to think he overheard some of our conversation.

I spend lunch lost in my own head. I'm vaguely aware of Nima sniffing the air around Zerah in between refilling my glass with more calamansi juice, and Rafi and Benham debating whether or not the House of Landowners should be done away with. But mostly, I'm trying to make sense of what the hell just happened in the kitchen. Rafi was all over the place. One minute, he was telling me that we don't need to consummate our marriage; the next, he was kissing me; and then the next, he was telling me that he's never wanted children.

How is it possible that a man with the parents he has, living in the Old City, has never pictured having children? At least now I know why he was so keen to marry me. Bringing home a wife from his travels cemented his role as trade minister within the old party. Perhaps I should feel some relief at this? Knowing that his expectations of me are true. That he doesn't expect me to have his babies. Especially in light of recent developments and the fact that I don't know if he played a part in that violent attack. My heart says one thing, but my brain . . . it's too much to process. So then why am I feeling uneasy—almost like . . . disappointment?

He has mentioned a previous relationship—surely having children has popped into his head once or twice before. Not that I can really picture Irina settling down and getting married. Or did he just mean that he's never pictured having them with me?

I should probably be relieved if that's the case. After all, I'm not in this for the long haul. Sure, there may have been a moment where it seemed plausible—or at least like it would be worth consummating the marriage enough to buy some contraceptive tea. But now? With all the mystery around what his job really entails, his vagueness around his comings and goings, and everything Zerah has reported from Whitey . . . I need to stay detached.

Rafi stands suddenly, and I realize everyone is looking at the front door.

Zerah leans over.

"What's wrong with you?"

"Wrong?"

"You've been in the clouds this whole meal. I'll think twice next time you try to talk me into staying for a family meal." She glares at Nima, who has just lit a candle and placed it next to Zerah's place setting.

"Thank you," Rafi says from the door, his eyes flickering over a piece of paper. A letter from someone local, most likely. I wonder if Zerah is thinking the same thing.

"I must apologize, but I need to excuse myself."

"What is it, Rafi?" Nima asks, her voice hitting the same decibel as I imagine it would if she were to say, *You're not going to leave me with these heathens, are you?*

"Just business," he says. But his voice is clipped, and gone from it is the levity from earlier. He rushes upstairs, presumably to collect his work bag and hat. But when he comes back down, he's only wearing his long raincoat.

"Is it raining?" I ask, rising from the table.

"Looks like it will be later," he says. I peer out the window, and the skies are blue. The first fall rains brought cooler winds off the Mittlesee, and I've needed a jacket, but if there is any rain in the forecast, it's not coming for a long while.

"You'll be gone long?" I ask.

He frowns. "I don't know. Is that a problem?" His expression is sharper than before, and I shake my head.

"Of course not."

He says his goodbyes and is out the door. We stay around the table quietly for a moment, when Zerah stands suddenly.

"I just remembered I have somewhere to be."

"You do?" I ask, frowning.

"Yes, but I need an escort."

"I cannot be spared, girl," Benham says, his tone much sharper without Rafi present.

"Of course, you cannot," Nima says, tutting her tongue.

"I'll accompany you."

"And how will you return home, then?" Nima says, aghast.

"I'll take a cab," I say, and before anyone can object—not that they would, as they both seem perfectly happy to say goodbye to Zerah—she and I are out the door.

"What is it you need to do?" I ask, trying my hardest to keep pace with her.

"Follow your husband."

CHAPTER TWENTY-SIX

"Follow him?" I frown, moving my feet at double pace to keep up with her long strides. She barely comes to my shoulder, and yet I'm the one who's out of breath.

"How do you know where he went?" I ask when she takes a violent right turn — not toward the market, but instead toward the jacaranda-lined boulevards of the financial district. The leaves flutter in the breeze that sweeps up from the waterfront. Being a Sunday, it's not a heavily trafficked route, and I suddenly realize how exposed we are, and what a mess we must look. Both of us in raincoats under blue autumn skies, speed walking on the wrong side of the road.

"I don't know where he went," Zerah says, barely casting me a backward glance over her narrow shoulder. "But I know where he didn't go."

"Where didn't he go?"

"To the left."

"To the left?"

"He turned right when he left."

"What if he was trying to throw us off?" I ask, finally catching up to her at an intersection.

"You think your husband expected you to follow him? Without trust, the marriage is doomed, Neve." Zerah tsks her tongue with a teasing glance. I glare at her as we wait for traffic to pass. I don't know what she expects to see, but I don't see Rafi anywhere.

"He was too rattled for that."

"Rattled?"

"You saw him. You heard him. He excused himself from Sunday lunch with his family and a guest. He was rattled."

"You don't think he went into his office?" I ask, but it's not really a question. We're approaching the government center. The old, plaster-cracked façade looms large, casting a formidable shadow over the south blocks. We cross into the intersection, and even as I follow Zerah toward the capital building, Zerah shakes her head.

"No, he didn't go there."

"How do you know?"

"Because he's over there."

I follow her gaze to where Rafi stands at the opposite end of the capital building, heading for the traffic circle. The green and yellow jacarandas rustle in the breeze, and the tiny leaves vibrate against one another like a rumor snaking through a crowd.

"Shit." Zerah knocks me to the side, and I nearly collide with a lamp post before she rights me and tugs me behind the round yellow building.

"What was that about?"

"He turned around."

"Maybe I should just catch up to him? Talk to him?"

"You think he'll tell you what he's doing? You think he'll be honest?"

I think for a moment. Just before lunch he told me that our wedding vows were important to him. That he would always be fair and just. But that he'd also always keep me safe. Part of me thinks that if I confronted him right now, out here on the streets, he would be honest. He would tell me the truth.

But there's another part, the part steeped in doubt and distrust, that questions whether or not anything he would tell me would be true. Even as he was reminding me of his wedding vows and how seriously he means to take them, he also tried to talk me down from us consummating our marriage — and then kissed me. That whole interaction left me spinning, and I can't imagine what could be going through his head — his usually steadfast head — to lead to that.

"I don't want to lose him," I say, something thick coating my words. Zerah stares at me, and then looks away abruptly, as if giving me a moment to myself. But I don't take the time to examine my turmoil as Zerah tugs me back toward the direction he was going.

We weave through the city streets at alternating breakneck and ultra slow paces. At one point, he ducks into a small flower shop. There's a tea cart down the block, and Zerah purchases us both paper cups of black tea. It's warm in my hands, and as I sip it, the earthy, floral notes warm my throat and fill my tummy. I hadn't realized how much of a chill had crept in, along with the dark clouds overhead.

"There he is." Zerah takes what's left of my tea from me and chucks it in the refuse can.

"I wasn't finished."

"I'll buy you another cup later."

By the time I look back, he's curved around the block, and I've missed it. Zerah takes off, tugging on my wrist, and we set off again.

He's carrying some sort of flower arrangement in his arms as he speed walks ahead of us, weaving through the side streets, toward the market. When we finally reach the market, most of the vendors are shutting down for the day, pulling tarps down over their stands and tucking away wooden stools and merchandise.

We serpentine between them, doing our best not to attract too much attention. I'm not sure we succeed, but when we reach the second traffic break, I don't see Rafi anywhere.

"Did we lose him?" I ask.

She shakes her head, brows pinched.

"Did we get ahead of him?" I look behind us, but there's no one there.

"This way," she says, pointing toward the unassuming stairwell that leads to the black market.

"What would—"

"There will be so much more time for questions like that when we're not pursuing our mark."

"He's not a—"

"Neve," Zerah hisses. There's a vigor in her eyes, passion mixed with fear. I nod quietly and follow her down the rickety metal steps, trying to keep my footfalls as light as possible.

The underground market is dark, and colder than the proper one, but at least it's shielded from the wind. Even more vendors have already closed and left for the day. Of course, someone who didn't know what to look for might not notice, but it's a clock in a window tipped on its side here, the backside of a doll in a window there, a doorhandle with a bit of fabric hanging from it. All clues that if you know what to look for are right there telling you that the merchants are coming back another day.

Except for one.

Dim yellow light illuminates the foggy, six-pane window on the door to the apothecary. And just inside, Rafi stands, hovering near the door.

"Over here," Zerah says, nudging me into a narrow vestibule outside what appears to be a tattoo parlor. It's not quite wide enough for us both to fit flush, so we squeeze together, her shoulder behind mine. We take turns peeking around the corner, trying to get a glimpse of what is happening.

"Are you having sex?" Zerah asks, a strange tone to her voice.

Her candidness surprises me, and I stutter a muffled, "No."

"It's not all they make it out to be, you know," Zerah whispers, her voice losing its sharpness. I feel her relax ever so slightly behind me, and when she presses her palm to the small of my back, I feel more than just her touch. I feel her support, her trust, her apologies for whatever it is that I'm feeling about not having been intimate with my husband.

"I never thought it was," I say with a snort. "My headmistress told me about my wifely duties, and even gave me a six-point list for how to 'make it end faster.'"

Zerah snorts and shakes her head. Her forehead brushes against my shoulder as a chilly breeze flutters a newspaper up the road. I lean back into her warmth, and she presses her chin into my shoulder.

"Well, I hope for your sake that when you do cross that bridge, you either remember those points, or forget them entirely."

I frown, trying to work through what she's said, when she pulls me back against her. Her hands press into my belly, and a new kind of heat coils beneath her touch. Her face presses into my shoulder blade, her breath coming hot and fast against my coat.

"Look down," she whispers. I do, just as I hear them: footsteps. Heavy ones with a metallic echo. I can't place the sound, but it's as if my instincts know them. Something that makes me think back to living in the slums in Gola Town. She pulls me back tighter, her hands curling up around my ribs. I wrap my arms around hers and let her tug me back into the shadows. We sink down the wall, slowly, slowly, slowly, until we're sitting together, me nearly on top of her slight form.

Still, the footsteps come closer, louder, more aggressive. The *thump-clink* cadence echoes in a nefarious crescendo. I'm certain it's no friend. The way Zerah's arms begin to shake, I sense that she thinks the same thing.

I peek out from where we squat against the cold, damp cobblestones, and just out of the corner of my line of sight, I see boots. They're heavy boots, and they have spurs on them. I follow the line up, up, up, and am just about to take in the person's face when there's a noise behind us. He turns suddenly, and the crack of gunfire echoes off the narrow walls. The boots run away.

I hold my breath until the footsteps are gone completely, and Zerah gives me a tight squeeze.

"Are you okay?" she whispers, turning my shoulders so that I face her. Her hazel eyes are bright, her cheeks are pink, and she looks invigorated.

"I'm okay. Are you?" I ask, brushing hair out of her face and cupping her cheeks. Something flashes in her eyes, and her skin flushes, warm and soft, beneath my touch.

She curls her fingers around my wrists, but doesn't push me away. Nor do I let go. It feels so right, holding each other, keeping each other still and safe in this moment.

The click of a door sounds, followed by muffled footsteps. But neither of us moves. I've never had truly close friends before. Perhaps this is what it feels like to finally find that rare breed of true female companionship that Headmistress Moyle hinted at. But as Zerah blinks up at me, a question in her eyes that I somehow instinctively know the answer to, I know that this is something else — something more.

A low voice clears behind us. We part quickly, and I look up, directly into the gruff, mustachioed face of the local constable.

"I think you ladies had better come with me."

CHAPTER TWENTY-SEVEN

*W*hitey arrives first.

He's embarrassed and flustered, but Zerah seems almost ambivalent about the whole thing. We were arrested for squatting in an exclusion zone. I know little about the laws of Osterstan, but it's enough to know that I should be embarrassed. We both should be. Exclusion zones were established in areas that were known to be high in non-violent crime.

"The man thought you were a night-worker," Whitey hisses at his wife as the constable retrieves her coat for her. Zerah looks disappointed that he remembered the feather-fringed coat. Since both of us were clearly not Osterstani, were new to the city, and were obviously "lost," we weren't truly arrested, much less booked into the system. Our husbands were simply called to come pick us up. Like we were misbehaving children in need of a stern talking-to.

"He did not," Zerah says, her eyes flaring as they meet mine.

"He did so!" Whitey's white-blond hair flaps on top of his head with the anger boiling beneath his pale skin. He looks like a wine-poached fig covered in corn silk. "He told me so himself."

"William," Zerah says, nudging my knee with hers as she

accepts her coat from the constable. "Look at how we're dressed. Do you truly believe anyone would think that we were 'nightworkers?'"

His nostrils flare, and if not for Zerah's pure look of amusement, I would be afraid for her.

"Zerah, I think it's time —"

"Have you checked on Stephen today?" Her voice is innocent, her eyes wide and blinking. The way the color drains from his face as he sputters has me covering my own laughter with my hand.

"He's fine," he says.

"Did he eat? You know it's important that they eat after they've been —"

"We should go," Whitey says, helping Zerah into her coat a little faster, ". . . check on Stephen." I frown, wondering what she was going to say. She's obviously talking about one of his emus. An emu named Stephen. As if she knows what I'm thinking, she leans over and presses a kiss to my cheek in farewell.

"A particularly nasty bird. He once kickboxed my virile husband. It might have been considered a knockout had there been a judge."

I snort and try to pass it off as a cough.

I watch them leave, my questions lingering between us.

"Neve." Rafi's voice is stony, his posture stoic. He stands next to the entrance, his expression the same mask he wore when we first met. He already has my coat, and he doesn't move as he waits for me to come to him. He helps me into my coat, and then holds the door for me.

We walk quietly as dark clouds gather overhead, blocking the setting sun. Icy gusts off the water hit sharper. It feels like both a longer and a shorter walk home than I remember. When we finally reach the steps of the townhouse, I pause, staring up at it. The yellow lights from inside fill the windows beneath the shades, and it's as if the house itself glowers down at me.

"What were you doing down there?" I ask.

He flinches from two steps up. Then he turns and reaches for my hand.

"We will talk inside," he says, his voice firm and soft. "The streets have ears." He gives my hand a tug, but I resist.

"Not in there," I say. It's too much all of a sudden. As if, by following him indoors, into his house, it gives him the advantage. I need to be on equal ground. Right now, I'm not the one who has done wrong.

He descends the steps and stuffs his hands into his pockets. Lamplight reflects off his glasses, and he leans a little closer.

"We will have this conversation, but we will have it inside our home."

"It's *your* home."

"It's *our* home, and we will have this conversation inside if it means I have to hoist you over my shoulder and carry you in myself." I flinch, but he doesn't so much as blink. "Though, I should warn you, if the neighbors see that, they'll be shouting out the window with their thoughts on how I should exact your punishment." He steps closer, lowering his voice. "Tell me, my love, would you prefer I paddle you, stone you, or brand your flesh? All would be my right as your husband under the laws of the old ways."

A swell of hot anger boils to the surface of my skin, scorching me, and I can't hold it in.

"That's barbaric!"

"That's the Old City." He sounds defeated and exhausted, but I can tell from the set of his shoulders and his jaw that he'll do it just the same.

"Fine." I stomp up the steps ahead of him and don't pause when I get inside.

"Rafi?" Nima pushes in from the kitchen, and when I meet her gaze, she looks ferocious. I don't slow, going up the staircase, not even so much as pausing when I hear Benham calling after Rafi. I tear through the door to our room and slam it shut. It doesn't catch though, stopping instead against Rafi's extended palm. He shuts the door slowly as I remove my coat and throw it on the bed.

"You wanted to talk inside? We're inside. So now, what were you doing?" I can't hold still. I pace, trying to release some of my boiling anger before I explode.

"I could ask the same of you," he hisses. "What were you thinking? Do you know how dangerous it is to be in the underground market?"

"Then what were you doing there?"

"What makes you think I was there?"

"Don't treat me like an idiot. I saw you."

He flinches and sputters for a moment.

"That's my business," he finally says, half-answering my question.

"I thought it was *our* business," I snap. His nostrils flare. He removes his glasses, pinches the bridge of his nose, and then resets them on his face.

"You need to tell me what exactly it was you were doing in following me."

"You left so suddenly. I—" *I followed Zerah.* But I stop myself from saying it out loud. I don't want to wrap her up in it. Still, it's as if he can read my mind. Of course, he would have been told that I wasn't alone down there.

"Do you plan to follow me every time I get an urgent notice? Because that's part of my job: putting out bureaucratic fires."

"Tell me, *Husband*," I hiss the word, and he flinches. "What sort of bureaucratic fire was there in the apothecary today?"

His pupils flash, and he sputters again, letting out a breathy scoff. Suddenly, it all comes together. He stopped for flowers on his way. When I made reference to the fact that we haven't consummated the marriage, he talked around it, telling me it wasn't important. As if it wasn't something he wanted. The way he said he'd never really considered having children. I try to remember what the chemist looks like, and she might be about the same age as Rafi now that I think about it.

"Oh my gods," I say, walking over to the table and chairs.

"I can explain," he says, all but confirming exactly what I've figured out.

"How long has this been going on?"

"This?"

"I saw, Rafi. You brought flowers . . ."

"Oh," he says, sitting opposite me. He squeezes the back of his neck as he removes his glasses.

The funny thing is that I don't feel angry. I don't even feel hurt. I feel . . . sorry.

"How long?"

"Well . . . I suppose it's been four years now."

"*Four years*?" I blink at him.

"Yes," he says, leaning back, pressing his forehead into his palm. "It's been exactly four years."

"Exactly?" It's their anniversary. I followed my husband to watch him bring flowers to the chemist who has given me contraceptive tea . . . on their anniversary. She must have been laughing at me when she talked about how handsome my husband is. The feeling of foolishness only fuels the fire burning in my belly.

"In some ways, it feels so much longer. In other ways, it feels as if no time has passed." His mouth curves into a sad smile.

"Was it—your mother? She doesn't approve?"

He frowns for a moment, and then lets out a short, sardonic laugh.

"Oh no, she did not approve. But you know how she is. 'Family is everything,' and all. plus, her history and everything."

"Her history?"

"Yes," he says, looking somewhat startled. He cocks his head, and then lets out another deep breath. "I had hoped that in your spending more time together, that she might tell you more about herself. About her pregnancies."

I frown again. Why would he hope his mother would tell me about her pregnancies? I thought he'd never considered having children? This man is giving me whiplash.

"I was her only successful pregnancy. There were others. Many others."

"Oh, no." He nods slowly, and I take it all in. The way she is constantly feeding me as if I'm carrying a child, the way she tracks my cycles. Perhaps it's not just nosiness—perhaps it's something far deeper and darker?

"She had me when she was twenty-two, but her first child—a girl—died when she was two months old. She had three miscarriages between us, and then another after me. There was a stillbirth, and then another live birth—my brother, Haluk. He died before he reached two weeks.

"The doctors couldn't tell her why she had so much trouble with childbirth. But then, she had a pregnancy of the Fallopian tube. It ruptured, and she almost died. This was when I was four years old, so I only remember seeing the bloody bedsheets carted out of her room. That was her last pregnancy."

"That's awful," I say, shaking my head. This godly woman, whose faith teaches her that the devout are those who bear as many children as they can.

"I thought perhaps that she would tell you herself. As a way to connect, or . . . I don't know. I thought she'd be pleased on that count."

"On what count?"

"That you might someday bear my children."

I frown. "But I thought you said you'd never considered having children."

"I haven't."

"But—but then, why would you want her to think about me

having your children? Why would that be a positive if you've never wanted them?"

"It's not that I never want them," he says, making a funny face.

"Is it the chemist? She can't have them?" I tilt my head, trying to be as sympathetic as I can. But then something hits him, and he wipes his hand down his face. The room is so quiet, and he leans back, looking out the window.

"The flowers weren't for the chemist."

"Oh?" I frown, not seeing where he's going.

"They were for the cemetery."

My heart sinks. He'd mentioned a past relationship before, but I hadn't realized.

"Dead?" I ask.

He nods, and I reach for his hand, squeezing it.

"What was her name?" I ask.

He lets out a sigh and a little laugh.

"Peter."

CHAPTER TWENTY-EIGHT

"*P*eter."

I repeat the name like it will somehow explain everything. And even before he can say anything more, I realize that it does make sense.

"Peter," I repeat. He nods.

Why his mother might not approve.

Why he hadn't pictured himself having children.

Perhaps even why his father has never warmed to me.

"Your father doesn't believe we're really together, does he?" He lowers his chin.

"I don't think so." The defeat in his shoulders makes it clear that whatever it was he was looking for from me, whatever discreet test he levied, I've failed.

He told me the name of his dead lover, and I made it about me.

"I'm sorry, Rafi. I didn't—"

"It's okay," he says as he sits back, sliding his glasses back on his nose. He's closing himself off. I've never seen him so shuttered.

"I didn't mean that—let me try again?"

He presses his lips together, and then shrugs.

"Peter."

"Peter."

"He's your ex?"

"He's my ex."

"You were together for four years?"

He frowns, and then something seems to occur to him, and he shakes his head.

"No, we were together when we were conscripted. It's actually —relationships in the military are more common than the older generation would have you believe."

"You were in the military?"

"I was."

"How long did you serve?"

"Three years." He frowns, and then thinks better of it. "I forget there is so much you do not know about Osterstan. It is required. All Osterstani men—and recently, women—must serve for three years. It's long enough for most, but some remain."

"Did Peter stay?"

"He did."

"And you didn't approve?"

"What?" He shakes his head. "No, I supported him. Always. But it is a dangerous life."

"He was sent somewhere dangerous?"

He frowns again.

"How much do you know about the invasion of the Osterstani corridor?"

"Invasion?" I frown, shaking my head. "I thought the Osterstani corridor was a free trade zone? Mutually regulated by a multinational treaty?"

He stares at me for a long, quiet moment—and then he snorts. For the first time, I see something in his expression that makes me curl in on myself. It's not anger, or hatred, or even annoyance. It's pity.

"About ten years ago, on All Saints Day—our holiest day, and a national holiday—Nordanian forces backed by Sudersbergian troops attacked the southern border of what is now the corridor. Meanwhile, unbeknownst to the innocent civilians in that part of the country, Swendish mercenaries had planted a string of bombs along the northernmost border.

"It was a planned assault, and the troops met less than two days later in the town of Ourocéu. The town councilor had no choice but to surrender in order to spare the twenty-five thousand innocents who lived within its borders. He negotiated a ceasefire, and a peace treaty that allowed other nations to use the railroad lines that spanned that stretch of Osterstan."

"They wanted to use the rail?"

"Yes. That was the problem in the first place."

"What were they shipping to Swendenland?"

"Drugs. Women. All sorts of illegal things, and in using our rail lines, we became complicit in the evil trade. You'd be shocked by the means people will take to ship illegal items. My father once told me of a train car full of chickens that arrived dead. Someone had hidden balloons full of unrefined poppyseed pods inside them, and the balloons ruptured."

"I don't understand. Why would they openly attack for illegal pursuits? Those things are illegal in Nordania, too."

"Are they? Are you sure?" He arches an eyebrow. "Would your institute girls say the same thing?"

I straighten my spine at the accusation. But I fumble for the words to counter it.

"Those aren't the same."

"Aren't they?"

"The girls from the institute accept public appointments. Or marry public figures. All of it is very public. They're not being shipped across international borders like chattel."

"It is a slippery slope." He presses his thumb and forefinger against his forehead and leans his elbow on the arm of his chair.

"A very slippery slope from using marriage contracts in lieu of trade concessions. Shipping women from workhouses to become Swendish house-women."

"Swendish house-women?" I say, frowning. But one look at his face tells me everything I need to know. And it's not a job I would ever want to have. With a chill, I recall Conrad mentioning workhouses being the natural progression for an Unchosen like me. They would take the girls that no one else wanted. But they must run out of space eventually. Or perhaps they just take a good deal when they see one.

"What does this have to do with Peter? This was ten years ago?" I ask, trying to shake the fear out of me.

"The invasion happened ten years ago, but it's been unstable ever since. Between the Nordanians sending weapons across the border and old believers fighting against what they see as 'evil progress,' or damnation, or whatever they see it as"—he shakes his head again—"it's an area that requires strict border control."

"Peter went to patrol the border."

"He did."

"And he never came back?"

He swallows around something thick as he shakes his head. "He did not."

"How long ago?" I ask, though I already know the answer.

"Four years."

"Four years today," I say. He nods. We're both quiet for a moment. I have questions about Peter, about what happened to him. But more than anything, I have questions about Rafi. About how he's dealt with this. About what this means for his future. For our future.

Our future. The thought hits me like broken glass, and I feel my cheeks pale. All I have to do is get through one year, and then I can leave. Not connect, not grow closer to him, not make our marriage stronger. And yet, even with everything that has happened, there is something here between us. Something that seems to be strengthening before my very eyes.

"Can I ask . . . ?" I stop, though, because I don't want to push him. He's only just admitted something very personal and private.

"You can ask me anything." As if the sun himself can hear Rafi's sincerity, the clouds break apart. His skin glows in the faint orange sunset.

"Was he—I mean, are you . . . have you ever . . . ?" I don't know how to ask the question, and I realize that I'm blowing this. Failing miserably. He opens his mouth to cut me off, but I raise my palm, shaking my head. He's given me so much. Maybe it's my time to give him something in return. Even if it's not much.

"I don't have experience with love," I say. I find it hard to meet his eyes, but he doesn't say anything as I stare at the table between us, so I continue. "My mother . . ." I take a deep breath, having never spoken to anyone about her. Conrad knew some details, just enough that he would occasionally hold them over my head to remind me he was in charge. But I never even confessed any of this to Arden, or even Carla.

"You don't have to say—"

"My mother was a whore," I say. The words tumble out, as if all it took was to remove the cork. "I mean, I don't think she always was. No, I know she wasn't. But I grew up in an Espancian slum—Gola Town—" He nods at this, understanding just what level of poverty I'm talking about. "I learned at far too young an age how to ice a swollen jaw, how to lie to the policemen so they wouldn't take me away from her."

He stares at me, and this time, I lift my eyes.

"I saw my father for the first time when I was nine. My mother put me in a dress nicer than any I'd ever seen. She dressed nicely, as well—a borrowed dress, I think? She even let me wear some of her lipstick. 'This is your armor, Neve,' she said." I touch my plum-color-stained lips as I fight the smile that forms.

"Then we went to a street festival. It was in celebration of the daughter of the mayor's wedding. It was a lovely celebration, and I remember shaking hands with the mayor's assistant. My mother said he was an important man, the one who called the shots behind the scenes. But he held my hand a little too long, stared a little too long, complimented my dress with a little too much enthusiasm.

"He was my father. My mother later told me that she wanted me to meet him just once, so I could see where I got my eyes. Such a strange way of putting it. But then she told me about his wife, and his children, and the life he led that had nothing to do with ours. 'You cannot expect a man to do what he says,' she told me. 'You must separate your heart from your will to survive.'"

I let out a long, shaky breath just as Rafi's hand curls over mine. He doesn't hold on to it, doesn't keep it in place. It's just his hand, layered over mine, warm and supportive.

"The point is, I realized at a young age that if I wanted to survive—no, not survive. My mother survived, and I wanted more than that." I shake my head, ridding it of the haunting questions that linger when I think about how long my mother survived—if she still survives.

"I've never been able to afford the luxury of romantic connections. So I've never considered it. People were people. They still are. I can appreciate when someone is beautiful, just like anyone else, but I don't know that I've ever been able to see someone as more than exactly who they are: a unique person who I either connect with, or I don't.

"I don't know where that leaves me. I can't honestly say that I'm attracted to men, or to women, or to neither . . ." For some reason, the thought that flickers through my brain is the memory of Zerah's face pressed against my shoulder blade, her breaths coming fast and hot against my coat, heating me from the outside in. My cheeks heat, and I shake it off.

"All I mean to say—rather ineloquently—is that I accept you

for who you are, simply because you are you. You've never been anyone different to me."

The smile that spreads across Rafi's lips is slow and lethal, utterly decimating the pallor that previously lived on his skin.

"Neve," he says, shifting out of his chair and kneeling on the floor next to me. "Your words are perfect."

"Yeah?"

"Yeah," he says, and the simple, informal word sounds funny on his tongue. He gathers my hands in his and presses kisses to my knuckles. They're soft and warm, and I smile.

"I feel the same. I like you, just as you are."

His gaze is searching, affirming something that makes my heart race. Something my brain is slow to connect to.

"And, like you, I only see a person. And the person I see before me right now?" He hesitates and cups my cheek. I freeze under his intimate touch, but it's not uncomfortable. "I don't know what these feelings are between us, but they startle me. I don't know how to navigate this. But I think it's possible that there could be a very sincere friendship between us. Or maybe even something deeper."

A flash of guilt creeps in.

"Even though I . . . haven't been the most trustworthy?"

He lets out a dark sigh.

"Yes," he finally says. "Even though you haven't been the most trustworthy. And even though I haven't been the best protector— I should have seen the signs. I shouldn't have expected you to make the choice I wanted, when you never had the free choice in the first place."

"Thank you," I say, softly.

"For what?"

"For all of this. For your understanding, your empathy . . . for your forgiveness?"

"Ah. Well, then thank you."

"For what?"

"For your trust, your openness, your . . . your compassion."

"Of course," I say, feeling a strange swell of hope.

He cups my cheeks and leans in. His lips brush against mine once, twice, and then, on the third time, I wrap my arms around his neck and hold him close. His lips are pillowy and warm, his tongue hot against my lips. His fingers thread into my hair, tilting me the way he wants.

He breaks the kiss and lowers his head, pressing his forehead into my sternum. I feel breathless, and my lips tingle, still buzzing off his heady kiss. I know I still have questions. So many questions. But maybe I don't need all the answers right now. Maybe I can just hold him on this bad day, and let him hold me in return. Maybe we can figure out what this is between us one day at a time.

CHAPTER TWENTY-NINE

"*What* do you think of this color, sweets?" Nima is back to thinking I'm pregnant, and judging by the pink skein of yarn she's crocheting with, she thinks this time it's a girl.

"Maman, leave my bride alone," Rafi teases her with a little wink. Then he kisses my cheek as he clears his plate from the breakfast table. Nima pretends to suppress a knowing smile as Benham stares at us with something like wonder.

It's been like this for the past two weeks, ever since Rafi and I had our talk. I still haven't asked the deep, digging questions I'm craving the answers to. Like whether he's only ever been with men, if he thinks what we have feels like a certain four-letter word, or if he's involved in the spate of violence across the city.

There have been two more incidents. Both minor, and thankfully, with no casualties. But the city has been tense, as if holding its collective breath, waiting for the other foot to drop. The first involved a man who attempted to enter a shelter for women and their children with a weapon. The newspapers didn't report what kind of weapon, but Rafi slipped and said it was Nordanian-sourced.

The second was the attempted kidnapping of a woman married to a local solicitor. Bystanders reported that the man spoke 'like a Nordanian.' Suffice it to say, I've allowed my Espancian accent to slip out a bit more than usual in public. Not that it seems to make a difference. Everyone knows that Rafi took a Nordanian wife. So, no matter that I look Espancian and sound Espancian, I'm still a Nordanian.

Still, we've attended a spate of events over the past two weeks. Despite them all being with different patronages, Rafi has gifted me a different gown for each occasion. He has a wonderful eye for colors that suit me, though I think my favorite is the one I wore to the war orphans benefit dinner last night. It was garnet red and bunched between my breasts before it fell to the floor. Red and black garnets dotted the fabric, increasing in density as they approached my feet, and when I moved, it looked as though I was dripping jewels.

I've never felt so admired—or so photographed—as I did last night. And when we returned home, Rafi and I kissed until we fell asleep. Anyone would think it was romantic. Even though there's still a fragile distance between us, padded by his secrets, it feels more and more possible that this marriage could actually work.

Not that everyone is happy to see us happy. When Rafi extracted himself to visit with a benefactor, pressing a kiss to my neck on his way, Whitey passed me a message for Conrad and hissed a warning that perhaps I should include in this message a postscript about how wide I've been spreading my legs. It was a disgusting, sobering reminder that there's more at stake here than just a little romance. I showed Rafi the message, of course. He nodded somberly, and then kissed my temple.

Over the past two weeks, the messages have been getting stranger and more cryptic, and I've noticed Rafi's name in them with increasing frequency.

Conrad wrote about ten days back, asking me to tell him how often Rafi went somewhere that wasn't the office. For a long moment, I considered ignoring him. And I would have. Except there was a postscript included about Carla. It said he was considering whether she would make a good wife, or a better worker. Now that I know what happens to the pretty girls in the workhouses, there's no way I would let that happen. I showed it to Rafi, and he said he would take care of it. I haven't asked for details, but he's been more tender with me since. As if my sharing Conrad's business has proven something.

I stretch my mouth wide as a yawn overtakes me.

"So tired already, pet?" Nima says with another knowing look. "I shouldn't be surprised after the creaking I heard last night."

I sit straighter.

"Creaking?" I ask, eyes wide and feeling nervous.

Rafi laughs from behind me, leaning down to wrap his arms around me and press another kiss to my cheek. "Maman, you tease too much. I had to use the restroom, and you know how creaky that door is."

"Don't patronize me, Rafi. I know the sounds of lovely music when I hear it. After all, it is a wife's duty to soothe her husband when he's up late working." Rafi frowns at this. But she continues. "Oh, I heard that blasted machine in the office again last night."

"I don't know what you're talking about, Maman," Rafi says with a tight smile. I shift, uncomfortable—I thought he fell asleep when I did. But it's Benham who launches to his feet, flustered. We all stare at him, quietly, as he seems to realize he has an audience.

"This is hardly breakfast table conversation," he mutters.

"It's hardly family conversation," Rafi says, wagging a playful finger at his mother.

"You forget how ravenous your appetite was when you were his age," Nima says to Benham. Rafi straightens, and an uncomfortable flush spreads to his bronzed cheeks.

"I don't need to hear this."

"Oh, don't be so scandalized." Nima smiles and blushes, and I see the pretty girl within who Benham must've first fallen head over heels for. "You know how many times I was pregnant."

It's the first time she's mentioned it in front of me. I don't want to ruin the moment, so I stay quiet.

"He saw me at the All Saints street fair. I was with my friends and far too young for him—and he'd already promised himself to another girl. Someone his family approved of who was much more age appropriate."

"You make me sound like a lothario," Benham says, a soft smile playing with the corner of his mouth. His rich brown eyes glint in the morning light.

"You were. You got what you wanted the same night we met!"

"Maman!" Rafi says, laughing through his mock scandalized expression. "Are you telling me you were a first-night affair?"

"Hardly," Nima says. "Does a first-night affair last thirty years? And besides, I knew he was my person, even if we skipped a step or two to get there."

"Thirty-two," Benham says, approaching his wife where she sits on the settee. He curls his fingers around the back of her neck.

"All I'm saying is that I think it is possible you inherited your father's unbridled passion."

"Okay," Rafi says, recoiling. I can't stifle my laughter, especially since I've seen exactly zero of his unbridled passion. "I believe that is my cue to leave."

"Oh, don't be so scandalized," Nima says again as Benham laughs, burying his nose in the crook of Nima's neck. She giggles —actually *giggles*—and I can see it. I can see how they have been able to survive all the grief over the years.

"Where are you off to?" I ask as Rafi gathers a jacket.

"Oh," he says, his eyes shifting, and then landing on a hat. He places the cap on his head, lowering it over his eyes to keep the impending rain from wetting his glasses. He leans and presses a kiss to my cheek, letting it linger. His breath is warm against my skin and, if I'm not mistaken, a little rushed.

"Are you okay? Did the discussion of your parents' lovemaking upset you that much?" I grin as he scrunches his face in distaste.

"No, I just have an appointment."

"On a Sunday morning?"

When he doesn't explain himself, I frown. He curls his fingers around the back of my neck and tilts my chin up to look at him. His brown eyes flicker with heat I'm not sure I've ever seen, and without another word, he presses a kiss to my mouth. There's an unfamiliar intensity to it, and I hold on to him as his free hand strokes up and down my spine. When he breaks the kiss, we're both a bit breathless.

"Hold that thought," he says with a nervous smile.

"Okay?"

He presses another kiss to my lips, then my nose, my forehead.

"Tell me where you're going?" I whisper, afraid to break whatever silent gift he just gave me. He squeezes my waist and leans in, his breath tickling the shell of my ear.

"It's a surprise. One I think—I hope—you'll like."

With that, he's gone. I don't know what just happened, but it's almost enough to distract me from the fact that once again, he left the house without me, and not for the office.

I help Nima clean up from breakfast, and then dress for the day. I'm not sure how long Rafi will be gone, but every time I think about his return, my stomach fills with a heady warmth that has me feeling almost nauseous. When he hasn't returned for lunch, I start to wonder, but then I hear the door shut.

I rush down the steps to find Benham there, holding a letter.

"It is for you, pet," he says. I freeze. He's never called me that before. Actually, I'm not sure he's ever even addressed me directly. He passes me the envelope, and I nod my thanks, still surprised. I move into the light next to the front window that looks out on the wet street. Autumn has moved in with a vengeance, bringing rain and wind and turning the jacaranda leaves golden-yellow.

The letter is from Conrad, but it's brief, and strange. I read it twice, and my blood runs cold.

Dear Neve,

I pray this letter finds you well. Arden has left us. She is no longer your sister. The weight of our family honor rests on your shoulders.

The seeds I planted this spring have thrived, although the flowers on your favorite tree — the one you admired from your bedroom window — have grown black. I suspect the soil under the ground has run red.

Perhaps your dear husband could advise? I hear he has a fondness for the cold. Perhaps he could recommend a compound or additive?

Your benefactor,

Conrad

I don't know what to think. He's clearly writing in code, but what is he trying to say? What did Arden do? She already left when she went to the institute. Did she get kicked out?

I call for Benham.

"Yes, pet?"

"Do you have any news from Nordania?" He frowns, his eyes narrowed, looking so much like Rafi that I almost flinch. "About the institute?"

"Oh, yes. I forget you do not read."

I do flinch then, tempering the smolder of anger that craves a spark in Rafi's absence.

"Did something happen?"

"Yes," he says, crossing the living room to pick up his newspaper. He flicks through it, but doesn't seem to find what he's looking for. "One of the girls—the one who people suspect is going to become the son's new wife—" He stops on a page, scanning the text. My heart races in my chest, waiting for more details. What if something happened to her? But wait—could it be possible? Was Arden really the one who was in the lead? There's no way . . . is there?

"Yes?" I try to nudge him.

"Here it is," he says, passing the paper to me and pointing to a small, buried clipping. "She's divorced her benefactor."

"What?" I frown, but he pokes the paper I'm holding taut. I read the article.

News out of Nordania's Women's Institute that Arden Thatcher, after an undisclosed incident, requested to be released of her beneficiary contract with her benefactor, Conrad Laarsworth. After a closed hearing, her request was approved, and she will continue as an independent candidate. Rumors abound that she is considered the front-runner. Time will tell if that changes with her new status.

"She's an independent candidate?" I ask, frowning at the minuscule bit of news. It's an archaic term, one that I learned about, but more as a theory. I don't think in the history of the institute that there's ever been an independent candidate.

"Such a ghastly system," Benham grumbles.

"What is?"

"That sham of a school. Nothing more than a front for human trafficking."

I stare at him in shock.

"It's a school," I say, and he stares at me, plain faced. "I mean, I know what it looks like. But it gives girls opportunities they might not otherwise have."

"So does regular compulsory school. But you don't see the Nordanian government mandating that."

His words hit me like a bolt of lightning.

The floor shakes beneath my feet. Literally.

I stare at Benham, and the only reason I know I'm not

imagining it is because his eyes go round with horror. For a moment, I think I'm still reeling from his words, but then he grabs onto my shoulders and pulls me down to the couch as a horrible, loud noise shatters the air around us, shaking the walls, rattling the hanging lights, and sending frames slipping from their nails.

"What was that?" I ask, as the noise ebbs. Benham looks around, his eyes frantic.

"Nima!" he calls, launching off the settee where I'm still on my side, shaking.

"In the kitchen. I'm fine, Benham!" Nima calls, but that doesn't stop Benham from racing to her.

I pull myself off the settee and move to the window. It's still intact, but when I look outside, I see that not everyone else has been so lucky. Neighbors pour into the street, looking left and right, and then settle on left. The air is already filling with smoke and fine dust as alarms ring throughout the city with an eerie dissonance. I see people pointing, and before I can think twice, I'm moving toward the door and through it. The noise outside is so strange. It's almost muffled. People stare to the left, but I can't see around the large tree at the base of the stairs. I nearly slip down them as I make my way into the street, and when I get there, I turn to the left.

And stare in horror at a large, mushroom-shaped cloud rising into the sky in the direction of the market.

CHAPTER THIRTY

*T*he neighbors fill the street, shoulder to shoulder. They weave between one another, blending into a potent cocktail of panic and shock. Some stand shellshocked. Others pray. Still others rush from one home to the next, shouting out the names of objects that should mean something to me, but in the mishmash of old Osterstani mixed with the common tongue, their words lose all meaning.

I don't know how long I stand there before Nima jostles me.

"Get back inside, pet. It is not safe out here."

Someone bumps into her, and she nudges into me, clinging to me and keeping me upright.

"Bandages, Nima? Can you spare bandages?" A neighbor who once spit in my direction interrupts us.

"Benham brought everything we have to the Costrapanis." Nima frowns, and then looks back at me. "Unless . . . I don't have time to be polite. Do you have supplies for your cycle?"

"We'll take anything. Nikita says he believes it to be a compound injury."

"Take it," I say, turning my eyes back to the plume of black smoke that seems to have no end in sight. It's coming from the direction of the market, but something sticks in my head. *Compound*.

"What kind of injury?" I ask as Nima rushes back toward the house. "Would a salve work? Or a compound—"

Compound.

Conrad's letter asked whether Rafi *could recommend a compound or additive*. It was written to sound as if Conrad was writing about soil. But he wasn't, was he? Why would he write to me about soil?

Soil.

Earth.

Underground. It was a warning.

I take off, weaving and pushing through the crowded street as fast as the huddled bodies will allow. I have to get to that market. Because, if there's any chance Rafi was there—he turned left this morning. There's a chance. There's more than a chance. Where else would he go? He went to get a surprise for me. Or so he said . . .

The air is full of dust and strange debris—paper, fuzzy bits of insulation, string. Traffic is stopped on the avenue, and I run along the pedestrian walkway, shoving past people who run in the opposite direction. Hurrying to safety. Time seems to slow down. My legs slog along, my forward progress slowed by other bodies, no matter the effort I put forth. My feet splash in water that spills unrestricted from a broken pipe in the sidewalk. The air is filled with the cries of chaos, the wails of pain, and the high-pitched sirens of emergency transports stuck in traffic—true harbingers of bad news.

My shoes weren't meant for running, and when I do get a chance to push through and run, my soles are slick and slip across the wet pavers. A rumble begins from ahead, like thunder rolling across the sky, except it never reaches my ears. The vibrations hit my feet. They rattle my teeth, but there's no boom. It's not an explosion. Something has collapsed.

I approach the market, separated by only one last avenue, when a hand clamps over mine.

"Neve?" It's Irina. She is covered in dust and dirt, the only recognizable part of her her sharp eyes.

"Irina! Are you okay?" I look her over, and she nods quickly as she clutches onto my shoulders, edging me away from the street. "What are you doing here? I thought you left."

She shakes her head, her dark eyes wide and panicked.

"Rafi. He helped me out of a collapsed stand." Her voice trembles. Even the unshakeable Irina is severely rattled.

"You saw him? He's okay?"

"Yes, he was fine — but — "

"Where is he?" I demand, squeezing my hands into fists.

"I don't know. He ran back in to help others."

I don't even wait for her to say more. I dart across the street, running in front of a cab that stops only just in time.

"Girl, get out of the road!" There's a whistle behind the shout, but I don't stop. I keep moving through traffic until I reach the other side.

The smoke pools between the pavers and the glass roof, the smell of wood and fibers and oddly, bacon, woven throughout. I press my sleeve against my nose and mouth and proceed carefully. The first block of the market is mostly empty of people, except for the few remaining who still make their way out. I'm the only one going in. Carts are knocked sideways, windows are uniformly shattered, and merchandise is splattered across the pavers like spilled popcorn kernels.

When I reach the next traffic break, there's nothing to wait for. But the next block looks far worse for the wear. Carts aren't just knocked over, they're broken into chunks like crude puzzle pieces. The ground is wet here, and I wonder if someone found water to put out a fire. Judging from the blackened ends of a splintered stand, I don't think it's a bad guess.

The further I push ahead, the denser the smoke, the heavier the floating detritus.

"Help." A scratchy voice comes from my left. I turn and stare into the darkness, trying to see where the voice could have come from. It takes me a long moment to see the elderly man whose leg is crushed under a heavy cart.

"I'm coming," I say, stepping as carefully as possible over the rubble of a once bustling market. When I finally reach the man, I see that it's not just his leg. The top of the cart has broken across his forehead and blood streams from his hairline into his eyes.

"Can you see me, sir?" I ask, squatting down next to him.

"I can see you just fine. Help me with this cart, will you?"

I don't waste any time. I give the bulky wooden cart a push, and he moans at the relief, but then the cart slips and falls back down on his leg. He wails in pain.

"I'm so sorry—"

"Don't apologize. Try pulling from the other side."

I do as he says, and I'm able to get a bit more grip on it, but it's still too heavy for just one person.

"Anyone down there?" A full voice calls from my left.

"Yes!" I yell back. I wait for a moment, until finally a tall, blonde-haired man wearing a porkpie hat and colorful scarf emerges from the smoke. He's strangely pretty to look at, even if he is covered in smudge and smoke.

"I can't get a good grip on this cart," I say.

"You push, I'll pull," he says, waiting for me to shift sides. "Give us just a moment, old man, and then you'll be out from under there and good as new."

"Who's calling who old?" The man hisses, and all three of us chuckle. Another low rumble comes from seemingly beneath our feet, and the laughter dies.

"Are you ready?" the blonde man asks. I catch his gaze and realize he's not as old as I first thought. My age, or a year older, but that's all. He tilts his head.

"I'm ready."

"Now."

I push the cart, leaning into the corner I can get with my shoulder, giving it the best shove I can. He pulls on it, and the cart shifts, leaning the direction we want it to go.

"Don't let up," he grunts. I lean into it even more, but my shoe slips, and I slide down the cart, knocking my ear into the edge. The pain cuts into my lobe and the hard bone behind it.

"Don't stop!"

"Trying," I moan.

"Can you move, man?" the blonde man asks.

"I don't think so," he says. I look down and see him try to slide, but then he hisses and seems to curl in on himself. "No, I can't."

"Okay, then it's gonna have to be me and you, girlie," the blonde man says. "Just a few more inches, and I can get it on my own."

"Okay," I mumble, fortifying myself with a deep breath. Then I push. I push with my shoulder and try to imagine pushing through my legs all the way to the ground beneath my feet. The thing shifts just enough that the man seems to be able to get momentum on his side. It starts to move in earnest.

"We got it, girlie," he says, pulling on it, and then knocking it over, away from the man. I fall to my hands and knees and immediately move to the older man on the ground. His leg looks bad. Smashed and tilted at the wrong angle.

"The name's Neve. *Not* girlie."

"Elm," he says with an amused grin. There's another low rumble, and his smile fades. "You need to get out of here."

"I need to find my husband."

Elm's blue eyes narrow, but he doesn't say anything else. Instead, he mumbles something to the old man, and then scoops him up in his arms as if he weighs nothing.

"I won't convince you then. Be safe."

"Thank you," I say. I watch him walk away while the man looks over Elm's shoulder as he's carried to safety. As they're swallowed by the smoke, I keep moving.

It's a ghost town, though. There's no one here, nothing to search for. And yet, there's a piece of me, buried deep within, that knows that if I walk out of here alone, I won't find Rafi out there. That Rafi is still in here somewhere. I pick my way through toppled carts and broken glass and smoldering stacks of who-knows-what, until I reach the next traffic passthrough. The smoke clears, and I stop, right where I am.

My heart stops.

The next block is completely destroyed. The buildings are rubble, and the carts and pedestrian street are completely covered in bricks and broken glass and splintered, smoldering wood. My heart in my throat, I turn around the corner to the stairway down to the underground market. It's roped off. The police have been here, and they've left it shut off. A hanging sign says that it's unsafe, inaccessible.

I stand there for a long moment, reading the sign over and over again, trying to understand. And then I duck under the rope.

"Oi!" a loud, barking voice calls. "Oi! You can't go down there!"

But I don't stop. I start down the steps, but I only make it three steps down when something gives out and the staircase groans, collapsing beneath my feet. Something hard clamps around my wrist, and my arm jerks as the floor literally falls out from beneath my feet.

The police officer pulls me up and through the door, setting me on my knees. He steps back and looks down at me like I'm a skittish fox.

"Didn't you hear me, girl? This area's been cleared! Gas leak."

"Gas leak?" I don't know who says it, but the way he looks at me, it's clearly come from my own mouth. "That was a gas leak?"

"No," he says, then looks left and right. He tugs me up to my feet and starts to walk me further from the market. I turn around, but his grip is firm. He keeps walking with me. "There's no mistaking it was a bomb. Nordanian likely." Then he frowns and stares at me. "Where did you say you were from?"

I realize I may have just walked into being a suspect, and nod —something I used to see my mother do whenever someone accused her.

"I am Espancian, sir." I don't even try to disguise my accent this time. He squints and tilts his head, not letting go of me, as if reserving his judgment.

"What are you doing here?"

"My husband is Osterstani, sir."

"Let's get you to safety. Perhaps we can find some information about your husband."

I know better than to fight him. And there's no way for me to get down to the underground market, anyway. I know without a doubt that Rafi was here—Irina literally saw him run back in. And the only place I can think that he would have gone, if he hasn't left for safety, is the apothecary.

The chemist is almost certainly dead. An entire city block collapsed. Right over top of the underground market. But I can't think about that. Because Rafi wouldn't just leave her. Even if he knew she died in the blast, he would be down there, trying to retrieve her body and give her a proper burial. Like they did for her brother.

"Neve!" Zerah is in front of me, rushing me, coiling her arms around my neck. I don't know how it is that she's here. How long I've been here . . . if I'm dreaming . . .

But as soon as I realize it's really her, that my face is buried into her neck, I'm sobbing uncontrollably. I don't know what has happened to Rafi, or to anyone else in this market. But the way my heart twists and aches, it's as if it already knows.

"You're okay," Zerah whispers into my hair, rubbing her

hands up and down my back. I clutch her, clinging on to her as if she might drift away. I'm vaguely aware of men talking around us as she continues to shush me and whisper that I'm okay, stroking my hair and my back.

But then she stills. And I know what has happened. I know. I know . . .

"Neve." Whitey's voice is right next to us. It's serious. He's sorry.

I break away from Zerah and look at him, at where he's standing with the same police officer who found me, and another in a formal-looking uniform.

"Neve, the officers have just told me — I'm so sorry, my dear. The officers need to ask you some questions."

"Questions?" I blink into the streetlamp. When did it get so dark? And so bright? Zerah squeezes me again, but says nothing. Whitey lets out a deep breath.

"They found Rafael. They found his body."

CHAPTER THIRTY-ONE

"*W*here? Show me."

Whitey and the officers exchange glances.

"Neve, did you hear me? They found his body. You don't want to see this." Whitey wipes a hand down his face. He looks pale. Paler than usual. "It's not a pretty crime that happened today. They're keeping it quiet for now, until the family can be notified. They sent someone to tell the family, but—"

"I'm his family."

"Yes . . ."

"I want to see him. It might not be him."

"Neve . . ."

"Miss?" the senior officer interrupts. "I understand you've had a shock, but if I may—I don't recommend that you see him right now. Not until they can clean the body."

"Rafi." The clarity with which I say his name is like a hot knife through a custard apple. Everything around me burns so hot, but my clarity, my thoughts, are crystal clear.

"Excuse me?"

"He has a name," I hiss, my bottom lip not cooperating. "His name is Rafi—Rafael. Family name Rostami."

"Yes, miss."

"I'm his wife. I'm not a *miss*."

Zerah squeezes my shoulders and tugs me closer as the men exchange an uncomfortable glance.

"Neve, this is a delicate situation," Whitey says. "I think it best if you go with the officer. They have a few questions is all. I will be present, if you like."

"As will I," Zerah says, her voice resolute.

"Actually, we need to speak with her alone," the officer who helped me says.

"We'll stay with her," Zerah insists.

"She's not under arrest, is she?" Whitey asks.

"No," the senior officer says, "but she's also not Osterstani."

"She is married to an Osterstani cabinet member."

"I'm sorry, sir," the senior officer says, stepping closer. "But she *was* married to an Osterstani cabinet member."

It hits like a wall of brick. Whatever clarity I had dissolves, melting into a puddle of bubbling, sticky fury. And fear.

"Please, let me see him. Give me that at least."

"I'm sorry," the officer says, and he does look truly sorry, "but his family has expressed the wish that nobody see the body."

"I *am* his family," I yell in his face. I'm somewhat aware of a calming presence pressing into my shoulders. But the fury and panic take over.

"We just need to ask you a few questions," the officer says, lowering his voice. "And then perhaps we can make an exception."

Whitey steps in as Zerah shushes in my ear. Her grip on my shoulders makes me realize that I'm shaking, sweating, ready to explode.

"It's going to be okay, love," Zerah says, pressing a kiss to the side of my head. I look at her, realizing what she's said, what she's called me.

"*Love*," I whisper. She cups my cheek and nods, her eyes glassy and aching. She doesn't realize she's used Rafi's nickname for me. And the kindness and care in her expression combined with this is enough to make me crumple. Zerah slips to the ground with me, holding me in one piece as we huddle on the ground. Again.

A sob, raw and aching, echoes off the brick buildings. As my knees hit the ground, I realize that it's mine.

Whitey awkwardly squats next to me.

"They're willing to let you go home and return in the morning. But they're worried you're a flight risk."

"Where would I go?" I ask.

"You can come to our home," Zerah says.

"She can't—"

"She *can*." Zerah's voice is loud and brash, and I would hate to be on the receiving end of it.

"We are not Osterstani. We are here on an Espancian diplomatic visa and cannot harbor guests. Especially not Nordanian ones, much less ones who no longer have ties to Osterstan—I know." He raises his palms. "It's just the facts. We will deal with all of this in the morning." He turns to me. "Let us take you home, and in the morning, we will help you sort everything out."

"You won't have to do anything you don't want to," Zerah says, her voice a low whisper.

"And you shouldn't make promises you can't keep, *dear*," Whitey practically hisses. The chill from sitting on the cold, wet pavement finally settles into my bones, and I shiver. I can't keep sitting here like this. So, I stand, and wait for someone to tell me where to go. A cab arrives, and we pass through the slick, shiny streets on our way back to the Old City. We're back to the townhouse faster than I expect, and Zerah hugs me at the car. Whitey escorts me to the door, which seems a bit much, but when he stops in front of the door, I realize he has a purpose.

"That was a lovely performance back there. I suppose I should congratulate you for reaching your end goal."

Hollow rage rattles within me, and I glare at him. How could he say something so cruel? So crude? He honestly thinks I might really be glad to have become a single woman. But I'm not just a single woman — I'm a widow.

"Of course, you haven't really fulfilled the other end of the bargain, now have you?" His lilting accent is gone, replaced by plain, unadulterated disdain. "Of course, things take time here in such uncivilized parts of the world. Everyone moves more slowly. Banks are a nightmare . . ." His ugly nostrils flare, and he shakes it off, as if thinking better. "I would suggest you refrain from sending your message tonight. Continue to play up your grief . . . or whatever this is."

I glare at him. His expression is cunning and stark. He thinks my grief is an act. He thinks I'm grateful for this turn in events. I can't stop my hand, nor would I want to if I could. The sound of my palm smacking his cheek is loud and echoes down the block.

His head knocks to the side with the force of my blow, and I swear I see blood in the corner of his mouth.

"Leave," I hiss. He looks like he's ready to say something else, but he doesn't. I wait for him to get in the car and go, watching Zerah's face in the back of the car disappear into the dark and the smoke.

CHAPTER THIRTY-TWO

I walk into the quiet vestibule and take a deep, shuddering breath. According to the officers, Nima and Benham have been told. They know about Rafi's death. Perhaps they'll let Benham view his body. I bite my lower lip as it wobbles, and with one last, fortifying breath, turn the handle and push into the townhouse.

It's a disaster zone. Clothing is scattered everywhere, fabric in every shade of green, gold, white, and red. No, not red, garnet. I pick up the dress from the floor, the one I wore at the last event we attended together. The night I started letting him in.

But why is it on the floor? Beneath it lies an emerald green gown I wore to a different benefit. Next to it is a flannel nightgown I haven't yet worn.

"Maman? Papa?" I call into the house, afraid for them suddenly. The kitchen door opens, and Nima pushes through, her chin tilted up, her shoulders back. Proud, even in her grief.

"Nima," I say, standing as she slowly approaches. As she gets closer, I see that her shoulders are shaking.

"How *dare* you come here."

"Nima?" My voice shakes. I know she's hurting, but I don't

understand. The door opens behind her. Benham passes through, and freezes.

"Nima," he says, his voice low. He approaches her from behind, cautiously.

"You killed him." Her voice is low and shaky, as if allowing any more airflow would cause her to explode.

"Nima, I promise you, I didn't. I got there—I was too late. I saw Irina, and she saw him. He helped her. She was stuck, and he helped her. But then, he went back to help other people." The words come out and won't stop. "He was always helping people . . . he went back, and I don't know what happened. They wouldn't tell me anything. They said they told you? Did he—" My panic and pain and sorrow catch up to me as I hiccup around a heavy sob. "Did you see him? Is he really . . . ?"

Both of Rafi's parents stare at me. Nima's vitriol doesn't ebb. It only seems to swell as her chin wobbles. Benham places his hands on her shoulders and gives a heavy nod.

"He's truly gone," Benham says.

"Forever," Nima says, her voice rising, unsteady. She steps out of Benham's hold and approaches me. An uneasy sensation spills over me as she gets nearer. "I'll never hold my son again, and I'll never hold my son's son either." My heart aches with a sudden and stabbing pain, as if it has actually broken.

"I'm sorry, Nima. I know what he—"

"You know *nothing*, whore!" She throws something at me, and a metal box strikes my head. I squat to retrieve it. "All this time, living under our roof, leading him astray from our Lord, and you've been killing them."

I stare at the green tin for a long moment. I don't have to open it to know it contains three sachets of contraceptive tea.

"I never—"

"Do not attempt to patronize me with your bald-faced lies. I have always seen the devil in you, girl. You're no better than the whores who eat these tinctures and sell their bodies at the Black

Magnolia. I knew from the first time I met you that that's where you belonged. I told him. And now, you'll pay for your crimes against my son and against my God."

The doorbell rings, and Benham pushes past me to answer it. The man who enters wears a police uniform, but he also wears the seven-pointed star of the old faith.

"Benham, Nima." He nods at each of them, and then his gaze lands on me. There's no kindness, no sympathy, only judgment.

"And you are the girl?"

I don't say anything, just stare at him. Benham shuts the door from the vestibule and steps between us.

"Nima, is this really necessary?"

"Don't you *dare* tell me what is and isn't necessary, Beni." Nima's grief overcomes her, and she sinks to the floor, shaking violently. Benham squats next to her, folding her in his arms.

"Am I to understand that you were found to be in possession of contraceptive tea, ma'am?" The officer's eyes are sharp and unforgiving.

"Yes," I say, trying to be as plain as I can. "Is that a problem? I did not think it was illegal in Osterstan?"

"The Old City has different laws that govern believers. I understand you are a believer?"

I frown at him. I don't know what this game is, or what the consequences are.

"I was not raised in the church."

"Your marriage was conducted in the old church, correct?"

"Yes," I say. "In Nordania."

He frowns at this, and his eyes flicker back to Nima, who is still huddled on the floor.

"I see," he says. "And you are not Osterstani." It's not a question. He retrieves a notepad and pencil and flips open a page. "If you are not a true believer, then it is not illegal to possess the contraceptive tea in Osterstan. It is, however, illegal to have consumed it in the furtherance of terminating life. Did you consume the tea with the intent of ending a pregnancy?"

"I'm not pregnant," I say. He frowns, and his eyes flicker between us again.

"Lies! I heard them. I watched her symptoms set in. She's lying," Nima wails from the floor. The officer looks uncomfortable. "Check her pockets! I bet she has more on her. Or something to help the morning sickness."

"Nima, this isn't going to change anything," Benham says.

"She's a killer!" Nima cries from the floor.

It's all too much.

"I suppose I'll have to ask you to let me search you."

"And if I don't?" I ask, crossing my arms over my chest. He arches an eyebrow and looks as if he's ready to write something down.

"Then, as a non-citizen, that's enough for us to take you in for the night."

"Fine." I hold out my arms and wait for the officer to pat me down, checking my pockets and examining bits of paper and taxi cards. Until he reaches a pocket in the back of my skirt and retrieves the envelope.

"What is this?" he asks. My stomach sinks as ice washes down my spine.

"A letter . . . from my former benefactor."

He reads the letter, and then his eyes flicker back up. He rereads the letter and holds it up.

"Can you explain this?"

I shake my head, helpless.

"What is this?" Benham asks, approaching. The officer lets him read it over his shoulder. "Arden? Who is Arden?"

"She was my roommate."

"The girl who has declared herself independent," the officer says under his breath with unmasked disgust.

"*Compound?*" Benham asks, noticing the same word I did. The one that made me think the letter was some sort of a warning. "And what is this talk about soil? What would Rafi know—" He stutters, and takes in a shaky breath. "What would he have known about soil?"

"I don't know," I mumble, looking away.

The officer pulls Benham aside, and the men talk in lowered voices. Nima is sitting on the settee, the settee that is also covered in my clothing. It's almost comical, if not for the fact that I realize I have no supporters and am completely at the whim of three people who seem to have no interest in my well-being.

"I think it best that you stay here for the night. Given the current climate toward Nordanians."

"What does that mean?" I ask, my eyes flickering from the officer back to Benham. But Benham averts his eyes, moving instead to stand behind the settee, resting his hands on Nima's shoulders.

"You're under house arrest until further notice."

"What?" The panic settles in, overwhelming me.

"You would ask us to keep a *criminal* like her under our roof? On the day of our only son's death?" Nima's voice warbles, but her meaning is clear. She wants me gone. I realize now that the clothes on the floor were likely her doing.

"So quickly you forget that he was my *husband*." I nearly choke around the word. "And I am your daughter."

She flinches, but vitriol floods her eyes as she spits at my feet. "You are no daughter of mine."

"It would be unwise and unsafe to take her into custody tonight. There are too many vigilantes out for justice." The officer sounds apologetic—to them, not me.

"Then take this!" Nima practically spits. She produces crumbled sheets of paper, and in a breathless heartbeat, I know exactly what they are. "Telegraphic messages this harlot was sending about the Osterstani trade minister to her contacts in Osterstan."

"That's not what — Rafi knew about — "

"Lies!" Nima screams, pointing a shaking fist full of paper in my face.

The officer takes the papers, gingerly, carefully, and reads over them. My heartbeat thunders against my chest as his brow becomes more and more furrowed.

"She can stay the night," Benham says. "Just the night. And you will provide protection?"

"Of course," the officer says. "She's clearly a flight risk. I'll send a guard over."

"You must be joking," I say. "Where do you think I'm going to go? I've done nothing other than search for my *dead husband* and come back to *my home*."

"This is not your home."

"It was Rafi's. I was his wife."

"You are not Osterstani. You cannot inherit Osterstani property if you are not Osterstani," the officer says with a sigh. "You aren't entitled to anything. You also will not be entitled to counsel at your trial."

"My trial?"

"Just assuming. Though, given the evidence . . . given what I have here" — he nods at the papers in his hand — "I probably shouldn't help you at all. But I suggest you keep your mouth shut. That will be the only warning I give. My recommendation would be for you to go to your rooms and to stay there until we return in the morning."

The room spins. It's as if I'm on a merry-go-round and everything is flying past faster than I can understand it, but I'm stuck in one place. I feel my mouth open and close, though I have no idea what I meant to do or say or what sound, if any, came out of it. Benham squeezes my forearm, and I meet his eyes. His brown eyes that look so much like Rafi's. Everything goes blurry as saline floods my eyes.

"Go upstairs, Neve," he says, his voice low and crisp. Gone is the drop of tenderness I'd finally earned from him. "There's nothing to be done now, and you can only make this worse."

His words are not unkind, but neither are they helpful. I climb the stairs without another word and lock myself in my room. This is insane. I don't understand what is happening. I don't understand why I'm being held on house arrest, or what will happen to me. There's no one to ask—no one to help. I'm completely and utterly alone.

Rafi's navy velvet slippers are in the middle of the floor, one slightly over top of the other. As if he kicked them off in a rush. Right where he left them this morning. Like he would return for them later tonight. I pick them up, ready to throw them as hard as I can, but then stop. I can't bring myself to do it. Everything hits me, and I sink to my knees, clutching his slippers to my heart. I cry.

In a flash, my world has changed, and once again, I'm left with no one and nothing.

CHAPTER THIRTY-THREE

$\mathcal{M}$y eyes ache, and my throat hurts as I curse the muddy green walls of my new prison cell. Someone left a tray of nigella bread and tea outside my room. When I retrieved it, the officer who's been sent to monitor my door eyed me warily. As if I was something to be feared.

The reality is, I feel like I'm slipping. It's only been a night, but no matter how heavy and tired my eyes were, no matter how dark the night and how much I rocked myself in the bed I once shared with Rafi, I couldn't seem to find sleep.

The bed still smells of him.

I hadn't realized until I climbed beneath the blankets last night and took a deep, shaky breath. When I'd been lying on the other side of the bed from him, I don't remember ever being able to pick out the notes of his scent. Whether it was his soap or his perfume or his natural essence, I'm left now with the fading embers of spiced tea and custard apple.

It's not just the bed linens that carry his scent, either. The wardrobe is thick with it, as are all my clothes. Benham at least had the courtesy to return them to me last night before I tried to fall asleep. He brought the pile up, the items underneath clumsily folded as if he tried and gave up. I'm not sure if he realized he was handing me a pile of Rafi's scent. Perhaps that's why he left so quickly. I spent a bit of time folding them, but when I realized that's what they smelled of, I left them on the floor next to the wardrobe.

Of course, when you're locked in a room that belonged to a ghost, there's nowhere to run.

There's a knock at the door, and I rise from the breakfast table where I leave my cooled tea and mostly untouched nigella roll. The tea smells too much like Rafi, and I couldn't bring myself to drink it down.

"Good morning, Mrs—I'm sorry, Miss Ruiz?" It's like a kick to the stomach, swift and sharp. The officer from the market last night is standing at the door, and behind him is Benham. I blink at the two of them. Benham's eyes are lowered, as if he has the good sense not to meet my gaze.

"How can I help you?"

"May we come in and talk?" He nods at the room behind me. I shrug. What am I going to say? No? Not likely.

Benham follows him in and sits on the settee. His eyes carry over the space, and as he takes in a deep breath, I see his grief in the way his features tighten.

"Shall we sit?" The officer points to the table and chairs where I do as he asks and wait.

"First, may I extend my condolences."

I nearly flinch at how rote his words are. But I school my face, trying to evoke as much of Headmistress Moyle's lessons on maintaining decorum in delicate situations as I can. Those lessons are a heap of emu dung in the moment. I nod and swallow around a thick lump in my throat.

"Can you tell me where he was found?"

The officer blinks, and his gaze flickers to Benham and back.

"I apologize. I don't know that I'm the best person to tell you the details—"

"No one has, so if you know how my husband died or where his body was found, you're as good as anyone."

Benham keeps his eyes fixed on the floorboards, and the officer clears his throat uncomfortably.

"Yes, well, he was found beneath the market, buried in rubble. We believe he was caught in a secondary explosion, as his skin was severely burned. Though, we believe it was the collapse of the market street that killed him, and the medical examiner does not believe he suffered."

"Oh."

I was close. He was where I thought he was. He found Irina and brought her to safety, and then went back—for Peter's sister, I suppose. I feel a tear tickle the corner of my eye.

"You said he was found in the underground market?"

Both men blink at me, their mouths tight. It's as if I've said something uncouth, as if we're not already discussing something traumatic.

"Between us, yes. But in official reports, we will omit that detail."

"Why?"

"Why?" Benham lets out a wry chuckle. "You really need a reason why we don't want it publicly known that he was found in the underground market? That he died among the sinners that fester and peddle their ungodly wares unfit for the light of day?"

"Were they not his constituents as well? And wasn't he down there to rescue them? Why shouldn't his last actions in his life be remembered accurately?"

"It would make a mockery of his life!" Benham roars. I shoot to my feet with the heat of my rage, and so does the officer. He raises his palms and motions for us both to stop.

"This will solve nothing," the officer says. "Let us sit and talk peacefully. After all, it's not as if you're going anywhere immediately."

"I'm not?" I ask, slowly lowering myself into my chair.

"No," he says, though his face still looks grim. "The evidence against you is mounting, and people want justice."

"They think I did this?" I ask, disbelieving.

His silence is answer enough.

"You can't be serious?"

"You are the Nordanian wife, the non-believer. Your mother-in-law made it well known that you have used—or at least possessed contraceptive tea. And Rafael was found with a small but concentrated amount of contraceptive elixir. It is considered highly sinful in the old faith. It's not hard to connect the dots and want to blame you for your sins."

"That's ridiculous," I say, shaking my head. But I'm not really listening now. Because Rafi bought contraceptive elixir. Meaning that he was thinking about what I wanted. Or what I didn't want. He was thinking about our future, about planning for our family. Even if it was planning to not have a family immediately. He was thinking about us.

Fresh tears spill over my eyelids, and the men's expressions darken, the way they always seem to when confronted with something deeply upsetting—or an emotional woman.

"I haven't broken the law," I say quietly.

He sighs. "The bigger problem is these communications sent to a contact in Nordania . . ."

"Rafi knew about . . . he was trying to help me."

"We've looked into them, and we have a warrant for the device."

Benham nods, as if giving the officer his permission to take the machine.

"Miss Ruiz," the officer says, and I flinch. "After a cursory read through, I can see that nothing vital was passed along. Nothing of confidential, or of national importance. But there are other coded messages. These . . . are problematic."

My stomach sinks.

"Let me explain. Please? Rafi was a good man. My benefactor

. . . he . . . Rafi only wanted to help. I'll swear under oath. I'll tell you what you want to know."

"I don't think that's in your best interest," the officer says. "And we cannot let this slide. In the eyes of the law, this is treason. I have with me . . ." He retrieves a folded piece of yellowed, official-looking paper from his pocket. "I have a warrant for your detainment. We need to take you into custody. But . . ." His eyes avert to Benham.

"But what?" I ask.

"As much as there is a mandate for your arrest, there is a strong interest that you not be treated like a common criminal. Other politicians would hesitate to set a precedent . . ."

"So this is all a political stunt?"

"I wouldn't say that," the officer says. "I would look at it as you've been granted a lucky break."

"What are you saying?" Benham's anger simmers beneath the surface.

"And in the meantime, we have to house her under our roof for no reason other than that she was once married to our murdered son?" Benham's voice shakes, and I wonder how near to bursting he is.

"This seems more humane," the officer says. His eyes flicker around the room, and then, thinking better, he shudders and says, "More humane than a widow in a jail cell."

"She has not been married long enough to be worthy of widowhood."

"That is not my place to comment on," he says, rising to his feet. "That said, you'll need to find someone to represent you in case charges are levied."

"I—" I look at Benham, who looks away from me, crossing his arms over his chest with the strength of an oak tree in a storm. "I don't know anyone. I cannot pay for one."

"That is a shame," the officer says, but he doesn't sound as if he means it. He turns to the door. "If there is anyone I can call on, on your behalf, let me know. It would be a shame to see the widow of the Osterstani trade minister go on trial without representation. But it wouldn't stop the process."

The men both move to the door, Benham's back to me as he leaves and doesn't turn around.

"Would you call on me again? Later today? I'll try to think of something."

"Yes," the officer says, begrudgingly. "Of course."

He starts to close the door and then stops, mid-motion. "Again, I am terribly sorry for your loss. Rafael was a good man. I personally heard him speak of you with fondness. You seemed a good match."

His words are like a blow. I can't seem to move from my spot next to the table after the door closes, after I'm once again locked alone with Rafi's ghost.

CHAPTER THIRTY-FOUR

othing changes.

The room I'm in doesn't change. The meals I'm delivered don't change. The bed and the way it smells doesn't change. I'm literally trapped. Benham and Nima take turns delivering my meal trays. At one point, I overhear them in the hall, having a tense argument. Nima wants me gone for good. The conversation ends abruptly with the sound of a toilet draining, and then the heavy footsteps of whichever guard has been assigned to me at the moment.

The officer who interviewed me returns as promised, but I don't have any ideas. I ask him to contact Zerah and Whitey, which he promises to do. But since they're not family and they're also only here on a diplomatic visa—a visa he hints may not last them much longer—he doesn't promise their visit. Especially since Zerah's Nordanian.

Late at night, when sleep eludes me yet again, I find a stack of books stashed away in the back of Rafi's wardrobe. I begin reading the first one, a story about a murder of crows that unites with an unkindness of ravens to bring peace to their homeland. It was strange, and yet poetic, and by the time the first rays of light hit the night sky, I had tears streaming down my cheeks. Not because the story was sad or particularly poignant, but because I could hear Rafi in it.

It's only been three days since his death, and I've started to realize what he meant to me. We weren't lovers. Not even close. But it was like he said—he promised to keep his vows to me, and he remained loyal to me throughout our short marriage. I've never felt that kind of loyalty before—not from any friends, and certainly not from my own parents. And yes, there was more to our relationship than just the loyalty. There was something undiscovered burning between us. And I'll never know now what it was.

Officer Koprihan makes a short visit that morning, with a warning that someone has spoken for me, and I might have a chance at a lawyer. I can't imagine who would do that, but I have my answer a few hours later when there's a sharp knock at the door.

Conrad enters.

"What are you doing here?" I ask, waiting for him to shut the door behind him. His gray suit is wrinkled, his pallor duller than the last time I saw him. Without suspenders like the Osterstani men, he looks strange—underdressed. I realize this is the first time a man has entered this room alone since Rafi. I'm not sure what he said to be allowed a solo audience with me, but I remain where I am, knowing he'll speak when he wants to.

"I'm sorry to hear of your husband's passing," he says, standing stock still for a moment. He looks older. More tired. He was always grayed, with his shiny bald head, thick gray eyebrows, and weathered features. But now, the lines etch more deeply around his eyes—eyes that were once so vividly blue and now lean into a blue-gray. His posture is affected, as if somehow both more tense and slumped more slack.

"Sit," he says as he moves to the settee and lowers himself. I stay where I am for another moment, waiting to feel him out before I relax. But when his expression doesn't change, I lower myself into my chair at the breakfast table and wait for him to speak again.

"It would seem you're in a bit of trouble."

"That's what they say."

"Hmm." He nods and studies me for a long moment. Then he gives me a vaguely appraising nod. "You did well for yourself while it lasted. Not that it matters. They want someone to hang, and your pretty neck will fit the noose." His words are crisp and acidic, sending a cold shiver down my spine.

"What do I do?"

"I can help you," he says, mock modesty layering over his skin like cheap makeup. "Of course. That's why I'm here."

I wait. He's not a man who does things out of the goodness of his heart. I'm honestly not sure he has one. There's a catch, and I won't let myself walk right into it.

"I had dinner with Jarls Von Brandt before I left Nordania."

A fresh chill rushes up my neck as I recall the horrible man who wanted to marry me—wanted to make me his third or fourth or whatever-eth wife. I say nothing again. Just sit and wait.

"He asked after you. Wondered how you were doing. I told him you were married to a cabinet official in Osterstan and living the high life. Of course, that has all changed."

I look down at my knees. They're shaky, knocking into each other. I press my fingers into them.

"You've been a good girl, Neve." I flinch at his description of me. I'm neither good nor a girl. "It would be unkind not to help you in your darkest hour. Therefore, I have a proposition for you."

"Which is?"

"I will help you get out of this mess. You will plead guilty to whatever charges they drum up. Duplicitous marital entrapment, political espionage, treason . . . you'll plead guilty to all of it. You will be deported, never allowed to return to Osterstan. Not that you'd want to."

A hot coal pulses in my stomach. But for what? What did he say that's wrong? Other than a small handful of people, I haven't been treated particularly well here. Nobody wants to see another Nordanian on Osterstani soil. And without Rafi here anymore, there's no reason for me to stay.

And yet . . . the thought of never being able to visit this home, never being able to walk the streets that Rafi did, of saying goodbye to him forever, breaks my heart.

"You will then return to Nordania. With me."

I flinch. He can't possibly mean *with* him, can he? He lets out a churlish laugh and shakes his head.

"Not like that, you fool. I have no need for an Unchosen girl to warm my bed."

Even just hearing those words from his mouth makes me feel queasy. But I suppress the shiver that rolls down my spine.

"Then, what? I return to Nordania, and then what?"

"Then I find you a new husband."

"What?" I frown, feeling a new wave of anxiety. I'd forgotten how this felt. This panic. This lack of control.

"You may find more suitors this time around. Now that you've been tried and proven."

"Nobody has *tried* me."

"Nobody will believe that. An Unchosen girl who was married to an Osterstani? Please. I'd have an easier time convincing them you snuck into the institute and danced with Declan Levington than that you, the Unchosen daughter of an Espancian whore, remained a chaste bride." Fury boils inside me, rising into my chest.

"Nobody else has to believe it. It's the truth."

"Well, good for you," he says, though it's clear he doesn't mean it. "I am simply offering my assistance. In exchange for using my resources to clear your case and get you out of a country that wants you dead, I only ask that you return to Nordania, and then allow me to find you a suitable husband."

It's too simple. Too easy. Why would anyone say no to this? Unless, of course, they don't want a husband. Which I don't.

That's when it hits me.

"And what else?"

He frowns, but his shoulders tense up, and it's clear I've nicked the right vein.

"What about my money?"

"What do you mean, *your* money?" He sneers and leans into his elbows over his knees.

"We had a deal."

"Yes, we did. You had a year. That is no longer possible. For obvious reasons. You're as useless to me now as you were before you managed to cast a spell on the Osterstani trade minister."

"But we had a deal. It's not my fault—"

"Do you want to take your chances with that defense in Osterstani court? I think you'll find you won't like the end result."

My stomach roils and spins and tightens with hot vitriol. It takes every spare ounce of energy and focus I have to take in a deep, cooling breath.

"Perhaps we could come to another agreement. Similar stakes."

"I will not marry Jarls."

He eyes me carefully.

"It's fascinating, watching someone with one leg to stand on try to leap."

His insult hits its target, but does nothing to cool my anger.

"Get out."

He looks unimpressed and underwhelmed. Both of which only serve to further infuriate me.

"The truth of the matter is, despite what you might think, I am not made of money. I would have to dip into your funds—which have been well invested—to cover your legal expenses. If we can then come to an agreement with a suitable man, I don't see any reason why I couldn't make whatever remains of your funds available. Of course, it's a nightmare trying to funnel Nordanian money through Osterstan . . . but I will do my best."

"You mean that? You'd give me the rest of my money?"

"Don't get your hopes up. Who knows what will be left after your expenses."

"And the rest of the deal. If I remain—"

"No one will believe that of a woman who's been married twice."

His words are like a bucket of seawater over my head.

"I will, of course, do all of this for you, but I need your word that you will return to Nordania with me. Allow me to find you a new life."

I'm not sure if he meant to phrase it that way, to make it sound so dire. Perhaps he did, and his effect has taken root. It feels like a godsend, really. And yet . . .

"I'll think about it."

His nostrils flare as he stares at me, as if trying to work something out. Whether he succeeds or fails, I'll never know, because the next moment, he stands and moves to the door.

"I'll come for your decision first thing in the morning. I've booked passage on an outbound ship at eleven in the morning, and if you know what's good for you, you'll be on that ship with me when it departs."

Then he's gone.

And once again, I'm alone, faced with a decision I can't see my way around.

CHAPTER THIRTY-FIVE

I don't know what I'm doing. It seems like I don't have another option. After everything I've done, everything I've achieved and all the things I've been put through, I'm right back to where I started. Well, not actually where I started, worse off. I'm stuck between two terrible options, two awful choices that I don't want to make.

If I tell Conrad exactly what he can do with himself, that leaves me to the whim of the Osterstanis who are mourning the loss of their market, of the people who perished when the bomb detonated, and the collapsed street that took their handsome trade minister as well. It seems pretty clear they won't go easy on me, that they'll be content to use me as an example simply because I'm Nordanian, whether I actually did have anything to do with the bombing or not. Which, of course, I didn't.

But if I go with Conrad, my life is over. I'll be married off to Jarls Von Brandt or, gods forbid, someone worse. There's no guarantee that the man Conrad chooses for me will have any humanity or even an inkling of compassion. Rafael was a one-in-a-million sort of man, and I still don't know how I was lucky enough to have met him the way I did. Or what it was about me that caught his eye. I can't expect or even hope for another good situation with anyone Conrad arranges for me.

I suppose there is another option, but I'm not even sure how I would go about it. I could try to run. But there's a police officer outside my door, and who knows if there are others standing outside on the street. I have no friends here, other than Zerah, and maybe Whitey— though Whitey is Conrad's business associate, so forget that. And who knows what Zerah and Whitey are facing at the moment. Plus, they have all those birds to deal with.

There's a knock at my door. I don't even get to tell people they can enter these days. Today's police officer stands there, holding an envelope with a broken seal.

"This just arrived for you, Miss."

"Thank you," I say, crossing the room to take it from him. He continues to stand there, watching me, as if waiting for me to read it aloud to him. I blink up at him.

"Is there something else you need?"

He stiffens, as if trying to convince me of his authority. But I wave him off.

"Clearly you've already read this. Can't you at least leave me in peace?"

He grunts, backing out of the room. I wait for him to leave before I move over to the window over the breakfast table and unfold the paper.

My dear Neve,

I am writing to express my sincerest condolences over the loss of your dear husband, Rafael. He was a truly good man. I feel lucky to have known him, and even luckier to have encountered him at the market when I did. I don't know that I would be writing this letter if not for that chance meeting.

I stop reading the letter and flip the envelope over. It's addressed to me, and the return address doesn't include a name, only an address. *6743-234 N. Breakers Ave.*

I try to picture where the address is. Breakers Avenue borders the ports, being split north and south by Market Street. The water taxis let off at the main port on Market Street, and the last time I ventured to that part of the city was with Zerah, when we had to place an order for more feed for the emus. But I can't picture it.

I continue reading.

I hear rumors that you are in need of assistance, and I would like to offer mine. I once asked if you were happy here in Osterstan. I would ask the same of you now. Although, I feel it safe to presume you are not. If I can offer my support, be it a good meal, kind word, anything at all, please let me know. You may write to me at the address on the envelope.

I do hope that you'll remember: it is in the darkest times that we discover how brightly we can shine. Rafi once remarked how brightly you shined, how you lit his world in such a way that he hadn't realized he'd been moving in the dark. Allow me to be the flint you need at this moment.

With sympathy,

I.

My fingers tremble against the paper, causing it to rattle loudly in the deathly quiet room.

Irina.

Irina is offering her help. But what does that mean? She runs a brothel. That's literally the only thing I know about her. That, and she had some sort of relationship with Rafi.

Or did she?

The past relationship he talked about was with Peter. Not Irina. So no, I don't think they had a relationship. Perhaps it was simply a friendship. But Rafi was so progressive, always looked to the horizon. Brothels and madams hardly seem progressive. Something isn't adding up.

I run my finger over the address on the envelope once more as I wonder whether or not I should write back. People would know I was in communication with her if I send a letter. And any correspondence I send will obviously be read.

The letter slips from my fingers as everything clicks into place.

I try to recall exactly what it was that Zerah said . . . what it was that Whitey had told her about Rafi. The reasons Whitey thought Rafi was involved with the terrorist acts . . . one of them was his travel. That goes without saying. He'd been gone for almost six months, a time during which people expected him to be learning his new role in the government. And instead, he'd been more or less missing in action, and had turned up in Nordania. Not just in Nordania, but in Peninsula City, where he'd met me. And then he'd brought home a Nordanian wife.

More than that, there's something Zerah said that is now buzzing like an alarm clock in my head—that they had documented evidence of his "correspondence with Nordanians." How would they have tracked that? How would they know? Could it be as simple as sending and receiving mail from Nordania? Would Whitey know the difference? Or would he intentionally blur those lines to make his point?

Something else sends heat down my spine, and I can't stand still. I pace the room, working it out. Something Conrad said earlier . . . that it was difficult to move Nordanian money through Osterstan. It's not *why* he said it. It's *that* he said it. And so did Whitey. Whitey said something about how it's near impossible to find a banker that'll move money from Nordania. But why is Whitey moving money from Nordania? He's Espancian.

I've been helping them. But with what? Sure, it started out easy enough, just sending telegrams and letters to Conrad with the information he wanted about Rafi. I assumed it would help Conrad make investments, or know when he should and shouldn't ship things. It didn't seem like a big deal at the time, but now . . .

But now, Conrad is leaving. In the morning. How can that possibly make sense? As far as I know, he's only just arrived. Is it possible he's been here longer? No, I don't think so . . . surely we would have heard that he was here if he'd arrived sooner. His clothes were wrinkled, as if he just got off a long passage. Zerah would have said something, if nothing else. But if Conrad only just arrived, and plans to leave on the eleven o'clock ship, how in the world does he think he's going to be able to wrap up the case against me?

Unless there isn't really a case against me.

Is that possible? Who would be holding me here, forcing my hand, making it seem as though the best option I have is to do what my former benefactor says, to go with him? The police are involved and everything . . . I just don't understand.

Unless . . . none of it matters. Unless Conrad is running this whole thing. Why would he do that? Why would he be behind bombings and shootings of Osterstanis? It makes no sense. But then, it doesn't make a whole lot of sense that he would ask me to report back to him on the comings and goings of Osterstani's trade minister, either. Especially when Rafi represented so much more than just trade with Osterstan. He represented hope, and progressive values, and . . . and a whole lot of anti-Nordanian values.

By eleven o'clock in the morning.

My heart hammers in my chest. Why was he so insistent on being gone by eleven? It makes no sense . . . unless there's a very good reason for it. A deadly reason.

CHAPTER THIRTY-SIX

I rush across the room and dig into the drawer of Rafi's nightstand. I know he kept pens somewhere in this room, because I'd seen him make notes of things he didn't want to forget. I find one buried at the very back of his drawer, next to a small velvet box. My heart twists as I feel the soft brush of the fabric against my cold and shaky fingertips. I open the box and clap a hand over my lips. Inside is a simple gold band, set with two rubies and one black diamond. It's an Espancian wedding band.

I press it against my chest for a long moment as I breathe through my nose, trying to calm my frantic heart. I need to do this, get a message to Irina. I can fall apart later.

I dig through his drawer, looking for a scrap of paper, but come up with nothing. I settle for the note Irina wrote itself. Flipping it over, I scribble a simple message.

Irina,

Thank you for your message. I welcome a visit, so long as my family will permit it. I don't yet understand their mourning customs.

I sign it quickly, tuck it back into the envelope, then write

Return to Sender on the front. I knock on the door and hand it to the officer when he opens. He looks baffled.

"Please send it back."

"Miss?"

"Just send it back. Read it if you want, I don't care. But please see that it gets to the return address."

The officer stares at the envelope, his forehead crinkling. "Who does it go to?"

"I don't know," I lie. But somehow, I know it will find its way to Irina's hands. "Send it quickly though, please?"

"Miss, I don't know if you realize, but—"

"I'll see that it gets there quickly." Benham is standing at the top of the staircase. His countenance is changed; he no longer seems enraged with me. I don't know what has shifted, but if he's willing, I need to take the chance.

"Wait, do you think you could take another? I just . . ." I look around for something else to write on, knowing that there's nothing. But I need to at least try to contact Zerah. If Whitey and Conrad are behind something, then she should know. A fresh wave of terror rolls through my body as my eyes scan the room.

"I can get you paper," Benham says, his voice still low, as if he's afraid of being caught. "Where would you like it to go?"

"Zerah. I—I saw her, but I think she must be concerned."

Benham's eyes flicker between the officer and me, and he lets out a low breath.

"All Nordanians have been instructed to leave Osterstan. Even though she's married to an Espancian man, she's Nordanian by birth. That's enough to revoke their papers. They'll be leaving soon, if they're not already gone."

My stomach drops. That would be the perfect excuse to get them out of town. The perfect alibi.

"Sir," the officer says, but Benham takes the envelope for Irina from his hands.

"She's not a prisoner," Benham says, his voice low and curt.

"I'll make sure this is sent. As for your friend . . . I'll ask after them. But no promises."

I nod, but tilt my head, uncertain what else to say. Or what has caused his shift in actions.

"Rafi would not have wanted . . . I'm doing this for him. For my son." His voice wobbles at the end. But then he turns and descends the stairs. The officer remains, alone, looking both frustrated and flustered.

"You should probably return to your post," I say with a smirk, shutting the door myself. I don't hear him turn the lock for another few moments. By then, I've started to dig through my clothes. I don't know what's coming, but I have a feeling I'm going to want to be dressed for anything.

Somewhere in this room, there's a ticking clock. I hadn't noticed it until now. After I lay out a long, waterproof raincoat with a scarf and hat, I hear it. As I'm changing into thick woolen tights and a forest-green belted dress that I can move in, I hear the ticking. I move through the room, checking in drawers and behind clothes. As I'm moving things around, I find a thick wool scarf that must have belonged to Rafi. It smells like him so deeply that I wonder whether he'd ever laundered it. I wrap it around my neck and tug on it, letting it coil around me like a warm hug.

I put on a heavy coat of dark red lipstick, my battle armor, and braid my hair, weaving it and pinning it back into a secure twist. As I walk back into the bedroom, my eyes land on the velvet box. I'd left it on the nightstand at some point, and it's still sitting there. I pick it up, ready to open it, to admire it once more, when there's a quick series of knocks at the door.

"Miss?" The officer is standing there, but so is Irina. And an unfamiliar man. No, wait—he looks familiar. He has blond hair and bright blue eyes, but he looks different from the last time I saw him. Where do I know him from?

"Neve, dearest." Irina bursts into the room and wraps her arms around me, turning us so that she's facing the door. The door closes behind us, and I can hear the man she's come with speaking in a low voice with the officer. She pulls back, and her eyes are shiny.

"Irina. Thank you for coming."

"Are you okay? Are you hurt?"

"No, of course not. I'm fine."

"Well, you're not fine. You're locked away in a haunted bedroom." Her eyes flicker from left to right, and she scrunches her nose. "Like a pathetic princess from a fairy story."

I cock my head, staring at this statuesque woman, wondering how she could possibly know the exact thoughts that have been going through my head.

"I understand. More than you would know . . ."

"I'm sorry, then," I say. She shrugs and steps back, her gaze moving over the room. It trails over the jacket I've laid out, and then back to me, eyeing my clothing. Her eyes stop on my hand, the way it curls around the velvet box. I hold it tighter, and she says nothing.

"It seems you're serious, then. You're ready?"

"Yes. That's . . . we have to go, Irina." I step closer, lowering my voice. "I don't know what's going on, but this thing that happened to Rafi . . . and not just at the market . . . I think it's—"

"Yes, I know. It's more than what anyone else is letting on."

"I think it's my benefactor."

She narrows her eyebrows.

"Why would your benefactor get involved in something like this?"

"That's just it. I don't know. I don't understand it. But he was here earlier."

"Your benefactor was here? From Nordania?" I nod, and she frowns.

"Neve, I need to ask you a question." She steps closer still, holding on to my biceps and squeezing gently. "I can make this all go away. I can get you out of here, to safety, but you should know you won't be welcome back."

"I know. That's what Conrad said, too."

"Conrad Laarsworth is your benefactor?" She stiffens, and I wonder what it is that caught her attention.

"Do you know him?"

"No," she says, too quickly. "He has a reputation, of course. But no, I don't know him. Not personally."

"I would hate it," I say, softly. "Not being able to come back. But I understand."

"Good," she says. "Then there's just one more thing." She reaches into the inside pocket of her duster and retrieves a folded bit of paper. "This may seem unfair, but I have a business to run."

My blood chills as I watch her press the paper flat against the breakfast table. She retrieves a gold pen from her cleavage and hands it to me.

"Your release will not be inexpensive. And I'm not in the business of charity. You will owe me the money I pay."

"Yes, of course," I say, taking the pen from her and leaning over to read the words on the document. But she stops me, holds me upright, meeting her gaze.

"You will come work for me."

"What?" My stomach drops. She runs a brothel. What she's asking is impossible. It's what my mother did. I swore to her I wouldn't end up where she did.

"You know what business I'm in, I take it?"

"Yes."

"Then you should know that the laws surrounding brothels in Sudersberg are very specific and particular to Sudersberg."

"How? How could they possibly be so different than in Espancia? In Nordania?"

"They are different in that a brothel is only defined as a group of independent contractors working for a manager—or madam, if you must—selling their services."

"And that is so different how?"

"It doesn't mean what you think it means. A service could be anything. Anything you can dream of."

"But the clientele—"

"The clientele is both men and women."

"Again, not so—"

"What is it you dream of doing, Neve? Do you dream of being someone else's wife? Of raising children?"

"No." My answer is so fast, so firm, it startles me. It hearkens back to when Rafi told me he'd never considered that he might one day have children.

"If you take me up on this, if you allow me to help you, you must continue to let me help you. You must come work for me. I will help you build a life for yourself. Yes, perhaps, it will not be one that you imagined. But it will be one that you have chosen.

"But in return, you will have to leave this life behind. You will have to leave your past lives behind and put in the work to make a new life for yourself. One that you would be proud of. It will not be easy, and you will pay me back every step of the way. But never at an unfair pace or rate."

I think for a long moment. If what she's saying is true, it doesn't sound so bad. I could do anything I want, so long as it's a service. I could earn my own wages. Which would be. . . well, honestly? It would be unbelievable. I can't quite wrap my head around it. And yet here is a woman, offering me everything I could ever dream of, right now.

"What do you say?"

"How long do I have to repay you?" I ask, my voice softer than I expect. Almost humbled.

"As long as it takes. So long as you're working under me, making regular payments in whatever amount you can manage." She nudges the paper toward me and then steps away giving me a chance to read what she's written.

The language is clear. It's plain and simple. I will repay her whatever amount she spends, in whatever time it takes me, by joining her business and working as an independent contractor in the field of my choosing. As long as I work for her, I will not owe interest.

Which reminds me of something else that upsets me.

"There's one other thing."

"What is it?"

"I have money. But my benefactor, he took it. Said I could have it back after. . . " I stop, wondering how much I can trust her with.

"You may as well spit it out now. If I don't already know about it, I'll soon find out."

I take a deep breath. "He asked me to report to him. Things I heard and saw. . . things that Rafi did."

Her gaze darkens, and she curls her hands together into a tight clasp.

"He asked you to spy on the Osterstani trade minister?"

"He did."

"And he said that if you did this, he would give you your money back."

"That's what he said. With interest."

"Over a period of time, I would assume?" Her gaze is dark, and I wonder if I should have said anything at all. If perhaps I haven't just sealed my fate, and she won't just walk me straight to the authorities and tell them what I've done.

"Yes." I say nothing more, and she nods, solemnly. After a long moment, she lets out a short sigh.

"I think I can help you get that money back."

"I would use it to repay you, of course."

"I'm not concerned with that," she says. "I would rather you use your own money toward your future and work for me to pay off this debt."

"Why?"

She sighs and purses her lips together. "Because I believe, above all other things, that everyone deserves a fair chance, and most of us deserve a second one."

I nod. Grateful. I sign the paper and pass it back to her. She doesn't even look at my signature as she tucks it away. It's as if it never existed.

The door swings open, and Benham stands there, Irina's man just behind him.

"You have company?" Benham looks surprised and confused.

"Yes," I say.

"We were actually just leaving," Irina says, picking up my jacket and handing it to me.

"You're going?" His brow furrows, so much like Rafi's used to. But he doesn't make as if to stop us, as I know Rafi would.

"Yes," I say, feeling a twinge of guilt for my sudden departure. Not that I owe anyone anything. After all, I've literally been imprisoned here.

"I have something to tell you," he says. He seems a little out of breath, his cheeks pale.

"What is it?" I fold the jacket over my arm as I check the laces on my boots.

"With Rafi . . . I've reassumed his title. I'm the acting trade minister . . . again."

"Congratulations," Irina says, crisply. Benham frowns at her.

"I received a message. From the National Security Advisory Council. There's going to be a lockdown tomorrow. All day."

"A lockdown?"

"Yes . . . good Lord, I don't know why I'm telling you all this. I don't know your plans. But please, whatever you do, avoid the Port of Albahar tomorrow afternoon."

Icy cold flushes down my spine. It all feels a little too real.

"What's happening at the Port of Albahar tomorrow?" Irina asks.

He flinches, but shakes his head. "I don't know. We've also been advised to stay away from the market and from any government buildings. It's not a Nordanian threat—the threat is believed to be domestic. Not that the public needs an excuse . . ."

He lets out a heavy sigh and approaches, pressing his firm hands into my shoulders.

"I don't know what happened between you and Rafi. I thought I knew my son, knew his mind and his heart. Then he returned with a pretty Nordanian bride. I didn't understand that side of him."

I understand what he's saying in a way that makes my throat thicken.

"But over the time you were together, I saw a new side of him. A side that had been left in the dark for too long. He found a new lightness about him, and I have to believe it was you who did that."

My heart feels as if it's breaking all over again. I bite down hard on my bottom lip to keep the tears at bay. But still, I fail.

"Thank you, Benham," I say, my voice thick with emotion.

"I know he wouldn't want me to send you into danger without at least a little bit of warning."

"Thank you," I say again. He pulls me into a hug, and it's so hard to let him go. But Irina clears her throat, and I know it's time.

"Thank you for everything," I say, kissing his cheek. He nods and touches my cheek, then backs away.

All that remains in the room I once shared with my husband are me, Irina, and her man.

"Where's the guard?" I ask.

"Something suddenly came up," Irina's man says. His voice is familiar, but I still can't pinpoint it. He grins as if he knows exactly what I'm thinking.

"The market," he says, catching my eye. "The man under the cart."

"Oh," I say, putting it together. "Elm, right?"

"Right."

"While I appreciate this beautiful moment, we need to move." Irina waves us on.

"One more thing," I say.

"Fantastic. What one more thing is it you need, princess?"

I struggle not to laugh at the nickname she gives me. "Zerah is my friend. She is also Nordanian, and I can't leave without making sure she's okay."

"She is married to the bird man, correct?" Elm says with a smirk.

"Emus," Irina says. "Regal creatures. Though his are detestable."

"Right. I just don't trust him. He was working with Conrad—"

"Yes, yes, I see." Irina frowns, and then catches Elm's eye. They seem to have a silent conversation. "It seems that these men, Conrad and William Whitey—that is his name, correct?" I nod, and she continues, "Perhaps they are the answer to all of this? Let me tap into my network and see what I can extract. Try to find a lead. Can I trust you?"

"Yes," I say. "With what?"

"Does it matter?"

I stand, awkwardly, waiting for more information.

"If we leave you to collect your friend, do you think she would join us?"

Something bubbles warm and sweet in my belly, a far contrast from the rest of the ice and stone that is filling my world at the moment.

"Yes, I think she might. I hope she would."

"Then go get her. Meet us at the address you sent the letter to. Do you need it again?"

"I—yes."

"No, she doesn't," Elm says. His blue eyes lock on mine as he lowers his hat. The corner of his feline mouth curves into a wicked smile. "Meet us at the lower level of the Black Magnolia."

"The Black Magnolia?" I remember the building from when I went with Zerah to order feed. It all clicks. Nima's comments about it, Zerah talking about how it's a known hotspot for all sorts of illicit activity. And now, it's my goal.

"Got it? Meet there by daybreak, or the deal is off." Irina's expression is hard and stony, but she extends a hand. I shake it, and then follow them, single file, down the stairs and out the front door.

CHAPTER THIRTY-SEVEN

*I*t's dark and strangely quiet as I make my way through the streets toward the south waterfront. The city feels rattled, as if it's holding its breath, waiting for the slightest shift in the current to either crumble or detonate. I'm not sure which would be better — or worse.

As I approach the house, there's a strange stillness to the air. No wind blows off the sea that's not far off; no pungent, briny odor in the air. Something critical isn't there, and it sends a tepid shiver down my spine.

The lights are out, as I would expect. But the preternatural emptiness of the air around the clapboard house is what triggers me. It's the thing that sends my pulse fluttering against my throat. I rush on soft feet to the side of the house, where I recall an entrance. I move as lightly as I can, so as not to rattle the emus. The last thing I want is to surprise them and have them start growling or try to attack through the fence. I make it easily. Either I'm better at this than I think, or there's something very wrong.

The yard is dark beneath the layer of tightly knit clouds, but it's also still. Too still. Why is everything so still? Doesn't the land know when things are all wrong? I stare for a long minute, or maybe five, or ten. As soon as it seems like the coast is clear, doubt creeps in. The easiest way into the house is through the yard. As far as I know, from what I remember, they don't keep that door locked. The emus are enough of a deterrent to would-be thieves.

The crazy thing is, I don't sense them. Or maybe I've come to be on the same wavelength as them, like Zerah. Whitey is terrified of them. But Zerah isn't. That's the only thing I can hold on to right now. I have to trust that Zerah is right, that there's nothing to fear among them. Slowly, cautiously, I slip my foot through a gap in the fence and pull myself up.

Even with as easy as my dress is to run and move in, the skirt still feels awkward and bulky climbing over the fence. I move quickly but carefully up the tall wall of link fencing. I swing one leg over the top of the fence, feeling my skirt stretch awkwardly over the top, and then nearly slip as I hoist my other leg over. Once I'm certain my skirt is over the fence, I descend slowly, nearly losing my footing once. Then I drop to the ground, landing hard.

A low *oof* comes from my lips, and I freeze. My eyes are more adjusted to the dark of the yard, my nose more attuned to the piquant odor of the birds. And yet, it's not as strong as I expect. Maybe there's more of a breeze than I realized? Maybe it's because they're sleeping . . . or maybe it's something else.

When nothing—and no one—attacks, I rise and move alongside the fence toward the house. As I approach the two-story building, it blocks what little light seeps through the cloud cover, casting me in even more darkness. I move as slowly and methodically as I can, trying to feel the ground with my feet before I commit to each step. When I finally do reach the house, then the door, I let out a small breath. I curl my fingers around the doorknob and twist, and it releases.

The door swings open, and I enter the sleeping house. I've

only ever been here once before, and never inside. I shut the door slowly and silently, waiting until I'm certain the door has latched before I turn to the house itself.

The air inside feels stale. It smells like dust and talcum powder and the faintest hint of decaying fruit. My stomach tightens into a tepid knot. Something is very wrong. The fear of what I might find crawls into my legs, and I can't seem to stop them from moving me through the mudroom and up the short staircase into the kitchen. Faint moonlight casts the long, narrow galley in silvers and grays, and there's nothing fresh or enticing about the space. It's as if no one has lived here or prepared food here in a long time.

I keep moving through the house, turning through a door that leads to the center hall. The house is deathly quiet. I don't hear so much as a clock ticking. I climb the stairs, where I assume the bedrooms must be, no longer worrying when my feet hit a squeak or a weak spot on a step. At the top of the stairs, I move down the short hallway, peeking into the first two doorways—a guest room and a den. I slow down as I reach the last two doors. I take a deep breath, and then turn the handle on the door to the right. Before me is the master suite. It's decorated in extravagant pieces done up in masculine tones. There's not a trace of Zerah in this room. Not even a jewelry box or a dress out of place. It feels like she's never even stepped foot in this room.

Backing out, I shut the door, and then turn to the last remaining room opposite the master.

I turn the handle on her door and hold my breath.

The room is empty.

Either she's in Whitey's room, something that sends a fresh set of chills down my spine while coiling my stomach in heated knots, or she's gone. Just then, light fills the room, and I blink. It's moonlight from outside, brighter than it's been all night, filling her room, casting it in silvery whites and blues. I move to the window and look up at where the clouds have parted, leaving a wide expanse of midnight blue sky between the murky gray clouds. But then I look down. My stomach drops.

The yard I tiptoed through, the one that houses twenty-odd emus and their coops, is empty. Completely empty. The doors to the coops are wide open, and startlingly barren.

I turn around to examine the room when I see it. Something lying on the bed, on Zerah's pillow. Something dark and strangely shaped. As I cross the room to examine it, I take note of the wardrobe—doors wide open, and empty within. I don't see a suitcase anywhere in this space. Or any personal effects.

I reach for the item on the bed and lift it. The flower is strange. Familiar in its shape, but with large, wide petals spiraling out from the center. I realize it's dusted in black as I rub my fingers against it. It's a black flower.

I drop it when I realize what sort of flower it is, and no longer fear that there's anyone else in the house. Because, while I have no idea why she left it, or why she thought it would convey a message to anyone, much less me, I can think of only one reason Zerah would leave a black magnolia sitting on her pillow in an empty bedroom.

Without another thought, I back out of the room, out of the house, and make my way down to the waterfront, praying that I can find a water taxi at this time of night. If I can't, I don't know that I'll make it in time—I don't know for what. As I reach the shore and persuade a sleeping driver to take me to the port, I try not to think about it.

Even from the water, the Black Magnolia stands just where I expect it to, as if it's been there longer than the town itself, rising from the earth and leaning a bit, as though it's not going anywhere no matter anyone else's intentions. Mist moves in from the water behind me as the water taxi driver sidles up next to the pier.

I reach into my pocket, looking for something to pay him with, when a shadow emerges from the mist.

"I'll cover that for you." Irina passes something to the taxi driver, and he nods, leaving before we even have a chance to leave the pier.

"She wasn't there," I say. Irina's expression shifts slightly, but she doesn't look surprised. If anything, it looks as though she expects it.

"Come, let's move onto solid ground. Secrets have a way of spilling over water." She loops her arm through mine, and I walk with her toward the esplanade. She finds the shadows along the seawall and keeps us to them, tucking our shadowy movements within all the secrets the city keeps.

"Whitey is missing as well," Irina says, a sharp note of distaste on her tongue.

"How do you know?"

"He wasn't at the Briny Pelican." I frown, having never heard of this place. "It's the brothel he's frequented since arriving."

A shudder crawls over my shoulders and up into my neck.

"Does that really surprise you? You would prefer a man like that get what he needs from an unwilling wife?"

"No," I hiss. "Of course not."

She's quiet for a moment, and gives my forearm a little squeeze.

"It happens more than you realize, of course. He may not be the most scrupulous of men, but it could be far worse for your dearest Zerah."

My chest contracts at the way she says it, *your dearest Zerah*, but I don't object, leaning into the small bit of comfort her words bring me.

"The bigger problem is that he hasn't been seen there since the underground market bombing."

"Do you think . . . ?"

"I don't think anything. Not until there's something to think. But I strongly suspect . . ."

"It wasn't just Zerah that was missing from the house. Everything was gone from her room. Her clothes, anything personal. It was as if she was never there." But that's not exactly true, is it? I frown, thinking.

"What is it?"

"Except, she left something on her bed."

"What?"

"A dried magnolia flower. It was covered in black powder. Like kohl."

"It doesn't take a genius to figure that one out," Irina says, turning us up a side street, cloaked in black.

"Yes, but there was something else."

She stops walking in the middle of the alley and cocks her head, waiting for me to speak.

"The birds were gone."

"The emus?"

"Yes."

"Where did they go?"

"I don't know. But how could twenty-odd emus be gone without someone noticing?"

"It could explain why Whitey wasn't there."

"He was somewhere else," a deeper voice interrupts. I jerk, but Irina remains as she is, solid and still against my arm. Elm appears next to us, and his sharp blue eyes catch mine. But he's in a disguise, wearing a heavy beard and a slouchy hat. He looks like he could just as easily be a dockworker out for a night of fun, or a vagrant looking for a warm corner in which to catch a bit of sleep. There's something about him that makes me want to ask a thousand questions, even if I doubt he'll ever give me the answers.

"Where?"

"The place with the aubergine door—over on Siletz Run

Road."

"Alone?"

"With his backer."

"Whitey has a backer?" I ask, but as soon as the words leave my mouth, it fits together.

"I believe he's your benefactor, dearie," Elm says, his words not unkind, but not feeling gentle either. "Talked to the girl he hired."

"Who?" Irina's voice hardens as she shifts into what I now recognize as her business-mode.

"Finola."

"Swendish girl?"

Elm nods. "She said he was in a celebrating mood, leaving town with less money in his pockets than he was used to having."

"Odd."

Elm snorts with another nod. "She said he was expecting the tide to turn very soon. But that he had to call it an early night as he'd be taking the first passage out."

"At eleven o'clock?" I ask, fidgeting with my pocket. It seems odd that the first passage out would not be first thing in the morning.

"No, at eight. He left early because he had an early morning." Elm cocks his head, and I feel his gaze penetrating me, as if he can somehow learn my fears, my weaknesses, my hopes, all with one glance.

"But Conrad said I needed to be on the eleven o'clock ship."

Irina and Elm share a guarded glance.

"Then you definitely don't want to be on the eleven o'clock ship. Can you get word to the authorities? Without drawing attention to us?"

"Wait," I say, squeezing Irina's arm. "Perhaps Benham . . ."

She nods.

"Yes, that's a good idea. You might start there, get at it from the outside instead of ruffling too many feathers."

"I'll start there. Thank you."

I nod at him, but he doesn't move. He stands there for another moment, until Irina motions for him to say whatever it is he wants to say.

"There's more."

"Go on, then," Irina says. She's still holding on to my arm, and I realize I'm leaning into her, letting her support me. When I try to readjust so that she's not bearing so much of my weight, she simply pats my forearm, as if to say, *it's okay, lean as much as you need to.*

"The girl also mentioned that Whitey had been there—like I said—but that he looked off. Spacey and glazed over. Probably snorted something."

I frown, trying to think of whether I'd ever noticed signs of an addiction within him, but nothing comes to mind. Elm continues.

"The girl said she offered her services, or to call for a friend, but he declined their offers. Mentioned that his wife needed a room to rest in before her passage the next day. Said she didn't need a wakeup call, just a decent place to sleep something off."

My stomach drops.

"Where is she?" I ask.

"Where do you think? The only place in town that rents rooms by the hour near the port?" His face darkens, and Irina nods, then glances to me.

"Shit," I say under my breath. I swear I see Elm's eyes flash with surprise, but when I look back at him, he's stoic, focused on Irina.

"Well, we've got our marching orders. You've got your portion covered?" Irina tilts her chin to Elm, and he nods.

"I'll find you once it's done."

"Good luck," she says, and then he's gone, just as quickly as he arrived. Irina gently tugs me in the direction we'd been walking, moving up the hill toward the high street above the lower esplanade.

"We'll want to split up. They know my face there, and while I'm not entirely unwelcome, I'm not welcome either."

I nod, as if I understand, even though it only makes me want to ask more questions.

"You go in the main entrance, see if you can buy a room. Whatever's available." She reaches into her bag and retrieves a few paper notes, pushing them into my hand and curling my fingers around it in a fist. "Then look, listen. I won't lie to you — you may hear or see things that will upset your sensibilities."

"I'm not a wilting flower," I say, even though I feel squeamish at the thought of what I might see. At seeing a hint of my mother's world. She nods, accepting me at face value, and then turns us left toward the hulking black behemoth ahead.

"I'll go back down to the low street and see if I can find anything in the port-side entrance. If someone has tried to move twenty-some-odd giant birds, someone down there is our best bet."

"Why do I get the impression there's something strange going on?"

"Because we're hunting down giant birds in the middle of the night."

Irina's face is plain, and it's hard not to laugh at what she's just said. But I keep it together, and she gives my forearms one last squeeze.

"You can do this. Just . . . read the room and play the part. You can do that, right?"

Her words are simple, and somehow, exactly what I need to hear. Because if there's one thing I can do, it's read the people I'm surrounded with and blend into the role I need to play. It's what I've been trained to do.

"Yes, of course."

"See you on the other side."

Then she's gone, before she can actually tell me where the other side is.

CHAPTER THIRTY-EIGHT

*T*he darkened, monolithic hotel looms ahead of me, ominously quiet. It may be the middle of the night, but I suppose I expected there to be at least one or two windows illuminated. The hairs on the backs of my arms stand as I approach the main entrance and realize that the glass doors are blackened. With paint or grime, I couldn't be certain. But with a ginger touch, I squeeze the latch and push through.

The reception area is modest and makes no pretenses about being a fine establishment. The faux-wood paneled walls are painted chocolate red, lending a macabre sense to the already icky sensation that coats my senses. A low wooden desk sits at the opposite end of the room; the legs are filigreed and indicate a once prestigious appointment. Now, those fine grooves merely collect dust, as though it's seen far better days. No one sits behind it, but a hastily hand-written paper tent says, *be back soon*. Another sign says there's no vacancy.

The foreboding silence tells me this isn't actually the case.

I wait another moment, and when I'm certain no one is about to pop out from behind a door I haven't noticed, I pass behind the desk and look out the window beyond. It's even darker outside, with the fading backlight behind me in the room, but I can just barely make out the largest of the piers in the port. It's quiet, and yet there's a strange, frenetic energy that tickles my senses.

Just then, a thunderous *thunk* jolts me. It came from below my feet, and I realize I've fallen to a crouch, as if trying to preserve my balance for when the floor crumbles beneath me. A high-pitched keening sound comes after that, and chills rush down my spine. There's something very wrong going on here. If I was wise, I'd run from it.

Another screeching sound fills the space from below, as if some creature is in gruesome pain. Without another thought, I start moving. There's a hall that stretches each direction off the lobby. Both look dark and desolate, and I take a guess, moving left. As I pass one room after the next, I brace myself for any sudden appearance that I would do well to run from. But nothing comes, nothing happens. The hall remains eerily still, and not so much as a sliver of lamplight escapes from beneath the doors to the hotel rooms.

At the very end of the hall, one door remains. Not enough space around it for a room. It looks as if it once held placard, perhaps one saying *exit* or *stairwell*? I turn the handle, holding my breath the entire time. But it gives, and the door swings out of my reach on an ear-splitting screech, slamming into the wall behind it.

I freeze as the noise echoes up and down the stairwell beyond. I look back down the hall. But the hotel behind me remains as dead as it was when I first entered. I push the door a bit more, and the squeal is just as loud as before. I push it only until it's open just enough for me to slip through.

The cold, concrete stairwell is lit by brownish-gray light through filthy windows that stack from ground to roof. The staircases are open, allowing dirty light to fill the columnar room, making it feel even more haunted than before.

A loud, grinding sound trumpets up the stairwell, and once I get ahold of my breathing again, I descend. The keening sounds that follow are pure animal, and I don't want to imagine what sort of torture would make a human sound so feral. At the bottom of the stairwell, there's an open doorframe. Beyond, the low, frantic rumbling of secrets and orders whispered in haste slithers across a large, cavernous space. Everything is still cloaked in darkness. It's impossible to see anything more from where I'm standing.

But what I can see is confusing.

It appears as though the basement level of the Black Magnolia is one large open space, with higher ceilings than I would have expected. I'm met with the distinct odor of wastewater and ocean brine. And something else. Something earthy and pungent. As my eyes adjust, I notice several large objects—perhaps boxes, or large pieces of furniture—that block my view from everything that's happening beyond.

A loud crack, like the sound of splintering wood, fills the space, and I flinch.

"Oi!" a deep voice calls over the space, but I can't make out the hurried low tones that follow. The ones that will surely tell me what exactly it is that's happening down here.

Another loud *thunk* fills the space, followed by one of the large items shifting before my very eyes. Lamplight fills its void, and I can just make out two hulking figures. One appears to be wearing robes, and a mask of some sort. The other is unrecognizable in an oilskin duster, hat, and boots. He appears to be very comfortable working on the pier at all hours of the night. The keening sound that follows is cut with something else far more human and far more terrifying.

"Keep her quiet!" The gruff noise seems to come from the man in the work clothes. A low voice seems to respond, too low for me to make out clearly.

The box continues to shift out of the basement storage space— I assume down to the docks.

"Found another one." A different low voice curls around the

corner, and I see another man in workwear walking in, dragging a woman by bound wrists. A woman who refuses to lower her chin.

"Shit," I whisper. The man jerks his head in my direction, and I close my eyes, as if the whites might somehow give me away.

"Where do you want her?"

"Put her in the back room with the other one." The voice that speaks is intimately familiar, and a shiver of dread winds its way down my spine as I realize that Conrad is here. Not just that, but there's an *other one* in the back room.

Zerah.

My heart rate picks up, hammering away faster than before, but as I breathe in slowly through my nose, I force calm into my veins.

I wait for Irina to counter, to fight back or spit in his face. But when she says nothing, I realize she must be bound in such a way that she cannot speak. My blood boils, and that familiar heated rage that fuels the deepest pit in my stomach churns into something instinctual.

As I watch the man lead Irina to a room on the opposite side of the space, I lean back, looking around for a way that I can get there without being seen. If I can just get into that room, wherever it is that they're being held, I can untie them, and we can escape.

"The job is done." Silver glints in the masked man's hand. A knife? No . . . it's far too small. It almost looks . . . medical. Like a scalpel?

The man in the robe and mask turns into the light, revealing his yellow surgical robes and matching mask. A doctor?

I shift back along the wall as the workers move to another crate. They shift it, clumsily, onto what I realize now is some sort of large wheeled platform. A thud and a crack sound from within, and the doctor yells at them in what I think must be old Osterstani. The only word I recognize is one I heard Nima say in my presence, so I assume it's an insult.

"They're only sedated, not unconscious! Their fight or flight instincts are enhanced. You must proceed with caution."

The workers move the crate with a touch more care. When the large crate is on the platform, they spin it slightly, and I realize that one side is almost open, but for the bars embedded across its expanse. And beyond those bars is a large bird.

My stomach tightens into a painful coil as I wonder what the hell is going on here that requires both a doctor and Whitey's birds. Irina mentioned this . . . asked Zerah about the birds, said she'd heard the vet had visited. Something else niggles at the back of my memory . . .

I don't have a chance to question it though, because just then, I feel a round of hard, cold metal against the side of my head.

"What a coincidence, meeting you here of all places." Whitey's nasal voice grates down my neck as his gun presses into my skin. I don't dare move my head to look at him.

"What's happening?" I dare to ask, trying to take in as many details as I can while I still have the chance.

"Taking care of loose ends, it would seem."

The gun digs into my back as he leads me onto a large, rickety ship. I don't know much about ships, but this one seems particularly unseaworthy. Never mind the fact that it's being loaded in the middle of the night with sedated emus.

"What are you doing with your emus? I thought they were important?"

"Never you mind that," he snarls. I've never heard him sound so unpleasant. Or so harried. He's nervous. It makes me wonder who is actually in charge here. He leads me along a long row of crates until he reaches an empty one.

"Sudersberg is a fascinating nation," he muses, as if we're just two people at a party discussing world cultures. He fumbles in his pocket for something until he produces a key. My stomach tightens into something both hot and cold.

"High style, high class. *Expensive*. They have a taste for the finer things in life there, and they produce the finer things, as well. Mink farms and gemstone mines and silk cocooneries producing finer threads than you've seen anywhere.

"They also, oddly enough, have a fascination with all things Nordanian. Especially trained Nordanian women."

A fresh chill shoots down my back, and I struggle against him. He pulls me tight against his short, squat frame, and a wave of revulsion twinges at my stomach.

"The funny thing is, the things that are hardest for them to get, no matter how mundane, are the things they'll pay a small fortune for."

"Let me guess," I hiss as he twists me around, squeezing the binding at my wrists tighter. "They like emu feathers?" He shudders behind me.

"Emu meat is a delicacy there, among the refined palates of the North Coast. And I suspect emu feathers will become haute couture soon enough."

He pulls a key from his pocket and works at the lock on the crate. My stomach drops, realizing what exactly is happening.

"Of course, Osterstan has become more and more difficult to deal with as of late. Although, I suspect it will soon become easier with the new trade minister."

My stomach drops. It all clicks into place.

"You set the bomb in the market?"

He sneers as the padlock snaps open.

"His policies were outrageous. He was sending the country into backslide. Do you know how much money Osterstan loses out on each year from shipments of things it deems 'unsavory'? How much money gets pilfered under the table? How many businesses go bankrupt because they can't ship goods to

Sudersberg? How much money it costs everyone else to do business around this stupid country?"

His tone grows higher-pitched and more frenzied. He pulls me to the side as he opens the gate, and then shoves me in. I trip over my own feet and fly into the wall, smacking my cheek against the hard wood. I hear the gate slam against the crate, and then the lock click shut behind me.

"You're one of the lucky ones, you know?" His voice is low, and his demeanor shifts. His pupils are dilated, and it occurs to me for the first time tonight that he might not be in his right mind.

"Osterstani weapons will be to blame, of course. Just as they were in the market attacks."

"Why Osterstani weapons?" I ask, trying to keep him talking. I look around, trying to find something, anything to get out of this crate that I have the worst feeling will send me to my death. If I can just keep him here a bit longer, perhaps I'll figure it out.

"Nordania is the enemy, darling." He lets out an ugly snort and curls his fingers around the wooden slats. "Or at least, that's what they think. But if it's actually native Osterstanis—freedom fighters—who set the docks ablaze, they'll realize that enough is enough. Once they follow the trail, they'll come to the conclusion that the progressive radicals who want Osterstan to lean even farther forward, even farther away from Nordania and Espancia and the rest of the damned world—they'll realize that they've pushed too far. It'll energize the fundamentalist old-party base into putting the brakes on its current isolationist dogma.

"And now, with the current Rostami vacancy, that's one less progressive vote."

"Watch yourself, Whitey." Conrad's sneer comes from around the corner, and while I can't see him, I can feel his vitriol. "This is starting to sound like the ravings of a lunatic."

"Isn't this what you wanted?"

"All I've ever wanted is my money," Conrad sneers. "The

money you owe me — repayment for me digging you out of debt so you could buy yourself an institute bride."

"I will get you that money," Whitey says with a shudder. Conrad shifts into view, leading a slight figure with a bag over their head.

"Enough is enough. It's not my fault you found yourself a defective bride." He nudges the person toward Whitey, and Whitey catches her. She lets out a low groan, and I realize it's Zerah. My stomach coils into molten lava, and I grit my teeth.

"You can't be completely neutral when it comes to global politics. Especially not when you've lost your credibility," Whitey sneers.

Conrad's shoulders tighten in a flash of anger, followed by something much harder, more calculated. It's as if he's trying to do quick math to figure out the cost-benefit analysis of losing me. When he averts his gaze, I can see he's changed his mind.

"Back up, whore!" Whitey points his pistol at me, and I back up against the back of the crate. He opens the lock again and pushes Zerah in. I fumble to catch her before she tumbles and hits her head, as he shuts the crate and clicks the lock shut.

"Conrad!" I shout. "You can't just leave me here!"

"Oh, yes, one of your cash cows. Would you like her back? I forget — was your plan to make a double profit on the girl? Very classy, by the way. Killing off her husband so she has no choice but to return to you and let you sell her again. I suppose . . ." Whitey leans in, his sweaty face pressing between the slats. "I suppose she could be a suitable second wife. Of course, she's also privy to a lot of information . . ."

"What will you do with the girls?" Conrad's tone is merely curious. I take the bag off Zerah's head, carefully, and examine her. Her temple is bruised, and her lip split, but otherwise, she doesn't look too bad. Other than being passed out.

"What difference does it make?" Whitey spits. "You've already turned your profit on her. I apprehended her, now she's my property. Do you have any idea how much she can turn in Sudersberg?"

"I do." Conrad nods, his eyes once again calculating. As if considering bargaining with the deranged man. "I also know what desperation sounds like when I hear it."

"Ha!"

"I'm not joking, Whitey. Do you really think anyone will buy this girl off a ship full of drug mules?" He snorts and steps closer. "Assuming you'll get your emus with their testicles packed with poppy powder past their enforcement teams."

Everything comes together at that moment. The emus, the doctor—veterinarian—the fact that the females have been so agitated. I don't understand how emus work, but it seems reasonable that the females might be able to sense that the males have been castrated, and their testicles filled with drugs.

"Don't be daft!" Whitey spits. "Sudersberg wants it all! I've been stuck between my damned mud flats and two dozen useless emus. If I can get them to Sudersberg, I can finally turn the profit I'm entitled to, particularly given that they're packed with the world's finest opium powder. Then you get the money you're owed, and after the terrible accident I'll be reporting to the coast guard . . ." He flashes a glance at Zerah, and my stomach sinks. I curl my fingers around her cold hand and squeeze. "It won't be a problem requesting a satisfactory replacement from the institute."

"You're disgusting," I shout. The men look at me, as if they've forgotten we're standing right here, listening to everything.

"She's not wrong," Conrad says, as if considering my point of view for a moment. "But I don't trust you. I've never trusted you. You're nothing more than a brown-nosing sycophant with an unfortunate inheritance and devastating halitosis."

Whitey flinches. Next to me, very quietly, Zerah snorts.

"I think I'll be taking my property with me before I leave."

When I realize what Conrad means, I squeeze Zerah's hand tighter.

"Conrad, no—"

"No, I don't think you will," Whitey says, cocking his revolver at Conrad. "Think I'll keep this one. Matter of fact, if I can't sell her for a decent rate, maybe I'll keep her until I can buy a better one."

My heart patters against my chest, and without another thought, I fly across the small crate and reach for Conrad. I catch him by surprise and cling to his wrist. He simply stares at my hands on his wrist and tries to yank his arm away. But my grip is stronger than he expects. I curl my fingers around his precious watch, feeling the latch dig into my fingertips as I keep him in place.

"You can't do this. Please. You promised. You said—"

"I made *no* such promises." He yanks his arm, and I let go as he stumbles backward, grabbing on to Whitey to keep from falling. I squeeze my fists into my sides, letting the pain of my clenched fingers keep me from falling apart.

"You'll get me what I'm owed, or you'll have bigger problems than me chasing down my debts."

"Don't make threats you can't keep, Conrad," Whitey says, but it's clear a detente has been reached. Conrad backs away, his eyes flickering to mine just once more, nothing but cold, detached emotion in them.

"I don't think I have to tell you," Whitey says, sauntering toward the crate as I back away, tucking my fists into my pockets. "But it would be very easy to 'lose' a crate in the seas."

"What is going to happen to the Black Magnolia?" I ask.

He cocks his head, a strange, detached grin curling his features into something truly evil, and for the first time, I feel fully afraid. "Why, I believe you'll be able to hear that soon enough."

Then he backs away, leaving me and Zerah locked in a wooden crate.

CHAPTER THIRTY-NINE

Zerah huddles in the corner as I press my cheek between the wooden slats. It's not that large of a crate. Frankly, the thought that a full-grown emu could fit inside seems unlikely, if not criminal.

I step back, next to Zerah and hoist my skirt. She doesn't say anything, still groggy as she eyes me and watches from the corner. I swing my foot and kick the slats as hard as I can. The impact shoots through my heel to my knee and hip, and I groan at the pain.

Around us, the squawk and guttural calls of pissed-off emus echo my own cry.

"You really think you can get through something meant to keep an emu in place?"

It's the first thing she's said, and it sounds so shockingly normal that I can't contain my laughter.

"Worth a try, isn't it?"

Zerah shrugs, hugging herself in the corner.

"What's he going to do?" I ask.

"He sort of just laid out all his cards. I think we both know that I'm not surviving this."

My stomach twists, and without thinking, I wrap my arms around Zerah. She winces, and when I step back, I realize she wasn't hugging herself—she's holding her right arm together. It looks all sorts of wrong, from the wrist, to the elbow, to the way it slants at an unnatural angle from her shoulder. I wonder if it's something that can actually be fixed.

"We'll get out," I say, squeezing her good shoulder.

I go back to the latch and try to examine the padlock. The slats are just wide enough that I can reach through and flip it upside down. I give it a good tug, feeling the raw edges of the thick slats scraping against my forearm. It's latched tight. It's not coming undone by force.

A foghorn sounds in the distance, and the ship rocks. I fall backward, but don't let go of the padlock. My thumb pinches between the lock and the wood. The emus aren't a fan of the movement either, and a chorus of angry squawks fills the air.

"Are they always this noisy?" I ask.

"No," Zerah says, thoughtfully. "I would say it got worse when he castrated them all."

"So, that's a thing people do?"

"That's a thing he does, apparently. And then he pays the vet to fill them with drugs so he can triple his payday. As one might do, I suppose, if one is a psychopath."

"I suppose I can't blame them. I'd be pissed if someone did that to me."

"Oh, that's not who's pissed."

"What do you mean?" I look over my shoulder, and Zerah wears a grim smirk.

"The females. Female emus are more aggressive. They're about to go into heat. And now, he's gone and castrated all the males. But the females can still smell them. They're confused, and panicked, and that makes for some really angry emus."

"I thought he was afraid of them? Why make them more angry?"

"Oh, that's not the worst of it."

"What could be worse?" The clouds overhead part, bathing the lock in more light. I look back down at the keyhole, trying to figure out how to get through it.

"He hasn't fed them in two days."

"Why not?"

"He didn't want them making a mess. He seemed to think that would make everything worse. I just think he's going to end up with some pissed off, ornery birds that want to attack the first person who opens that crate."

I reach into my tangle of braids and pull out one, then two hairpins.

"Do you know what you're doing?" she asks.

I grin and nod. It's one of the few questionable skills Headmistress Moyle taught me. I can do this with my eyes closed.

With the hairpins inserted into the padlock, I wiggle them around and feel for the gears, searching for the indentation where a key would fit. The pins are almost too short, but when I feel the first groove engage, my stomach flips with excitement. I can do this.

The second one takes more work, and I wiggle it around, feeling all around the first. The emu chatter picks up, loud enough that I can't hear the gears in my own hand. But then it clicks. I hold the pins where they are and twist.

Nothing.

My heart plummets as I realize this might be a three-pronged mechanism. I look back at Zerah, and there's something so tragically beautiful about the way she watches me with a mix of horror and hope.

"Usually, these locks are two pronged. But this one . . . I just need something . . ." I lean into the slats when I hear it. A dull, muffled *thunk* against the crate.

The cold metal watch swings in my pocket, and I nod toward it.

"Reach in there. Grab that, will you?" Zerah frowns, but does as I've asked, retrieving Conrad's flashy timepiece.

"What do you want me to do with this?"

"Can you get me another pin? Maybe from the strap?"

She squints as she holds it in the palm of her right hand, turning it left and right to examine the close. Gritting her teeth, her left hand moves over it with astonishing deftness. It takes only a few seconds for her to release the spring on the golden strap and hand me the pin that had been holding it in place.

"Here," she says, reaching through the slat to place the pin in my free hand. "Try this."

I nudge the short pin into the lock, feeling around for the spot where it will fit into place and solve the puzzle. It feels close . . . so close . . .

"Will it work?" Zerah whispers, hope evident in her voice.

The pin clicks. I push to engage the indentations more fully, and turn hard.

The lock clicks open.

"You've got to be kidding me," she says, laughing around her words. She opens her mouth to say something else, but whatever she says is drowned out by a wave of emu calls. I pull the lock off completely, and then slowly, gently, open the door.

The crates are stacked in long rows, lit only by the fickle moon. We must still be in the bay of Albahar, because the ship is only rocked with the gentlest of waves. I motion for Zerah to follow quietly, and together, we step out of our crate and into the lane between the rows. I look around us and meet large, round amber eyes. The emu's head is bowed over in its crate, its huge, feathery body practically filling the space from side to side. It looks hungry and uncomfortable and pissed off.

"Shhh . . ." I say to it, as if it can understand my need for discretion. It snorts at me, and its throat wobbles, as if it's trying to get enough air to yell out our location. We freeze and wait a moment. But the emu keeps staring, not actually making a sound.

Carefully, slowly, I step to the left, toward the rear of the ship —the stern, I think? The emu watches us, but does nothing more. I step past its crate, letting out a short breath. But my relief doesn't last.

The next emu screams. I shush it, but Zerah grabs me by the yoke of my jacket, pulling me back against the row of crates whose backs are to us. We thud against it, and the emus inside those crates start screaming.

"Shut up!" Whitey's thin voice flies over the crates, and from the narrow strip of darkness Zerah has pulled me into, I see someone walk past our row.

"They're going to give away our location," I hiss. "You've lived with them for the past—how long?"

"Three months," she says with a shiver.

"How can we stop them from screaming like that?"

"I don't think we can. And I don't blame them. They just want to be able to stretch their legs, drink some water, and eat something."

I pause for a moment, thinking about what she's said.

"They eat, what? Birdseed?"

"That's what we feed them. Sometimes fruit, if William is willing to spare it."

There's something about the way she says it that starts an idea churning in my gut. Whitey is terrified of these birds, but they tolerate Zerah. Perhaps we can use them to keep him away?

I move down the aisle, keeping to the shadows, and when the next emu screeches, I thud against the crate next to me. The emu in the crate, who can't see me, screeches even louder.

"Will you shut that damn thing up!" Whitey squeals from somewhere near the prow of the ship.

"They's wild animals. They's gonna squawk whenever they's wants!" A gruff voice calls from the row behind us. We keep moving, and Zerah slowly, slowly approaches the next emu, at the end of the row. He bobs his head and cocks it funny, as if he's under the influence of something.

Perhaps he is. My stomach twists with the thought that some of the drugs that Whitey has filled them with might leak inside them.

Zerah reaches through the thick wooden bars and strokes the large bird's feathery nose, just above his beak.

"Sweet boy," she says, her voice soothing, sending a wave of calm even through me.

"Do you know where the galley is?" I ask. She nods, but doesn't take her eyes off the clearly sick bird.

"Downstairs, in the back." She's distracted, petting the bird, mothering him.

The bird wobbles, clearly having a difficult time keeping his balance in such tight quarters.

"They're omnivores," she adds. "They like seeds. Fruit is a treat."

"I'll be back—"

She grabs my arm and narrows her eyebrows. "You're going to lure them? As a distraction?"

I nod, grateful she understands what I'm doing.

"You said Whitey is afraid of them, right?"

"Terrified."

"I just need to get some treats to lure them—"

"You need to get them out of the crates. I can go get food."

"But your arm—"

"I can carry things with the other arm. What I can't do is pick a lock. You pick the locks."

"But . . ." I hesitate, feeling foolish for the thought I'm having.

"What?"

"What if they don't like me as much as they dislike Whitey?"

She frowns, thinking. Then, with her good arm, she very carefully, gingerly, uncoils the long black scarf she was wearing and wraps it over my shoulders.

"You'll smell like me. That should help." Her scarf immediately brings me a flush of warmth as she shivers. But she doesn't look cold. She is right, though: I can smell her sweet, floral-and-cinnamon scent. It might just work. I tighten the scarf around my neck as I give her a side hug, avoiding her bad arm.

"Be careful."

"You, too."

She takes off around the corner, and I let out a breath of a prayer. Then I get to work.

I pull the pins from my pocket and start on the lock for the sick bird. I'm nervous here on the very end. Not just that, but because of the angle of the moonlight, I can't stand in the shadows as I'm working on the lock. All it would take is one person walking around the corner to see me or my shadow standing there, attempting to pick at this lock. The emu within eyes me, warily, but when he gets close enough, he calms. Probably scenting Zerah's scarf.

The first pin clicks, and then the second and the third. I twist it hard, like I did the first lock. The mechanisms unlatch just as I hear footsteps around the corner slow. I unhook the lock and open the door. The footsteps get louder, heavier, closer, and I duck inside the crate with the emu. I press myself against the side, and the emu stays where he is. Cagey, suspicious, but ultimately too tired to object.

The footsteps stop. There's a pregnant pause in the air. I swear I can hear someone breathing, sniffing the air. The emu makes a gurgling sound and ruffles its feathers. Then the steps sound again, moving away . . . they keep going, getting softer and quieter. When I can no longer hear them, I slowly push the crate door open, and step out. Then I open it wider and motion for the emu to get out. He studies me with a wary expression.

"Come on, you dumb bird," I whisper, waving for him to get out. "Don't you want to be free?" Leave it to me to find the one emu who doesn't actually want to escape his prison cell.

"Please," I beg, reaching my hand out to him. Slowly, he lowers his head to my hand. The hard, smooth edge of his beak rubs against my palm, and his oily, smooth feathers scratch my skin. Then, he snorts. Stretching out one long leg at a time, he exits the crate. He stretches his neck up, and I realize just how tall these creatures are. He's much taller than the crate. It's a crime to have these birds locked up this way.

"Go!" I hiss. "Don't just stand there! You should be indignant after what they did to you! Make chaos!" As if he understands, but won't be bothered, he slowly turns the corner, and then he's gone.

So much for chaos.

I move on to the next crate. This emu is far less cerebral. She makes low groaning sounds as I fumble with the lock. But having already unlatched two of them, this one comes a little faster. When I open the gate, she nearly knocks me over rushing out. But incredibly, she's quiet. She goes the same direction as the other bird.

As I'm unlatching the next lock, I hear a clattering, like something tumbling over, followed by shouts from the prow of the ship. The birds must've been spotted. The lock I'm working on clicks, and I open the gate. The bird rushes me, nearly tripping and knocking me back into the crate behind me. The back of my head *thunks* against the wooden slats, and I see stars. The bird in the crate I've knocked into screeches, but then a loud string of feral screams and human shouts comes from the front. I start working on the next lock when I hear the sounds of panic from across the deck. I move the pins around, trying to focus amidst the clamor.

"They're out!" a low, gruff voice — one of the deckhands — calls from the prow.

"How did they get out?" Whitey's voice has a note of panic in it.

"Shit if I know."

The lock I'm working on clicks open, and I don't wait around once I've unhooked the lock from the crate. I maneuver to the shadowy side of the row, passing the crate we once occupied. And I keep running. I don't know where Zerah is, but I have to find her.

I stop at the end of the row and peer around the corner, looking for enemies — foul or fowl.

There's nothing. Except . . . there's a boat. A lifeboat?

I know exactly what I'm going to do.

I take off, darting into the moonlight, crossing to the vessel that could be our salvation. When I reach it, I examine the rusted metal boat. It hardly looks seaworthy, but it may be our only option. I start to examine the frayed knot securing the boat to the ship, trying to figure out how to undo it.

"They're gone!" The voice roars out across the ship. My heart flutters in my chest as an alarm rings out.

CHAPTER FORTY

*T*he alarm hits a decibel that leaves my ears alternately ringing and aching. But I can't slow down. I say a little prayer to the old gods and the new ones, just to cover my ass — if there are old ones, there must be new ones, right?

I tug at the rope, unwinding the knot as quickly as my frozen fingers will allow. I don't know when they got so cold or so stiff, but they will hardly bend to uncoil the knot. Once it's done, I move my way down the lifeboat to the next knot. At the rear of the ship, where I am, it feels like I have room to work. As long as I don't fixate on the fact that it only took me about thirty paces to get here from the row of crates we were housed in, I feel like I can keep myself from panicking.

"Neve! Hurry!" Zerah runs from around the corner, where I assume the stairwell down was. She's carrying a mass of fruits. Pomegranates, figs, a grayish-toned melon, and a couple of calamansi. I don't know if this will be enough to attract the emus, but I do know that I need to leave the fruit to Zerah and focus on untying these knots. Especially since Zerah is working with only one functioning arm.

"What do you want me to do?" Zerah hisses.

"Watch for them, and call the emus."

Out of the corner of my eye, I see her freeze in place.

"What?"

"Your plan relies on me *calling the emus?*"

"Can you do it, or not?" I fumble with the third knot and let out a deep breath as I shift to the prow of the upside-down boat, trying to figure out how I can get it overboard and get us into it.

"How do you feel about jumping?" I ask.

"Not great," she says, but then she rises. "Neve."

"What?"

"Quite the plan here, *dearest.*" Whitey's acidic tone cuts through the chaos from about twenty paces down the deck. I tug on the lifeboat and realize it's not moving. I tug again, and still it remains in place.

"Funny," he says, moving past an open aisle of crates. Only two more aisles remain between us, and I have no idea where anyone else is. But I need to shift this lifeboat. If we can just get this thing overboard and jump into it—but my mind won't even let me finish the thought. It's impossible.

We've lost.

This is it. This is where it was either going to work or fall apart.

I look up at Zerah, and she meets my gaze. But there's no defeat in her eyes. She lifts her chin and stares him down.

"We thought it was really quite smart." I can't stop the snort at her bravado. I've never heard her so bold, and a flutter of hope blossoms in my chest. My hands don't stop; I keep working on shifting the lifeboat.

"And yet," Whitey says, sweeping out his hand with a flourish, "here we are. Given your predilection for picking locks, I'd have thought you'd be further along with this one here."

A lock. Of course, this is locked. Although, how macabre is that? A lifeboat locked to the ship? It was never meant to be used; that can be the only reason.

I look around the floor, running my hands along the shadowed lip around the lifeboat for the hint of a lock. I don't feel anything. There's nothing there.

"There's really only one thing to be done now, you understand." He sounds sympathetic, but I don't even so much as glance at him as I crawl beneath the lifeboat and feel around for a metal lock. Sure enough, there's a bar attached to the side of the boat halfway down, another lock on it. I reach for my pins and start working.

"Now, that's unimaginative," I hear Zerah say from the other side of the lifeboat. "And certainly less imaginative than what we came up with."

The first pin settles into place with a click. I push the second pin into the keyhole and move it around, feeling for the spot that will unleash the boat.

"Unimaginative? Why does drowning need to be imaginative?"

A chill shuttles down my spine, despite the sweat that slicks my hairline as I keep pushing and nudging, turning and checking, trying to open this stupid lock.

"Who says we're the ones who will drown?" Zerah's voice is light and almost playful, stronger than I've ever heard. I want to squeeze her. But not until I get this damned lock open. I can't find the right spot for the pin to work. There's just nothing in there. It's as if I'm trying to find something that doesn't exist, or something that's already been found.

I gasp.

I remove the second pin and turn the first, hard. The lock clicks open. Just like a lock that's been picked so many times that it's been filed down. I unhook the lock and shuffle myself backward, out from under the lifeboat, so as not to give away the fact that I've solved it.

I stand, and when Zerah shoots me a questioning look, I school my face into an apologetic expression.

"I'm sorry," I say, but I shoot her a look that I hope she reads correctly.

"Now, now, don't be so sad, girls. There was never any way out of this. Perhaps, there's still an opportunity for resolution?" He steps closer, approaching the second to last aisle between the crates. Somewhere behind him, a wild screech rings across the ship, followed by the stunted yelp of a man caught unawares. Then a splash.

Whitey looks over his shoulder, and when he turns back around, his face is white.

"Or perhaps it's best to nip this in the bud." He sneers and approaches closer.

"Zerah," I whisper. "The calamansi."

She passes me the round, yellow citrus fruits, and I dig my fingernail into the side of it.

"You don't have to do anything, you know?" I say, stepping closer.

"Neve," Zerah hisses, but I ignore her. Instead, I tip my head at the lifeboat and hope she gets the hint.

"Is that so?" Whitey asks, hesitating in front of the second to last aisle. "I can't wait to hear what the Unchosen whore thinks I should do." I suck in a breath. Zerah freezes, taking in her husband's words.

But his reveal is the least of my problems. The problem is that I don't know who else is on this ship backing him up. I don't know how many minions he has, and I don't know if they've caught any of the emus. All I can do is hope that my instincts are correct.

"You've sacrificed your entire inheritance for this journey, after all. Why not get the most money out of it as you can?"

His lip curls into an ugly sneer, and he steps closer. I keep dragging my thumbnail around the fruit until I've made a full circle. I step closer still, listening for a sign of something. Anything to tell me I'm not crazy.

"So, you're telling me you want to be sold to a Sudersbergian? Like the whore you are? Like the whore your mother was? Oh yes, your benefactor told me all about the daughter of the Espancian whore who was supposed to be sent to the institute. But instead, her competition went, because she simply wasn't good enough." I feel Zerah's eyes on me as I try to focus on the task at hand, digging my nail into the thick skin of the fruit, feeling the juice drip down my thumb. "You expect me to believe you'd go willingly? When you wouldn't even go willingly for your own benefactor?"

I shrug. "Of course not."

"Then what are you saying?"

I rip the calamansi into two ragged, juicy pieces and throw them as hard as I can down the first aisle between us. He stares at me, his eyebrows knitting together, his nostrils flaring beneath the gray moonlight.

Nothing happens.

Not a sound. Not a cry, not a movement. Not a damned wingbeat. Just nothing.

Whitey laughs. Laughter fills him, shaking his belly and his shoulders and his chin. He wipes tears away from his eyes, and I reach behind me, holding my hand out, hoping against all hope that Zerah sees me. That she knows what it is that I want.

"That was your brilliant plan? Your creative, imaginative plan to secure your safety?" He keeps laughing and steps closer, his feet moving faster, with more confidence. I step back just as Zerah places something heavy and round in my hand.

"It didn't quite go the way I expected," I say, waiting for him to take just a few more steps. Then I pull the melon around, crash it against the lifeboat once, twice, and a third time, until it's split in two, the juices running down my arms.

"I should've just killed you the moment I had the chance. You were a sitting duck, unaware and completely inconvenient at that party. It should've been you and Rafael at that party. Would've saved me all the trouble of the market bombs."

I lift the melon, letting the juices wash down the anger, the grief, the hatred that threatens to boil over.

He pauses, but I don't. I toss one of the halves at him, and throw the other down the aisle. He catches it and stares down at it. It's not much, just long enough. He doesn't see the bird until he hears her hungry, angry cry. The emu rushes down the aisle and charges at him, hitting him and sweeping him straight off the deck and over the railing.

I don't hear his cry until just before I hear the splash.

Zerah quickly breaks apart the rest of the fruit and drops it for the other emus.

"They won't be content with that for very long, will they?" I ask.

"Not even a moment."

"Can you help me shift this?" She hesitates, looking at me with a new, unfamiliar expression. But then she takes the opposite side of the lifeboat. It's lighter than I expect. We push the lip up onto the rail of the deck, and slowly, slowly, we nudge it over the side. Beneath it is a rope, and if there was more time, I would tie it so that we could climb down slowly. But there is no time. The emus have finished the fruit, and they're back to looking pissed off.

"Oi! Where d'you think you're going?" a gruff voice calls from the deck. We have to jump.

"Go!" I yell. I help Zerah over the railing, and then climb over it myself.

"Together," she says, curling her good hand around mine.

"Now!" I call. We push off the ship and fall, crashing hard against the boat. She lands inside; I splash into the frigid water next to it. Water rushes up my nose when I plunge beneath the surface. But she doesn't let go. She tugs on my hand, and when I breach the surface, coughing harder than I've ever done, I grab on to the side of the lifeboat. It begins to tilt as I pull myself up and I yell something at her that makes her move to the opposite side. Carefully, counterbalancing, I climb into the lifeboat while the ship we just left roars with the sound of angry emus and panicked men.

"Here," Zerah says, passing me an oar. The other one is strapped to the bottom of the lifeboat, and I unhook it before she can. I put them in the water and begin rowing. I feel her watching me for a long moment.

"Where are we going?"

"Back," I say. She nods. And I take us back to where it began.

CHAPTER FORTY-ONE

*T*he port is a mess of activity when we return. But it's still there. I hadn't realized that I doubted that it would be until we rowed up to the lowest dock, where Officer Koprihan was waiting for us with two of his colleagues.

"You're just the woman I was looking for," Koprihan says, his tone serious, his gaze unreadable.

"Help her first, please," I ask, nodding toward Zerah. An officer helps me tie the boat to the dock, while the other steps down into the rocky vessel and helps Zerah to her feet. I'm still not sure what Whitey gave her to knock her out the way he did, but her legs are shaky as she stands. Or maybe it's just her sea legs. Either way, she stumbles to get out, and Koprihan has to step in and help her to the pier.

He reaches his hand out for me next, and I steel myself for whatever is coming. He helps me out of the boat and onto the dock, then nods for his colleague to go on with Zerah.

"Where are you taking her?"

"Don't worry. You'll be reunited soon enough," he says. His eyes flash out toward the sea. It's clear I'm in trouble, that I'm not free to leave, and yet, he doesn't actually detain me.

"It might be best if you tell me everything, from the beginning, before we find ourselves somewhere with ears for walls." He speaks low and casually. "But before you begin," he says, scratching the side of his nose, "we've already spoken with two people who implicated your benefactor and Mrs. Whitey's husband in quite the scheme."

"Zerah had nothing to do with any of it," I say quickly.

He lifts his chin, and then lowers it in a meaningful nod. "That's what they said. But I'd like to hear what you know."

I stuff my hands into my trench coat pockets and snort.

"From the beginning?"

"It would seem that's a natural place to begin."

So, we stand on the end of a pier at the edge of Albahar, shrouded in marine layer as I tell him a story about an unchosen girl who wanted everything, and the boy who patched up her cracked heart. I tell him about the friends she made along the way, and the trouble she found herself in. The villains who sought to control her, and the truly good man who tried to help.

Then I tell him about the outsiders whose desire to help may have led them into more trouble. The dark and strange business that pushed the girl and her closest friend into trouble, and how they managed to escape.

I answer his questions until the sun breaks through the fog, and I listen in as he orders border patrol agents out onto the choppy waters to look for confirmation that my strange story is, in fact, true.

When I've answered all his questions, and he's sent away everyone it seems he can think to, he walks me up the dock and to a coffee cart. Quietly, he orders two cups, passing one to me, and then he finds a bench and asks me to sit.

We sit on the bench, sipping our coffee, watching the thin, lingering fingers of fog descend.

"The Black Magnolia is safe," he says, quietly.

I sigh, relieved, and take a deep sip of my coffee. It tastes good unadorned. Bitter and hot and honest.

"It doesn't seem fair," he says, the frown heavy in his voice, "that you should be punished for something of this magnitude." I say nothing, hoping that he really means it. Still, I can hear the *but* coming. "But . . ."—there it is—"it also seems unfair that no one would be punished for the secret communications. After all, you are an accessory to their drug trade scheme."

I swallow hard. But it doesn't sting the way it might have before.

"I understand."

He sighs and scratches at the side of his nose.

"That's the problem, Neve," he says, using my given name for perhaps the first time. And with a gentleness I'm not prepared for.

"What's the problem?"

"You understand? I understand, as well. You weren't given a choice. Here in Osterstan, we have our own battles. Our country is deeply divided. Part of it is a generational gap, and perhaps that's the simpler way to consider the issue. The old party longs for the simplicity of the days when Godliness was the national creed, and gender roles were clearly defined. But our God teaches about lifting the downtrodden and showing respect and compassion to all of God's creatures.

"Rafael—your husband," he allows, and his small concession brings tears to my eyes. "He was a good man. Possibly the best man our country has known. Even before he took office, he stood up for what was right. I'm not sure if he ever really explained what happened before he left Osterstan?"

I shake my head, but don't say a word, afraid that if I say the wrong thing, he'll stop, and I'll never know more about the man who saved me in more ways than one.

"A woman was beaten in the streets. It was violent and brutal, but her neighbors did nothing. They said it was justified because she had displeased her husband. It happened in your neighborhood — in the Old City. People are a little different in the Old City.

"Rafael came to me and asked if there was anything that might be done for this woman. Unless she made a formal complaint against her husband, I could do nothing. And even then, it would be her word against her husband's. Which shouldn't matter — I know this, and you know this. Rafael knew this, as well. And so, he agreed to sponsor her divorce."

I can hardly keep the gasp to myself. It's not something anyone speaks of in the Old City. But thankfully, it doesn't stop him from speaking.

"He paid for her legal fees, moved her into a safe apartment on his bill. It caused problems within his family, as I understand it. His parents — his mother, in particular — were upset that he would spend money in such a way. They cut his access to the family accounts just before the woman could go to trial."

"What happened to her?"

He frowns, but doesn't look unhappy.

"I believe that is where your other friend steps into the story."

"Irina?"

He nods. "She has her ways. I cannot say for certain, but I believe she lets people see what they want to see. When people expect to see a money-hungry madam, they don't look beneath the surface. And therefore, they don't see all the donations she accepts from likeminded Osterstanis who fund the home she's built in eastern Osterstan for women who are truly out of options."

Everything falls into place, and my throat becomes thick. That's why Rafi and Irina knew each other. He had worked with her to help this other woman. Maybe more than just this one?

"He was able to divert the funds he'd set aside for this woman's legal defense to move this woman to the safe house. But when his parents discovered what he'd done, it was . . . well, let's just say it didn't go well. He came to see me before he left.

He said he needed to clear his head. That everything was dark and murky, and he just needed to catch his breath and find his way.

"Then, three months later, he returned. With you."

I nod.

"As you may have figured out, he would not become the head of his household until he returned . . . with a wife." He frowns and cocks his head. "I do not mean to imply that your marriage was anything other than—"

"I understand," I say, blinking back tears. "I understand more than you know. I don't think he wanted to be married. And he didn't want the job. I really don't think that mattered to him."

"I don't think he would have married someone just for the money." Koprihan turns to face me.

"He saved me," I say with a little shrug. "He was always thinking about others."

He shakes his head.

"Neve." He reaches over and squeezes my hand. "I believe it was you who saved him."

"I don't understand." But I want to. I want him to make me believe it.

"He paid off your contract, correct?" I nod. "He could have left it at that. But he didn't. I really do believe that when he left, he was without a purpose. You gave him a new purpose."

"Me? I think you give me too much credit. I'm not a purpose . . ."

"I think you inspired him. He suddenly wanted to do all the things he was meant to do, to live up to all the things he was meant to live up to. There was talk before he returned that perhaps a new trade minister would have to be appointed. Without his voice to energize the nation, it was assumed that it would be an old party member, and there was fear we would return to our archaic old ways.

"I don't know what made him do what he did, but you moved

him. He had no plans to return to Osterstan when he left. And that changed."

My mouth hangs open. "He said he was returning the next day . . ."

Koprihan smiles. "Seems something you did moved him tremendously. You saved him, and in saving him, you saved our country."

He lets out a heavy sigh as he releases my hand.

"Which is why it pains me more than you could possibly understand to tell you that you have twenty-four hours to pack your things and leave, and you may never return."

I blink at him, trying to keep the hurt off my face. I'm pretty sure I fail.

"I have a day?"

"You have a day. It's the best I could do." He takes my empty cup and stands, walking them both over to a refuse bin to toss them. Then he returns and squats in front of me, pressing his warm hands against my knees. Deep lines crease his forehead as a rare smile flickers across his mouth.

"I cannot accept that this will be the last time we meet. But it will, likely, be the last time we speak so frankly with one another. I wish you the very best, Neve Rostami."

I smile, but I don't fight the hot tear that slips from between my lashes. I squeeze his hands, and then we walk away from the sea, toward the rest of my life.

CHAPTER FORTY-TWO

"*A*re you ready?" Irina stands in the doorway, not deigning to such trivial manners as knocking before entering one's private room.

"Yes," I say, nodding toward my small suitcase. Even though Benham had told me I could take anything that belonged to me as Rafi's wife, I didn't pack much. The red dress, of course. The makeup, obviously. Although, as I was packing, I realized that my favorite colors were the ones I blended myself.

"I hate to be the bearer of bad news, but life in Sudersberg will hardly be as interesting as being married to the trade minister and wanted for domestic terrorism." Irina's wry grin matches her humor.

"I could use something a little quieter, I think," I say.

Koprihan brought me straight to the townhouse, where he said Irina would meet me. Benham let me inside, explaining that Nima had gone to church for the morning. Part of me was sad that I would not see her before leaving, but perhaps it is for the best. What would possibly provide me closure may only enrage her, and I don't want to leave hearing angry words.

I can tolerate leaving without saying goodbye to Nima, but the thought of never seeing Zerah again churns my gut.

"Do you know—"

"Zerah is safe," Irina says, though she looks troubled. "She did ask me to give you this."

I turn as Irina reaches out her hand, Conrad's precious gold watch lying in her palm in two pieces. I laugh and shake my head, taking the damned thing and examining it. I reach into my pocket to retrieve the pin and slowly, gently, reassemble it.

"It's a nice watch," Irina says.

"I know." I check the latch. It seems secure enough.

"She can't return to Espancia," Irina says, softly. My shoulders tighten. "Nor can she return to Nordania. William Whitey's creditors are many and far-reaching." Irina frowns, and there's a weight to her brow that I haven't often seen.

"Can she come with us?"

Her smile is sad as she shakes her head.

"I can keep my women safe from a great many things within my walls. But Sudersberg is not a haven for the indebted. If someone wants to find her there, they will."

"What will she do?"

She purses her lips as I open the drawer to my nightstand and remove a novel and two sanitary pads.

"I wish I could tell you I have everything worked out."

"You don't?"

"I'm working on it." She looks tired. I'm sure she hasn't slept in at least as long as it's been for me. For now, I'm running on adrenaline, but I know I'll crash here soon enough. I pack away my things and for some reason, open Rafi's nightstand drawer. Lying at the front is the small velvet box that I'd almost forgotten about. I pick it up, running my fingertips over the cool, soft velvet.

"He was a romantic at heart," she says, standing next to me. She takes the box and opens it, *hmm*-ing to herself, as if the ring was exactly as she expected. "It's beautiful. Suits you." She takes it out of the box and reaches for my hand, slipping it onto my middle finger. It fits perfectly. But it doesn't feel right to wear it. He never asked me to. He may have bought it with me in mind, but he never gave it to me.

"How much do you think it's worth?" I ask, ideas running through my head. Irina tenses, but folds my fingers into a fist, as if to keep the ring on my hand.

"He would not want anyone else to wear that ring—of that, I am certain." Her words are clear and final. "And besides, I told you, I do not wish for you to pay me back immediately."

"Is it too much to ask whether we might be able to track down Conrad and get my money?"

"Probably," she says. "Maybe someday, but right now, he is missing. He'll turn up somewhere eventually. I have eyes in many places, and when I learn of his whereabouts, I'll share that with you."

I frown. "Why?"

"Why what? Why would I share that information with you?"

Her features cloud, and something truly sad passes across them.

"Because I am a reasonable person. I don't intend to trap you. If I hear news of where the man who stole from you might be, I will tell you. But also, you must learn to trust me. I let people believe what they want, but there is a fundamental difference between me and the other people who have helped you in the past."

"You're a woman," I say, with an obvious shrug.

"Precisely. And unlike a man, I know what it is to be truly vulnerable." Something dark passes over her features. I wonder how this woman, who is stronger and bolder than any man I've encountered, could have ever found herself in a vulnerable situation. But then, I suppose we all come from somewhere.

I nod, and it seems to be enough for her, for now. I put the velvet case back in the nightstand and close the drawer, keeping the ring on my left hand. I doubt I'll wear it again. But for the last time, as I stand in this room still thick with Rafi's ghost, I'll wear it.

As I go to latch my suitcase, I realize there's still a weight in my hand. Conrad's watch.

"Where can Zerah go?" I ask, staring at the watch.

"There is a place to the east. For the right price, papers can be drawn up, names changed."

"Names changed?" I frown as a wave of sadness hits me.

"She is in danger. I can only guess as to who Whitey's creditors might have been. Assuming my guesses are good — which, they usually are — she is in far graver danger if she leaves Osterstan. But . . ."

"But you don't have enough money to help her?"

She hesitates. It's as good as an answer.

I balance the watch in my hand. I don't know how valuable it truly is, but I feel confident it would supply me with enough money to start a proper business in Irina's brothel. Without it . . . I don't know.

"How do women start their businesses with you?" I ask, still staring at the watch.

She's quiet for a long moment. Then she steps closer, lowering her chin.

"They take out a loan. I am not a shark. I do not charge interest until the primary loan has been paid off." She lets out a muffled chuckle. "I make enough interest on the men who take out loans to cover their expenses."

"Would I qualify for a loan?" I look up at her, holding her gaze. Slowly, she nods.

"You would."

"And this? Would this be enough? For Zerah?" I hold up the watch.

"I do not believe she would want you to use this on her," Irina says, but she doesn't refuse it either.

"Perhaps she doesn't have to know? If you could sell it? The proceeds could be from an anonymous donor?"

"If that is truly what you wish," Irina says, and then nods.

"It is."

I press the watch into her hand. It's the last thing Conrad would want to spend money on: freeing a girl and sending her somewhere she can be safe from the influence of men like him. It feels right.

It also sends an ache through my chest.

"Then, it is done. There should be more than enough. I can bring you the remains—"

"No." I shake my head, stepping back to latch my suitcase. I walk to the chaise where my trench coat lies and slip my arms into it. "Give it all to her. Let her decide how to spend the rest. Call it whatever you must. Just make sure it goes to her."

Irina doesn't say another word, and I don't see the watch again as she opens the door and steps through.

"Shall we be on our way, then?"

I take one last look around the room I once shared with Rafi, the place where I hid, where we bonded, and where we shared our short life together.

"Yes."

CHAPTER FORTY-THREE

*I*rina goes her separate way, putting me in a cab with Elm. He gives me a hat and suggests I keep my face down in case anyone spots me. It's with this idea of a threat that we ride to the port. I have yet to find out exactly how they were able to stop the Black Magnolia from exploding. I suspect this is a story for another time. Though I also suspect that if I asked him, he would tell me a wild story, leaving me to wonder which parts of it are tall tale and which parts are strange enough to be the truth.

When we arrive at the port, I stay in the cab for a long time while he sorts things out. I sit there, watching the dockworkers come and go, as if nothing had been about to change their entire world only a few mere hours ago. Everything looks as it should, though perhaps a bit lighter in traffic than normal. Men smoke hand-rolled cigarettes as they talk in small groups on the docks; a few women pass on the esplanade with hurried glances.

I wish I had paid more attention on the ride here. I wish I'd taken a moment to memorize the exact yellow of the jacaranda trees that line the boulevards. I wish I'd rolled down the window and breathed in the scent of the roasted nuts and spiced tea carts along the market district. I wish I'd had the courage to ask

Benham where Rafi would be buried. And if I could arrange for flowers to be placed on his grave on his death day. And on Peter's.

The door opens, and I look up, but it's not Elm.

It's Zerah.

"What are you—"

"What have you done?" Her voice is frantic, but her eyes water.

"Are you okay? What happened?"

"Suddenly, there's an anonymous donor who has paid enough money to get me to a safe house in eastern Osterstan. I'll have a home, a new name—and enough left over to start a new life."

I blink back hot tears and shake my head.

"That's wonderful, Zerah. Irina told me—"

"You sold the watch, didn't you?"

I frown. I shake my head. She won't accept it if I tell her. She's too proud.

"You're going to a safe house?" I ask, my voice softer than hers.

She swallows hard. And nods. And then she smiles. It's different from any smile I've seen on her before. It makes her look . . . free.

"Yeah," she says with a hurried nod. "I don't have a lot of time. But someone"—she shoots me a glare—"stepped in at the last minute and provided more than enough money for new papers, transportation, everything I need. And then some."

"That's wonderful, Zerah."

She nods, but something catches in her throat.

"Yeah, it really is. But I can't ever repay this kindness." She looks distraught.

I wrap my arms around her and hug her tight.

"I don't think anyone expects you to. I think that's the point of it coming from an anonymous donor."

She wraps her arms around my waist and squeezes me tight to her.

"I'll miss you more than you know," she whispers into my ear. I squeeze her just as tight, inhaling her warm cinnamon-and-floral scent, feeling her warmth for perhaps the last time.

"I'll miss you more," I say. She laughs. She pulls back, but hesitates, her eyelashes clumped with tears as her gaze flickers to my lips.

"Shideh."

"What's that?" I whisper.

"My new name. *Shideh*. It means 'bright.'" She cups my cheek. "Same as Neve."

My chest expands with sweet warmth, and I cup her cheeks as well, pressing my forehead to hers.

"I'll come find you."

"You'd better," she says. Her eyes flicker to my lips once more, and then she leans in. Her lips brush mine, soft and warm. They feel so different from Rafi's. And yet, so right. She pulls back, her hazel eyes uncertain, hesitant. I smile, and a smile flickers at the corner of her lips. I kiss her back, pressing my lips to hers with more of everything. I suck on her bottom lip, taking it between my own and tasting the sweet berry of her lipstick. I lick the seam of her lips, and she yields to me, threading her fingers through my hair as I deepen the kiss. A small moan slips between us as I try to memorize the feel of her soft skin, the way her touch alights against mine, the soft heat of her tongue.

She is the one to break off the kiss, and she does so with a giggle.

I've never heard her giggle before. It fills me with the most joyful warmth. I grin and cup her cheeks, running my thumbs over them as if I can memorize the exact lines of her joy.

"I'll never forgive you for this, you know." Her words are shaky, but they're not angry.

"I know," I say, kissing the tip of her nose, her forehead, each of her eyelids. There's a knock on the window behind me, and her expression confirms that our time is nearly over. Her lipstick is smudged, and I smile at the fact that she's wearing it at all. I reach into my pocket and retrieve my favorite muted red.

"Here," I say, opening the tube and applying it to her lips. I don't know how I never realized that my favorite color would look so perfect on her skin. I apply a second layer, wiping at the perfect bow of her top lip with my fingertip.

"Keep this," I say, pushing it into her pocket. "Always good to have a little extra armor when you need it."

She smiles, pressing a kiss to my fingertip. Then her eyes turn round and afraid.

"Find me," she says.

"I promise."

The door behind me opens, and the cab is filled with the cold port wind.

"This is our cue to swap places," Elm says. I take one last look at Zerah, and she squeezes my hand. I squeeze back. Then I take Elm's and exit the cab.

"You're going with her?" I ask as he sets my suitcase on the ground next to me.

"I am."

"You'll keep her safe?" I ask.

"Of course." He says it with an easy shrug. I watch him settle into the cab as the driver returns. The engine rattles, and then they pull away. Zerah stares out the back window, and I hold her gaze until the car turns back toward the city.

☙

"Are you ready for an adventure?" Irina says. I don't know how long I've been standing here, staring at the Zerah-less street. I don't know how long she's been standing there watching me. She wears a hip-length, white fur coat over a long, slate-blue dress.

She looks ready for a cold journey, and I wonder if she knows something I don't. She nods at my suitcase, and I carry it, following her toward the large ocean liner.

We board the ship and find our rooms. They're both more modern and more elegant than the ones on the ship I rode with Rafi after our wedding. I've barely had a chance to settle in when the horn blares three times. I open the long curtain in front of the window, revealing a small balcony, and step outside. To my right, I watch Albahar and Osterstan move away as the ship sets out to sea.

It hurts more than I can bear to stare at the land as it fades away, growing smaller with every passing minute.

"Look forward, instead," Irina says. I don't know when she joined me, or how she entered my room. She threads her fingers through mine and squeezes. "Always look forward. Know that what's behind is there, but always look ahead."

I nod, and heed her advice. I turn my gaze away from the land and out to the sea, to the unending blue horizon ahead. I don't know what the future holds for me. But I do know that as long as I'm still moving, as long as I'm still heading forward, I'll be closer to reaching a future I have chosen. And one that has chosen me.

ACKNOWLEDGMENTS

Thank you to Kisa Whipkey for her unwavering support in this story, and every other story that passes through my brain in this universe. Your love for these characters reinvigorates my love for these characters, and I couldn't do this without you.

To Ash Ruggirello, thank you again for a stunning cover.

To my writing community: Jefna Cohen, Desiree Granzow, Mari Hotchkiss, and Heather Penner—thank you for talking through the many plot holes (some emu-sized) in this one with me.

To my readers: thank you for bearing with me as I took an unexpected detour to tell Neve's story. This story spoke to me in a way that nothing has in a very long time (not since Arden first appeared on the page), and I'm so grateful to have you still with me.

As always, thanks to my husband, Chris, and my favorite boys, Elliott and Walt. Your enthusiasm, cheerleading, and (at times) sheer toleration is often the difference between the doing and the not doing.

ABOUT THE AUTHOR

Erin Riha writes young adult fantasy novels about ambitious girls who don't know they're not supposed to exceed expectations. She has an undergraduate degree in Political Science, a Law Degree, and a deep reverence for the power of using exactly the right word in exactly the right moment. She lives in wonderfully weird Portland, Oregon, with her super dreamy husband, where they're raising a future train engineer and a future chicken whisperer. When not writing, she's a music director for a teen theater company, traveling the world, or dreaming of traveling the world.